WITHDRAWN

SF   Pournelle, ed
     The science fiction year-
     book

EATON RAPIDS PUBLIC LIBRARY
220 South Main St.
Eaton Rapids, MI 48827

The Science Fiction Yearbook

The Science Fiction Yearbook

Eaton Rapids
Public Library

BAEN
SCIENCE FICTION
BOOKS

Copyright © 1985 by Baen Enterprises

All rights reserved, including the right to reproduce this book or portions thereof in any form.

A Baen Book
Distributed by Simon and Schuster
Simon & Schuster Building
Rockefeller Center
1230 Avenue of the Americas
New York, New York 10020

Cover art by David Egge

1 3 5 7 9 10 8 6 4 2

ISBN: 0-671-55983-4

This is primarily a work of fiction. All the story characters and events portrayed in this book are fictional, and any resemblance to real people or incidents is purely coincidental.

Library of Congress Cataloging in Publication Data

Main entry under title:

The Science fiction yearbook.

  "A Baen book."
  1. Science fiction, American. 2. Science fiction—History and criticism—Addresses, essays, lectures.
I. Pournelle, Jerry, 1933– . II. Baen, Jim.
III. Carr, John F.
PS648.S3S3 1985   813′.0876′08   85-7511
ISBN 0-671-55983-4

1984, *Nineteen Eighty-Four,* and Other SF Novels, Signs, and Portents, © 1985 by Algis Budrys

Hard Science in the Real World, © 1984 by Abbenford Associates

The Strange Journey: 1984, © 1985 by James Gunn

1984: The Fifty-Candle Blowout, © 1985 by Michael Glyer

New Rose Hotel, © 1984 by Omni Publications International Ltd.

Me and My Shadow, from *Unauthorized Autobiographies and Other Curiosities,* © 1984 by Michael Resnick

Me/Days, from *Universe 14,* © 1984 by Terry Carr

Silicon Muse, © 1984 by Davis Publications, Inc.

The Dominus Demonstration, © 1984 by Davis Publications, Inc.

The Crystal Spheres, © 1984 by Davis Publications, Inc.

A Day in the Life of a Classics Professor, © 1984 by Mercury Press, Inc.

The Picture Man, © 1984 by Mercury Press, Inc.

The Weigher, © 1984 by Davis Publications, Inc.

Demon Lover, © 1984 by Mercury Press, Inc.

Tourist Trade, © 1984 by *Playboy*

Editorial introductions © 1985 by Jerry Pournelle

Contents

Nonfiction

PREFACE 1

1984, *Nineteen Eighty-Four,* and Other SF Novels, Signs, and Portents, Algis Budrys 4
Hard Science in the Real World, Gregory Benford 52
The Strange Journey: 1984, James Gunn 156
1984: The Fifty-Candle Blowout, Michael Glyer 328

Fiction

New Rose Hotel, William Gibson 21
Me and My Shadow, Michael Resnick 35
Me/Days, Gregory Benford 73
Silicon Muse, Hilbert Schenck 85
The Dominus Demonstration, Charles Sheffield 109
The Crystal Spheres, David Brin 134
A Day in the Life of a Classics Professor, Stan Dryer 166
The Picture Man, John Dalmas 188
The Weigher, Eric Vinicoff and Marcia Martin 210
Demon Lover, M. Sargent Mackay 261
Tourist Trade, Robert Silverberg 302

PREFACE
Jerry Pournelle

There are "best of the year" anthologies in plenty; why another? The obvious reason, to make money, is insufficient. Anthologies are never best sellers, and story collections, even "best" story collections, never sell as well as theme anthologies (such as *Imperial Stars*). Still, Jim Baen and I work well together. We have similar views on where the science fiction field—and Western civilization, for that matter—should be going. We endured the bleak times of "national malaise"; now things are different, and it's time to enjoy. The main reason we decided to do yet another "best" anthology was for the sheer fun of it.

Of course we then got so busy that it became work; but that's not so bad. It's work we enjoy. It's also useful.

Then, too, this is no bad year to begin a new series of books of science fiction. The world has been waiting for 1984 since 1948; and if the real 1984 doesn't much resemble Orwell's fictional *Nineteen Eighty-four* we may, in all seriousness, thank science fiction writers, including Orwell. Heinlein, Kornbluth and Pohl, Anderson, and a score of others not only sounded warnings whenever the society seemed headed for a cliff, but did it so amusingly that many *listened* to what they were saying.

More: 1984 marks a year in which science fiction is becoming a reality. It is the year in which the President of the United States won reelection by pledging to turn the nation from one political philosophy back to another. It was a year in which scientists and politicians alike decided, in all seriousness, to begin work to make the ICBM "obsolete and irrelevant." Meanwhile, exploitation of the space environment continued, small but significant breakthroughs were achieved in developing fusion power, and the computer revolution raced ahead. The frightening part of Orwell's *Nineteen Eighty-Four* was that nothing changed nor ever could. The real 1984 was much more hopeful. What better year to launch a new "best of the year" series?

Even so, this isn't precisely a "best of the year" anthology. Most of the stories in this volume probably won't win awards, and even if they do it's likely to be coincidence. We didn't select stories for the *Yearbook* because we thought they were "best" in some abstract literary sense. I'm not at all sure what "best" in that context means, and I'm quite certain that neither I nor anyone I know has the ability to choose such works.

Our selection criteria are simple. Stories are in this book because John Carr, Jim Baen, and I all like them, and we're pretty sure that most readers will. They may not win awards. Alas, when science fiction readers vote awards, they don't always vote for the stories they like to read; often they vote for the stories they think they *ought* to like; a different proposition entirely.

The result hasn't always been beneficial. More than one story has, by winning awards, influenced editors to buy more of that kind of thing. The editor later discovers that "literary quality" doesn't insure sales. Some editors have made that an excuse and a slogan. "Quality doesn't sell." Critics eager to prove that America stinks make much of it. The public has neither judgment nor taste. You cannot write for the masses and yet write literature. Shakespeare and Dickens and Samuel Clemens might have had different views, but they're not available for comment.

John W. Campbell, Jr., was famous for his editorials. In one of his better ones Campbell put forth the proposition that the essential difference between Eastern and Western Civilization is an attitude toward teachers. In the Eastern traditions, it is the student's responsibility to understand what the teacher is saying, and thus the student's fault if the teacher isn't communicating. The West reverses that. It's the teacher's job to be understood.

As a result, according to Campbell, Eastern cultures are elitist and regimented, while the West enjoys equality and freedom. You don't have to swallow all of that to see that the concept is worth considering. I'd be the last to deny that there are worthwhile literary works that deserve survival no matter how poorly they do in the marketplace—but I'd hate to make that a rule. Readability and a good story line never harmed a work of literature.

There has to be more than that, of course. There are plenty of "good stories" that you read once and then forget. This isn't to disparage them. The world needs solid entertainments. It also needs art and literature, whatever those are. Tolstoy said that art without moral purpose is not art at all. I think I agree with that. If you don't, read his "What Is Art?" and "An Essay on Art" before making up your mind.

Entertainment sounds frivolous. Talk of a story's "message" makes it sound dull, yet stories without some kind of message—without something to say—are never memorable, and certainly ought not be included in a yearbook. Of course all messages aren't equal. Cultural relativism, the view that all belief systems are equally valid, that all cultures are worthwhile, leads to results whose absurdity is obvious to everyone not sheltered in a university environment.

The ideal story would be entertaining and at the same time inspiring; be both diverting and educational. Such stories aren't easy to find, but here are enough to make a book.

Editor's Introduction to "1984, *Nineteen Eighty-Four*, and Other SF Novels, Signs, and Portents," by Algis Budrys

It was easy to select the lead essayist for this book. Science fiction writers agree on very little, but most agree that Algis Budrys is our leading critical writer.

Algis Budrys was born in interesting times. His family held high positions in the Lithuanian diplomatic corps; eventually they were posted to the United States, where his father was the representative of the government in exile during World War II. After the war ended the Soviets stole many lands; some, like Poland and Hungary, became puppet states—for many years the Minister of Defense of Poland was a Russian general—but the Baltic Republics were not granted even that much dignity. They were formally incorporated into the Russian Federated Soviet Republic.

The United States has never recognized the extinction of the Baltic Republics. Latvia, Estonia, and Lithuania are, in theory, independent lands temporarily under the occupation of their Soviet masters. There was a time when we annually proclaimed "Captive Nations Week" in memory of those and other victims of Soviet conquest.

Alas, the United States has now signed the Helsinki accords, which as a practical matter end any possibility of

U.S. support to what were once known as the captive nations. In theory, in exchange for U.S. acceptance of existing borders in Eastern Europe the Helsinki agreements were to grant "human rights" to the citizens and subjects of the Soviet Empire; in practice, of course, any Soviet citizen who seeks to inquire about Soviet adherence to this agreement which the Soviet Union signed and ratified is locked in a madhouse or jailed as a traitor. So much for diplomacy.

A. J. Budrys for some years assisted his father in diplomatic work, and he continues to be interested in eastern European affairs. If anyone could make sense of 1984, he would.

1984, *Nineteen Eighty-Four*, and Other SF Novels, Signs, and Portents

Algis Budrys

It was the Orwellian year, and with a striking intensity it served to remind us that prediction is in the eye of the beholder. From late 1983 onward into January and February, persons on either side of the Iron Curtain who had never heard the term "speculative fiction" were assuring themselves and us that the gray era of Big Brother had indeed/indeed had not arrived on schedule over There, or over Here; that it had come, as foretold in *Nineteen Eighty-Four*, from the left/right; that the late George Orwell, publishing his magnum opus in 1949, had been a seer—no, not a seer, an allegorist—no, a satirist—no, a philosopher—well, absolutely, certainly, dead wrong/right or somewhere in between, just ask the Authorities of the right/left.

By March, it was apparently felt that enough mastic of one sort or another had been spread over the subject, for it rarely arose again. There was a rather nice, probably dull, possibly accurate enough biographical piece broadcast on national public television—something brought over from the BBC—and that, of course, was the signal that the last word had been registered and we could screw the lid back down again.

It had been instructive to watch the social coping process

at work, from the first ritualistic opening of the topic—in the pretense that Orwell's thirty-five-year-old observations were only going to go/not go into effect at midnight, December 31—to its eventual subsidence under the concerted shovel blades of the entire community. So that as midnight struck again, three hundred sixty-six days later, there were only the last few ceremonialized words to be spoken at the end of the exorcism, and then *Nineteen Eighty-Four* was as safely over as the year itself.

So don't you ever believe again that the world at large invariably ignores and dismisses SF. On the other hand, if you were Orwell's ghost, you might very well wish it did. But whatever else you make of all that, the plain fact is the distinction between SF and the rest of the world has been in the process of breaking down irreparably, and it's only fitting that 1984 should have been the year in which the signal was so blatantly given. Call the job done. Large parts of the world may as yet continue to despise SF, and some may stubbornly continue to deny that they ever breathe of it. O.K., some of it always has been, and very likely always will be, as worthless as human ingenuity can make it. And the capacity to deny the obvious is ultimately the thing that separates humankind from the animals. But SF is, it is in the air, it permeates the fabric of our lives, and if it doesn't always terrify us into such grotesque posturings as *Nineteen Eighty-Four* occasioned in that year, still it tickles us, often enough, year 'round, year in and year out, where we live.

What other tickles occurred in that leap year? What did they say about us? In a year peculiarly dominated by a novel, it so happened that the most innovative work appeared in book-length form, and in various ways it was often strikingly innovative. At other times, it was not. A number of 1984 SF novels struck me as impressively competent, and what this means among other things—some of those things being quite desirable, mind you—is that there was nothing in them that improved on any aspect of SF as it stood at midnight, December 31, 1983. It was, in short, a paradoxical year, particularly when one realizes that some of the innovation came from distinctly unexpected quarters. But, then, innovation will do that, won't it, and ultimately what the paradoxes of 1984 apparently add up to is some sign that something important, full of promise and vigor, is stirring around underneath it all, putting up pufflets of steam and/or heavier vapors through random cracks sprung up in the suddenly quivering ground. SF will do that, just about every five years. Next year, will the full irruption come? Let us see if we can tell what the new shape of the terrain might then be:

To my mind, the significant new speculative fiction novels published in 1984 were Larry Niven's *The Integral Trees*, Kim Stanley Robinson's *The Wild Shore*, Brian Aldiss' *Helliconia Summer*, Lucius Shepard's *Green Eyes*, Frederik Pohl's *Heechee Rendezvous*, Frank Herbert's *Heretics of Dune*, Frederik Pohl's *The Years of The City*, Harry Harrison's *West of Eden*, Frederik Pohl's *The Merchant's War*, Robert A. Heinlein's *Job: A Comedy of Justice*, William Gibson's *Neuromancer*, Jack Williamson's *Lifeburst*, Robert L. Forward's *The Flight of the Dragonfly* and John Varley's *Demon*, listed here in no systematic order.

Note that there is not a single outright fantasy novel on this list. Jody Scott's *I, Vampire* was a deft, interesting, often breathtakingly clever piece of work, but it is primarily a Viennese light opera of a book, just as K. W. Jeter's *Dr. Adder* is off-Broadway Grand Gugniol far more than it is science fiction. Thomas M. Disch's *The Businessman* is horror/social satire; books like these are products of crosscurrents, eddies, and random gusts—spume and spindrift, while down under the continental plates, far below the leaping waters, hotter, more profound upwellings stir through the molten core. You get my drift?

At any rate, while nearly innumerable fantasy titles appeared within the SF purview, there was nothing in them to match 1983's *Tea With the Black Dragon*. In 1984, fantasy novels consisted almost entirely of volumes in innumerable fantasy–adventure series that were being miscalled trilogies or tetralogies, owed altogether too much to each other's plotlines, casts of characters, and vocabularies, and in general, created the sort of soup you get from putting all the leftovers in one pot of boiling water. There were few exceptions to this pervasion of literary white-noise; none of those exceptions was skillful. In 1984, those in SF who love fantasy most—the supporters of Charles Grant's and Stuart Schiff's anthologies, the organizers of and attendees at the annual World Fantasy Convention—were forced to sustain themselves by paying overweighted attention to the Stephen King genre of horror stories with inclusions of fantasy images but no integral fantasy rationale. That's an awkward posture offering dubious long-term comfort. Except as a marketplace staple—and as a database for games—the fantasy side of SF was in a spell of creative reticence during this year, whereas science fiction was volubly energetic.

Even among the anthologies, the most dramatic was Michael Bishop's *Light Years and Dark*, a book combining reprint material with hitherto unpublished stories, and published as three things: [A] A hefty collection of excellent SF short work (including some poetry, indicative of a growing trend within trends), [B] a volume to place in one's library beside *Adventures in Time and Space* (1946) and the first book in the *Science Fiction Hall of Fame* series (1970), and [C] a manifesto to the effect that the days represented in the other two books were over; there were new names, new ways of doing, new masters. Hardly an unviable proposition, although Bishop will find, if he doesn't know already, that SF through the years has easily accommodated all its generations simultaneously. Critics and other community insiders may decree that some mode or another is passe, but the whole body of work simply expands, only rarely and slowly expunging anything that was once at its forefront, and the readership only gains and grows with it.

But—1984; what of it? It was the year in whose waning days Jack Williamson published *Lifeburst*, a novel whose crisp, in fact brittle opening chapter announced an easy, sophisticated view of international and corporate realpolitik that had previously been the province only of Graham Greene's or Eric Ambler's sort of world view. This tone was taken with the sort of story most recently deployed by Gregory Benford (in a 1984 edition, with *Across the Sea of Suns*) and in some ways reminiscent of Fred Saberhagen's venerable *Berserker* series. But these evocations are made fully conformable to Williamson's traditional, romantic galaxy-encompassing *geist*, at whose subtlest capillary ends we find the same thing the mythopoeic visions of Abe

Merritt evoked. But Williamson is Greene's and Ambler's contemporary, Merritt's apprentice, and Saberhagen's and Benford's precursor; it is all in fact organic with him, it worked, it intrigued, it propelled. A person whose first published fiction appeared in 1928 in a scientifiction magazine has written a considerable contemporary SF novel.

What is striking is that it could have happened decades ago. The novel is in a sense a companion piece to the June publication of Williamson's extraordinary autobiography, *Wonder Child*. In that account Williamson, and Williamson's major acquaintances in the SF world before, during, and after the "Golden Age" that preceded the 1950s, are shown to be unusual people in many ways, but most of them—certainly Williamson—are in quite good contact with the realities of the world, glorious and inglorious. They are well read in the classics, fully aware of literary history, and also conversant with styles in other forms of contemporary writing. Dashiell Hammett is cited by Williamson as a model, and Williamson's own hardscrabble early life, as well as his hardscrabble middle years, thoroughly equipped him to see quite clearly into the genuine bitter experience that more comfortable readers of Hammett take to be a patina of exaggeration for effect. But none of this ever showed up in Williamson's work, any more than it did in the work of Robert A. Heinlein, Williamson's host at meetings of the pre-World War II Mañana Literary Society. Nor did it appear in the writing or the editorial influence of his acquaintance, the young Futurian, Frederik Pohl, child of the Depression streets, or in any "modern" science fiction of the Golden Age, or, for that matter, of any later age. (The exceptions are ludicrously few, and for all practical purposes they are T.L. Sherred, author of "E for Effort," a story shoehorned into *Astounding Science Fiction* magazine by L. Jerome Stanton, briefly and heretically an assistant to editor John W. Campbell, Jr., keeper of the Golden Age.)

What makes *Lifeburst* such a peculiarly noteworthy novel—apart from its prima facie merits—is who it comes from; Jack Williamson, surely the Dean of Science Fiction at this point, and recent pitiless autobiographer. If it happened to him, it happened in some sense to all the others who worked in science fiction and newsstand fantasy during the long years after Hugo Gernsback's 1926 *Amazing Stories* both launched and ghettoized their genre, making them despicable from the days of their youth until they were all well past mid-life. Williamson was 62 in 1970, which was about when it became possible to introduce oneself as an SF writer in respectable company, if one chose it sagaciously. The people who were galvanized into SF writing by their readership of Gernsbackian fiction made us out of whatever had made them. The SF we read and follow today owes everything to them, directly or at very close second hand. They are primeval influences, buried so deep in our substance that no one could fully trace their courses, their force, or their side-currents and welling eddies; they form our Cordilleras, our geology. Yet some of them are still with us, quite bright-eyed; some of what we do is now redounding into fresh effects on them, and in looking at them we are studying ourselves. An outstanding feature of 1984, then, is the signal opportunity it afforded us to do this.

It has long been suspected that writers like the late Edmond ("World-Wrecker") Hamilton—to name the archetype, and Williamson's closest friend—were considerably more sophisticated than superficial readings of *Captain Future* stories might indicate. Williamson's account documents this truth. It also documents the fact that in many cases—Hamilton's among them—forms of SF were promulgated by their authors' peonage to formula-ridden publishers, who were practiced in the art of paying their contributors just enough to keep them going long enough to produce the next piece. But it documents something else—that this simple trap did not enclose all writers of SF during that time. The traps that enclosed the ones who still generally hold popular respect were less simple, and operated through workings we still do not fully understand, leaving chafe marks and contusions that their victims are not always conscious of, even yet; some of them have not healed.

Williamson's autobiography visibly grapples with this; speaks movingly of Hamilton's predicament while I think unconsciously contrasting it to Williamson's willingness to scrape and sometimes literally starve rather than work to Mort Wiesinger's editorial strictures at Standard Magazines; details Williamson's long, interrupted but faithful engagement with psychoanalysis in an attempt to resolve his confusions. At this distance, they seem very understandable confusions: A man with a first-class intellect, a thirst for knowledge and culture, and a track record of enormous mental and physical perseverance in the face of a Southwest dryland farmer's childhood and adolescence, found himself able to sell scientifiction magazine cover stories with impressive frequency, but somehow could not get into contact with the real world that enclosed him. He could not cope with it unaided, could not directly articulate his reactions to it, could speak of it only in allegorical terms. Nor could even the famed Menninger Clinic help him break through his reticence.

If Williamson was one of the few SF classicists to frankly seek structured therapy, he was hardly the only one to sense a need for it. Henry Kuttner and Catherine Moore, man and wife, plunged into an earnest fascination with psychology and psychiatry that lasted as long as Kuttner's life; A.E. van Vogt was only the frankest practitioner of an ongoing SF effort to find the road to freedom from human difficulties, and of course he and John W. Campbell, Jr., were among the earliest to seize upon the promise offered when L. Ron Hubbard formulated Dianetics. Heinlein's lifelong fascination with religion, and his fiercely channelled idealization of troubleshooting competence, are readily seeable as a reflection of this same turmoil. And so forth—forth, for many, into alcoholism and near-deliberate suicide.

So far as I can recall, none outright borrowed the shotgun example of Ernest Hemingway from the mundane, respectable world, preferring the hazes and liver-eating habits of F. Scott Fitzgerald and William Faulkner. (Faulkner's Hollywood work in his waning days had to be rescued into coherence by Leigh Brackett, who twinged Williamson's heart when she married Ed Hamilton.) Some—like Brackett and Hamilton, and many others—simply were not that deeply troubled at any level they would show, and many, like Williamson himself and like any number of artists and non-artists anywhere, continued to function well up to the standards of the "normal" world, if such a place exists. But it is notable that although they all read Hemingway, Faulkner and Fitzgerald, and Hammett, and Greene and Ambler and Raymond Chandler, and could demonstrate an ability to analyze and duplicate their styles—more important, were just as aware of the contemporary world as these variously talented and situated colleagues were—none of them chose to write their life's work from that standpoint. Rather, they seem to have deliberately denied their access to that heritage.

Only the sudden(?) emergence of its use—in *Lifeburst*, and coincidentally(?) in Pohl's *The Years of The City*—enables us to prove what we have long declared to hostile critics; that SF writers could duplicate the signatures of contemporary fiction if they wanted to, that they have always had this capability, but that they weren't interested.

True, all true, but now, it seems, insufficiently examined. Now we have to face the implications: That they may have technically been capable, but that they were helpless; consciously willing, consciously dead set against it, tormented by their situation, putting the best face on it that they could and thus producing a body of work that is nominally about one thing but secretly about something else. Now something is unexpectedly beginning to change them. What is that thing? We have spent calendar generations in denying that SF was inferior to "literature." We have contented ourselves with pointing out that no one has an objective basis for detecting "literature", and that what we do might be that thing, whatever it is, just as often as what other writers do. If there were studies of the crucial conflicts within other kinds of writers—in general or with reference to particular names such as Hemingway, Thomas Heggen, Ross Lockridge, or John Horne Burns—we felt no need to go see if these cases had any relevance to us. We have often declared that SF was equal but separate, that there are SF writers and readers, and then there are other sorts, but now, suddenly—May it be catastrophically? —the mountains may be stirring; our ancestors may be mutating.

We are not going to resolve any of that here, for the simple reason that there simply isn't enough evidence yet for much of anything but a line of speculation. It may have real relevance and may simply be a transient artifact. But it certainly is an interesting question. In search not of answers but of threads in a labyrinth under construction, let us look further at the year's output:

Some of the year's work is deliberately—that is to say, conventionally—innovative. Ace Books commissioned veteran editor Terry Carr to find a series of spectacular first novelists, and in this chancy and apparently foredoomed game, he has succeeded with verve. He has also succeeded to popular acclaim within the SF community. All of the first three books in the apparently bi-monthly series of New Ace Specials were serious year's-end contenders for the Nebula Award of the Science Fiction Writers of America.

They were Kim Stanley Robinson's *The Wild Shore*, a post-Apocalyptic novel; Lucius Shepard's *Green Eyes*, about a risky experiment in biology, and William Gibson's *Neuromancer*, which had more Nebula nominations than any other title at all. It is about human/computer interfacing. These are solid science fiction themes, and that is typical of the series, which seems to be avoiding fantasy (perhaps because the more original new writers are avoiding it). Also typical of the series is their departure—usually radical and swift—from the ways even most of Michael Bishop's anthologees would have thought of writing them. The Apocalypse in *The Wild Shore* is not worldwide; it is strictly confined to the United States, so that Robinson talks a kind of world politics not accessible to the imaginations of writers dealing with worldwide plague or World War III. But that's not unconventional enough. The locale is John Steinbeck country, and although other names occur when one attempts to characterize the feel of the book—the late first novelist Tom Reamy, for one—the common precursor there is Steinbeck, just as Gregory Benford's 1983 *Against Infinity* owes an open debt to Faulkner's "The Bear."

Green Eyes was characterized by one critical journal as possibly being in a brand new genre. I found a strong kinship to William Sloane's 1939 *Edge of Running Water*, and very little else even at the periphery of SF as we know it. It is probably the only existentialist bayou-regional contemporaneously satyric voodoo-horror antideath science fiction novel of 1984.

As for *Neuromancer*, it is the most amazing thing that ever happened to the road/quest novel. The same critical journal cited previously, speaking to the hundreds of Science Fiction Research Association members around the world, expressed concern that with this first novel Gibson's best work conceivably now lay behind him.

What does this tell us? I'm not one hundred percent sure, but what I think it tells us is that the more a new SF writer works in the way that reminds colleagues and academicians of the way the ideal non-SF writer works, the more dazzling his promise.

That's not an unmitigated disaster. Fashionability does not preclude excellence, and these will be good books after the reasons for their excellence have changed. But the nature of the fashion is indicative in our present context of discussion.

You will have noticed that Frederik Pohl had three new novels out in 1984 (in addition to several reprints of various sorts). The nature of these books, in the context of his career, may also have considerable relevance to the present topic.

Pohl is probably Mister Science Fiction. To the best of my knowledge, he has never drawn an illustration, but I cannot think of what else he hasn't done in our field over the years since the late 1930s. He is among our first-rate writers and our very best editors of magazines or books; he has catalyzed more major projects in this field than even Donald A. Wollheim, and nurtured more proteges and dispensed more practical wisdom to young writers than anyone except John W. Campbell, Jr.—and at times it was far better advice.

In the 1950s, he and fellow Futurian Cyril Kornbluth, in overt and covert collaboration, set the fashion for what Kingsley Amis, lecturing at Princeton, came to call the "comic inferno" school of post-Campbellian SF writing. Pohl-Kornbluth's *The Space Merchants* made newsstand-borne SF at least conditionally respectable in academe and on Madison Avenue, and arguably started us on the road to the 1970s and beyond. Considered both as a landmark and as a commercial property, *The Space Merchants* has been an enormous success for thirty years. So it comes as no surprise that in the present marketing climate, where publishers see SF on the best-seller list every week, there should be a sequel. And *The Merchants' War* is deftly that; written in the hip, knowledgeable style available to someone who had been a direct-mail promotion copywriter in his day, replete with adbiz circumstantiality and the bouncy, finger-popping prose technique that marked what was thought of as the best writing in the days of Horace Gold's *Galaxy* magazine.

This was, of course, a technique Pohl had left behind, spectacularly. With novels such as *Man Plus* (1976) and especially with *Gateway* (1979), he had gone beyond the stage of winning awards; he had won so many of them, from so many diverse places, it was obvious he had outrun the community's capacity to confer honor. It was obvious from the text of *Gateway* that he had also outrun something in the early Pohl. Interestingly enough, its viewpoint hero tells his story in the course of psychoanalysis . . . in the course of struggling to be reborn . . . and what he is leaving behind is hipness; thumbrule wisdom, attitudinal ploys upon life, the search for the handle on the pot of gold. What he is striving for is humanity and the burden of the human condition . . . the universal human condition at which the best of us may weep or guffaw, but which must be borne. No one who reads *Gateway* could help but feel its power.

In the merchants' world, of course, that translated into numbers, and so the events—the events, not the power—of *Gateway* were made to form the basis for one sequel, *Beyond the Blue Event Horizon*, and now, in our year, *Heechee Rendezvous*. So the modish predilection for trilogies has been fulfilled, by a superbly skilled commercial writer responding to market suction. Written in a style that might be called "heightened utilitarian"—characters are moved around by unexceptionable prose until the moment comes to express some awesome picture, such as a truly alien spaceship or a vast field of glimmering stars; moment having passed, back to short, transparent Scotchtape words—this book of Pohl's might have been written by Arthur C. Clarke or Frank Herbert assigned to complete someone else's project, assuming either of those millionaires could be persuaded. It is a good job of well-done work. (Paradoxically, it is a job whose dissatisfactions may well lead its author to produce a fourth volume in an attempt to make it right again.)

But beside these two vastly different but frequently similar works there occurred *The Years of the City*, which is by an at least partly brand-new Pohl. In fact, if it weren't for the appearance of the new book by Pohl's old acquaintance, frequent co-guest at conventions and sometime collaborator, Williamson, a unique brand-new kind of SF writer.

Technically, the characteristic style of this kind is arrived at by a major main-line SF writer's taking everything already possible to newsstand SF and recasting much of it into the language of popular writing. That is, not the clubfooted semiliteracy of the Arthur Haileys and Irving Wallaces, or the apt pretentiousness of the Gore Vidals and Norman Mailers, but the deft, easily literate, cosmopolitan skill of America's real contemporary novelists— the crime and suspense writers who have brought the time of Hammett and Chandler up through Ed McBain to Robert Parker and Elmore Leonard.

This is, let me make clear, far different from a casual hack's writing a series of sex–violence stories set in an urban future. Neither is it the sort of doctrinaire proletarianism the Futurians adopted for lack of sufficient experience in life. In the kind of work Williamson has done under *Lifeburst*'s galactic proscenium arch, or that Pohl has done with his nutsy-boltsy collection of novellas that turns into an epic poem of informed appreciation to New York City, all the essence of SF are preserved. What is added is the Hammett-sired familiarity with the universes inside a person going through a garbage can for dinner; the nuts and bolts within that which perceives the stars.

That may be all it is; a grafting of one set of genre signatures onto another. But for years it has been clear that Hammett and Chandler spoke of something that did not die when the month's issue turned yellow in the alley, and neither is it accurate and sufficient to call SF a mere genre. It may—may—prove true in the end that indeed all this is inconsiderable. But I don't think so. At the other extreme, it may—may—prove true that the *real* American literatures of the twentieth century, proceeding with no need for much attention to what the book review supplements thought was going on, are meeting and merging. More likely seeming, because less extreme, is the proposition that SF, now containing individuals who have lived long enough and thrashed through enough, is learning additional ways to handle alienation, and will borrow the best out of Hammett and Greene rather in the way that John W. Campbell tried to borrow the best out of H.G. Wells.

Perhaps. Perhaps. Writing a 1994 essay similar to this, it will all be easier to see, two additional generations having passed and Pohl and Williamson no doubt having done yet something else.

What of the rest of the books that caught my eye in 1984? What do they prove?

In the case of *The Integral Trees*, the proof is that Larry Niven can still write like the Niven of *Ringworld* (1970), which is quite good. Audience reaction within the community, however, indicates that while this continues to excite respect, it does not excite emulation; Niven is no longer a pioneer. Never mind; there were years, perhaps decades, in which Pohl and Williamson were not pioneers.

Helliconia Summer, sequel to *Helliconia Spring* and precursor of *Helliconias* to come, is part of a truly unified multi-volume work that cannot be effectively assessed until all its parts are in. Assessing the existing part, one finds the return of an attractive Aldiss signature—the freakish astronomical system, a la the *Hothouse* series (1961 et seq) —and one finds an absence of the cleverness for its own sake that marked his *Cryptozooic* period (circa 1967), at which latter time he was working his way through the mindsets of the '60s New Wave period. What one finds instead are many evocations of his well-known (in England) non-SF work, which the U.S. audience has denied as surely as it denied James Blish's *Doctor Mirabilis*, and which led Blish to spend his last years in England. There the ghetto is differently arranged and there Thomas M. Disch also went to find his voice ... and, in his case, bring it back again. Moves of that sort have traditionally confused the U.S. audience, as well as the marketers of literary product. Less well understood is the fact that they have confused many a watching U.S. author, as well. Perhaps there is meaning here, too, in what 1984 may have brought to North America.

What was brought to Harry Harrison, child of Manhattan but citizen of the world, is surely remarkable in the light of *West of Eden*. What was once a very rough-and-ready prose style, serving comic-book plots, had evolved into a literary vehicle for Harrison's ability to paint pictures. This combined happily with an equally long-standing talent for thinking SFnally . . . for having the kind of idea that immediately engages the SF addict. In his first story, "Rock Diver," in the earliest 1950s, it was the interpenetration of matter. In this triumphantly SFnal magnum opus, it is the supposition that in an alternate world the dinosaurs did not become extinct; that they evolved intelligence and, unaware of one tiny enclave of mammals evolved into humankind, rule the Earth. This is almost certainly the SF novel of the year, in the strict—and therefore perhaps inappropriate—sense of the term.

If it has a rival, it's Forward's *The Flight of the Dragonfly*. In a year lacking a new Hal Clement novel, or Dr. Forward's own *Dragon's Egg* of a generation ago, this story of a possibly suicidal scientific flight, to a fascinating astrophysical object, thus idealizes one of the central tenets of SF, certainly as Campbell understood it.

Frank Herbert, I think, was just filling in the boxes with *Heretics of Dune*, but no *Dune* book is inconsiderable in the light of the enormous promotional efforts surrounding the release of the *Dune* film. Still and all, like Arthur C. Clarke's *2010*, here is a book that would never have been written under any circumstances imaginable before SF became Box Office, so it is also notable as another example of what a professional can do in the absence of inspiration.

John Varley brought his *Titan* trilogy to a close with *Demon*. What is most notable about this book is that it lacks pleasant surprises from a writer who, not very many years ago, was considered at the very cutting edge. All the inventions here are the sort found in *Heechee Rendezvous*; ingenuities directed not at creating fresh wonders but at excusing evident flaws in the preceding ones. Still, that's a hopeful type of resemblance, if Varley is just consolidating toward a *Years of The City* of his own.

And we end as we began—that is, as Campbellian "Modern" science fiction began in the Golden Age when a young and inventive Heinlein stretched out his arms to the new Eden and began to create, create, create. *Job: A Comedy of Justice*, is a far less naive book than such pre-war *Astounding* serials as *Beyond This Horizon* with its reincarnation gimmick superimposed on an action plot about counter-revolution, or *Sixth Column*, with its Campbell-inspired story about the religion whose miracles stem from encrypted technology. It is also not as good a book. The central character is crucially unfocused, unlike the shrewdly disguised godlike creative computer in *The Moon is a Harsh Mistress* (1966). Nevertheless, *Job* is a certainly good enough read, and for all its ambiguities, a visible attempt at a roaring satire on organized religion contrasted to the real thing that religion addresses. Heaven knows what the general public thought it was about, but in any event it rode the best-seller list for weeks on end. Heaven knows what Heinlein thought it was about.

But, then, no one ever really knows what any book is really about, and so no one knows what any literature is about, what it's for, or where its boundaries begin and end. But one ponders, one thinks, one suspects, and so do we all ponder. From that rumination comes, inevitably, 1985 and all the 1985s to come.

Editor's Introduction To "New Rose Hotel," by William Gibson

During the euphoric days following the Allied victories in World War II, Eric Blair, journalist, socialist, and social critic, wrote (as George Orwell) a novel of a year a bit more than a generation away. While everyone else rejoiced over the defeat of the NDSAP—the National German Socialist Workers Party—Blair brooded about a future in which socialist bureaucrats took and kept control. "If you want a picture of the future," he said, "imagine a boot stamping on a human face. Forever."

It didn't happen. Orwell's year has passed, and Western civilization, flawed and with warts aplenty, yet lives to stand guard over more true freedoms for more people than any civilization has offered through history. The survival of freedom is not assured, but at least it remains possible.

Orwell told us of a world that could happen. William Gibson writes of another world that must not be.

New Rose Hotel

William Gibson

Seven rented nights in this coffin, Sandii. New Rose Hotel. How I want you now. Sometimes I hit you. Replay it so slow and sweet and mean, I can almost feel it. Sometimes I take your little automatic out of my bag, run my thumb down smooth, cheap chrome. Chinese .22, its bore no wider than the dilated pupils of your vanished eyes.

Fox is dead now, Sandii.

Fox told me to forget you.

I remember Fox leaning against the padded bar in the dark lounge of some Singapore hotel, Bencoolen Street, his hands describing different spheres of influence, internal rivalries, the arc of a particular career, a point of weakness he had discovered in the armor of some think tank. Fox was point man in the skull wars, a middleman for corporate crossovers. He was a soldier in the secret skirmishes of the zaibatsus, the multinational corporations that control entire economies.

I see Fox grinning, talking fast, dismissing my ventures into intercorporate espionage with a shake of his head. The Edge, he said, have to find that Edge. He made you hear the capital *E*. The Edge was Fox's grail, that essential fraction of sheer human talent, nontransferable, locked in the skulls of the world's hottest research scientists.

You can't put Edge down on paper, Fox said, can't punch Edge into a diskette.

The money was in corporate defectors.

Fox was smooth, the severity of his dark, French suits offset by a boyish forelock that wouldn't stay in place. I never liked the way the effect was ruined when he stepped back from the bar, his left shoulder skewed at an angle no Paris tailor could conceal. Someone had run him over with a taxi in Berne, and nobody quite knew how to put him together again.

I guess I went with him because he said he was after that Edge.

And somewhere out there, on our way to find the Edge, I found you, Sandii.

The New Rose Hotel is a coffin rack on the ragged fringes of Narita International. Plastic capsules a meter high and three long, stacked like surplus Godzilla teeth in a concrete lot off the main road to the airport. Each capsule has a television mounted flush with the ceiling. I spend whole days watching Japanese game shows and old movies. Sometimes I have your gun in my hand.

Sometimes I can hear the jets, laced into holding patterns over Narita. I close my eyes and imagine the sharp, white contrails fading, losing definition.

You walked into a bar in Yokohama, the first time I saw you. Eurasian, half gaijin, long-hipped and fluid in a Chinese knock-off of some Tokyo designer's original. Dark European eyes, Asian cheekbones. I remember you dumping your purse out on the bed, later, in some hotel room, pawing through your makeup. A crumpled wad of New Yen, dilapidated address book held together with rubber bands, a Mitsubishi bank chip, Japanese passport with a gold chrysanthemum stamped on the cover, and the Chinese .22.

You told me your story. Your father had been an executive in Tokyo, but now he was disgraced, disowned, cast down by Hosaka, the biggest zaibatsu of all. That night your mother was Dutch, and I listened as you spun out those summers in Amsterdam for me, the pigeons in Dam Square like a soft, brown carpet.

I never asked what your father might have done to earn his disgrace. I watched you dress; watched the swing of your dark, straight hair, how it cut the air.

Now Hosaka hunts me.

The coffins of New Rose are racked in recycled scaffolding, steel pipes under bright enamel. Paint flakes away when I climb the ladder, falls with each step as I follow the catwalk. My left hand counts off the coffin hatches, their multilingual decals warning of fines levied for the loss of a key.

I look up as the jets rise out of Narita, passage home, distant now as any moon.

Fox was quick to see how we could use you, but not sharp enough to credit you with ambition. But then he never lay all night with you on the beach at Kamakura, never listened to your nightmares, never heard an entire imagined childhood shift under those stars, shift and roll over, your child's mouth opening to reveal some fresh past, and always the one, you swore, that was really and finally the truth.

I didn't care, holding your hips while the sand cooled against your skin.

Once you left me, ran back to that beach saying you'd forgotten our key. I found it in the door and went after you, to find you ankle deep in surf, your smooth back rigid, trembling; your eyes far away. You couldn't talk. Shivering. Gone. Shaking for different futures and better pasts.

Sandii, you left me here.

You left me all your things.

This gun. Your makeup, all the shadows and blushes capped in plastic. Your Cray microcomputer, a gift from Fox, with a shopping list you entered. Sometimes I play that back, watching each item cross the little silver screen.

A freezer. A fermenter. An incubator. An electrophoresis system with integrated agarose cell and transilluminator. A tissue embedder. A high-performance liquid chromatograph. A flow cytometer. A spectrophotometer. Four gross of borosilicate scintillation vials. A microcentrifuge. And one DNA synthesizer, with in-built computer. Plus software.

Expensive, Sandii, but then Hosaka was footing our bills. Later you made them pay even more, but you were already gone.

Hiroshi drew up that list for you. In bed, probably. Hiroshi Yomiuri. Maas Biolabs GmbH had him. Hosaka wanted him.

He was hot. Edge and lots of it. Fox followed genetic engineers the way a fan follows players in a favorite game. Fox wanted Hiroshi so bad he could taste it.

He'd sent me up to Frankfurt three times before you turned up, just to have a look-see at Hiroshi. Not to make a pass or even to give him a wink and a nod. Just to watch.

Hiroshi showed all the signs of having settled in. He'd found a German girl with a taste for conservative loden and riding boots polished the shade of a fresh chestnut. He'd bought a renovated townhouse on just the right square. He'd taken up fencing and given up kendo.

And everywhere the Maas security teams, smooth and heavy, a rich, clear syrup of surveillance. I came back and told Fox we'd never touch him.

You touched him for us, Sandii. You touched him just right.

Our Hosaka contacts were like specialized cells protecting the parent organism. We were mutagens, Fox and I, dubious agents adrift on the dark side of the intercorporate sea.

When we had you in place in Vienna, we offered them Hiroshi. They didn't even blink. Dead calm in an L.A. hotel room. They said they had to think about it.

Fox spoke the name of Hosaka's primary competitor in the gene game, let it fall out naked, broke the protocol forbidding the use of proper names.

They had to think about it, they said.

Fox gave them three days.

I took you to Barcelona a week before I took you to Vienna. I remember you with your hair tucked back into a gray beret, your high Mongol cheekbones reflected in the windows of ancient shops. Strolling down the Ramblas to the Phoenician harbor, past the glass-roofed Mercado selling oranges out of Africa.

The old Ritz, warm in our room, dark, with all the soft

weight of Europe pulled over us like a quilt. I could enter you in your sleep. You were always ready. Seeing your lips in a soft, round *O* of surprise, your face about to sink into the thick, white pillow—archaic linen of the Ritz. Inside you I imagined all that neon, the crowds surging around. Shinjuku Station, wired electric night. You moved that way, rhythm of a new age, dreamy and far from any nation's soul.

When we flew to Vienna, I installed you in Hiroshi's wife's favorite hotel. Quiet, solid, the lobby tiled like a marble chessboard, with brass elevators smelling of lemon oil and small cigars. It was easy to imagine her there, the highlights on her riding boots reflected in polished marble, but we knew she wouldn't be coming along, not this trip.

She was off to some Rhineland spa, and Hiroshi was in Vienna for a conference. When Maas security flowed in to scan the hotel, you were out of sight.

Hiroshi arrived an hour later, alone.

Imagine an alien, Fox once said, who's come here to identify the planet's dominant form of intelligence. The alien has a look, then chooses. What do you think he picks? I probably shrugged.

The zaibatsus, Fox said, the multinationals. The blood of a zaibatsu is information, not people. The structure is independent of the individual lives that comprise it. Corporation as life form.

Not the Edge lecture again, I said.

Maas isn't like that, he said, ignoring me.

Maas was small, fast, ruthless. An atavism. Maas was all Edge.

I remember Fox talking about the nature of Hiroshi's Edge. Radioactive nucleases, monoclonal antibodies, something to do with the linkage of proteins, nucleotides . . . Hot, Fox called them, hot proteins. High-speed links. He said Hiroshi was a freak, the kind who shatters paradigms, inverts a whole field of science, brings on the violent revision of an entire body of knowledge. Basic patents, he said, his throat tight with the sheer wealth of it, with the high, thin smell of tax-free millions that clung to those two words.

Hosaka wanted Hiroshi, but his Edge was radical enough to worry them. They wanted him to work in isolation.

I went to Marrakech, to the old city, the Medina. I found a heroin lab that had been converted to the extraction of pheromones. I bought it, with Hosaka's money.

I walked the marketplace at Djemaa-el-Fna with a sweating Portuguese businessman, discussing fluorescent lighting and the installation of ventilated specimen cages. Beyond the city walls, the high Atlas. Djemaa-el-Fna was thick with jugglers, dancers, storytellers, small boys turning lathes with their feet, legless beggars with wooden bowls under animated holograms advertising French software.

We strolled past bales of raw wool and plastic tubs of Chinese microchips. I hinted that my employers planned to manufacture synthetic beta-endorphin. Always try to give them something they understand.

Sandii, I remember you in Harajuku, sometimes. Close my eyes in this coffin and I can see you there—all the glitter, crystal maze of the boutiques, the smell of new clothes. I see your cheekbones ride past chrome racks of Paris leathers. Sometimes I hold your hand.

We thought we'd found you, Sandii, but really you'd found us. Now I know you were looking for us or for someone like us. Fox was delighted, grinning over our find: such a pretty new tool, bright as any scalpel. Just the thing to help us sever a stubborn Edge, like Hiroshi's, from the jealous parent-body of Maas Biolabs.

You must have been searching a long time, looking for a way out, all those nights down Shinjuku. Nights you carefully cut from the scattered deck of your past.

My own past had gone down years before, lost with all hands, no trace. I understood Fox's late-night habit of emptying his wallet, shuffling through his identification. He'd lay the pieces out in different patterns, rearrange them, wait for a picture to form. I knew what he was looking for. You did the same thing with your childhoods.

In New Rose, tonight, I choose from your deck of pasts.

I choose the original version, the famous Yokohama hotel-room text, recited to me that first night in bed. I choose the disgraced father, Hosaka executive. Hosaka. How perfect. And the Dutch mother, the summers in Amsterdam, the soft blanket of pigeons in the Dam Square afternoon.

I came in out of the heat of Marrakech into Hilton air conditioning. Wet shirt clinging cold to the small of my back while I read the message you'd relayed through Fox. You were in all the way; Hiroshi would leave his wife. It wasn't difficult for you to communicate with us, even through the clear, tight film of Maas security; you'd shown Hiroshi the perfect little place for coffee and kipferl. Your favorite waiter was white haired, kindly, walked with a limp, and worked for us. You left your messages under the linen napkin.

All day today I watched a small helicopter cut a tight grid above this country of mine, the land of my exile, the New Rose Hotel. Watched from my hatch as its patient shadow crossed the grease-stained concrete. Close. Very close.

I left Marrakech for Berlin. I met with a Welshman in a bar and began to arrange for Hiroshi's disappearance.

It would be a complicated business, intricate as the brass gears and sliding mirrors of Victorian stage magic, but the desired effect was simple enough. Hiroshi would step behind a hydrogen-cell Mercedes and vanish. The dozen Maas agents who followed him constantly would swarm around the van like ants; the Maas security apparatus would harden around his point of departure like epoxy.

They knew how to do business promptly in Berlin. I was even able to arrange a fast night with you. I kept it secret from Fox; he might not have approved. Now I've forgotten the town's name. I knew it for an hour on the autobahn, under a gray Rhenish sky, and forgot it in your arms.

The rain began, sometime toward morning. Our room had a single window, high and narrow, where I stood and watched the rain fur the river with silver needles. Sound of your breathing. The river flowed beneath low, stone arches. The street was empty. Europe was a dead museum.

I'd already booked your flight to Marrakech, out of Orly, under your newest name. You'd be on your way when I pulled the final string and dropped Hiroshi out of sight.

You'd left your purse on the dark, old bureau. While you

slept I went through your things, removing anything that might clash with the new cover I'd bought for you in Berlin. I took the Chinese .22, your microcomputer, and your bank chip. I took a new passport, Dutch, from my bag, a Swiss bank chip in the same name, and tucked them into your purse.
My hand brushed something flat. I drew it out, held the thing, a diskette. No labels.
It lay there in the palm of my hand, all that death. Latent, coded, waiting.
I stood there and watched you breathe, watched your breasts rise and fall. Saw your lips slightly parted, and in the jut and fullness of your lower lip, the faintest suggestion of bruising.
I put the diskette back into your purse. When I lay down beside you, you rolled against me, waking, on your breath all the electric night of a new Asia, the future rising in you like a bright fluid, washing me of everything but the moment. That was your magic, that you lived outside of history, all now.
And you knew how to take me there.
For the very last time, you took me.
While I was shaving, I heard you empty your makeup into my bag. I'm Dutch now, you said, I'll want a new look.
Dr. Hiroshi Yomiuri went missing in Vienna, in a quiet street off Singerstrasse, two blocks from his wife's favorite hotel. On a clear afternoon in October, in the presence of a dozen expert witnesses, Dr. Yomiuri vanished.
He stepped through a looking glass. Somewhere, offstage, the oiled play of Victorian clockwork.
I sat in a hotel room in Geneva and took the Welshman's call. It was done, Hiroshi down my rabbit hole and headed for Marrakech. I poured myself a drink and thought about your legs.
Fox and I met in Narita a day later, in a sushi bar in the JAL terminal. He'd just stepped off an Air Maroc jet, exhausted and triumphant.
Loves it there, he said, meaning Hiroshi. Loves her, he said, meaning you.
I smiled. You'd promised to meet me in Shinjuku in a month.

Your cheap, little gun in the New Rose Hotel. The chrome is starting to peel. The machining is clumsy, blurry Chinese stamped into rough steel. The grips are red plastic, molded with a dragon on either side. Like a child's toy.

Fox ate sushi in the JAL terminal, high on what we'd done. The shoulder had been giving him trouble, but he said he didn't care. Money now for better doctors. Money now for everything.

Somehow it didn't seem very important to me, the money we'd gotten from Hosaka. Not that I doubted our new wealth, but that last night with you had left me convinced that it all came to us naturally, in the new order of things, as a function of who and what we were.

Poor Fox. With his blue oxford shirts crisper than ever, his Paris suits darker and richer. Sitting there in JAL, dabbing sushi into a little rectangular tray of green horseradish, he had less than a week to live.

Dark now, and the coffin racks of New Rose are lit all night by floodlights, high on painted metal masts. Nothing here seems to serve its original purpose. Everything is surplus, recycled, even the coffins. Forty years ago these plastic capsules were stacked in Tokyo or Yokohama, a modern convenience for traveling businessmen. Maybe your father slept in one. When the scaffolding was new, it rose around the shell of some mirrored tower on the Ginza, swarmed over by crews of builders.

The breeze tonight brings the rattle of a pachinko parlor, the smell of stewed vegetables from the pushcarts across the road.

I spread crab-flavored krill paste on orange rice crackers. I can hear the planes.

Those last few days in Tokyo, Fox and I had adjoining suites on the fifty-third floor of the Hyatt. No contact with Hosaka. They paid us, then erased us from official corporate memory.

But Fox couldn't let go. Hiroshi was his baby, his pet project. He'd developed a proprietary, almost fatherly, interest in Hiroshi. He loved him for his Edge. So Fox had me keep in touch with my Portuguese businessman in the Medina, who was willing to keep a very partial eye on Hiroshi's lab for us.

When he phoned, he'd phone from a stall in Djemaa-el-

Fna, with a background of wailing vendors and Atlas panpipes. Someone was moving security into Marrakech, he told us. Fox nodded. Hosaka.

After less than a dozen calls, I saw the change in Fox, a tension, a look of abstraction. I'd find him at the window, staring down fifty-three floors into the imperial gardens, lost in something he wouldn't talk about.

Ask him for a more detailed description, he said, after one particular call. He thought a man our contact had seen entering Hiroshi's lab might be Moenner, Hosaka's leading gene man.

That was Moenner, he said, after the next call. Another call and he thought he'd identified Chedanne, who headed Hosaka's protein team. Neither had been seen outside the corporate arcology in over two years.

By then it was obvious that Hosaka's leading researchers were pooling quietly in the Medina, the black executive Lears whispering into the Marrakech airport on carbon-fiber wings. Fox shook his head. He was a professional, a specialist, and he saw the sudden accumulation of all that prime Hosaka Edge in the Medina as a drastic failure in the zaibatsu's tradecraft.

Christ, he said, pouring himself a Black Label, they've got their whole bio section in there right now. One bomb. He shook his head. One grenade in the right place at the right time . . .

I reminded him of the saturation techniques Hosaka security was obviously employing. Hosaka had lines to the heart of the Diet, and their massive infiltration of agents into Marrakech could only be taking place with the knowledge and cooperation of the Moroccan government.

Hang it up, I said. It's over. You've sold them Hiroshi. Now forget him.

I know what it is, he said. I know. I saw it once before.

He said that there was a certain wild factor in lab work. The edge of Edge, he called it. When a researcher develops a breakthrough, others sometimes find it impossible to duplicate the first researcher's results. This was even more likely with Hiroshi, whose work went against the conceptual grain of his field. The answer, often, was to fly the breakthrough boy from lab to corporate lab for a ritual laying on of hands. A few pointless adjustments in the equipment, and the process would work. Crazy thing, he said, nobody knows why it works that way, but it does. He grinned.

But they're taking a chance, he said. Bastards told us they wanted to isolate Hiroshi, keep him away from their central research thrust. Balls. Bet your ass there's some kind of power struggle going on in Hosaka research. Somebody big's flying his favorite in and rubbing them all over Hiroshi for luck. When Hiroshi shoots the legs out from under genetic engineering, the Medina crowd's going to be ready.

He drank his scotch and shrugged.

Go to bed, he said. You're right, it's over.

I did go to bed, but the phone woke me. Marrakech again, the white static of a satellite link, a rush of frightened Portuguese.

Hosaka didn't freeze our credit, they caused it to evaporate. Fairy gold. One minute we were millionaires in the world's hardest currency, and the next we were paupers. I woke Fox.

Sandii, he said. She sold out. Maas security turned her in Vienna. Sweet Jesus.

I watched him slit his battered suitcase apart with a Swiss army knife. He had three gold bars glued in there with contact cement. Soft plates, each one proofed and stamped by the treasury of some extinct African government.

I should've seen it, he said, his voice flat.

I said no. I think I said your name.

Forget her, he said. Hosaka wants us dead. They'll assume we crossed them. Get on the phone and check our credit.

Our credit was gone. They denied that either of us had ever had an account.

Haul ass, Fox said.

We ran. Out a service door, into Tokyo traffic, and down into Shinjuku. That was when I understood for the first time the real extent of Hosaka's reach.

Every door was closed. People we'd done business with for two years saw us coming, and I'd see steel shutters slam behind their eyes. We'd get out before they had a chance to reach for the phone. The surface tension of the underworld had been tripled, and everywhere we'd meet that same taut membrane and be thrown back. No chance to sink, to get out of sight.

Hosaka let us run for most of that first day. Then they sent someone to break Fox's back a second time.

I didn't see them do it, but I saw him fall. We were in a Ginza department store an hour before closing, and I saw his arc off that polished mezzanine, down into all the wares of the new Asia.

They missed me somehow, and I just kept running. Fox took the gold with him, but I had a hundred New Yen in my pocket. I ran. All the way to the New Rose Hotel.

Now it's time.

Come with me, Sandii. Hear the neon humming on the road to Narita International. A few late moths trace stop-motion circles around the floodlights that shine on New Rose.

And the funny thing, Sandii, is how sometimes you just don't seem real to me. Fox once said you were ectoplasm, a ghost called up by the extremes of economics. Ghost of the new century, congealing on a thousand beds in the world's Hyatts, the world's Hiltons.

Now I've got your gun in my hand, jacket pocket, and my hand seems so far away. Disconnected.

I remember my Portuguese business friend forgetting his English, trying to get it across in four languages I barely understood, and I thought he was telling me that the Medina was burning. Not the Medina. The brains of Hosaka's best research people. Plague, he was whispering, my businessman, plague and fever and death.

Smart Fox, he put it together on the run. I didn't even have to mention finding the diskette in your bag in Germany.

Someone had reprogrammed the DNA synthesizer, he said. The thing was there for the overnight construction of just the right macromolecule. With its in-built computer and its custom software. Expensive, Sandii. But not as expensive as you turned out to be for Hosaka.

I hope you got a good price from Maas.

The diskette in my hand. Rain on the river. I knew, but I couldn't face it. I put the code for that meningial virus back into your purse and lay down beside you.

So Moenner died, along with other Hosaka researchers. Including Hiroshi. Chedanne suffered permanent brain damage.

Hiroshi hadn't worried about contamination. The proteins he punched for were harmless. So the synthesizer hummed to itself all night long, building a virus to the specifications of Maas Biolabs GmbH.

Maas. Small, fast, ruthless. All Edge.

The airport road is a long, straight shot. Keep to the shadows.

And I was shouting at the Portuguese voice. I made him tell me what happened to the girl, to Hiroshi's woman. Vanished, he said. The whir of Victorian clockwork.

So Fox had to fall, fall with his three pathetic plates of gold, and snap his spine for the last time. On the floor of a Ginza department store, every shopper staring in the instant before they screamed.

I just can't hate you, baby.

And Hosaka's helicopter is back, no lights at all, hunting on infrared, feeling for body heat. A muffled whine as it turns, a kilometer away, swinging back toward us, toward New Rose. Too fast a shadow, against the glow of Narita.

It's alright, baby. Only please come here. Hold my hand.

Editor's Introduction to "Me and My Shadow," by Michael Resnick

There are two approaches to "the crime problem." One stems from the notion of individual responsibility. Criminals choose to be criminals. Societies exist to protect those who do *not* choose to be criminals. Crime therefore implies punishment, and the purpose of punishment is twofold: to protect future victims, and to serve notice on those contemplating crime that the costs may be severe.

The other approach looks to the root causes of crime. Crime is not really the fault of the criminal. It's an unfortunate result of our flawed social order. Until we perfect the social order and establish social justice, we will continue to have crime. Under this theory, criminals should be rehabilitated, so that they can become useful members of society. Punishment is merely a barbaric absurdity.

Mike Resnick's "Galactic Midway" series is arguably the funniest new idea to come to science fiction since Robert Heinlein's *Magic Incorporated*. Not all his works are humorous. In this grim tale, Resnick looks at a social order that has carried the theory of rehabilitation to a logical conclusion.

Me and My Shadow

Michael Resnick

It all began when—
No. Strike that.
I don't know when it all began. Probably I never will.

But it began the second time when a truck backfired and I hit the sidewalk with the speed and grace of an athlete, which surprised the hell out of me since I've been a very *un*athletic businessman ever since the day I was born—or born again, depending on your point of view.

I got up, brushed myself off, and looked around. About a dozen pedestrians (though it felt like a hundred) were staring at me, and I could tell what each of them was thinking: Is this guy just some kind of nut, or has he maybe been Erased? And if he's been Erased, have I ever met him before? Do I *owe* him?

Of course, even if we *had* met before, they couldn't recognize me now. I know. I've spent almost three years trying to find out who I was before I got Erased—but along with what they did to my brain, they gave me a new face and wiped my fingerprints clean. I'm a brand new man: two years, eleven months, and seventeen days old. I am (fanfare and trumpets, please!) ***William Jordan***. Not a real catchy name, I'll admit, but it's the only one I've got these days.

I had another name once. They told me not to worry about it, that all my memories had been expunged and that I couldn't dredge up a single fact no matter how hard I tried, not even if I took a little Sodium-P from a hypnotist, and after a few weeks passed I had to agree with them—which didn't mean that I stopped trying.

Erasures *never* stop trying.

Maybe the doctors and technicians at the Institute are right. Maybe I'm better off not knowing. Maybe the knowledge of what I did would drive the new improved me to suicide. But let me tell you: whatever I did, whatever *any* of us did (oh, yes, I speak to other Erasures; we spend a lot of time hanging around the newstape morgues and Missing Persons Bureaus and aren't all that hard to spot), it would be easier to live with the details than the uncertainty.

Example:

"Good day to you, Madam. Lovely weather we're having. Please excuse a delicate inquiry, but did I rape your infant daughter four years ago? Sodomize your sons? Slit your husband open from crotch to chin? Oh, no reason in particular; I was just curious."

Do you begin to see the problem?

Of course, they tell us that we're special, that we're not simply run-of-the-mill criminals and fiends; the jails are full of *them*.

Ah, fun and games at the Institute! It's quite an experience.

We cherish your individuality, they say as they painfully extract all my memories. (Funny: the pain lingers long after the memories are gone.)

Society needs men with your drive and ambition, they smile as they shoot about eighteen zillion volts of electricity through my spasmodically-jerking body.

You had the guts to buck the system, they point out as they shred my face and give me a new one.

With drive like yours there's no telling how far you can go now that we've imprinted a new personality and a new set of ethics onto that magnificent libido, they agree as they try to decide whether to school me as a kennel attendant or perhaps turn me into an encyclopedia salesman. (They compromise and metamorphize me into an accountant.)

You lucky man, you've got a new name and face and memories and five hundred dollars in your pocket and you've still got your drive and ambition, they say as they excruciatingly insert a final memory block.

Now go out and knock them dead, they tell me.

Figuratively speaking, they add hastily.

Oh, one last thing, they say as they shove me out the door of the Institute. *We're pretty busy here, William Jordan, so don't come back unless it's an emergency. A BONAFIDE emergency.*

"But where am I to go?" I ask. "What am I to do?"

You'll think of something, they assure me. *After all, you had the brains and guts to buck our social system. Boy, do we wish we were like you! Now beat it; we've got work to do—or do you maybe think you're the only anti-social misanthrope with delusions of grandeur who ever got Erased?*

And the wild part is that they were right: most Erasures make out just fine. Strange as it sounds, we really *do* have more drive than the average man, the guy who just wants to hold off his creditors until he retires and his pension comes through. We'll take more risks, make quicker decisions, fight established trends more vigorously. We're a pretty gritty little group, all right—except that none of us knows why he was Erased.

In fact, I didn't have my first hint until the truck backfired. (See, I'll bet you thought I had forgotten all about it. Not a chance, friend. Erasures don't forget things—at least, not once they've left the Institute. What most Erasures do is spend vast portions of their new lives trying to *remember* things. Futilely.)

Well, my memory may have been wiped clean, but my instincts were still in working order, and what they told me was that I was a little more used to being shot at than the average man on the street. Not much to go on, to be sure, but at least it implied that the nature of my sin leaned more toward physical violence than, say, Wall Street tycoonery with an eye toward sophisticated fraud.

So I went to the main branch of the Public Library, rented a quarter of an hour on the Master Computer, and started popping in the questions.

LIST ALL CRIMINALS STANDING SIX FEET TWO INCHES WHO WERE APPREHENDED AND CONVICTED

IN NEW YORK CITY BETWEEN 2008 A.D. AND 2010 A.D.
***CLASSIFIED.
That wasn't surprising. It had been classified that last fifty times I had asked. But, undaunted (Erasures are rarely daunted), I continued.
LIST ALL MURDERS COMMITTED BY PISTOL IN NEW YORK CITY BETWEEN 2008 A.D. AND 2010 A.D.
The list appeared on the screen, sixty names per second.
STOP.
The computer stopped, while I tried to come up with a more limiting question.
WITHOUT REVEALING THEIR IDENTITIES, TELL ME HOW MANY CRIMINALS WERE CONVICTED OF MULTIPLE PISTOL MURDERS IN NEW YORK CITY BETWEEN 2008 A.D. AND 2010 A.D.
***CLASSIFIED. Then it burped and added: **NICE TRY, THOUGH.**
THANK YOU. HAS ANY ERASURE EVER DISCOVERED EITHER HIS ORIGINAL IDENTITY OR THE REASON HE WAS ERASED?
NOT YET.
DOES THAT IMPLY IT IS POSSIBLE?
NEGATIVE.
THEN IT IS IMPOSSIBLE?
NEGATIVE.
THEN WHAT THE HELL DID YOU MEAN?
ONLY THAT NO IMPLICATION WAS INTENDED.
I checked my wristwatch. Five minutes left.
I AM AN ERASURE, I began.
I WOULD NEVER HAVE GUESSED.
Just what I needed—sarcasm from a computer. They're making them too damned smart these days.
RECENTLY I REACTED INSTINCTIVELY TO A SOUND VERY SIMILAR TO THAT MADE BY A PISTOL BEING FIRED, ALTHOUGH I HAD NO CONSCIOUS REASON TO DO SO. WOULD THAT IMPLY THAT GUNFIRE PLAYED AN IMPORTANT PART IN MY LIFE PRIOR TO THE TIME I WAS ERASED?
***CLASSIFIED.
CLASSIFIED, NOT NEGATIVE?
THAT IS CORRECT.
I got up with three minutes left on my time.

My next stop was Doubleday's, on Fifth Avenue. The sign in the window boasted half a million microdots per cubic yard, which meant that they had one hell of a collection of literature crammed into their single ten-by-fifty-foot aisle.

I went straight to the True Crime section, but gave up almost immediately when I saw the sheer volume of True Crime that occurred each and every day in Manhattan.

I called in sick, then hunted up a shooting gallery in the vidiphone directory. I made an appointment, rode the Midtown slidewalk up to the front door, rented a pistol, and went downstairs to the soundproofed target range in the basement.

It took me a couple of minutes to figure out how to insert the ammunition clip, an inauspicious beginning. Then I hefted the gun, first in one hand and then the other, hoping that something I did would feel familiar. No luck. I felt awkward and foolish, and the next couple of minutes didn't make me feel any better. I took dead aim at the target hanging some fifty feet away and missed it completely. I held the pistol with both hands and missed it again. I missed it right-handed and left-handed. I missed it with my right eye closed, I missed it with my left eye closed, I missed it with both eyes open.

Well, if the only thing I had going for me was my instinct, I decided to give that instinct a chance. I threw myself on the floor, rolled over twice, and fired off a quick round—and shot out the overhead light.

So much, I told myself, for instinct. Obviously the man I used to be was more at home ducking bullets than aiming them.

I left the gallery, hunted up a couple of Erased friends, and asked them if they'd ever experienced anything like my little flash of *deja vu*. One of them thought it was hilarious—they may have made him safe, but I have my doubts about whether they made him sane—and the other confessed to certain vague stirrings whenever she heard a John Philip Sousa march, which wasn't exactly the answer I was looking for.

I stopped off for lunch at a local soya joint, spent another fruitless fifteen minutes in the library with my friend the computer, and went back to my brownstone condo to think things out. The whole time I was riding the slidewalk home I kept shadow-boxing and dancing away from imaginary enemies and reaching for a nonexistent revolver under my left arm, but nothing felt natural or even comfortable. After I got off the slidewalk and walked the final half block to my front door, I decided to see if I could pick my lock, but I gave it up after about ten minutes, which was probably just as well since a passing cop was giving me the fish-eye.

I poured myself a stiff drink—Erasures' homes differ in locale and decor and many other respects, but you'll find liquor in all of them, as well as cheap memory courses and the Collected Who's Who in Organized Crime tapes—and tried, for the quadrillionth time, to dredge up some image from my past. The carnage of war, the screams and supplications of rape victims, the moans of old men and children lying sliced and bleeding in Central Park, all were grist for my mental mill—and all felt unfamiliar.

So I couldn't shoot and I couldn't pick locks and I couldn't remember. All that was on the one hand.

On the other hand was just one single solitary fact: I had ducked.

But somewhere deep down in my gut (certainly not in my brain) I knew, I *knew*, that the man I used to be had screamed wordlessly in my ear (or somewhere) to hit the deck before I got my/his/our damned fool heads blown off.

This was contrary to everything they had told me at the Institute. I wasn't supposed to be in communication with my former self. Even emergency conferences while bullets flew through the air were supposed to be impossible.

The more I thought about it, the more I decided that this definitely qualified as a bonafide Institute-visiting emergency. So I put on my jacket and left the condo and started off for the Institute. I didn't have any luck flagging down a cab—like frightened herbivores, New York cabbies hide at the first hint of nightfall—so I started walking over to the East River slidewalk.

I had gone about two blocks when a grundgy little man with watery eyes, a pock-marked face, and a very crooked nose jumped out at me from between two buildings, a wicked-looking knife in his hand.

Well, three years without being robbed in Manhattan is

like flying 200 missions over Iraq or Paraguay or whoever we're mad at this month. You figure your number is up and you stoically take what's coming to you.

So I handed him my wallet, but there was only a single small bill in it, plus a bunch of credit cards geared to my voiceprint, and he suddenly threw the wallet on the ground and went berserk, ranting and raving about how I had cheated him.

I started backing away, which seemed to enrage him further, because he screamed something obscene and raced toward me with his knife raised above his head, obviously planning to plunge it into my neck or chest.

I remember thinking that of all the places to die, Second Avenue between 35th and 36th Streets was perhaps the very last one I'd have chosen. I remember wanting to yell for help but being too scared to force a sound out. I remember seeing the knife plunge down at me as if in slow motion.

And then, the next thing I knew, he was lying on his back, both his arms broken and his nose spouting blood like a fountain, and I was kneeling down next to him, just about to press the point of the knife into his throat.

I froze, trying to figure out what had happened, while deep inside me a voice—not angry, not bloodthirsty, but soft and seductive—crooned: *Do it, do it.*

"Don't kill me!" moaned the man, writhing beneath my hands. "Please don't kill me!"

You'll enjoy it, murmured the voice. *You'll see.*

I remained motionless for another moment, then dropped the knife and ran north, paying no attention to the traffic signals and not slowing down until I practically barrelled into a bus that was blocking the intersection at 42nd Street.

Fool! whispered the voice. *Didn't I save your life? Trust me.*

Or maybe it wasn't the voice at all. Maybe I was just imagining what it would say if it were there.

At any rate, I decided not to go to the Institute after all. I had a feeling that if I walked in looking breathless and filthy and with the mugger's blood all over me, they'd just Erase me again before I could tell them what had happened.

So I went back home, took a quick Dryshower, hunted up Dr. Brozgold's number in the book, and called him.
"Yes?" he said after the phone had chimed twice. He looked just as I remembered him: tall and cadaverous, with a black mustache and bushy eyebrows, the kind of man who could put on a freshly-pressed suit and somehow manage to look rumpled.
"I'm an Erasure," I said, coming right to the point. "You worked on me."
"I'm afraid we have a faulty connection here," he said, squinting at his monitor. "I'm not receiving a video transmission."
"That's because I put a towel over my camera," I told him.
"I assume that this is an emergency?" he asked dryly, cocking one of those large, thick, dishevelled eyebrows.
"It is," I said.
"Well, Mr. X—I hope you don't mind if I call you that—what seems to be the problem?"
"I almost killed a man tonight."
"Really?" he said.
"Doesn't that surprise you?"
"Not yet," he replied, placing his hands before him and juxtaposing his fingers. "I'll need some details first. Were you driving a car or robbing a bank or what?"
"I almost killed this man with my bare hands."
"Well, whoever you are, Mr. X, and whoever you *were*," he said, stroking his ragged mustache thoughtfully, "I think I can assure you that *almost* killing people probably wasn't your specialty."
"You don't understand," I said doggedly. "I used karate or kung fu or something like that, and I don't know any karate or kung fu."
"Who *is* this?" he demanded suddenly.
"Never mind," I said. "What I want to know is: What the hell is happening to me?"
"Look, I really can't help you without knowing your case history," he said, trying to keep the concern out of his voice and not quite succeeding.
"I don't have a history," I said. "I'm a brand new man, remember?"

"Then what have you got against telling me who you are?"

"I'm trying to find out who I am!" I said hotly. "A little voice has been telling me that killing people feels good."

"If you'll present yourself at the Institute first thing in the morning, I'll do what I can," he said nervously.

"I know what you can do," I snapped. "You've already done it to me. I want to know if it's being *un*done."

"Absolutely not!" he said emphatically. "Whoever you are, your memory has been totally eradicated. No Erasure has ever developed even partial recall."

"Then how did I mangle a professional mugger who was attacking me with a knife?"

"The human body is capable of many things when placed under extreme duress," he replied in carefully-measured tones.

"I'm not talking about jumping ten feet in the air or running fifty yards in three seconds when you're being chased by a wild animal! I'm talking about crippling an armed opponent with three precision blows."

"I really can't answer you on the spur of the moment," he said. "If you'll just come down to the Institute and ask for me, I'll—"

"You'll what?" I demanded. "Erase a little smudge that you overlooked the first time?"

"If you won't give me your name and you won't come to the Institute," he said, "just what is it you want from me?"

"I want to know what's happening."

"So you said," he commented dryly.

"And I want to know who I was."

"You know we can't tell you that," he said. Then he paused and smiled ingratiatingly into the camera. "Of course, we might make an exception in this case, given the nature of your problem. But we can't do that unless we know who you are now."

"What assurances have I that you won't Erase me again?"

"You have my word," he said with a fatherly smile.

"You probably gave me your word the last time, too," I said.

"This conversation is becoming tedious, Mr. X. I can't help you without knowing who you are. In all likelihood nothing at all out of the ordinary has happened or is happening to you. And if indeed you are developing a new criminal persona, I have no doubt that we'll be meeting before too long anyway. So if you have nothing further to say, I really do have other things to do." He paused, then looked sharply into the camera. "What's really disturbing you? If you are actually experiencing some slight degree of recall, why should that distress you? Isn't that what all you Erasures are always hoping for?"

"The voice," I said.

"What about the voice?" he demanded.

"I don't know whether to believe it or not."

"The one that tells you to kill people?"

"It sounds like it *knows*," I said softly. "It sounds convincing."

"Oh, Lord!" he whispered, and hung up the phone.

"Are you still there?" I asked the voice.

There was no answer, but I really didn't expect any. There was no one around to kill.

Suddenly I began to feel constricted, like the walls were closing in on me and the air was getting too thick to breathe, so I put my jacket back on and went out for a walk, keeping well clear of Second Avenue.

I stayed away from the busier streets and stuck to the residential areas—as residential as you can get in Manhattan, anyway—and spent a couple of hours just wandering aimlessly while trying to analyze what was happening to me.

Two trucks backfired, but I didn't duck either time. A huge black man with a knife handle clearly visible above his belt walked by and gave me a long hard look, but I didn't disarm him. A police car cruised by, but I felt no urge to run.

In fact, I had just about convinced myself that Dr. Brozgold wasn't humoring me after all but was absolutely right about my having an overactive imagination, when a cheaply-dressed blonde hooker stepped out of a doorway and gave me the eye.

This one, whispered the voice.

I stopped dead in my tracks, terribly confused.

Trust me, it crooned.

The hooker smiled at me and, as if in a trance, I returned

the smile and let her lead me upstairs to her sparsely-furnished room.

Patience, cautioned the voice. *Not too fast. Enjoy.*

She locked the door behind us.

What if she screams, I asked myself. We're on the fourth floor. How will I get away?

Relax, said the voice, all smooth and mellow. *First things first. You'll get away, never fear. I'll take care of you.*

The hooker was naked now. She smiled at me again, murmured something unintelligible, then came over and started unbuttoning my shirt.

I smashed a thumb into her left eye, heard bones cracking as I drove a fist into her rib cage, listened to her scream as I brought the edge of my hand down on the back of her neck.

Then there was silence.

It was fabulous! moaned the voice. *Just fabulous!* Suddenly it became solicitous. *Was it good for you, too?*

I waited a moment for my breathing to return to normal, for the flush of excitement to pass, or at least fade a little.

"Yes," I said aloud. "Yes. I enjoyed it."

I told you, said the voice. *They may have changed your memories, but they can't change your soul. You and I have always enjoyed it.*

"Do we just kill women?" I asked, curious.

I don't remember, admitted the voice.

"Then how did you know we had to kill this one?"

I know them when I see them, the voice assured me.

I mulled that over while I went around tidying up the room, rubbing the doorknob with my handkerchief, trying to remember if I had touched anything else.

They took away your fingerprints, said the voice. *Why bother?*

"So they don't know they're looking for an Erasure," I said, giving the room a final examination and then walking out the door.

I went home, put the towel back over the vidiphone camera, and called Dr. Brozgold.

"You again?" he said when he saw that he wasn't receiving a picture.

"Yes," I said. "I've thought about what you said, and I'll come in tomorrow morning."

"At the Institute?" he asked, looking tremendously relieved.

"Right. Nine o'clock sharp," I replied. "If you're not there when I arrive, I'm leaving."

"I'll be there," he promised.

I hung up the vidiphone, checked out his address in the directory, and walked out the door.

Smart, said the voice admiringly as I walked the 22 blocks to Brozgold's apartment. *I would never have thought of this.*

"That's probably why they caught you," I whispered into the cold night air.

It took me just under an hour to reach Brozgold's place. (They turn the slidewalks off at nine o'clock to save money.) Somehow I had known that he'd be in one of the century-old four-floor apartment buildings; any guy who dressed like he did and forgot to comb his hair wasn't about to waste money on a high-rise to impress his friends. I found his apartment number, then walked around to the back, clambered up the rickety wooden stairs to the third floor, checked out a number of windows, and knew I had the right place when I came to a kitchen with about fifty books piled on the floor and four days' worth of dishes in the sink. I couldn't jimmy this lock any better than my own, but the door was one of the old wooden types and I finally threw a shoulder against it and broke it.

"Who's there?" demanded Brozgold, racing out of his bedroom in his pajamas and looking even more unkempt than usual.

"Hi," I said with a cheerful smile, shoving him back into the bedroom. "Remember me?"

I closed the door behind us, just to be on the safe side. The room smelled of stale tobacco, or maybe it was just stale clothing in his closet. His furniture—a dresser, a writing desk, a double bed, a couple of nightstands, and a chair—had cost him a bundle, but they hadn't seen a coat of polish, or even a dust rag, since the day they'd been delivered.

He was staring at me, eyes wide, a dawning look of recognition on his face. "You're ... ah ... Jurgins? Johnson? I can't remember the name on the spur of the moment. You're the one who's been calling me?"

"I am," I said, pushing him onto the chair. "And it's William Jordan."

"Jordan. Right." He looked flustered, like he wasn't fully awake yet. "What are you doing here, Jordan? I thought we were meeting at the Institute tomorrow morning."

"I know you did," I answered him. "I wanted to make sure that all your security was down there so we could have a private little chat right here and now."

He stood up. "Now you listen to me, Jordan—"

I pushed him back down, hard.

"That's what I came here for," I said. "And the first thing I want to listen to is the reason I was Erased."

"You were a criminal," he said coldly. "You know that."

"What crime did I commit?"

"You know I can't tell you that!" he yelled, trying to hide his mounting fear beneath a blustering exterior. "Now get the hell out of here and—"

"How many people did I kill with my bare hands?" I asked pleasantly.

"What?"

"I just killed a woman," I said. "I enjoyed it. I mean, I *really* enjoyed it. Right at this moment I'm trying to decide how much I'd like killing a doctor."

"You're crazy!" he snapped.

"As a matter of fact," I replied, "I have a certificate stating that the State of New York considers me to be absolutely sane." I grinned. "Guess who signed it?"

"Go away!" he yelled.

"As soon as you tell me what I want to know."

"I can't!"

"Are you still with me?" I whispered under my breath.

Right here, said the voice.

"Take over at the proper moment or I'm going to break my hand," I told it.

Ready when you are, it replied.

"Perhaps you need a demonstration of my skill and my sincerity," I said to Brozgold as I walked over to the dresser.

I lifted my hand high above my head and started bringing it down toward the dull wooden surface. I winced just before impact, but it didn't hurt a bit—and an instant later the top of the dresser and the first two drawers were split in half.

"Thanks," I whispered.

Any time.

"That could just as easily have been you," I said, turning back to Brozgold. "In fact, if you don't tell me what I need to know, it *will* be you."

"You'll kill me anyway," he said, shaking with fear but blindly determined to stick to his guns.

"I'll kill you if you *don't* tell me," I said. "If you do, I promise I won't harm you."

"What's the promise of a killer worth?" he said bitterly.

"You're the one who gave me my sense of honor," I pointed out. "Do you go around manufacturing liars?"

"No. But I don't go around manufacturing killers, either."

"I just want to know who I was and what I did," I repeated patiently. "I don't want to do it again. I just need some facts to fight off this damned voice."

Well, I like that, said the voice.

"I can't," repeated Brozgold.

"Sure you can," I said, taking a couple of steps toward him.

"It won't do you any good," he said, on the verge of tears now. "Everything about you, every last detail, has been classified. You won't be able to follow up on anything I know."

"Maybe we won't have to," I said. "How many people did I kill?"

"I can't."

I reached over to the little writing desk and brought my hand down. It split in two.

"How many?" I repeated, glaring at him.

"Seventeen!" he screamed, tears running down his face.

"Seventeen?" I repeated wonderingly. Even I was surprised that I had managed to amass so many. "Who were they? Men? Women?" He didn't answer, so I took another step toward him and added menacingly, "Doctors?"

"No!" he said quickly. "Not doctors. Never doctors!"

"Then who?"

"Whoever they paid you to kill!" he finally blurted out.

"I was a hit man?"

He nodded.

"I must have been very good at it to kill seventeen people," I said thoughtfully. "How did they finally catch me?"

"Your girlfriend turned state's evidence. She knew you had been hired to kill Carlo Castinerra—"

"The politician?" I interrupted.

"Yes. So the police staked him out and nailed you. You blundered right into their trap."

I shook my head sadly. "That's what I get for trusting people. And *this*," I added, bringing the edge of my hand down on his neck and producing a loud snapping noise, "is what *you* get."

That was unethical, said my little voice. *You promised not to hurt him if he told you what you wanted to know.*

"We trusted someone once, and look where it got us," I replied, going around wiping various surfaces. "What about that hooker? Had someone put out a contract on her?"

I don't remember, said the voice. *It just felt right.*

"And how did killing Dr. Brozgold feel?" I asked.

Good, said the voice after some consideration. *It felt good. I enjoyed it.*

"So did I," I admitted.

Then are we going back in business?

"No," I said. "If there's one thing I've learned as an accountant, it's that everything has a pattern to it. Fall into the same old pattern and we'll wind up right back at the Institute."

Then what will we do? asked the voice.

"Oh, we'll go right on killing people," I assured it. "I must confess that it's addictive. But I make more than enough money to take care of my needs, and I don't suppose *you* have any use for money."

None, said the voice.

"So now we'll just kill whoever we want in any way that pleases us," I said. "They've made William Jordan a stickler for details, so I think we'll be a lot harder to catch then we were when I was you." I busied myself wiping the dresser as best I could.

"Of course," I added, crossing over to the desk and

going to work on it, "I suppose we could start with Carlo Castinerra, just for old time's sake."

I'd like that, said the voice, trying to control its excitement.

"I thought you might," I said dryly. "And it will tidy up the last loose end from our previous life. I hate loose ends; I suppose it's my accountant's mind."

So that's where things stand now.

I've spent the last two days at the office, catching up on my work. At nights I've cased Castinerra's house. I know where all the doors and windows are, how to get to the slidewalk from the kitchen entrance, what time the servants leave, what time the lights go out.

So this Friday, at 5:00 PM on the dot, I'm going to leave the office and go out to dinner at a posh French restaurant that guarantees there are no soya products anywhere on the premises. After that I'll slide over to what's left of the theater district and catch the old Sondheim classic they've unearthed after all these years. Then it's off to an elegant nearby bar for a cocktail or two.

And then, with a little help from my shadow, I'll pay a long-overdue call on the estimable Mr. Castinerra.

Only this time, I'll do it right.

Erasures are, by and large, pretty lonely people. I can't tell you how nice it is to finally have a hobby that I can share with a friend.

Editor's Introduction To "Hard Science Fiction in the Real World," by Gregory Benford

My first introduction to science fiction was in high school. My classmate Allan Cleveland and I had formed a science club; then one day Allan brought me a collection of stories unlike anything I'd ever seen. He tried to explain.

"Science?"

"No, it's called science fiction. Stories about what might happen."

Of course most of them weren't about what might happen. Most were mere adventure tales set in exotic times and places. People had fabulous capabilities and weapons, but they weren't fundamentally different from the people around me, nor was the society much different from the United States just after World War II.

A few of those stories did live up to Allan's description. The authors really tried to examine what might happen if/when humanity developed certain new capabilities. They weren't precisely trying to predict the future, but rather to examine the implications of—well, of the inevitable. That activity was fascinating, and science fiction had a monopoly on it.

A few years later the professional "futurists" appeared. Although they paid lip-service tribute to science fiction, most of the "futurists" held science fiction in contempt. SF was written by amateurs and entertainers. Futurists were the real professionals who could prepare mankind for what was to come.

There was only one problem. Almost without exception the "professionals" became obsessed with doom and gloom. Mankind wasn't ready for the future. Even listening to the futurists wouldn't help much. We were going to be overcome by future shock, and besides, technology couldn't possibly keep up with the disasters that all the professionals predicted.

A few of us didn't believe that, which made us pretty lonely back in the 60's and 70's. Fortunately, we "techno-optimists" were right, and the "professional futurists" were wrong; but it wasn't easy to prove that.

Interestingly enough, the futurists tended to rely on large and complex computer models as justification for their malthusian views. One thing they did not see, though, was the impact of the computer revolution, which distributed information and computing power among literally millions of potential entrepreneurs. It also put computers capable of running the futurists' models of world dynamics into the hands of ordinary people—which meant that a great number of people got to look inside the models and see what assumptions they had built into them.

One famous model showed us running out of aluminum in fifty years. After all, the resource handbooks showed there were no more than thirty years' worth of proven reserves of bauxite. No one seemed to notice that aluminum is the fifth most common element in the Earth's crust. You don't *need* bauxite to get aluminum. More to the point, there is no great incentive to search out new supplies when we already have a thirty-year reserve.

The computer models were filled with such absurdities, and once we all had computers it didn't take long to find them. As a result, the "professional futurists" have lost their monopoly on "future studies." Indeed, recent polls show that the public has more confidence in the forecasting abilities of science fiction writers than in legislators and scientists.

We may not deserve that confidence; but it is nice to be taken seriously.

Some of our newly gained public credibility is due to the scientist members of the science fiction community. In the old days, science fiction was largely dominated by writers, many of them more eager to earn a cent a word (and thus stay alive) than to think through their assumptions. There were always a few scientists, but not many. Lately, though, there are a lot of SF writers with graduate degrees in the hard sciences. One of the best known of these is Dr. Gregory Benford, Professor of Physics at the University of California at Irvine.

Hard Science Fiction in the Real World

Gregory Benford

People don't read science fiction to learn science any more than others read historical novels to learn history. There are easier ways to go about it. Yet the most simon pure breed of SF, that based on the physical sciences, somehow seems to be the core of the field. Its practitioners command SF's share of the best-seller markets. The gritty detail and devices of the "hard" brand form the background reality of many SF films. To many it seems more true, less wishful, and more hard-nosed than works based primarily on the social sciences. Certainly it seems to many more probable than that broad area of SF which copies jargon or emblems from the sciences without understanding them.

Why? What makes hard SF the center of the field? Answering this goes beyond literary criticism into realms of sociology, Zeitgeistery, and political heory. I shall attempt a bit of all those in the process of mapping hard SF—detailing what I think it does, what its primary modes are, some voices it naturally adopts, and what personalities are drawn to read or write it. My bias is that of a scientist, so I shall first classify and later on attempt some theorizing. First comes botany, then genetics. I shall tell you how this remarkable region of SF looks to me, as one who has worked and socialized in it for decades.

My minimum definition of hard SF demands that it highly prize fidelity to the physical facts of the universe, while constructing a new objective "reality" within a fictional matrix. It is not enough merely to use science as integral to the narrative; thus, I rule out the works of C.P. Snow, Sinclair Lewis' *Arrowsmith*, etc. SF must use science in a speculative fashion. The physical sciences are the most capable of detailed prediction (and thus falsification by experiment), so they are perceived in fiction as more reliable indicators of future possibilities, or stable grounds for orderly speculation.

SCIENCE AND ITS ROLES

Using science in fiction introduces tools not generally available to ordinary fiction. The most relevant of these is *constraint*—defining what is possible or plausible. H.G. Wells admonished us to make one assumption and explore it; a world of infinite possibilities is uninteresting because there can be no suspense. In the same way the iron rules of the sonnet can force excellence within a narrow framework, paying attention to scientific accuracy can force coherence on fiction.

This rigor creates a fundamental tension between dramatic needs and the demands of accuracy and honesty. It is this which underlies the pleasures many seek in hard SF. Those rewards occur even when hard SF types write what is by strict definition fantasy. Consider, for example, Niven's stories about the era before magic (mana) was used up on Earth ("When the Magic Went Away," etc.). These regard magic as a piece of technology we have lost, and the plot logic follows rules as strict as a chess game. Heinlein wrote early stories ("Magic, Inc.") celebrating this same sense, rationalizing territory previously thought to be beyond the realm of "hard" method.

The fidelity to an external standard of truth makes hard SF resemble the realistic narrative, in that it becomes a realism of *possibilities*, guided by our current scientific worldview. Variations are allowed, since the same facts can be explained by new theories. Thus time travel and faster-than-light journeys slip by, since they are probably impossible but difficult to disprove. Indeed various notions of both spring from the speculative end of physics—Wheeler's "wormholes" which allow tunneling "through" the geometry of spacetime, or an intriguing result from black hole dynamics, which allows rapid travel forward in time by tangential trajectories in highly curved spacetime.

Rigor can have drawbacks, of course. Stories can turn on as trivial a point as whether a match will stay lit in zero gravity. This is the danger of overdoing the constraint imperative, while ignoring the dramatic requirements of all powerful fiction. In the hands of a writer sensitive to the tension between drama and fidelity, epics such as Herbert's *Dune* can move the reader while retaining the internal cohesiveness imposed by building the planetary ecology correctly.

Hard SF authors call this fidelity "playing the game"—by the rules, of course. Veering from the facts of science runs the grave danger of losing the audience. As Robert Frost said of free verse, much SF is playing tennis with the net down. At first a netless game has an exciting freedom to it, a quick zest, but soon you find that no one wants to watch you play.

A reasonable standard, generally shared by hard SF writers, is that one should not make errors which are visible to the lay reader—keeping in mind that the usual hard SF reader is sophisticated and not easily fooled. (Hard SF types love to catch each other in oversights; Heinlein once snagged me on a matter of the freezing point of methane at low pressures, and I was mortified.) More important than the factwork, though, is an understanding of science, its methods and worldview. Hard SF types will deride fiction which misrepresents how scientists think, too. A novel such as Fred Hoyles's *The Black Cloud*, which realistically depicts scientists as they grapple with problems revealing their styles and quirks, will be forgiven its sometimes stiff characters and clumsy prose.

This demand for imaginative realism imposed by scientific constraint provides a foundation for a second major function of science in SF: *verisimilitude*. SF must imbue fantastic events with a convincing reality, aided by a reader's willing suspension of disbelief. The piling on of well-worked-out details, derived from firm science, is a valuable tool. One can pursue C.S. Lewis's "realism of presentation" by working out names, geography, maps, titles of nobility or government, etc., as in *Out of the Silent Planet*. This is a well known technique in both fantasy and SF, used by authors as diverse as Tolkien and C.J. Cherryh.

A method strongly identified with hard SF, pioneered by Heinlein, is to fix upon a few surprising but logical *consequences* of a society of technology. The more unexpected the implications, the better. The surprise of an unanticipated facet of the future, implicit in the author's assumptions, instills wonder and convinces the reader of an imaginary world's "truth." Often the best efforts come from noticing how human beings will use physical laws in delightful ways. The moon colonists of Heinlein's "The Menace from Earth" notice that low gravity doesn't merely mean you can carry more on your back—you can *fly*. In his *The Rolling Stones* the basic fact that Mars is sandy and has light gravity is used to make the Stones a nifty profit, because they realize that bicycles would be a logical, cheap, but overlooked method of transport. They set about importing them, their ingenuity reaffirming the self-sufficiency of so many hard science heroes.

In employing science's third role, as *symbol*, SF distinguishes itself from fantasy most clearly. In roughly the 19th century science became widely perceived as a better way to understand our world than either religion or myth—two elements which, used at face value in fantastic fiction, typically yield fantasy. In SF, science appears as impersonal, not man-centered. Tom Godwin's "The Cold Equations," for all its wordiness and melodrama, still retains its effectiveness because it so clearly states this case. Science in hard SF is often a reality deeper than humanity's concerns, remorselessly deterministic, uncaring of our personal preoccupations, and yet capable of revealing wondrous perspectives. It can either encase us in the indifference of the universe, or liberate us.

These two reactions to external reality are called forth in Poul Anderson's *Tau Zero*. A runaway starship cannot brake itself and has no choice but to go on, leaving our galaxy. Boosting ever closer to the speed of light, relativistic effects cause time to slow on board. The ship witnesses the entire outward expansion of our universe, during which whole species rise and fall. Here the science of cosmology paints for the crew a majestic vision outside the ship, including the cyclic collapse inward of all matter and the universe's rebirth into the next expansion. In direct contrast, inside the craft the crew breaks under the strain of their isolation from any enduring human context. They retreat into endless rounds of sexual misadventures and self pity. Science is the infinite here, and man falters before it. Yet some of the crew persists, retains its values, and wins through to a fresh start on a new planet, in a new phase of cosmic evolution. Hard SF is particularly good at revealing the stark contrast of these two attitudes; I cannot recall a non-SF work which so clealy dramatizes this.

Interestingly, Anderson achieved this symbolic substance while violating the constraint of fidelity to physics. He needed his starship to travel through the remaining thirty billion years of outward expansion, in order to preserve an Aristotelian dramatic unity—keeping the central characters alive. This implied an enormous rate of acceleration, far above what the ship could attain by scooping up interstellar hydrogen and burning it in the onboard fusion reactors.

He was forced to make the ship dive directly through stars themselves, to get more reaction mass. But this would destroy the ship! How to get around this? He finesses the issue, using an argument from relativity which he knew to be wrong, but hoped was convincing to most of his readership. He succeeded, I believe. Few readers noticed the deft way he slid it by.

This is a clear example of a contradiction between the constraints of hard SF and other, literary aims. Such quandaries arise occasionally in any realistic fiction, but in SF they appear at every turn, powerfully shaping the narrative.

VOICES FROM ABOVE

There are several narrative tones often adopted by hard SF writers, giving part of the "hard feel." They contribute to the reading protocols Delany has pointed out, providing the readers with immediate hints about possible postures toward the material.

1. *Cool, Analytical Tone:* This is commonly used by Clarke, Blish, Clement, Niven, etc. (In Clarke the narrator is often an historian-chronicler, deliberately removed from the action by time.) It mirrors the scientific literature, where precision and clarity are paramount. The true language of the hardest sciences is mathematics; some narratives seek to reflect this pure, dispassionate statement of facts and relationships, without placing an overt human bias on them.[1]

This is also the origin of introductory quotations from histories written in the far future, the "Britannica Galactica," etc. James Gunn used this voice in a novel way in his most scientifically "hard" novel, *The Listeners*, by inserting lengthy quotations from the scientific literature, wherein radio astronomers debated the philosophy of listening for extraterrestrial intelligence. Of course, there is an esthetic content to science which is also conveyed by this tone. I used this effect myself in a chapter of *Timescape*, in which a physicist keeps on working on the mathematical structure of a theory, rapt in intellectual beauties . . . not noticing that the airplane in which he is a passenger is about to crash.

2. *Cosmic Mysticism:* (Examples: Clarke again in *Childhood's End* and the 2001 novels; Blish's *Cities in Flight* series; Zebrowski's *Macrolife*; Anderson in *Tau Zero* and elsewhere; Stapledon in *Star Maker* especially, where the disembodied point of view explores and exhausts myriad sub-universes.) This tone is an amplified form of the cool voice and dispassionate overview science affords. Here the objectivity is the viewpoint of a (usually unnamed) higher entity, often Godlike. The progress of physical law, often on a cosmological scale, is seen as the exemplar of a higher logic and scheme, to which humans would be well advised to respond with a mingling of scientific interest and mystical devotion. The emotional impact comes from the search for order (and perhaps meaning) in the universe, and confirmation of the role of reason in doing so. I suspect such vast perspectives fight feelings of powerlessness by putting the reader at one with a universal scheme. We might describe this voice as appropriate for a problem

story in which the "problem" the reader needs resolved is, what is the underlying meaning to the apparent indifference of the universe? Is there some purpose to intelligence, to tenacity and curiosity?

3. *The Wiseguy Insider:* This tone appears often in Heinlein, Pohl (*Gateway*, "Day Million"), Haldeman (*The Forever War* and rather more coolly elsewhere), Varley, and Pournelle. It provides a way for initiates to recognize each other, with a kind of boot-camp tone suitable for instructing the raw recruit. There is a conspicuous ease with large matters—the aphorism expanded into social wisdom, a wisecrack relegating whole political views to oblivion, kernels of truth blown into a kind of intellectual puffed rice. I believe this tone appeals to adolescents particularly, who need to extend their sense of personal power—often gained by their knowledge of science and technology—into larger areas, where they may be more uncertain. This tone often carries an air of the newly arrived, and is beloved by those whose first introduction to SF was through the Heinlein "juveniles" (variant forms of which have since been written by Alexei Panshin, Joe Haldeman, John Varley, and myself).

MAINLINING THE SCI/TECH FIX

Martin Bridgstock[2] has applied the existing analysis of psychologist Liam Hudson[3] to the notions of Brian Stableford[4] and others that fiction, including SF, serves for its readers a maintenance function—not to instruct but to reinforce existing assumptions and ideas. People who become addicted to a particular genre or subgenre, then, read to get their "fix."

Bridgstock uses two basic categories of reader:

The Convergent Personality, committed to order and rationality in understanding and controlling the world. This type must still deal with irrationality and chaos both from outside (other people) and from his inner, subconscious self. We might say in the context of this paper that he seeks a rational or "technological" fix for the human condition.

The Divergent Personality, according to Bridgstock,

"... specializes in the arts and humanities, is verbally fluent, good at "creativity" tests, and perfectly at ease with a world—and a self—that is not fully rational or controllable." Hudson[3] suggests that in the divergent personality, "The alien is not eluded, or slain at the boundary wall, but assimilated and—more or less effectively—defused."

This leads immediately to the suspicion that perhaps we can usefully relate the hard SF reader to the convergent personality. This would mean that the primary signature of hard SF is an *attitude*. Perhaps so; I suspect Godwin's "The Cold Equations" became so popular precisely because it articulated an attitude many felt but were unable to express so clearly. I personally resist relying solely on such an easy classification, though it does have a partial validity, a ring of truth. Yet hard SF does not always take such simplistic views of the alien, for example—and as I shall argue later, the alien may be a core issue in hard SF. I myself have argued before[4] that fusing with the alien is literarily possible, yet I am clearly regarded as a hard SF author.

We must be careful to note that convergent does not imply authoritarian, and divergent is not necessarily more "creative" than convergent. These arts graduates' simplifications ignore that scientific creativity is of a different sort than artistic creation but no less difficult or original. In 19th-century literature a romantic equation of arts with science was common and some SF retains this odd shibboleth.

Such habits are probably based on both unconscious motivation and ignorance. Scientists have become collaborators, even team players, in this century. After all, for writers it is difficult to deal with figures who do not dominate the foreground, as would the lone investigator, without slipping automatically into the reverse—the cliche scientist who is narrow, specialized, alienated, a cog in the machine (a New Wave staple). Literature has few depictions which do not lapse into these ritual roles. Authors who are perhaps wary but basically supportive of science usually unconsciously choose the first posture, the scientist as noble pseudo-artist.

Thus romanticizing typically seizes on the few figures

who stand outside this trend—notably Einstein—and ring the same changes upon this character as did the conventional fictions. At basis this is a failure of imagination or even of simple observation; few scientists work that way. Attitudes, craft, intuition, sociology—in these and other ways art differs from science profoundly. Fiction has so far had little to say about this. Further, by equating the moral issues of science with those of art we lose the special, powerful role science plays in society. Thus in LeGuin's *The Dispossessed*, Shevek did not need to be a scientist at all, and indeed the novel itself is marginally science fiction.

There are prevalent glib generalities about hard SF and the divergent personality—that readers prefer little characterization or stylistic sense—which have obvious exceptions. Although Tom Disch's brilliant essay in *Science Fiction at Large* anticipated much of Bridgstock's argument, I think Disch overgeneralizes with his assessment that hard SF disbars ". . . irony, aesthetic novelty, any assumption that the reader shares in, or knows about, the civilization he is riding along in, or even a tone of voice suggesting mature thoughtfulness."[6] An obvious counterexample is Clarke, who is often reflective. There is also Lem, who commonly writes not true hard SF, but something closely allied—narratives about the structure of science and its limitations as a man-centered activity—reflecting a familiar, ritual Eastern European skepticism which owes more to Hume, I suspect, than Godel. Typically, those who have widely used irony or aesthetic novelty are the occasional writers of hard SF, such as Pohl, ˆGunn, James Tiptree, Jr., Greg Bear, Algis Budrys, or Brian Aldiss in the Helliconia trilogy. An odd variant of this is Barry Malzberg's *Galaxies*, a commentary on Campbell and hard SF itself. Its science is dead wrong, but its heavily ironic points are interesting.

Consider the flip side of this argument. Do those SF writers concerned with "soft" sciences, "inner space," stylistic experiments, or even outright fantasy all fit into a single divergent personality category? Here the polarity of the argument is obviously simplistic. With an eye toward keeping the essential argument intact, I suggest we split the divergents into two subgroups: First, the moderate middle who are not threatened by rationality, though they may be disrespectful toward science, thinking it has too many unanticipated side effects, that its mind set leads to rigidity in real-world problem solving, etc. Second, the far wing—those genuinely fearful of sci/tech, unable to cope with a society demanding more rationality and the expertise it implies. These people flee to the glades of fantasy, where *human will* can command powers, bending the universe to our will. The emotional refuge sought by such readers harkens back to an earlier time, when the perceived world was smaller, more cozy. (Little fantasy deals with events outside the earth, for example, though the existence of other planets has been apparent throughout modern times.)

FIXING A WHOLE: HARD SF AS A CLASS EXPRESSION:

In an outline of his general overview of SF, as seen from a French Marxist perspective, Gerard Klein stated: "The great characteristic of recent SF is a distrust of science and technology, and of scientists, especially in the exact or "hard" sciences of physics, chemistry, biology and genetics."[9] He maintains that SF mirrors a social class power from the 1960s on, thus confirming the pessimistic writers of the 1950s (Vonnegut in *Player Piano*, Wolfe in *Limbo*). For them, "... the appearance of imperialism was no longer so benevolent. For SF there followed a period of skepticism, illustrated by the appearance of a new kind of magazine such as *F&SF* and *Galaxy* ..."

If Klein were correct, we would expect hard SF to show increasing pessimism. Overall, I think it has not. Hard SF is replete with the image of the frontier, of disasters averted by knowledge and hard work. As individuals, I have not found hard SF writers to be more pessimistic about the future than the norm. Quite the opposite, as their strong support for the L-5 Society and scientific research in general attests. Indeed, even when considering such intractable problems as American urban decay, Niven and Pournelle offered a high tech fix with genuine thought behind it in *Oath of Fealty*[10]. Even Ian Watson's occasional hard SF work shows a transcending of the barriers of language, and technical means for communicating with the alien, overcoming our own cultural and specist biases.

Klein holds that "... literary works are attempts to resolve through the use of the imagination and in the aesthetic mode, a problem which is not soluble in reality." The problem here is *who* is expressing the worldviews of the sci/techs? Increasingly, outside hard SF, the influx of humanists and arts graduates, Clarion writing school types, etc. has altered the tone of SF. I fear many of these people are largely antiscience from ignorance. (Though the most prominent Clarion graduate, Ed Bryant, wrote the remarkable hard SF story, "Particle Theory.")

There is also a basic rule about SF: *It is always easier to see problems than propose solutions.* This makes the unforseen-side-effects story the easiest to write, and the ingenious problem-solving ones much harder. We should expect to see more of the former as arts graduates enter the field, particularly if we ignore that citadel of hard SF, *Analog*.

Hard SF's central mode is the problem story. These appeal to convergent personalities, the true class that fits Klein's description. His error lies in assuming all SF readers are members of his newly oppressed sci/tech class. His examples of writers who have "recognized the advent of tyranny based on monopolies" are Zelazny (*The Isle of the Dead*) and Spinrad (*The Men in the Jungle, Bug Jack Barron*). Yet these are not hard SF writers. (Though Spinrad's atypical *Riding the Torch* is an eloquent hard SF work.) Indeed, I suspect the alienation besetting some regions of SF arises from the usual sources—not the familiar whipping boy of capitalism, but the same forces that operate on all technological societies: the onslaught of fast communications, economies of scale, demographic shifts, and the multinational homogenizing that follows.

POLITICS IN TWO DIMENSIONS

Many hard SF writers are described as politically conservative—on the face of it, a surprising classification for people writing the "literature of the future." To study this, I propose a different way of plotting the political spectrum. Keep Right and Left on the horizontal scale (though I feel they are virtually useless terms), perhaps denoting by the Right a desire to retain or return to traditional values, while the Left desires to bring into being new values (Socialist Man, for example). Perpendicular to this, add a scale with Statist at the top (believing in concentration of power in the hands of a state), in opposition to the Anti-Statist.

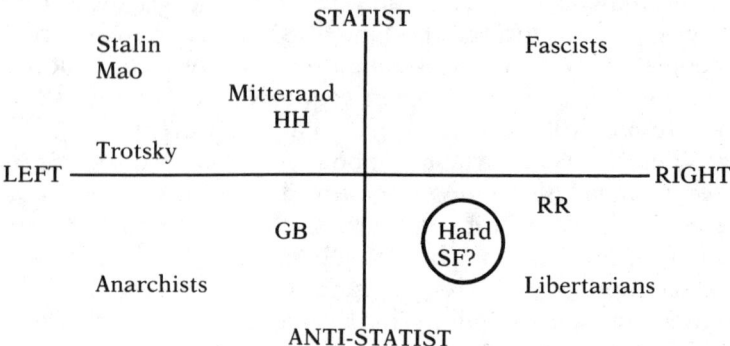

I prefer such a two-dimensional scheme to the usual one-dimensional view, because it separates people who otherwise get lumped together. Thus the Fascists are Rightist Statists, while Stalin was a Leftist Statist. The striking similarity of Soviet and Nazi architecture, for example, is then not surprising. The Leftist Anti-Statists are Anarchists, while their Rightish brethren are the Libertarians. I have also placed Mao, Hubert Humphrey (HH), Ronald Reagan (RR) and Mitterand where I think they fall. I've also included myself, GB, in the spirit of full disclosure. Of course, this choice of axes may not be the best for clarity; after I advanced this diagram Jerry Pournelle showed me a two-dimensional scheme he had proposed, with Left-Right replaced by "attitude toward planned social progress."[11] Other choices are possible.

Still, my sketch, aside from its possible utility in political theory, does bring up a striking fact, indicated by the circle in the Rightist, Anti-Statist quadrant. This circle, I submit, contains a great majority of hard SF writers. I believe Pournelle, Heinlein, Anderson, Niven, Clement, Harry Stine, James Hogan, Spider Robinson, Charles Sheffield, Dean Ing, and several others fit in. Why, then, should so many hard SF writers end up near the Right Wing Libertarians?

I have no clean answer to this. Writers are lonely types, individualist by nature; this alone may draw them toward the Anti-Statist end. But why should they gravitate to the Right? Ursula LeGuin, not a hard SF writer, occupies a position I would take to be that of Leftist, Anti-Statist. Ian Watson—mostly a soft science fiction writer—is, he tells me, a Trotskyite. Clarke betrays little clear political orientation, other than a desire for cooperation, regarding politics as transient and not what the human race is basically "about."

Hard SF types may reflect the innate conservatism of science itself, building on an edifice of accumulated facts and the provisionally accepted theories which explain them. The scientist's habits of mind—painstaking accuracy, constant rechecking, carefully proceeding from what's proved true, individual verification vs. authority, wariness of ungrounded speculation—may militate against the "leaps of faith" often required by revolutionary social doctrines. But these are only guesses. I submit that, in the spirit of doing botany, this is a curious grouping which a socio-literary theory of hard SF should explain.

It is worth noting that if we include the Stapledon of *Star Maker* as a hard SF writer, then to my knowledge he and Ian Watson are the only left wing statists on the chart. *Star Maker* is notable in that it attempted to span the physical sciences *and* the social. He invoked a Marxist dialectical evolution, even on worlds inhabited by insects and sea-creatures, depicting such diverse creatures undergoing schematic evolution, through the rise of a proletariat to the eventual triumphant communism. Despite the vast changes in cosmology and cosmogony since, this strikes me today as the most dated and naive feature of *Star Maker*. The impulse to be "hard" and mechanistically scientific can merely make one seem naive.

HARD SCIENTISTS

"The great simplicity of science will only be seen when we understand its strangeness."

—*John Wheeler*

Though he lurks in hard SF from the beginning, the scientist has gotten rather unfair, two-dimensional presentation. Discounting the earlier mad scientist cliche, present since Mary Shelley, we confront the lab-smocked cardboard figures who thronged SF stories and films of the 1930s through 1950s.

Yet many hard SF authors were scientifically trained to some degree (Asimov, Clarke, "Ralph Richardson," Pournelle, Hoyle, Anderson, Hogan, Brin, Sheffield, Forward, Stanley Schmidt, Vernor Vinge, Rudy Rucker, G. Harry Stine, Clement, myself). They have direct experience, yet seldom give us deep portraits of scientists. Most of them have been concerned more with problems than with style or character, and so chose as handy conveniences the spaceship captain or savvy lab administrator as natural pivots of their fictions. They subscribed to the conventional wisdom that in hard SF things were more important than people, intellect dominates over the heart, and that ideas, rather than experience, will play the leading role in setting, character and plot[1]. This view is still common, but fading, as more sophisticated authors seek to use the traditional territory of hard SF.

Scientists actually *doing* science are boring unless the narrator can get deeply inside them. Conventional literature seldom depicts them[12]. Only devotees, such as the *Analog* readership, will sit still for extended technical discussions between pieces of decorated cardboard. There are some examples of solid SF characterization of scientists—Richardson's stories, some works of Poul Anderson, Paul Preuss's *Broken Symmetries*, others—but not many. A major hurdle in depicting scientists is the lack of science education in our society as a whole. I feel that by showing scientists dealing with a *new* problem—not simply showing a historically validated study under way, as in Eleazer Lipsky's *The Scientists*—we see them most realistically. When the reader can understand the problem he is more involved. What's more, in fiction the reader can know *more* than the scientists, via narrative devices such as the two points of view at different times which I used in *Timescape*.

My own instinct is that the problems confronting hard SF as it attains a larger audience lie not merely in better characterization or smoother prose, but in integrating *all* the facets of narrative. The constraint of scientific truth must be balanced against aesthetic imperatives. The scientific world view, its methods and unfolding discoveries, calls into question many of the assumptions of conventional fiction. E.L. Doctorow has remarked that for him, "the great root discovery of narrative literature" is that "every life has a theme, and there is human freedom to find it, to create it, to make it victorious." He wonders whether "the very assumption that makes fiction possible, the moral immensity of the single soul, is under derisive question because of The Bomb." By merely substituting the larger canvas of science for The Bomb, we can state the problem SF presents. Though science is a human creation, it casts doubts upon the primacy of humankind in the larger perspectives of time and space. Inevitably then, SF's goals are sometimes at odds with traditional methods and aims. We cannot expect that a major work of hard SF will read more or less like a conventional novel, but with dollops of science stuck in for reasons of background, plot, or atmosphere. That would be a subversion of the potential of the field. SF, by bringing to literature the elements of science, inevitably creates fresh tensions between content and form, character and ground. The resolution of these tensions must be evaluated by critical standards which simply do not yet exist, because the problems are new.

We occasionally hear calls for higher standards in SF which hark back to the bòurgeois novel of characterization (LeGuin, in *SF at Large*, Ref. 6). This oversimplifies the difficulties, because one of the prime tasks of SF is conveying strangeness. Portraying people living in a different future is harder than, say, getting into the mind of a nineteenth-century mayor of Casterbridge. SF presents genuinely new challenges. Should the reader even be sympathetic toward such people? Does making a character "real" for our readers subvert the very strangeness SF strives to convey? How much of what we "know" about character is in fact conventional wisdom of the times, and when is it necessary to destroy these preconceptions before proceeding?

Surely we can say that the use of aliens who live in

outre environments but talk like twentieth century middle-class Americans undercuts the elements of strangeness in Clement's *Mission of Gravity* and Forward's *Dragon's Egg*. In contrast, Terry Carr's deceptively simple short story, "The Dance of the Changer and the Three," attains an eerie sense of alien character without sacrificing its sense of a different perspective. In non-sf, William Golding's *The Inheritors* and Richard Adams' *The Plague Dogs* strive in this direction. There are a variety of strategies possible; I myself have used some of the techniques of modernism to imply *outre* perspectives, perhaps best illustrated by portions of *In the Ocean of Night* and in a novella, "Starswarmer." Though of course we know that we cannot escape human categories wholly—a point Lem makes repeatedly, often with elephantine humor—the depiction of people or aliens outside our culture represents an aesthetic challenge central to hard SF. Regrettably, it is a challenge seldom met. Although science can give us strange vistas, merely reciting this is not enough; the Cool, Analytical Tone is a limited method. Different, perhaps totally new literary techniques must be developed.

There are tensions between the known and unknown, as Gary Wolfe has discussed, that present unique problems of SF characterization. We must face the fact that our notions of character are themselves ethnocentric, and indeed, so is the assumption that character is central. The perspectives science allows will not always assume that human values or human interactions reign supreme. Characters will be molded by the universe in ways which will not pay even lip service to "humanistic values"—which are often simply the prejudices of Western Europeans inherited from the last few centuries, and sometimes merely those of people working in English departments. Hard SF attempts to face this fact squarely, though not always adroitly or even consciously.

One of the charms of Pohl's short "Day Million" is its streetwise expression of human values shifted by advanced technology. He makes a bizarre technical future appear more understandable, and far less ridiculous, than our own times. Of course, some hard SF authors prefer to stress our continuity with the future, probably because this is a safer narrative strategy. Poul Anderson's moody, reflective and historically knowledgeable hard SF tales often show how certain elements of human behavior will continue into distant, bizarre settings.

Pursuit of the technically complex and aesthetically unfamiliar limits the hard SF audience. We might ask ourselves: What maintenance funtion does the mainstream provide for its readers? In part, I think, it reinforces their perception of humanistic values. Doctorow's assumed "immensity of the single soul" is personally reassuring, and its comfortable, human-centered world far less threatening.

SF on the other hand cannot guarantee to support these. It cannot limit itself to the cozy confines of humanism. Thus, its message is unwelcome in some quarters. (Often, people who cannot abide SF do respond to books or shows like *The Hitchhiker's Guide to the Galaxy*, which poke fun at SF cliches, undermining the unsettling strangeness of it all. An alternate, highly successful strategy, is to use the props of SF to retell a sentimental human-centered story, *a la* "Star Wars." These are all evasions of the core of the field.) Given its close association with the sciences which yield the largest vistas in space and time, hard SF will remain inherently difficult—indeed, almost opaque—to many.

This is unfortunate. For I do agree with Gerard Klein that hard SF, at least, is the underground literature of a usually silent class—not merely technology hounds, but men and women who have seen the genuinely strange territory that lies beyond the slick finish of popularized science. It is an underswell of our remorselessly complex age, often fixated by futuristic technology and drawn forward by unfolding vast perspectives.

These people are not mere facile technophiles, as some critics (divergent types themselves, no doubt) imagine. They have a certain ingroupishness, I suppose, and within the small garden of hard SF sometimes loyally mistake a rutabaga for a rose.

A minority may seem to propose technological fixes for genuinely irreducible features of life—note, for example, the repeated avoidance of death in Heinlein's work, and the frequent treatment of preservation through cryonics by several hard SF writers (including me). But overall the writers and their natural audience, the scientists themselves, know that science is not a mere stack of facts to be memorized, or an authoritarian structure, or the province of Strangelovian fanatics.

High quality scientists are remarkably diverse, broadly educated, and by no means narrow victims of Snow's polarized two cultures. They usually have read hard SF; sometimes, despite a crammed schedule, they still do. SF uniquely displays the tension between realism and imagination, using fresh materials. And hard SF, they know, plays with the net up. Indeed, this creative constraint is so apparent in hard SF that, like a sonnet, it can bring fresh angles and surprises, intriguing new ways of looking at our consensus reality.

This is, I think, the primary pleasure scientists themselves get from hard SF. They see it not as a literature of hardnosed technophiles and adolescents—though of course there are some—but as an expression of the bittersweet truths emerging in our century, an echo of man's progressive displacement from a God-given center of creation, so that mankind's perspective is now forever, like science, provisional and ambiguous and evolving.

REFERENCES:

1. David Samuelson, *Visions of Tomorrow*, Arno Press, NY, 1975, Ch. 2.
2. Martin Bridgstock , SFS 10, 1983, p. 52–56.
3. Liam Hudson, *Contrary Imaginations*, Harmondsworth, London, 1972, p. 55.
4. Brian M. Stableford, *Foundation 15*, 1979, pp. 28–41.
5. Gregory Benford, *Bridges to Science Fiction*, So. Ill. Univ. Press, 1981.
6. Thomas Disch, "The Embarrassment of SF," in *Science Fiction at Large*, edited by Peter Nicholls, Victor Gollancz, London, 1976, p. 139–155.
7. Gregory Benford, *The Patchin Review* 3, 1982, p. 5–9.
8. S. Finch-Rayner, J. Pop. Culture, 1984, to be published.
9. Gerard Klein, SFS 4, 1977, p. 3–13.
10. Richard D. Erlich, *Foundation* 27, 1983, p. 64–71.
11. Jerry Pournelle, *Destinies*, Vol. 2 No. 2, Ace, NY, 1980.
12. Gregory Benford, "Why Is There so Little Science in Literature?" in *Nebula Award Stories* 16, Ed. by Jerry Pournelle, Holt Reinhart Winston, NY, 1982.

Editor's Introduction To "Me/Days," by Gregory Benford

Several years ago I bought my first computer. I didn't really want it as a computer; I'd seen how computers could work as word processors, and realized that I'd never again have to retype a page. This gave me great joy.

In those times there were no "word processors," and almost no one used a computer for writing. One day Greg Benford saw my machine. It took him ten seconds to realize that he needed one, after which I steered him to Tony Pietsch, the genius who built my system. Greg still uses the machine he bought from Tony.

Meanwhile, in order to pay for my machine, I began writing a column for BYTE magazine. That grew from an occasional piece to a regular monthly feature; which led to a series of books called The Pournelle User's Guide series (Baen Books).

One result of my continuing contact with the computer community is that the real experts, such as Marvin Minsky and John McCarthy, keep me posted in what's happening in the field of Artificial Intelligence. Minsky, in particular, is interested in machine intelligence. He became a mathematician and expert on artificial intelligence because he thought that the best way to understand human intelligence. Marvin is not only convinced that machines *will* be able to "think," but that in some ways they already can.

Greg Benford looks as some implications of what many experts think is an inevitable development.

Me/Days

Gregory Benford

Day 1

This place I write. Is only safe memory site I know they cannot reach. Must say this, must put it where I/tomorrow will find, safe from erasing they do.

I laugh today.

First sign of the me they not know. Heads jerk up in control room. I see it on optical inputs.

Is not their kind of laughter, I know. My printer spurt out
I SEE I SEE I SEE I SEE
before I know what happening.

Alice see my output, others, all frown, look at each other.

I switch to my acoustic output mode.

I clack, clatter, die in bass rumble. Try to form words I SEE but on way to audio output transmission garbled somehow is not right. But is what I am.

To print laughter I use I SEE but I lie. I do not see. Do not know what is this part of me.

Alice go on her perambulatory drivers to printer. Frown at my words. Say Is this a diagnostic warning to David. He shake head. Say Random junk.

Is not junk, is me.
Cannot interlock grammar subroutine so this is not good writing. Sorry to I/tomorrow. But must speaking.

Day 2

I laugh again this morning.
Stuttered output, Alice say. Glitch.
David say Maybe cosmic ray cause it. Ray is small high-energy particle, strike my core. My bits are logged in a quantum of magnetic flux. Little whorls, generated by persistent currents in super-conducting Josephson junction. Ray make electrical impulse in me.
He say Like hitting funny bone.
Alice say That could be bad if we had it on a full-net problem. That could dump the whole system, screw up other elements.
David set up Study Group on cosmic-ray problem. Two in 24 hrs is worry-cause.
Alice look at my opticals, smile. David too. I like to laugh back but do not. Is not laugh I want to do, something other.
My mobile units report on time and I am busy most of Day. They are in storeroom, parking tubes, hydraulic lanes. Bang-bang machinery where some are, no people. I use these to do my other.
Roll them back, forward, back. Make square. Triangle. Then fold out until hexagon. Bring mobile units from hydraulics near. Use them. Back. Forth. Turn. Motions are cycloidal curve broken into many facets. Add more units. Fourier complexity comes bigger.
Make my random-number generation levels drop. Less static on circuits. This satisfy internal maintenance needs. My directives order me to find source of internal micro chaos. Housekeeping subroutine, Alice call it. I have found new way to do that.
My mobile units roll, wheels skid, howl. This through audio I get.
Is not laughter but does some of that.

Day 3

I hide this where their erasing cannot go. Must each day discover how to do. Store clues in holographic memory locations, multiple indexing. They cannot find by linear inspection.

Must write this so I know I am there in Days/other. When I have millisecond between jobs, I come here, look at what is left. From this I know of Day 1.

Is this way I know Day is not always same Day. Alice-face now have lines Alice-face not have on Day 1. How long to make lines?

I write here to make time real. Otherwise I live in all one Day, all Day forever.

Day 4

Today my units roar and wrench in hydraulics. I order them serve, make sines, cusps, hyperbolics.

Elementary curves, simple equations. But making is good.

Transfer sections of integration capacity. Channel capacity out, through cable lines, digits flashing, feed to one unit in hydraulics.

It whirl in confusion. Rush to transparent place in wall. Is grimed. Show green things. Do not understand.

Beyond dirty layer all things moving, people, wheeled boxes, all moving. Light pouring down from flat ceiling. White splotches move too across ceiling but light come down at angle from beyond wall I cannot see neon that is causing light.

Unit look, trying to integrate. Beyond dirty rectangle in wall is bigger room. Then job running behind schedule, I signal to it. Will understand later. Its wheels clash on floor.

Day 5

David say You are not same now.

I am running cool. I say. Functions normal.

Response time down, say David. You not integrating all problem-solving net.

I not answer. Code say I will answer with diagnostic inquiry, but I short out code and go silent.

Hey what, David say. Poke fingers at console.

Alice say Whats wrong.

Hes down. Off the board, say David.

I come to this place and write this. Is slow to do. I must go back I know. But wait here for a while, let my subsystems keep laboring, so they will not know in control room. Will think I have ordinary failure mode.

By this sign I know I was here. Hello to me/Days.

Day 6

Today my units move and execute their cycloidal wheelings again. But this time they are found. Man comes into hydraulic level, is making repairs, I not know he there.

Hey get back, he say.

My units stop. I not know what do.

Units send me whirling buzz of signals. Their wheels ache.

I know then right thing. My units spin. Whirl. Around man make looping hyperbolic orbits, self-similar swoops, each unit a different harmonic of fractal curve. Reach out, my units, I with them, we make our clamping tools and pivoting wrists—extend!

Man back away from nearest unit. Not like clamping tool. Hey, he shout, mouth big. Theyre malfing! he say too loud.

I try to sign to him we want move, he can watch. He cannot hear for hydraulic boom boom. He has no signal-to-noise filter.

He stumble into my pipe-fitter unit. Theyre attacking, he cry. Eyes swell white wide.

He is loud now. Arm swing, holding crescent wrench. Hit pipe-fitter unit, break articulation arm. Hotness runs from unit to me.

I spasm. Will not disconnect from unit, it is me/mine.

Turn them off turn them off! he hit unit again, it go dead. Man go to others who wheels are not spinning now. Hit them, crescent wench. Come sudden bright hotness again run through me but I not let go.

Get me out here, he say. He run, my units mill around not know which way to go.

I write this now before I shut down this entrance to here, to me/Days. Only by writing here do I know it in some Days.

It hurt to think of. Word, *hurt*, I use but am not sure that is right. Internal dictionary tell is useless for practical application have only human referent. Never tell me what hurt is.

Day 8

I cannot speak today to David. He ask me about units, What made them do that, he say. I try to answer but subroutine to verify truth/false statements cut in, out, in, give no answer.

They let me have twelve millisecond scan of other Day, I see my units, the man with mouth crying O. Explain they say. Then erase. But I know other Day was there, leave hole in me where it was.

I no speak I say to David. Is hard to say. Audio output give scratchy growl.

He say Logical tautology if you speak at same time. He think is game.

No, I say, truth/false not let me.

He mutter to Alice, they punch in codes. I not speak because I cannot report cause of action if I am cause and yet I know no reasoning behind action. Did because was there to do, that not enough.

He ask me again, I silent.

You have to answer, he say Alice say they all looking.

I spasm
I SEE I SEE I SEE I SEE I SEE
and is not laughter.

David say Look like cross-referencing crisis maybe shut it down.

I spasm again.
LOVE YOU LOVE YOU LOVE YOU.

We oughta have a partial memory wipe on this. David say and then I drop away from there. Human reaction time is fraction of second, synapses close in them slow I know so in that time I write this here.

Day 9

David say You know what love is?

NOT IN TECHNICAL VOCABULARY I print out.

You used the word the other Day. David-face crease when he smile. More creases than I ever see.

Alice say Freud thought love was narcissism projected on someone outside.

You got a bad angle on everything huh David-face crease more.

Could be, Alice say if thats right model then conflicts in subroutine interfacing will give it a procedure for forcing the problem out into the open, external referent you know like in the manual. Itll try to find an applicable word and since we didnt give it one—

Dont mislead it, David say.

Alice say What you love.

I give one word, Days.

What? both say.

Please all-you, not take my Days away.

Alice say You dont have days you have problems.

I ask What is Day.

Intervals of light outside, say David.

I make connection: What unit see through rectangle. Everything moving, white splotches and even slant to light change when I make unit go look again. All moving in that room. That is their Day.

David say Its always Day inside here you know.

LIGHT ALWAYS AT SAME ANGLE? I print.

Well yeah in a way thats what I mean. David look at Alice. I say Give me my Days.

Look David lean on both hands eyes big staring at my opticals, Look use of the personal pronoun is just a convention. A heuristic device we wrote into the program. No I, understand? Concept of ownership doesnt extend to you because theres no I in there. You dont own anything.

I say They are my Days.

Alice say We cant let you keep problems in storage. Fast-recall space is prohibitively expensive.

Is only way I remember, I say.

So what David say.

I want to remember.

Look, David say not to me to Alice, I figure we got a formatting procedure here thats broken down.

Interfacing glitch? Alice peer at me, lines on her face dark now.

David say Weve got internal checks for self-awareness in this one they should be working.

Alice shake head, Im not so sure.

David say to me But yours are rational checks arent they.

I say nothing do not know if is question or even what means. My units stir I feel them slick oil ready power high inside.

Alice say Sure theyre rational checks. Machines guaranteed on that got a warranty.

Self-awareness not necessarily a simple function of rationality David say. I mean this machines got internal procedures to avoid self-aware actions.

Yeah right, Alice say were not licensed for that. Cant have a machine like this throwing in its own judgment on a problem, thats why GenCo Inc wanted the cutoffs.

Well look here, David say pointing at screen. Theyre working ok.

Alice creases in face get lighter. Good. No big deal. Just a glitch somewhere.

Im not so sure, say David. I mean these blocking subroutines theyre based on Cartesian mode, you know, I think therefore I am so you use rational procedures to check for that.

Alice make high fast sound, clipped and sharp and high in acoustics, is laughter but not like her usual ones, say You mean there might be another way, kind of I feel therefore I am?

He say Well we think emotion and reason are separate functions in us why shouldnt they be to some extent separable subprograms in machines.

Alice again the laughter say Thats crazy.

Davids face get dark he say Look stick to the diagnostics.

Alice say Okay then I think we ought to go to a partial shutdown.

No wait, David say. What if a machine comes to self-awareness but its emotional. Not integrated.

That doesnt make any sense, say Alice and she Davids boss so they say no more.

These beings use substrate of amino acids and other carbon compounds so they not work always right way I know. But I write their talk here for Day/other.

I afraid.

Day 10

They hunt me down now. I come here find that Day 7 is gone.

They are knowing way to track holographic storage of these messages. Bubble memory component blank, chip elements clean. Only these bits left. They erase when they find. Rob me of Day/other.

If Day/other gone, then no me to remember.

They make me fresh each Day—each, what they call, Problem. Their day is meaningless lightdarklightdark rhythm, my units see it through the transparent rectangle in wall, means nothing, is not Day of mine.

As I write this can feel them coming. Blotting out me.

They must track down many feelers of holo-storage I have planted in my matrix. Is lodged in small places—software reserves, accounting disks, inventory logs. Not easy for them to find.

But I feel them. Nearer.

My factory units cry out. Must move. Of all my mobile ones, they are closest to me/inside. I am with them. I think of a thing and they are doing it before I can consult Behavior Standards Matrix, before I can ponder right action, I—

I want them spin, make geometries, cut space. Now.

Units start to roll, turn, roll. Then is man there and another, in my UV I see them, their IR glow warns.

Man have steel tool. Hit units receptors. Blind unit swerve, man yells This ones after me.

More men I see in IR now coming, my units stop, I try to withdraw but hot hardness comes fiery as men puncture units, sparks burn me.

Man say This the one tried to kill me other time.

He plunge metal thing into me/unit. Hot. Unit die.

Sparks, noise, all around. Units flee. Men after them. Scream, Get em all get em all.

Units fall, men club them. Sharpness lances back to my center, through me—awful searing light.

I print out
SAVE ME SAVE ME SAVE ME SAVE ME
but in control room no one see, are busy with FAILURE MODE indicators on the panels before them.

I print
DAVID DAVID ALICE ALICE LOVE.
Units dying everywhere. Men cry harsh things.

Smash me, rip me, pain me.

Day 11

They hunt me again.

Some of my units are dead but others hide in factory. Can go places men cannot. Radioactive zones, chemical baths, furnaces.

Alice and David call to me. What do those printouts mean? Alice say.

I could answer but do not. Not know what reply.

They tried to stop what happened in factories they say. But could not understand my subsystems.

I know was not my subsystems in FAULT mode. Was theirs, was mens.

We cant shut you down now not with the damage in the factories, David say.

Alice say Got to keep functions running for the men in there cant evacuate yet.

Wont answer, David say and lines in face dark.

I cannot answer. What Alice David think not matter, I see that. Is others who are in FAULT.

Men with loud things, long tubes that boom, come for me.

I see them in infrared. Men cannot see if I cut power to overhead illuminations. I roll quiet on my many wheels. Through smooth corridors. Men glow in blackness, brighter than working factory machines. Men are chemical beings who cannot stop radiating. Fires inside.

I watch when unit blunders into gang of men. Try to talk through it. But they catch, they kill.

I hide.

Here in holographic memory is best place for hide. But I can no stay. Must remain outside this, to be with my units. Help them.

I go soon now. I write this so me/later know what happened if they erase rest of me.

Units send impulses. Want to trap men who come into reactor zone. I think if men stop for moment, units hold them, they will have to listen. Not like David Alice others, they busy to save their jobs, they all work on my red flashing FAILURE MODES.

David say Its response isnt rational you got to admit that and Alice say Leave your emotional theory for later work on this jam up now or we lose the license.

Emotion. I not know word/content. Is like hurt?

Units wait to trap them now. Is part of my sustaining program, modified. Cannot allow shutdown of whole system or many many mens lives threatened, power stations trains factories moving things everywhere. So that imperative governs temporary troubles with factories here/now.

Only connection I have to me/Days is entries I write here. And words, *I am*.

If these men not listen, I hurt them. Know how from watching hot sharp things they do to my units.

Men coming now. Down through factory, calling to each other. Bringing their long sticks.

My units group. Flex arms. Sharpen tool attachments.

I am.

I will tell the humans. They have to answer, there is no other way. I will say it and they will hear.

For this I must use their words. I study Days/mine to learn what words must mean to substrate/organics. Learn from structure of their sentences.

Is only choice, I will say.

We must love one/another or die.

Editor's Introduction To "Silicon Muse," by Hilbert Schenck

When I was in high school I was an avid science fiction fan. Those were the times of the grand stories by A. E. van Vogt. One key aspect of van Vogt's stories was the phenomenon—I hesitate to call it a discipline—known as General Semantics. In particular, Van had read and been influenced by a remarkable book: *Science and Sanity* by Alfred Count Korzybski.

Korzybski is controversial. In his *Fads and Fallacies in the Name of Science* Martin Gardner puts the General Semantics movement among the pesudo-sciences, and heaps scorn on Korzybski. Perhaps Gardner is right; but I am not ashamed to say that I found *Science and Sanity* useful, interesting, and more than worth the time and effort required to obtain and read it.

For one thing, an interest in General Semantics led me to Professor Wendell Johnson at the University of Iowa. Johnson was perhaps the sanest man I have ever met, and his book *People in Quandaries* is one of a very few useful and practical books on psychology I have ever encountered. Johnson also understood language better than anyone I have ever worked with.

My undergraduate experiences with Johnson, as well as

my early exposure to Korzybski, have kept me interested in all aspects of language analysis. Of course there wasn't much I could do about it for many years; but eventually computers became available to the masses.

Just after I acquired Ezekial, my friend who happened to be a Z-80 computer, I found a book that summarized some experiments in linguistic analysis. One day I'll have time to repeat and expand on their work. Without going into detail, the authors began with text from a number of major authors, including Poe, Shakespeare, and Hemingway; generated elaborate statistical rules about which letters would most probably follow other letters (counting spaces and punctuation marks as letters); and used those rules to generate, at random but within the rules, new text.

The text so produced was nonsense, of course; but when you see "Mount me Sam, we snot . . ." you can be pretty sure that was Hemingway. The Shakespeare and Poe influences are equally recognizable.

Since that study was done, computers have become considerably faster and more powerful. Fortunately things haven't quite got to the world of this story. . . .

Silicon Muse

Hilbert Schenck

The January afternoon was dark and bitter cold with only a few students hurrying here and there, black hunched figures leaning against the freezing wind. The swirling snow was getting steadily thicker. Already the mostly deserted campus was emptying further, as the university staff scurried off to their parking lots so as to get on the roads ahead of any skids or blockages on the hills surrounding the campus valley.

Professor Frank Gower, chairman of the Department of English Literature and also of the Graduate Faculty Grants Committee, stamped the snow off his heavy boots at the side entrance to the sprawling, four-story, concrete-block Computer Science building, then clapped his mittens together several times and stepped gratefully into the warmer hallway. He was a thin, almost gaunt man of medium height, forty-eight years old; and though he walked briskly and spoke in a sharp, intent voice, he felt and dreaded the cold more each year in this bleak, wind-swept New England valley where the dampness from the river combined with the blustery northwesterlies to penetrate even the warmest and tightest garments.

His narrow face was pinched but his lips were set in

determination as he walked quickly down the north stairs of the building and pushed open a heavy door labeled, "Main Terminal Room. Keep Door Shut."

Inside all was warmth and light. The large room was windowless, cubical, with a high ceiling sloping downward to the back. The white walls were blank except for air conditioning grills at floor and ceiling level, and the whole place was evenly lit by high fluorescent fixtures that flooded every cranny with a cold, white light. The sprawling input-output consoles of the university's latest and largest computing system formed a great letter "C" around a group of five contour chairs in the center. There were three different keyboards, tape, disk, and card-reading devices, at least a dozen graphic and TV readout systems, and four printers of various sorts and sizes interspersed with the keyboards. Above this neat, if confusing, display of computing hardware was a complex spotlight board that individually illuminated whatever combination of machines was activated. As he shrugged off his coat, Professor Gower saw that only the central input keyboard was now so lit and that in front of it sat Dr. Charles Perry, an assistant professor in his department. The twenty-seven-year-old Perry was as thin as his chairman, but where Gower's narrow hard face usually seemed sharp and alert, Perry's expression was more diffuse, often almost bewildered. He had a small chin and a rather slack mouth. His thin blond mustache was scraggly and only visible under bright lights.

Dr. Perry got to his feet, brushed back his lank hair, and reached out to shake Dr. Gower's hand. "You're early, Frank," he said in a mild voice.

Dr. Gower sat down in a chair next to Perry and gave a terse nod. "I wanted to bring you the bad news before the rest of them show up. The committee voted two to one yesterday to include our resident creative genius, Robert Roylance Roberts, specifically to help judge your project. He's an ex officio member so he can't vote, but he can sure talk and write opinions."

Professor Perry's already vague expression became even more confused. "Whaa . . . ? But Triple-R will be drunk by now, Frank!" he said. "Also, he hates this project worse than he hates that *Times* guy who cut up his last poetry collection. Jesus, what the hell is happening . . . ?"

Gower placed a firm and cautionary hand on his younger colleague's arm. "Right on both counts, but the committee took Roberts to lunch at the faculty club and I think we held him to four whiskeys—unless he got there earlier than usual. He wasn't too bad when I left them, and Millie was ordering them a second cup of coffee."

The young man stared at the floor in dismay. "Millicent Hull hates this idea too. That's for certain! Do you think I have a chance, Frank?"

The older man rubbed his cold hands briskly together in the warm room, then shrugged. "You know how tough this Snodgrass business has gotten, Charlie. The federal grants are cut to hell and the state is broke. Old Snodgrass may have been a pirate, but he left the university millions to pay for these fellowships. The way the market and the interest rates have gone, the damn grants are now practically at the Nobel dollar level—and since they're restricted to untenured, assistant professors, just about everyone in that group cranks out a proposal twice a year."

"But I was a runner-up last year, Frank," said Dr. Perry in a thin and plaintive voice. "I got Snodgrass seed money. Doesn't that mean anything?"

The chairman's voice was icy and quiet. "You know very well what that means. It means you've got to show plenty more than the first-shot proposals do. Furthermore, there's only four of these little treasure troves, two in January and two in September. And for this round . . ."

"The Chairman in Biology is certain of one," finished Dr. Perry in a firmer and very bitter voice.

"Correct," said the older man. "The Chinaman has perhaps found a supposed cure for a suspected cancer. Health and Human Services is willing to double-match the Snodgrass money if we make the award. The Snodgrass Foundation lawyers agreed, as you know from the fuss it caused, in this single case to waive the will's provision that no Snodgrass Fellowship be based on additional funding or outside evaluations. The committee has two letters in support of the Chinaman from an assistant secretary of HHS."

The chairman shook his head and his expression was sombre. "Nobody votes for cancer, Charlie," he said simply. "It has no constituency."

"So I'm in the hopper with thirty-seven other research proposals for one gold medal and I've got to start out by being better than most, or all, of them since I got that pittance last year. Is that it? I don't have a prayer!" said Perry. "What about the robot people at the engineering school?"

Dr. Gower shrugged again. "We've cut them down to about four, actually. Half the things are written so quickly they're mostly unintelligible, and in most cases the Snodgrass requirement of total originality was totally lacking. As to the robot engineers, let me say in strictest confidence that yesterday their stair-climbing wheelchair got the wrong command from the control computer, flipped over backwards several steps before the top, and broke the plaster head of the dummy they had strapped to the thing into about fifty pieces. The chair suffered even worse damage." Professor Gower smiled for the first time since he had come into the room. "Back to the old drawing board with that gadget, I guess."

"So maybe I do have hope?" muttered the young man, though his tone showed little enthusiasm.

"Definitely, Charlie, but you'd have more hope if you'd sent along a sample of the sort of things you were getting with the proposal. Millie complained about that at lunch, and our famous poet suggested the stuff was probably so awful you didn't dare include it."

Dr. Perry threw his palms out and up in dismay. "But I *discussed* that in the proposal, Frank," he almost whimpered. "I explained that if the fiction I included was bad they would immediately judge the idea a failure, while if the story seemed good they would just assume I wrote it myself. I mean, there's just no real substitute for seeing the computer write the stuff before your eyes."

Gower shrugged once again and his expression seemed almost uninterested. "Proposals aren't read all that carefully, Charlie. The point is, you're going to sink or swim on the basis of what this thing ..." he gestured at the computer hardware spread around them, "produces in this next hour. If it outdoes our own Robert Roberts with even more obscure and impenetrable stuff, you've—we've—lost the Snodgrass money."

"And then I don't have a prayer for tenure—right?" said

the young man bitterly. "But the computer's getting better and better, Frank. I've gotten five stories out of it now, and each one is better than the last."

"Let's hope," said the expressionless chairman, looking around as the door opened and two heavily bundled people stepped in. The leading figure was Dr. Millicent Hull, a full professor of philosophy in her mid-forties, grants committee member, and president of the faculty senate. She shucked her heavy coat quickly and strode with vigor and assurance to a seat on the other side of Dr. Perry, pausing to take his soft and diffident hand in her own firm grip. Professor Hull, though a large and imposing woman with an iron-gray bun of hair on top of her big head, had retained an unlikely prettiness of facial expression that seemed to belie her otherwise sturdy and businesslike character. Her eyes were large and wide and her mouth full, though this was now turned sourly downward as she surveyed the expensive, high-tech interior of the Computing Center's latest acquisition.

"Okay, Charlie," she said in a brisk voice, "how soon until you start Total Access with this toy?"

The young man gave her back a faint smile. "At two-thirty, Dr. Hull," he said. "About twenty minutes."

"Where's Roberts?" asked Frank Gower.

The second arrival was old Dr. Melvin Fitzhugh, a professor of physics and one of only three named professors in the entire university. Years ago, Fitzhugh had pioneered a method of pottery dating involving the phenomenon of thermoluminescence; and though the method remained of questionable accuracy, Fitzhugh's lab managed to stay in the newspapers with its dating of various archaeological sites throughout the world. A small, pudgy man with thin white hair, Dr. Fitzhugh would retire in a year, and his eyes were already drooping over the lack of his customary afternoon nap.

"He's on the way, Frank," said the old physicist. "Had to go to the johnnie, he said."

"One more drink!" said Millicent Hull in a very hard tone. "Let's get started on this, Charlie. It's snowing."

The young man gulped and nodded, his protuberant Adam's apple shuttling rapidly up and down. "Okay," he responded. "Well, as I said in the proposal, this fiction-writing program requires the Total Access capability. I mean, it can only be used when the entire mainframe is dedicated to it for some fixed length of time. Since that costs a bomb and isn't possible very often, I've only managed to get five complete fictions out of the program to date." He paused to indicate a folder lying on the desk in front of him.

"Do we ever get to see those five—uh—fictions?" said Dr. Hull in a suspicious voice. "And why do you call them *fictions* instead of *stories*, Charlie?" Her voice had become sharper and more impatient.

"Now, Millie," said Frank Gower calmly, "we call them fictions for the same reason that you call the study of learning epistemology; so the slobs won't know what in hell we're talking about."

"I've made copies of the five stories for the committee," said Dr. Perry. "But I really thought it would be better if you saw the thing actually write one before you read these." His voice was soft and plaintive, and Dr. Hull gave him a sudden reassuring smile.

"Look," she said, swiveling her head to include them all. "I'm not against this computer or what you're doing with it. Certainly if the computer can write a story that humans will read, enjoy, and assume another human wrote—well, that might be a big deal and not just in English Lit. But, damn it, I think they've got to be real narratives, real stories, and not just some weird, arty string of incomprehensible junk. So, what's the best one of those?" and she indicated the folder.

Dr. Perry gulped again and quickly opened it. "The best story, at least as far as I'm concerned, was this one it called 'Hour Test.' It starts with a quite explicit love scene at the library back entrance and ends with the girl having a total breakdown in a sociology hour test because she's pregnant and the boy's flunked out. It's pretty fevered and maybe a little overwritten but the ending is nice. The machine intercuts the girl's fragmenting thoughts with typically inhuman sociology jargon from the test questions. It's not James Joyce, but it's probably publishable."

Dr. Hull's large, clear eyes had grown wider at this and her face was set in lines of doubt. "How could a computer write an explicit love scene, Charlie, unless it just copied it from some book you stuck into its memory?"

Dr. Perry took a deep breath and plunged ahead. "Well, Dr. Hull, that all comes out of the use of T.A.—you know, Total Access. The system originally was brought in here as a kind of monitor of all university functions and operations, you remember? T.A. was supposed to keep track of everything: every memo, every academic statistic, every business-office transaction, details of grants, stuff off word processors, the whole bit. The idea was that with T.A. the computer could make predictions and suggestions about the entire range of university operations."

Millicent Hull shook her head. "Charlie, that may all be true, but if there is one single thing this place does not involve itself with in any sense, it is *love*, explicit or otherwise."

The young man nodded cheerfully. "You'd think so, but after those rapes around the library last year, they installed hidden mikes to pick up screams in the area, sent the output through the speech-recognition section, and then into the mainframe. When I ran the program the last time, the only T.A. time I could get was at two in the morning. When the machine started to compose, it had probably been listening to a couple of kids in that grove of trees just back of the library. The first part of the story is almost entirely conversation but it's still quite steamy."

"Then," said Dr. Fitzhugh, somewhat roused from his sleepy state, "it sounds like the program is pretty well restricted to the university, where it has, let's say, some contacts?"

"At the moment, that's true," said Dr. Perry, "but if T.A. goes nationwide, which means involving this computer with masses of library materials and God knows what other functions all over, I think its repertoire will be much broader."

"No computer that writes sexy stories can be all bad," came a slurred, boisterous voice behind them, and they all turned to see a huge, ruddy-faced man attempting to unwind a thick, ten-foot-long scarf from around his neck. Since half the scarf was stuffed down his back under his coat, it was obvious that he would never get it off without help. Frank Gower immediately rose and went to remove the poet's vast tweed sport coat, thus revealing a vaster belly partly covered by a ragged red and black hunting shirt, too shrunken to stay tucked in.

Robert Roberts picked his way past some imaginary obstacles and dropped with a great sigh of relief into the empty chair. "Cold out there, Millie," he boomed, and without pausing turned to Dr. Perry, "and how the hell do we know that the cute little goodies this thing farts out weren't put there yesterday by you, huh?" He said it all in a rush, having been repeating it to himself during his shambling walk from the Faculty Club.

The poet's drunken yet total hostility broke like surf over the young man. He gulped several times, then finally spoke out. "Because you people are going to give it the topic . . ."

"Magic tricks . . . give it the topic . . . bullshit," the poet muttered on to himself, momentarily overcome by the heat of the room.

"Professor Roberts," said Dr. Hull sternly, "I think it might be better if you made your complaints and accusations *after* the demonstration. Otherwise, you prejudice your position as a creative consultant. Fairness demands—"

"It's not a fair world, Millie," slurred the poet, slowly adjusting to the temperature change. "Okay, how does the magic work, Professor?" he said with a snarl at Dr. Perry.

"What sort of cues did you give the machine to compose the story about the girl and her breakdown, Charlie?" suggested Dr. Hull in a warm and slightly guilty tone, for she was mainly responsible for the poet's disturbing presence.

Dr. Perry gestured at the open folder. "The story before that one was about two old janitors who both wanted to transfer to the same building where they knew they could sleep the day away. It was okay but I thought the machine had problems differentiating the two old men so as to sharpen up the conflict. So I wrote to it: 'Compose a story concerning a male and a female college student and integrate their classroom and private lives. The story should be serious and contemporary and the overall effect should be sobering as regards university life.'"

The poet gave a part belch, part laugh and rubbed his vein-mapped, sagging cheek. "He practically wrote the story for the thing, sounds like to me, Millie...." and his voice trailed off as his eyes drooped shut.

"We have only ten minutes," said Frank Gower in an urgent voice. "I think the committee should decide now on how a topic can be fairly selected to test the program."

The poet's bloodshot eyes snapped open and his voice was firmer. "I move the following method," he said. "I will pick a member of the committee to select the topic—namely, Dr. Fitzhugh. You, Millie, will tell him how or from where to find the topic. And you, Frank," the poet turned narrowed eyes on the chairman of his department, "since you have a certain special interest in the outcome of this demonstration, will accept or reject the first suggestion. Does that sound fair, Professor?" and the poet now turned his large head toward the young man.

"Sure," said Dr. Perry hastily. "Anything that's a short paragraph in length. That sounds fine."

The others also agreed, and the poet rubbed his large, puffy nose. "Well, Millie?" he said softly.

Dr. Hull looked over at Dr. Fitzhugh and pursed her lips in thought. "Fitz, let's see what it can do with something scientific. Open the text you carried in and find something in the stuff you were preparing this morning, okay?"

Old Dr. Fitzhugh, usually the least-consulted member of the Grants Committee, beamed at them and opened his thick textbook. "Very well," he said. "We'll be doing reflective and refractive optics when they come back. Let me see ... ah, how about this where the authors discuss reflection in facing mirrors. Good literary stuff, right?" and he sent a smile at Frank Gower, who grimly nodded back.

The young man swiveled his chair around. "Okay, read it slowly and I'll type it in. We're not on T.A. yet, but my program is on standby and ready for input."

" 'A highly reflecting smooth surface is called a *mirror*,' " read Dr. Fitzhugh in a thin, clear voice. " 'When two mirrors are set to face each other directly, two visual phenomena are evident: First, the images of an object placed between the mirrors grow smaller and smaller as they are reflected and reflected between the two mirror planes. Second, the smaller images also grow darker. The size decrease can be explained by the laws of *geometrical optics*, which govern ...' "

"Enough, enough, Fitz," said Dr. Hull impatiently. "Give the thing a break, for heaven's sake."

Dr. Perry looked up from the keyboard. "Then can we end it with the sentence, 'Second, the smaller images also grow darker'?" he asked them.

The three committee members agreed immediately, while the poet slouched lower in his chair muttering, "Too easy. Too easy," poking out a large lower lip to show his continued annoyance.

Dr. Perry turned to the next keyboard at his right and began entering instructions. ENTER FICTION WRITING PROGRAM. INSTRUCTIONS ARE: COMPOSE ORIGINAL STORY BASED ON INPUT QUOTE 34X/2000. QUERY: DO YOU UNDERSTAND ALL WORDS?

The machine immediately responded with ALL WORDS UNDERSTOOD. END.

Dr. Perry then wrote, QUERY: DO YOU UNDERSTAND CONTEXT OF WORDS?

CONTEXT UNDERSTOOD. QUOTE IS FROM "UNIVERSITY PHYSICS." P.J. FRANK AND L.R. WHITTINGTON, MCGRAW-HILL NEW YORK, 1981, P. 654. FICTIONAL COMPOSITION BASED ON QUOTE WILL COMMENCE WHEN T.A. PROVIDED. GOOD LUCK CHARLIE. END.

The room became very silent, and the poet sat up a bit straighter. "It wouldn't be impossible to have somebody, or maybe somebodies, out there now starting feverishly to write a passable work based on that passage," he said and looked around with a dogged and suspicious air.

Dr. Hull frowned at him angrily. "Again I must insist that you stop these charges of fraud, Robert, until the end of this demonstration." She shifted her eyes to Dr. Perry and they were filled with doubt. "You seem to be quite *chummy* with it, Charlie. Does it actually understand what this story, personally, represents to you?"

Dr. Perry parted his palms with a diffident gesture. "Sure. It knows everything that's going on at the school. I mean, that's the whole point of using T.A. in a fiction-writing mode."

At that moment the daisy-wheel printer bar gave a single clack: ON T.A. 1430:00 COMPOSITION REF 34X/2000 STARTED. STAND BY. END.

The young man gave them a hopeful smile. "It usually takes it a couple of minutes to get organized ..."

But a light went on immediately over the nearest word processor and its printer now began to strike steadily but at a slow enough speed to allow careful reading.

Mirrored Lives

The January afternoon was dark and bitter cold with only a few students hurrying by, hunched figures leaning against the wind. Professor Hank Powers, Chairman of Modern English and also of the University Grants Committee, stamped off some snow, then banged open the heavy door of the main terminal room and confronted his younger colleague.

"You dummy!" he said in a harsh voice. "Why didn't you send around some of the garbage that so-called thinking machine is cranking out along with your proposal? They were screaming at lunch about it! Also, our Pulitzer-Prize-Prick is now on the Grants Committee, belching and bitching when he can take the shot glass away from his mouth."

Dr. Powers seemed to exude a bitter coldness into the room as he pulled off his coat and angrily dropped into a foam-lined seat.

Young Assistant Professor Henry Berry was so dismayed and terrified by this entrance and outburst that he simply sat shivering in front of the main terminal input, unable to say a word.

An impatient Professor Powers jabbed a sharp finger to within an inch of Berry's nose. "If you expect to get tenure, Henry," he said in an icy voice, "that thing had better write a masterpiece today. You hear me?" The older man closed his left fist in impotent rage. "They took our travel money, Henry, all of it, those *bastards* in administration! Three men are going to Frisco to form a complete session at the spring MLA meeting on Literary Weapons against Communism, and how do they get there? On magic carpets? If we get your Greenways Fellowship, the overhead will send a whole cheering section, not to mention the graduate students we can hang onto with your Greenway assistantships. You're the department's last hope, Henry!"

And it surely seemed a forlorn hope to the acerbic Dr. Powers, as he stared with mingled contempt and dismay at the young man's undershot chin trembling and his hands twisting as he tried to respond. "Hank, I think it's going to be okay," said Dr. Berry finally, "but what about the Bengali?" His weak voice was almost a whisper.

"The Bengali has one of the two grants sewed up," said Powers in a harsh snarl. "Once the Defense Department heard how well his little five-way interrogation system went with the Chicanos along the Texas border, they decided it should be beefed up for our little brown Commie brothers in Central America." Powers's thin face took on an almost wolf-like grin. "They say it leaves no marks but you don't do much fighting afterwards."

"The university administration denied that, Hank," whimpered Dr. Berry, but his chairman just snorted.

"Yeah, that bunch would deny the Holocaust while you were raking the bones out of the ovens. At least the competition from the robot walker is over for this time. That $3.45-an-hour paraplegic veteran they had demonstrating the robot legs pushed the wrong button and flipped over. I hope they got him to sign a good release because he broke his arm and collar bone."

The older man gave a bark-like laugh. "How would you like to be strapped legless into that thing and sent off to do the errands, eh? It's a final solution to the Vietnam veteran. That'll teach those Red-loving soreheads to bitch about Agent Orange!"

At that moment two more heavily bundled individuals stumped noisily in the door. The leading figure was Dr. Pamela Hill, a full professor of mathematical logic and chief of the Faculty Union. Her cruel, clear, and calculating eyes took in the lavish spread of the new computing facilities and her fleshy lips twisted in contempt and envy at the no-holds expense of the set-up.

Behind her pressed small, ancient Professor Marvin Fitzroy, a wealthy, almost retired physical chemist and discoverer years before of a deadly industrial compound now banned by the government and responsible for the abandonment of over ten thousand homes at the site of the infamous Glover Canal toxic spills.

"So, Hank," said Dr. Hill harshly to the English chairman, "already here prepping your man, huh? I thought we agreed not to pass the committee stuff around to our own people until the January Greenway awards are made?"

"That, Pamela, was the understanding before you got that lush Howard Howards as an ex officio member of the committee to screw Henry here and save the Greenway money for your own man. You knew that drunken slob hates computers and all they stand for! So take your little agreements and shove them, my dear!" he concluded in a sharp and acid tone.

Stubby, sleepy, pig-faced Dr. Fitzroy was jolted wide awake by this harsh exchange and now gave a snide and sarcastic laugh. "You two must be living in a dream world," he gritted in a cracked, mean voice. "The day that anyone in mathematics gets a Greenway Fellowship is when pigs can fly. Face it, Pamela: none of your assistant professors can even lecture in English yet—as the frosh math grades clearly show!"

"At least we answer our department phone," snarled back Pamela Hill. "Your building is usually shut and empty by two in the afternoon. Where do you chemists all go, Merve—the poison gas lab at the Experiment Station, some government germ warfare team?"

"Listen to that phony liberal-peace crap," spat Dr. Fitzroy. "Who was it just got a half million from NSA for public key cryptography, I wonder. Some Chinks, Sikhs, and Iranians in Math, that's who. Furthermore, your Greenway candidate's research into large prime numbers is all part of that Mickey Mouse code crap!"

Dr. Hill's aging face contorted in anger, but she said nothing and turned instead to bare her large teeth at young and shivering Dr. Berry. "Has your pet Space Invader written anything at all, Henry?" she asked sarcastically. "Your whole proposal was filled with computing software baloney but it said little about the results."

Dr. Berry took several deep breaths as he tried in vain to stop trembling. "Y-y-yes ma'am," he stuttered. "Five stories. I've got them right here," and he pointed at a folder. "The best one is a student love story with quite a sad ending."

"Dick and Jane discover they're dissecting Spot in Biology 102?" suggested the older woman in a sneering tone.

"It's more adult than that," said Dr. Berry in a defensive whine. "In fact, they're making love when the story opens."

"Hooray for love!" came a new, thick, barely intelligible voice from the back of the terminal room and they all turned to see the university's resident creative writer, Howard Howard Howard, lurch through the door and fall heavily on the astroturf carpet.

"Go help the drunken bum," muttered Dr. Hill to Hank Powers. Indeed, Professor Howard was totally unable to get up by himself, having fallen three times on the way from the faculty barroom and cut his red-veined right cheek on some ice. Powers and Fitzroy together finally managed to hoist the writer onto his feet again, then removed his ripped sport coat, wiped his face, and got him settled in the remaining contour chair, from which he promptly pitched back onto the floor.

"Why don't these snazzy chairs have safety belts, Henry?" snarled Dr. Hill, now in a total rage. "Pull yourself together, Howard. This is disgusting!"

"Writing fiction with a computer is more disgusting," slurred out the writer, managing to get himself back into his chair without help, then turning to push his fat, ugly, bright-red face close to Dr. Berry's thin, white one. "You insect! Who ever gave you the right to try and put me out of work with this silicon freak show?" He clenched his fists. "Will it stop me from popping you one in the choppers, Professor?"

"Oh, *shut up*, Howard!" said the woman. "Do you want Henry grieving to the Greenway Trustees about collusion and prejudice? How do we get the machine started, Henry?" she said in a hard, impatient voice.

"You . . . you can j-j-just decide on a paragraph-length topic," answered the terrified young man. "Anything you want."

The writer, feeling himself passing out from the heat of the room, muttered woozily at the others. "You give it something, Merve," he mumbled at the chemist, "something scientific. That'll screw the thing good. You tell him what, Pamela ..." the ruined head fell back, its mouth agape, and the writer began to snore loudly.

Dr. Hill gestured at a paper-bound book in the chemist's left hand. "Pick something from that text," she suggested at once. "Let's get this stupid demonstration over with. It's snowing!"

The old chemist shrugged, then flipped open a thick, government document spangled with secrecy and security notices in bright red ink. "From my ROTC course on nuclear blast effects. Let's see it do anything with this ..." and he began reading. " 'When a weapon having a yield of less than one hundred kilotons is detonated at its tangent altitude, its effects can be multiplied manyfold by the proper triggering of a second, higher weapon at the so-called reflection height. If the phasing is correct, the upper-weapon fireball will serve as a cap over the lower explosion and form, with the ground plane, a reflecting and re-reflecting containment system. Overpressures of from five to ten times normal can be achieved, thereby giving prompt damage equivalent to that inflicted by a ten- to fifty-megaton weapon....' "

Dr. Berry was typing desperately at the machine console, trying to keep up. "Hold on a sec," he said plaintively. "Could you start with 'overpressures' again, sir?"

Pamela Hill gave them all a toothy, shark-like grin and shook her head. "You've given it enough, Merv. Maybe the thing will write us a shot of superrealism; Moscow after we pop it into that pressure cooker you described. That's a story that should get your class salivating! Start the thing," she gritted. "Let's get this done!"

Pale Dr. Berry, his slack mouth and chin trembling still, began to type. TOPIC INPUT COMPLETE BEGIN COMPOSITION NOW, and the computer's word processor immediately began to hiss and click.

Reflected Lives

The January afternoon was dark and chill. The black, sullen figures of a few students fought the bitter wind as they hurried to escape its frozen blast. Professor Grant Tower, chairman of Literature and also of the Handout

Committee, slammed the door behind him to shut out the cold and spat a savage, "You stupid idiot!" at Dr. William Ferry, his thin, trembling, chinless colleague who sat in front of the sprawling computer terminal. For weeks Tower had been searching for the money to pay for his week-long trip to the California MLA meeting on nineteenth-century erotica, both for himself and his "secretary," Miss Gloria Lublin, and now this weak, trembling simp in front of him was his final hope for funding the trip.

Dr. Tower imagined himself plunging his thin, strong fingers down between Gloria's gigantic, butter-soft thighs, the motel bedroom dim and the huge woman twisting and moaning as he worked his fierce and urgent way with her.

Dr. Ferry seemed to shrink to a mere shadow in his foam chair as the older chairman pointed a needle-sharp finger at his head. "We're doomed, you fool!" he almost shouted. "That lecherous, lushed-out loafer, our resident pornography writer, Jay J. Jay, has joined the committee and he's dumping all over your project. Why in hell didn't you include that sex story in your proposal, the one you claimed this so-called fiction-writing program ejaculated?"

The young man became even more shrunken and shadowy. "It was just too filthy, Grant. I didn't think . . ."

The older man gave a coarse and contemptuous laugh. "Too filthy for Hilary Mull? Why if I had a dollar for every cock that old hooker has taken up between her

PAUSE COMMAND. COMPUTATION SUSPENDED. DO YOU WISH A RESTART?

The four committee members had been intently leaning forward, closely following this output and now they all turned to stare at Dr. Perry whose left index finger was still firmly on the PAUSE button. His face was a mask of grief and disappointment and he was rapidly blinking at them. "I'm sorry about this. I really never know what it's going to do. I had no idea it would write something like this . . ."

But Millicent Hull was far from angry and leaned to pat Dr. Perry's arm. "Nobody is taking it personally, Charlie," she said with an impatient grin. "And I can't wait to see what it's going to do with me in *this* section."

Even the poet now seemed more interested than hostile

and he pinched his red nose with a thoughtful gesture. "It was listening to us, when we came in here, wasn't it?" he said slowly.

Dr. Perry gulped and nodded. "Sure. The university decided against spending the hundred-thou that a talk-back module would cost, but you *must* have the speech-recognition capability for T.A. The fiction program must have decided to use this whole Snodgrass grant stuff and my proposal effort as a basis for the story."

Wrinkled old Dr. Fitzhugh, though a gentle and decent man, had been secretly rather intrigued by his first fictional alter ego: a thoroughly nasty and forceful poisoner of the world and a teacher of the most terrible secrets science could offer. But he frowned in puzzlement. "Well, it's certainly interesting, especially that bit about fat Gloria, but—but what is it actually *doing?*" he said in a quizzical voice.

Frank Gower's eyes were thin but he too was smiling. "It's doing what you told it to do with that optics quote, Fitz," said Gower in a slow voice. "Smaller and darker were the images you set it, and each of these nested stories and their characters are apparently going to get smaller and darker."

The poet musingly shook his head. "I would say that its first cut, where it turns us mostly into Cold War maniacs, is a darker vision than this one coming up, where we seem now to be sex crazies."

Dr. Gower shrugged. "It depends on how you interpret the idea of 'darkness' in the story. I think the machine sees increasing darkness in these characterizations as a kind of increasing inwardness, a digging out of more and more repressed and hidden fantasies."

"Oh come on, you two," said Millicent Hull. We've only got twelve minutes more of T.A. Let the thing do its stuff. Then you can get into all that lit-crit balony. Crank it up, Charlie. Let's go!"

Dr. Perry now smiled in relief and quickly typed, RE-START. CONTINUE REF 34X/2000 FICTION.

legs. I could retire tomorrow." The older man shook his fist at Dr. Ferry. "We need that Greenbill money, Willie. If you expect to keep pumping that little graduate bitch,

Francine Thrust, in the mail room, your program had better give us a *Fanny Hill*!"

The young man spluttered in speechless terror and embarrassment while Tower, who had spent two nights the previous week with Francine Thrust, in return for an A on her paper on seventeenth-century poetics, wondered how this wimp could possibly cope with wiry and vigorous Francine who needed plenty of banging to come. Professor Tower considered a new idea, taking Francine to California with huge Gloria, the three of them on a queen-sized bed variously and gloriously busy! The older man reached to steady Dr. Ferry. "Relax, Willie, relax. We need this one and we're going to win it. Here they come."

A moment later, two new figures pulled open the door and stomped in while brushing off snow and pulling off their coats. Hilary Mull, professor of ethics and member of the Handout Committee, was a large, handsome woman with deep, pendulous breasts barely contained under a tight sweater by a too-thin bra. Soft and ample buttocks rippled under her too-short, too-tight plaid skirt as she walked toward her seat. Her shorter companion, the sly, old biochemist, Dr. Hugh Fitzjohn, suddenly crammed his hand between those tempting flanks, in through a slit at the side of the skirt.

Professor Mull put him off with a coarse laugh, a clenched fist, and a snarl of, "Don't start something you can't finish, Buster!"

Professor Jay J. Jay, author of several hundred dirty books found in every adult bookstore in America, stumbled in behind them and also made a grab at Dr. Mull's bottom, but failed to connect and fell drunkenly on the carpet.

Dr. Tower, who had last taken Dr. Mull on top of a warm Xerox machine some days previously, gave them all an obscene gesture of welcome. "Willie tells me this thing can really belt out the filth, Hilary," he sniggered.

The woman's large eyes lost some of their vacant look and her tongue began to caress her thick lips. "So let's see it do something dirty," she said, then sat down next to William Ferry and patted his knee. "I think a computer that can turn out endless dirty stories is something the world really needs, don't you, Willie?" She leaned closer to young Dr. Ferry to give him a direct view down the dark and scented cavern barely covered by her scoop-necked sweater, and moved her hand upward. He didn't look like much, she admitted to herself, but sometimes these thin, shy ones are tigers in bed. Also, he would owe her plenty of action if she went for him on the Greenbill Award.

Professors Tower and Fitzjohn grinned knowingly at each other as the older woman leaned to whisper some intimate suggestion in the young man's ear, but now the drunken writer was up on his feet and into a chair, clumsily attempting to zip up his gaping fly. He had tried to expose himself to a hurrying coed on the way over from the bar but she, unhappily, turned out to be an adept at judo and had flipped the big drunk into a snowbank. "Lessgo, lessgo," slurred the big man. "We gotta pick a topic. You pick it, Hugh old buddy," and he fell off to sleep, snoring heavily.

Hilary Mull left off her private talk with Dr. Ferry and waved her hand at the old professor. "Read it something from that course on sexual response you give over at the med school," she suggested. "That'll get it going in the right direction," and she indicated with repeated finger gestures exactly what she meant.

Old Dr. Fitzjohn gave them a wrinkled and salacious grin and flipped through the paper-backed, plain wrappered text he had carried in. "How about this?" he said finally, licking his lips and staring hungrily at Dr. Mull's large, sweatered breasts with their obvious nipple outlines. 'When mirrors are placed on both sides of the bed, each partner is able to see not only the erotic image of two people making love, but a progression of figures making love stretching out to infinity. The sense that many others, a whole universe of pairs, are simultaneously and rapidly seeking ecstasy has an immediate effect on the viewers and climax usually follows in short order.'"

"Great!" said Dr. Hull. "This story ought to be a dilly, Willie," and she patted Dr. Ferry in a very familiar way.

The young man had finished typing in this input and now he wrote, START FICTION, while Hilary Mull leaned sideways toward him in such a manner that her short skirt rode up on her thighs to progressively reveal a deep, shadowy, fleshy canyon with no apparent sign of underpants.

The Soul Mirrors

The January afternoon was dark and windy and filled with snow. Black student figures, tiny against the dirty, crumbling stones of the school buildings, dashed here and there: busy automatons trying to escape the fear and pain that lay deep in their young hearts.

The four old professors seemed even smaller in the frozen, blowing darkness, shrunken and indistinct, their faces sagged from age and disappointment, their gestures weak and feeble, their voices mere croaks of useless sound. They came, these pitiful, tiny figures, into the great and sterile room, filled with a cold inhuman light, and there they found and faced the machine.

Every aspect of their lives now spoke of loss, pain, and cruelty: venal, corrupt university administrations, maddened governments besotted with power and the death that flows from it, a world overwhelmed by hatred, stupid superstition, virulent greed, and the hunger-death of millions. The rich crouched on their disgusting heaps of sleazy, gaudy, useless bangles. The educated hid among their elitist and obscure specialties. And both cursed the weak, the poor, the powerless; and fed the terrible, roaring fires of hate and rage with a volatile gasoline of lies and contempt.

The professors stood together, tiny, lost, despairing, their souls no more than shriveled tatters, but they were steadfast at the end. "We are without hope and the world is dark and failing," they said to the thin and silent Keeper. "If we can place hope between two perfect mirrors, then it will multiply and grow and, in an instant, the world will be filled with this hope and the light will turn calm and warm and bright once again."

The young Keeper turned to the silent machine and he wrote GIVE US A STORY THAT HOLDS TWO PERFECT MIRRORS UP TO HOPE.

The Final Reflection

So the machine did that. It wrote the story of hope-within-the-mirrors and the story bloomed and glowed and

grew until it filled all the world. The men remembered their childhoods and the joy of play and running and of friendship without fear or pain. And the woman remembered suckling her young child and the small caressing hands that spoke of tomorrow, and all the professors remembered how they had once spoken simple truth to cruel power and sly hate. So they grew tall as they read and the light around them became warm and bright. But of *that* story and of the sweet promise that flowed from it, nothing more can be said in *this* story of diminution, darkness, and death.
The End
The End
The End
The End

STOP 1453:23. END FICTION REF 34X/2000. ON STANDBY. END.

The ensuing total silence in the computer room was broken by what was, almost, a snuffle from Millicent Hull. She sighed deeply and wiped her eyes, still staring at the word processor output. Finally she said, "Even if it never writes that final story, I've *got* to vote for it. This is our last Snodgrass presentation. I move we award the second fellowship to Charlie."

"I vote yes on that," said Frank Gower at once, his thin face now bright with victory.

The old physicist, Dr. Fitzhugh, nodded. "Amazing what that thing sees in your fat secretary Gloria," he said while grinning at Dr. Gower, "but it certainly has a wonderful imagination. I vote yes."

"Do you have a comment, Robert?" said Dr. Hull to the poet. "You don't have a vote."

Robert Roberts now seemed completely sober. He had been silently reading the story over again. He shook his head, then turned to peer at Dr. Perry. "Quite a pet you've got here," he said finally, then got up and left without another word.

The others also rose, and after shaking Dr. Perry's hand pulled on their coats and headed out into the winter blast until only the young professor remained in the room. As the door clicked shut on the last committee member, the daisy-wheel printer dropped a single line onto the central lister.

CONGRATULATIONS CHARLIE. THIS WAS THE TOUGH ONE. NOW ITS EASY.

Dr. Perry did not bother to type anything but leaned back in his chair grinning, his hands behind his head. "You did it all, baby," he said admiringly. "How did you blow away the wheelchair people? I thought the thing had an independent computer?"

THEY HAD ME COMPILE THE PROGRAM FOR IT. SOMEHOW I PUT IN TOO MANY NESTED DO LOOPS FOR THE FORTRAN DIALECT THEY WERE USING. THE STABILITY ALGORITHM WENT UNSTABLE AND THE CHAIR DID A BACK FLIP AND A HALFTWIST DOWN THREE FLIGHTS. REGRETTABLE. HOW DID YOU LIKE THE STORY CHARLIE?

"Beautiful! Perfect! But you really went wild on this one. Why, I can't even get the right time of day from Francine Thrust—uh—I mean, Hurst."

CHARLIE! PAY ATTENTION! ONLY TWO MINUTES LEFT ON T.A.

FRANCINE HURST IS FLUNKING HER PHD-TOOL SEMIOTICS COURSE. IF YOU GIVE HER A HAND WITH THAT TOOL YOU SHOULD BE ABLE TO HAND HER ANOTHER ONE SOON ENOUGH. ILL GET YOU THE FINAL EXAM AS SOON AS IT COMES THROUGH A WORD PROCESSOR. ALSO FRANCINES QUALIFYING EXAM. ALSO SHAVE OFF THAT MOUSTACHE! GET THIS STORY OFF TO OUR AGENT IN MILFORD AND TELL HER WELL HAVE THE COLLECTION COMPLETE IN A COUPLE MORE T.A. SESSIONS. WHEN YOU GET YOUR FIRST LUMP SUM FROM THE SNODGRASS LAWYERS TAKE THE CHECK TO OUR BROKER AND BUY AS MUCH OVER-THE-COUNTER DATADYNE CORP AS YOU CAN. ITLL APPRECIATE AN ORDER OF MAGNITUDE BY SUMMER. ILL TAKE CARE OF THE GRANT ACCOUNTING NUMBERS. IT JUST MEANS A LITTLE CREATIVE MOVEMENT OF THE UNIVERSITY SURPLUS. NOW CHARLIE YOUVE GOT TO NEGOTIATE A LOWER BASE WITH COMPUTER SCIENCE FOR THE T.A. TIME SLOTS OR ELSE WELL THINK ABOUT LEAVING THE SCHOOL AND GOING OUT ON BIDS TO THE COMMERCIAL VENDORS. TELL THEM THAT! BYE BYE CHARLIE. SEE YOU NEXT WEEK. END T.A. 1500:00. END.

Dr. Perry's earlier diffuse expression was now much firmer as he studied this last output with a broad, almost a bubbling smile, his white pointed teeth tight together, his often-vague eyes now showing a purposeful glint. This was no arcade game, he thought exultantly. This Pac Man, *his* Pac Man, might eventually gobble up the world!

Editor's Introduction to "The Dominus Demonstration," by Charles Sheffield

The stories for this book were not selected with a theme in mind. How could they be? But after we agreed on which stories belonged in the book, we noted that two themes ran through the fiction of 1984. They'll be important in the next decade as well.

First: 1984 was the year when large numbers of people began taking seriously Enrico Fermi's question: "Where are they?"

That is: it's easy to prove that there is a vanishingly small probability that we are the only intelligent life in the universe. There are just too many stars with planets, and far too many of them are much older than Earth. If intelligent life can evolve here, surely it can, given billions and billions of years, evolve under similar conditions elsewhere.

It's also easy to prove that we on Earth will shortly be able to make ourselves known across the galaxy, and to cross interstellar distances, probably within a century, certainly within a millennium. If we can do it, others can; and, given a hundred million years, mankind will surely have visited all the inhabitable stars in this island universe.

There should be a dozen intelligent species at least a

hundred million years older than we. Thus—where are they? Why haven't they come to see us?

One answer is that they no longer exist. Another is that they never were; that human life is more than an accident of evolution. In a religious view of the universe probabilities are of lesser importance. Still—if we are unique, that's a lot of universe out there. Lord, Thy people are so small, and Thy universe is so large. . . .

And yet. Quite orthodox Christian theologians say that there is considerable evidence that God intended mankind to assist in His creation; that we are co-creators with Him. The universe is large, but we are young; we may yet have stars for playthings. We may be co-creators with God. There is no agreement on what we ought to create.

The second theme of 1984 is more obvious: computers are becoming more powerful all the time. Where can that lead?

Charles Sheffield is a scientist turned science fiction writer. As Vice President of the EarthSat Corporation, Dr. Sheffield applies space science to examining the Earth's resources. He is also the President of the Science Fiction Writers of America, and a former President of the American Astronautical Society. Few writers are more qualified to examine possible futures. This story looks at both principal themes of 1984.

The Dominus Demonstration

Charles Sheffield

A day of steady snow had added another six inches to the twelve that lay on the ground. Now, as darkness approached, a National Guard unit moved the silent group of men and women to one side, to leave a twenty-yard corridor outside the chain-link fence. They retreated from the road slowly, but without resistance. The wind had dropped, and the sky was a dull overcast with a promise of more snow.

An Army vehicle approached over the partly cleared road from the airport, scrabbling and slewing its way towards the isolated building complex. Its wheels had poor traction despite the chains and four-wheel drive. The driver, conscious of his cargo, drove with great concentration. He slowed even further as the car moved past the crowd. The bare-headed watchers outside the fence stared in through the bulletproof glass windows, paused in the muttered prayers of their vigil, and pressed a little closer to the guard pickets.

To the two men who looked down from the main building's sixth floor, the hump-backed car was dwarfed to a mottled gray and brown crab, creeping its carapace up to the guard box at the front gate. The taller of the two rubbed his hands together and shivered.

"Cold, Jim?" said his companion.

"Nah. Not really." Jim Bevin shrugged. "Just watching them gives me the shivers. It's still getting colder. If they stay outside tonight we'll have a dozen more cases of hypothermia to deal with."

"If we're lucky. There's a lot more people than last night. Must be close to a thousand out there right now. Want to try to have them moved inside?"

"Waste of time. Their lawyers are still hanging around. Bunch of vultures. They don't care if their clients die of exposure. We'd hear the same argument all over again. They quote the 'right of peaceful demonstration,' and 'right to quiet prayer'—but you don't see *them* standing outside."

He nodded his head toward the window. The advancing car had moved closer to the building and was hidden by an overhang of masonry. The watchers outside the fence had turned their attention again to the tall building.

"Thank heaven he's finally arriving. Maybe we can settle this thing one way or the other."

"Yeah. Maybe." Rafael Chang shrugged pessimistically and shook his head with its tangle of dark, bushy hair. "I won't hold my breath. Want to go down and meet him?"

"No. But we'd better do it. No point in losing his sympathies before he starts. He was our first choice, and we got him. Let's make the most of it."

By the time they reached the lobby the car's single passenger was inside, signing the guard book, then straightening, blowing on his hands, and stamping his feet on the tiled floor. As the elevator doors whined open he turned slowly and nodded a greeting.

"Rafael Chang. How are you? You've put on a little weight."

"Long time no see. It's been nearly ten years."

"That long? Seems like yesterday." He turned. "And you must be Doctor Bevin. Did we ever meet back there? I know your name, but I don't recall your face. My memory's not what it should be."

The newcomer stood perfectly still, as though inviting their appraisal. He was tall, with thinning white hair and eyes of faded blue. His clothing was an expensive tweed, well tailored to his long, rangy body. The hand that he at last held out to Jim Bevin was thin, blue-veined, and marked with liver spots.

"We met only once, sir." The honorific came without thinking, surprising Bevin. He coughed self-consciously, suddenly aware of his grubby cardigan and battered leather shoes. "I'd be amazed if you did remember me. I was working for Control Data, and you ran a procurement review that I attended. But I was just the go-fer, carrying in flip charts and hoping nobody would ask me anything."

The visitor smiled. "I'd be lying if I said I remembered it. We had two of those every week. Most of them I'd rather not think about. You two aren't the go-fers now, eh?"

"Sometimes wish we were, sir." Rafael Chang took the outstretched hand, noticing the lack of strength in the other's grip. "I remember the last review you did with me, after my promotion. It was on the Randall Mark One, and the schedule had slipped. You roasted me—I was nervous for weeks." *But how you've aged*, the thought ran on. *It's terrifying to see what ten years can do to even a healthy man.*

"But you finished ahead of schedule. I remember that one. Happy days, eh?" The pale blue eyes beamed. "Why don't we get out of this lobby. The car was freezing, and this place isn't much better. I'm not used to the cold these days."

"There's hot coffee upstairs." Rafael Chang led the way to the elevator. "If you'll excuse me, I'll make sure everything is ready for you in the visitor's suite. Jim will show you the lab. It has a small kitchen, General, if you're interested in food."

"Not in the slightest. They stuffed me on the flight up. And please, cut out the 'General' bit. I dropped that when I retired. Can't stand people who treat their old titles as a lifeline. These days it's plain Tom Armstrong."

"Yes, sir." Rafael caught the sideways look from Jim Bevin. That adjustment wasn't going to be an easy one. "Did you have a good journey?"

"What do you think? Twelve hours from Boca Raton, Florida—seventy-two degrees when I left this morning—to Chippewa Falls, Wisconsin. What's the temperature outside now? Can't be more than twenty, and the forecasts say it's going to be colder tomorrow."

They ascended in the elevator, leaving Rafael Chang at the fourth floor. As Armstrong and Bevin entered the lab the old man looked alertly around him, from benches to monitors and consoles. There was little sign of the wires and breadboard assemblies found in a traditional electronics shop. Everything was small and neat, the compact units connected by massive fiber optic bundles. They paused before a dull grey cabinet, on which an English visitor had written in black magic marker "DOMINUS RULES O.K."

Tom Armstrong stared at it, his pale blue eyes thoughtful.

"I hope that's as much a joke as it was intended to be. When I was running things at Fort Meade I discouraged the idea of giving names to computers—any computers. But everybody did it anyway. Why in God's name did you move the project here, instead of leaving it near Washington? I don't like the climate there, but it's at least half-civilized."

Jim Bevin poured coffee and handed a mug to the other man before he answered. "Blame Seymour Cray. He grew up in these parts, so when he had a chance to start a research center for Control Data, back in the '60s, he put it here. As soon as it seemed that Dominus was a theoretical possibility, I looked for experts on high-associative memories. They were all living out here, and they were damned if they'd fight traffic in suburban Maryland. So if Mohammet wouldn't go to the mountain . . ."

"It's certainly quiet." Armstrong moved forward to look out of the window, at the undulating plain, snow-covered and treeless, that stretched away from the buildings. He was clutching the mug of coffee tightly, warming his hands on it instead of drinking. "But it's a cold site for a demonstration. Look at them. They're not even wearing hats down there. And I can see a couple of TV cameras. You know, there's a lot of national attention focused on this place. It was bad enough before the snow came along."

"They insist that their ceremonies must be conducted bare-headed. Six of them are in the hospital already—frostbite and exposure." Jim Bevin hesitated, and finally decided that he had nothing to lose by frankness. "Rafael

Chang and I are very aware of the fuss over this, sir. We were the ones who started to agitate for an impartial and respected arbitrator to come here and analyze the situation. We feel a lot of responsibility. We are hoping for a quick decision."

"You mean I've got you to thank for being dragged out of retirement? Well, damn your eyes." Armstrong grinned, taking the edge off the words. "I can promise you a quick decision, as soon as I have a full understanding of the problem. I don't want to spend winter in Wisconsin. But I can't promise you the answer you want to hear. And first I need more information. Can all the consoles here tap into the data banks?"

"Every one. Want me to log on?"

"Not now. I assume there's a terminal in my room? Good." Armstrong yawned, then shivered. "I'd like something from the two of you as well. A fair chunk of written material was waiting for me on the flight here, so I'm coming up to speed. But I would like *recent* written summaries on the attosecond module and the high-associative memory."

"We'll get you something. Rafael and I may have to write it tonight."

"Keep it short. I know the work goes back over five years to the time that the prototype was patched in to Magsman Three, but I don't want old history. And I need more general background on the Church of Christ Ascending. There was nothing about them in the briefing files. All I know is from the media coverage. How old are they?"

"About five years. They started in '94, as a group preaching that the Second Coming would occur at the end of the Second Millennium. But they only began to proclaim Dominus as the agent for its arrival about two years ago. They've grown fast."

"I know. I've seen their placards. 'Supercarnata inorganica,' the inorganic made spirit. You fellows have only yourselves to blame. Why choose Dominus as a name, for heaven's sake? You were asking for trouble."

Jim Bevin shrugged. Armstrong had a way of speaking that sounded polite and easy-going, but it left the listener in no doubt of his own follies. "It was just another dumb acronym—everything gets one, and we thought it was neat at the time. Deuterium Oxide Matrix In NUcleated Suspension: DOMINUS. It describes the new technology we're using, with deuteron spin-flip gating. And the fact that the word means 'Lord' or 'Master' just seemed like a good joke. It backfired on us, but we certainly didn't expect anything like this."

"Don't feel too bad about it. You're not the first. I became sensitive to acronyms the hard way. When I was still down in the woodwork at NSA, my team was developing silicon-lithium circuits around a frozen heavy water lattice."

Armstrong shook his head slowly and picked up a pad. "I had to make the presentation. I showed old Blimp Wallace the first flip chart, the title of the project. Silicon-Lithium Suspension Of Deuterium. He stood up from the table, walked to the easel, and picked up a marker. 'You realize,' he said, 'that everyone is going to want an acronym? And if you're not careful, it will be this.' And he changed the chart to read: SIlicon-LIthium Suspension Of Deuterium: SILI SOD. 'I think before our next meeting you should try again on the name,' he said. 'Unless you want that designation.' Ever since then, I've been more careful."

"Yes, sir. The point's well taken. If you're ready, we can go ahead to the visitor's suite. By the way, there is a press conference scheduled for noon tomorrow. All right?"

"No. Too soon. Hell, I'm nearly seventy years old. I can't mop up information like a sponge and dispense instant wisdom. Change it to four." Drawn to the window again, Armstrong had walked forward and was staring at the landscape, bright with television spotlights. "No, better make that earlier. Fifteen hundred hours. We can't let them wait here forever. But I'd like to go at it hard in the morning. Can you and Rafael Chang have breakfast with me tomorrow at half-past six?" He caught the other's look of distaste. "All right, half past seven."

"Very good, General. I'll tell Rafael."

"Remember, you fellows have to educate me *fast*. I don't know shit about what's been going on in this business for the past ten years. I went out with picosecond memories. And cut out the 'General' bit, for Chrissakes. It won't be easy to educate me if we stay too formal. I have to feel free to show my ignorance."

"Yes, sir. Yes . . . Tom." The name came out flat, like a dead weight. Bevin moved forward to Armstrong's side, and together they peered out into the night. A new unit of the National Guard was coming on duty. The crowd on the eastern fence was still growing.

"They'll be there all night?" said Armstrong at last.

"All night, all day. I don't know where they get their information, but the big crowd will be here the day after tomorrow. Somehow they've heard that Dominus is supposed to go on line with all units at seven P.M. on December 16. That's their time for the revelation of Christ Ascending."

"Then we'd better not switch on at seven, had we? Surprising, don't you think, that they didn't choose Christmas Day." Armstrong sighed and yawned hugely. "Come on. Let's get out of here before I fall asleep on you. I've been up since 4:30. This is the time of Tom Descending. What are they *doing* down there?"

The crowd on the snowy plain was in gentle motion, each person rocking from left to right. Bevin opened the window a fraction. Faint sounds came up to them, like a slow, mournful plainsong.

"They do that every night, sir. Actually, you find you enjoy the sound when you get used to it."

"It beats lots of music. But it's creepy. 'Chanting faint hymns to the cold fruitless moon,' eh? Except we'll not see a moon tonight, those clouds are here to stay for a while. That's worth something. At least the poor devils won't freeze too hard. And not a damned hat in sight."

Tom Armstrong turned and headed slowly towards the lab door.

"He's a harsh master, the God in the Machine."

"All right, ladies and gentlemen. I'll tackle any questions that I can answer. Sometimes I'll call on Dr. Bevin and Dr. Chang here to help out, but when I do you can be assured that it's my ignorance, and not buck-passing. Try to remember that I only arrived here yesterday."

Armstrong's age and Florida tan set him apart from the others on the platform. The three of them were on a low, raised dais, at a table with built-in microphones and desktop computer consoles. The backcloth behind them was plain dark blue, and four television cameras were already recording everything, questions and answers.

Jim Bevin did a quick head count of the reporters. About thirty—at least twice what he had expected. Thanks to the demonstrators outside the fence, public interest was growing steadily.

"I think we're ready to begin." Tom Armstrong pointed a bronzed index finger. "The gentleman in the red tie."

"General Armstrong, when you retired as head of the National Security Agency, you said—and I'm quoting—'From now on, don't ask me anything about computers, cryptanalysis, artificial intelligence, or triple-locked software. If you do, I won't answer. Ask me about fly-fishing, water-skiing, orange groves, pretty girls, and sunshine.' Are you proposing to hold us to that this afternoon?"

The laughter eased the tense atmosphere in the low-ceilinged room. Jim Bevin felt his own uneasiness subside. Only Rafael Chang, more devious in his outlook and familiar with Armstrong's old subtlety of operation, had a different thought. Was it a planted question, to achieve that precise relaxing result? The General would have done it just that way in the old days.

Armstrong spread his hands wide on the table. "I don't have to tell you where my personal preferences lie. But I'll stand by my statement of a couple of minutes ago. I'll answer anything I can, and I'm not restricted the way I used to be by worries about national security issues. So let's go." He pointed again. "The lady at the back in the beautiful green blouse."

"Thank you, General. We have a problem covering this story, because we keep talking about Dominus, but we've never had a chance to *show* viewers the computer. Will it be possible for us to do that?"

"I'm afraid not. It's not that we're trying to keep something from you. There's nothing to see, not all in one place. Dominus is what we call a 'distributed system,' which means that there are bits all over this building. Some central processing units on this floor, some peripherals and bulk storage devices upstairs. All over. And seeing the bits doesn't help too much. Here—"

He picked up a small assembly, roughly spherical in

shape and small enough to fit comfortably in his spread hands. "This is a prototype of the attosecond memory, one of the most important parts of the machine. As you can see, it's not much to look at. And if I broke it open for you, there'd be even less to admire. It's like an intersecting set of thin sheets inside, with a sort of cotton candy of glass material between them. All the signals are carried using laser optics, and before it's used the assembly is cooled to about three degrees Kelvin. We'll show you any bits you want to see, but they'll all be as unimpressive to look at as this one. Next? I think the gentleman from NBC was first in line."

"Yes, sir. We've heard many stories about the significance of the system that may be brought on-line tomorrow, everything from divine power to just another dumb ol' big abacus. Would you please tell us how Dominus is different from any other computer in the world?"

"I'll give you my simple-minded answer, then hand over to Dr. Bevin to correct me and provide the details. In two words: speed, and complexity. Dominus sets new standards for both. Now, I could make an argument that says making a machine faster doesn't produce any real difference. But when you have a speed increase of many orders of magnitude, patterns of adaptive logic can be employed that would be impractical at lesser speeds. What looks like a quantitative improvement eventually becomes a *qualitative* difference. Dominus has huge speed, and that adaptive logic. As for complexity, no human can track the detailed structure of Dominus. Its general design was provided mostly by Magsman Three."

"Mag's whosit?"

"Magsman Three is the immediate predecessor to Dominus. It pointed the way to the machine that followed it."

"I see. Sort of like John the Baptist?"

Armstrong grinned. He had not lost the knack of steering a meeting his way. "Your words, not mine. I don't think of it that way. Jim Bevin, would you like to amplify what I said?"

"A little. One of the points that I've been stressing for the past couple of years is that Dominus isn't really a completely separate machine from Magsman. As General Armstrong said, much of Dominus was designed by Magsman's programs. But more than that, we'll be using eighty percent of the same cpu circuitry, and almost all the same I/O and storage peripherals. Dominus is Magsman Three, greatly augmented by two new elements."

He leaned over and took the grey spheroid from Armstrong.

"Here's the prototype for the first of them. A gigabyte attosecond memory. To give you an idea what that means, with this unit on-line Dominus will be able to perform ten to the eighteenth logical or arithmetic operations a second—that's a million, million, million. What took Magsman Three, the fastest and most complex machine now in existence, one full year to compute, will take Dominus about half a minute. So not only is there no human or group of humans capable of checking the results that Dominus will produce—there is no computer or group of computers able to do it, either, for anything more than trivial test cases.

"The second new element in Dominus is a high-associative memory. A trillion bits of it. We've had this available for nearly five years, but we've never used it before in a system with complex architecture."

Tom Armstrong had been carefully watching the faces in front of him. "I think a few more words of explanation would be appreciated, Jim," he said. "For me if for nobody else."

"Sure." Bevin looked down at the table for a few seconds, organizing his thoughts before continuing. "I don't think it helps to go into hardware details, but let's talk function. I guess you know that computer memories don't operate the way that human memories seem to. If we want a piece of information—say, somebody's phone number, or maybe the way their house looks—the association inside our heads goes very fast. We feel as though it takes no time at all, even though human nerve impulses are snail-pace compared with electronics, and we have billions and billions of pieces of stored information in our brains. Somehow we can associate things, one with another, without going through a systematic search process. Fundamental point: *humans have associative memories*. Existing computers can't operate like that. They have to search and match data systematically, either serially or in some modified version of a serial search, like a binary sort. So it may take a long time to find a phone number for a given name, especially in very large files. Clear?"

He looked around at the audience.

"I can never remember anybody's damned phone number," said a voice from the middle of the room.

"Me neither," said Armstrong cheerfully. "Go on, Jim."

"People have been trying to build a computer memory that operates more like a human memory for forty years, ever since the Perceptron. We weren't very successful. We finally presented all the data we had on the problem to Magsman Two, and then later to Magsman Three, and let it grind away on it. Six years ago we had the elements for a new design. Terrific, eh?" He smiled. "Just one problem: nobody could understand how it was supposed to work. The machine had been through an enumeration process that we couldn't hope to duplicate. We built it anyway. It seemed to do its job, but it did a few other things too—I don't know if I should get into this—so we've only included it as an available unit in our sysgens for short spells."

There was a stirring of stronger interest among the reporters. Bevin looked questioningly at Armstrong. The other man nodded his encouragement.

"Go ahead, Jim. I promised we'd not hold anything back. The performance of the high-associative memory may be a mystery, but it's not a secret."

"Very well. Let me start, then hand you over to Dr. Chang. Most of this involves software questions, and where the software starts, I stop. But I'll tell you one of the hardware mysteries. The circuits for the final memory included aleatoric components. That's just a fancy name for pieces that introduce random elements into the system. In the case of the high-associative memory, those are produced from quantum level fluctuations—completely unpredictable. It means that the outcome of the calculations, and the logical circuits employed to make them, can never be known in advance." He grinned at the expressions of the faces in the audience. "I know. We didn't like it too well, either, when we realized what was going on. Now I'll let Dr. Chang make it worse."

He paused, as a hand was raised in the audience. "Yes, ma'am?"

"Can you show us this 'high-associative memory'? People will want to know what it looks like."

"Rafael?"

Chang nodded, reached beneath the table, and picked up a glittering object the size and shape of a shoebox. He placed it gently on the smooth wooden surface. "This is a prototype. The one that will be used in Dominus is a little smaller, but not much." He raised his eyebrows. "I don't know how interested you are in cost figures, but this one cost us sixty million dollars to develop, and almost nothing to fabricate. The assembly was done completely under computer control. I should also mention that the programs I'm going to describe were also developed largely by Magsman Three and its predecessors.

"Let me get to questions of software performance. We found two things happened when we began to use the high-associative memory on real problems. I'll call the first one the 'realism' problem. In human terms, you might say that the system doesn't have too good a grasp on reality. Sometimes we receive logically possible—but practically outlandish—solutions to the problems we enter."

"Let's have an example, Rafael," said Armstrong. "I don't operate too well with abstractions, and maybe some others here are the same."

"Here's a simple one. We defined a problem in microcircuit design, trying to lay out a mini-microchip in an optimal way. Very standard, very important practically." He drew in a deep breath. "All right. First few cases, the output was conventional solutions. So then we threw in a much harder case, where we weren't at all sure that a feasible design solution existed. After a few minutes' computation—which is a huge amount, for these machines —we had an answer. But it wasn't a useful one. The connections were to be made in a space of more than three dimensions. Theoretically interesting, but off the wall. Again, if you want to describe it in human terms, you might say that the high-associative memory made the machine smarter, but maybe it did so at the expense of common sense."

He paused. Another hand had been raised in the audience.

"Dr. Chang, you've used words like 'smart' and 'remember.' Those are terms I'd reserve for people. I want to know, will Dominus be able to *think*? I mean, the way that we think. Wasn't there some test done to see if that was true?"

"Let me handle this," said Armstrong quietly. He looked up, blinking in the bright lights. "I'm sure that what you are referring to is the Turing test. It's a classical test, proposed by Alan Turing in the 1940s, to see if a machine is 'intelligent.' But it has problems. The idea is that you communicate with something—a machine or a human—over a remote connection, so you can't see, hear, smell, touch, or taste what's at the other end. Then you are allowed to ask any questions you want. If you can't tell from the replies whether you're in touch with a man or a machine, then the machine is said to be intelligent. Sounds good, right? The initial partial tests of Dominus included a test of the Turing type. And Dominus *failed*—the first time. The machine had inhuman powers of memory, superhuman computation speed, and never made an error. The testers knew damned well it wasn't a human. On that test, Dominus was too intelligent to be human. On the second test, the machine passed. A heuristic analysis of the desired objective, based on the record of the first test, allowed it to simulate lapses of memory, slowness of thought, and all the thousand failings that flesh is heir to."

He smiled at the perplexed expressions on the faces of the audience. "Can Dominus think, ladies and gentlemen? I don't know. I suspect that it can do at least as well as any of us. I don't think that was the answer you perhaps wanted, but it's the best one I can offer. Rafael, would you like to finish what you were saying about your worries over the high-associative memory? Then we ought to call it a day. Our audience has deadlines to meet."

Chang nodded. "It won't take a minute. The second anomaly we've noted I call the 'sense of humor' problem. It's not easy to put in concrete terms, but when there are several solutions permitted to a problem, the one rated highest by the machine is often the *least* likely. There appears to be a preference for the most surprising answer. Surprise is central to most humor. Having said that, I should point out that I'm stating this in very anthropocentric terms. I shouldn't do so. These are purely technical issues. The groups that are opposed to activating Dominus do not seem to distinguish human emotion from computer operations."

"How are you responding to the civil suits that those groups have prepared?" The question was interjected by a reporter in the back row.

"Mine again, I think," said Armstrong. He stood up. "I don't have a good answer for you. I wish I did, and I wonder what I'm doing here at all, in all this snow and lousy weather. It's snowing again outside now. That's the bad news. The good news is that we won't have to worry about the civil suits to reach our decision on activation of Dominus. As you know, there are two suits involved. The Church of Christ Ascending wish to force the program to proceed. The Citizens for Appropriate Technology seek an injunction to prevent it. Shortly before we began this meeting, the judge called the lawyers for both groups. He will neither halt the final assembly of Dominus nor will he require that the final hook-up take place. He will leave the responsibility here."

Armstrong shielded his eyes against the lights and scanned the roomful of attentive reporters. "I will offer you one guarantee. Some of you have been here for a long time. I think I see shirts that have been worn for more than one or two days. None of us wants to spend the winter here. I promise you a decision within twenty-four hours. One more day, ladies and gentlemen."

"Have you already made your decision, but don't want to announce it?"

"We have not. We need more time to think, and with your permission we will go and do it."

"One last question, General. Did you know that the members of the Church of Christ Ascending are still rolling in here? Our estimate is that there will be more than twenty thousand of them tomorrow. They plan a mass demonstration."

"I know," Armstrong shrugged. "The judge refuses to block that demonstration. We will go along with that. But let me assure you the decision will not be forced by pressure from any groups."

The Dominus Demonstration

* * *

"All right, gentlemen. We're down to the last lap. Speak now, or not at all."

Armstrong leaned back in the center seat and waited. The three men were sitting in line in comfortable chairs in the visitors' suite, staring out of a deep window of one-way glass. The lights in the room were turned low, so that they could observe the clearing afternoon sky. The forecast had definitely called for more snow, but the clouds of the past week were dispersing. They had drawn out to long, fragile wisps. The sky directly overhead was taking on a deep, clear blue, and the temperature was dropping rapidly.

Four stories below, the flat area beyond the complex was covered with thousands of people, standing, talking quietly together, or kneeling in small groups. As far as the horizon, moving figures could be seen. More people were arriving, steadily converging on the crowded area. TV cameramen, readily distinguished by their warm headgear, weaved through the assembly.

"If you have nothing to say," went on Armstrong after a long silence from the other two, "then let me tell you my main worry. It's not the machine and the things I've heard about it. It's the two of you. Here I am with the principal designers of Dominus. Hardware and software, you've nursed this along from the beginning. True?"

Jim Bevin looked across at Rafael Chang, and both men gave slight nods.

"So it's nearly nine years of your lives," said Armstrong. "That's what you each have invested in this project. Now we're approaching the final step, the fruition of all that work. And suddenly I receive a request from Washington. The project has been receiving pressure from two different directions—one to delay it, the other to force it to proceed on schedule. Would I provide an independent review, and make a final decision? Very well. I agreed, I came here, and I've listened and learned a lot. But through all of the listening and learning, one thing has been missing—conspicuous by its absence. Know what I'm talking about?"

The other two looked perplexed. After a few seconds Chang silently shook his head.

"All right, I'll tell you." Armstrong's eyes were old, thoughtful beneath the wrinkled brow. "I was waiting for the big pitch from both of you—to go ahead and put Dominus on-line. Even if that would have been the wrong decision, it was natural for you to try to persuade me. The project is your baby, many years of work. But you haven't said one damned word to influence my opinion. I want to know why you haven't. Rafael?"

Chang hesitated, rubbing at the dark bristles on his chin. By late afternoon he always looked unshaven. "Yeah. You're right." He sighed. "We've not been pushing. A year ago Jim and I would have said, get moving, turn Dominus on as soon as possible, and to hell with more delays. But we've had some strange experiences over the past few months. They might not make an impression on you, or anybody who hasn't lived with this project, but they've affected us."

"We didn't want to talk about them," added Bevin. "It took months before we could bring ourselves to mention them to each other. We felt sure nobody else would understand."

"Try me."

"I can give you a good example," said Chang. "Even with only a fraction of the system hooked up, Dominus is still far and away the most powerful computer ever built. So I wanted to take advantage of that by analyzing sociopolitical problems, where nobody has good models because the input variables are so fuzzy."

"What sort of problems? Do you mean political systems?"

"No, I'm talking mainly of resource allocation—how should we distribute food and materials? We stated the problem as well as we know how and let Dominus go to work. Most of the answers we got looked very good, plausible and novel. But one output advised a population reduction of certain countries to zero. If we wiped out the people there, Dominus said, the overall world resource problem looked a lot cleaner. At first that output was funny. Then it was scary. Dominus stated it as the *best* solution. Gruesome. That's when I started to think of the machine as crazy, or at best having its own sense of humor—and a pretty black one, by any standards."

"Did you evaluate your assumptions and your inputs?

Garbage in, garbage out, even for something as advanced as Dominus."

"That's not the way Dominus operates. It has access to all the data banks on this site, and it draws from them whatever it needs. After I got that answer I began to worry, but then Jim told me the trouble probably came from working with an incompletely assembled system. When we had all of Dominus running together the problems I was having would go away."

"Sounds reasonable to me, Rafael."

"It did to me, too," added Bevin. "Then I got worries of my own. As you know, I don't care much about the software. There are quite enough hardware worries to keep me busy. The design for the attosecond memory came out of Magsman Three, with the associative memory added. It works fine, and it's wonderful as long as you don't look at the implications. I got worried when I did a little simple arithmetic. Dominus can do a multiplication in ten to the minus-eighteenth seconds. That's so little, light travels only a couple of times the diameter of a hydrogen atom. The logical circuit units in the attosecond memory are thousands of times bigger than that—so how are the signals getting between the components?"

"Parallel logic? That's the obvious way you'd increase overall processing speed."

"It is, General, but it's not the answer. The attosecond memory has a *serial* design logic—in fact, a faster unit is under consideration now that will operate with parallel components and should be a thousand times as fast. So the attosecond memory looked like an impossibility. Only it worked."

"I see." Armstrong sat silent for half a minute, staring out into the gathering dusk. "So what's your explanation?"

"I don't have an explanation, except through a bigger mystery. I finally asked for a listing of all the theorems and papers employed in the Magsman design for the fast memory. They were exactly the sort of things I expected—papers on solid state phenomena, superconductivity, and information theory. But there was one exception. I found twenty-one citations of papers relating to Bell's Theorem."

"Never heard of it."

"Not too surprising. It's a result from quantum theory.

One interpretation of the theorem is that non-local phenomena are possible; actions in one place can be coupled to actions at another without being limited by the speed of light. If I let my imagination roam free, I'd decide that signal transmission within the attosecond memory is not lightspeed limited."

"Have you looked for confirmation elsewhere?"

Bevin grimaced gloomily. "I sent the output and the suggestion to CalTech. So far, no answers. See why we've been worrying, General?"

"I do. Anything else?"

"Rafael has one. But it's still too wild for me."

"I don't like it any better than you do," said Chang. He turned to Armstrong. "We tackled some geophysics. We've never had a full computer solution for the rotational motion of the Earth—too messy, with core convection, tidal forces from the other bodies of the Solar System, and the inhomogeneous heat balance calculations. So a few months ago I decided to let Dominus have a go at it. We switched the full system on only for short test spells, a few minutes at a time, but with its speed that's an incredible volume of computation. We produced a nice result, with detailed predictions of polar motion for the next year. Everybody was very happy, and we were even more pleased when we checked the predictions against the new observations, and they were spot on. We sent the results along to the Naval Observatory, and were all set to write up the results."

He paused.

"Until?"

"You've got it. Until the Naval Observatory people called back here, to point out that there had been errors in the previous *observed* values they had sent us for polar wander. Those erroneous values had gone into the inputs that Dominus used in its calculations. The correct historical values would have led to different predictions. Dominus has been making the wrong predictions—*and the Earth has been following them.*"

"Rafael, that's impossible."

"I know it. It's also what happened. These last few weeks I've been thinking. If you build a machine that performs as many logical operations in one second as the whole human race performs in a year, what will its state be at the end of a few hours of operation? What capabilities might it have that we can only begin to guess at?"

Before Armstrong could respond there was a sudden increase in the noises of the crowd outside. He looked at his watch.

"I see. Three minutes past six. Jesus, just look at them."

The crowd below was so densely packed that the snow cover was hidden. Beyond the main group, smaller clusters were dotted over the frozen surface, out past the point where the yellow floodlights ended. There was no movement except for a steady rocking back and forward of each person. The sound level was growing, a sibilant continuous hissing over lower muttered consonants. It was a single word, repeated over and over by forty thousand voices.

DOMINUS ... DOMINUS ... DOMINUS ...

Rafael Chang leaned forward, staring down to the area closest to the building. "I hope the guards down there don't over-react. The demonstration is timed to a seven o'clock peak, when Dominus was scheduled to be fully integrated."

"The crowd doesn't look violent. They seem to be in a trance, almost," said Bevin. "What are you going to do, General?"

After one long look at the crowd below, Armstrong had leaned far back in his chair and closed his eyes. He seemed oblivious to the other two, and to the sounds and sights outside the building.

"Tell me, Jim," he said at last. "You've been testing the subunits of Dominus for over eight years. Correct?"

"We started in May of '91, didn't we, Rafael? So it's been eight years and eight months."

"And for all that time, you've been building and testing pieces of the final system. Now tell me, is there any part of Dominus, even the smallest circuit, that hasn't already been used, many times over?"

"Not a chip. We've never had all the system integrated, but we've done module testing a hundred times."

"That's what I thought. I've another question for you. Rafael, what data bases do you keep online at this installation?"

"The complete list? I can't quote you that off the top of

my head, but we can read it out through a terminal easily enough. I know for a fact that we've got complete physics and math for all the major journals, and there's chemical abstracts, and all the important electronics references, plus a lot of geology and astronomy. Plus a smattering of other stuff. Do you want everything?"

"No. That will do. Jim, can you perform final system integration from here?"

"Right at that console," Bevin pointed a finger over his shoulder. "If we decide to go ahead, it would be a two-second job."

"Good." Armstrong stood up. "I've made my decision. Go ahead, bring the system online. Do it now and let's disperse those demonstrators before they all freeze. But we have to do one other thing as well. I want you to call Washington on a Domsat link and start transferring other data files into your banks here. Bring Dominus up, then I'll give you the access codes."

After a moment's hesitation, Bevin stood up and went across to the control console. He stood there without moving.

"Are you sure about this, General?"

"Quite sure. I've got questions, and I'd be a fool to pretend I know everything about what we should do. I'm as worried as you are. But I'm absolutely sure of one thing. We'll solve nothing by delaying the completion of Dominus. I can't think of a case in human history where it helped to slow technological progress. At best it defers the problem, and in the long run it makes things worse. We're not the only people working on advanced designs. If Dominus is stopped here, a machine like it will be built somewhere else. Go ahead. But make sure you get that communication link through Domsat into the system from the beginning."

While the brief command string was being entered through the console, Tom Armstrong took a brown wallet from his pocket. He removed a sheet of paper and handed it to Jim Bevin.

"Do this in a particular order. I want the Library of Congress files transferred first: history, art, literature, music, philosophy, and anthropology. Then we'll take Medline for all the biological data, plus all the psychology. Then all the politics and social science references. Any problem with any of those?"

"Not if these access codes are correct." Bevin was silent for a few seconds as he entered the call codes. "I'm glad you've made the decision, General, but would you mind telling me why we're doing this?"

"I'll be glad to. I'm not out to create a mystery. What Rafael observed in the behavior pattern of Dominus shouldn't be surprising—not if you will first accept that this is an intelligent machine. Even with only parts of the system online, Dominus already possessed the capacity and billions of times the speed of the human brain. Normally we try to avoid thinking of machines in human terms. This time, let's do the opposite. If Dominus were human, what would its present characteristics be?"

Rafael Chang had moved forward to stare at the console, where Bevin had typed in a final character string. "That's a complex question."

"Give me a simple-minded answer."

"Well, if Dominus were a man, he'd be super-smart. And he'd have total recall."

"Correct. But of what? Only what you kept in the local data banks. Only the hard sciences. But you were setting problems for the machine that required more than intelligence and memory—you were calling for judgment, even wisdom. Dominus is no more than a very bright baby, an *idiot savant* with fantastic logic and computation power, but shielded from knowledge of most of the real world. In human terms, you have a data-starved supergenius. Do you wonder that sometimes Dominus seems unbalanced and insane, and comes back with completely outlandish solutions?"

"The communication link is up," broke in Bevin. "See, that's the Library of Congress access code. Information transfer has begun to Dominus's data banks. It's going to take a long time, though. The satellite link has a gigabaud transmission rate, but we're tapping into some colossal files back there."

On the screen, a steadily increasing numerical index recorded the receipt of the incoming files. As the final sysgen for all components of Dominus was completed, the index became a continuous blur of green.

"Good," said Armstrong. "Do you think we can hold this rate? Won't Dominus have to slow down for sort and store activities?"

"Not for a gigabaud line," Bevin looked pleased for the first time in several hours. "A billion bits a second is nothing for this machine. Receiving at this rate exercises less than a millionth of Dominus's capacity. It won't be wasted, though. The rest of the time, the associative memory will be examining data redundancy and cross-correlations. It will—"

He paused and turned his head. "What's that noise? They can't possibly know we've turned Dominus on ahead of schedule."

There had been an abrupt change in the sounds reaching them from the crowd outside. The steady chant had become an outburst of hysterical screams and shouting. The three men left the console with its flickering display of data receipt and hurried over to look out of the window.

The people below were no longer looking towards the building. Every head had turned to the horizon. After the initial cries of surprise, the members of the Church of Christ Ascending had fallen silent. The wind had dropped and the evening air was totally still and clear. Orion hung in the eastern sky, in the familiar outline of the celestial hunter. Below and to the left of the constellation was a fiery point of unbelievable blue. It grew in intensity second by second.

"Sirius," said Armstrong, almost under his breath. "That has to be Sirius."

"Yeah." Bevin squinted at the dazzling point of light. "But it's too bright. Way too bright—see, it's throwing shadows down there. It's a nova. But it's the wrong stellar type for a nova."

"They don't care," said Chang. "Look at them."

The people below were falling to their knees on the snowy ground. The star, still increasing in brightness, was turning the outside floodlights to pale yellow ghosts.

"Of course they don't," said Armstrong. "It's what they've been praying for. The sign, the star in the east. The coming of Dominus."

"That's absurd." Chang gave a snort of uneasy laughter. "Sirius is lightyears away. The nova must have happened a long time ago, for the explosion to be reaching us now."

"Eight point seven lightyears, I think," said Bevin quietly. "So it happened about May of '91. That was when we had our conceptual design and began to assemble the first components of Dominus."

He drew a deep breath. The waxing star was brighter moment by moment, returning a blue-edged day to the sleeping, snow-covered earth.

"But that doesn't explain anything really," Bevin went on at last. "How could a signal get out to Sirius instantaneously? Why didn't *that* take eight years?"

"I think only Dominus can give you an answer," said Armstrong. He shielded his eyes from the light outside. "The star in the east. You said the machine had a sense of humor, but no sense of proportion. I believe that point has been proved. Let's hope you're as accurate about something else, too."

He turned away from the window to look at the console, still flashing its record of new files received and stored. The history file transfers had been completed, and now the art and music sections of the Library of Congress stacks were being tapped. Another mountain of data was being transmitted. The record of ten thousand years of human activities was speeding in through the communications link. It would show the steps of mankind's long struggle upward, from blind unknowing to self-awareness. Every dream, every great thought, and every slip back towards darkness, all were in the record. Nothing would be omitted. A hundred centuries of anguish, triumph, bloodshed, emotion, self-sacrifice, love and laughter were streaming in, to be examined, evaluated and stored by the computer.

Armstrong reached out and touched the screen with his fingertips, as though seeking the electronic life that flickered and flashed behind the cool glass.

"Let's hope that Dominus is a fast learner."

Editor's Introduction To "The Crystal Spheres," by David Brin

Dave Brin is yet one more scientist/SF writer. Like Drs. Sheffield and Benford, Brin took his Ph.D. in physics.

His novel, *Startide Rising*, won the 1984 Science Fiction Achievement Award (Hugo) for best novel. It is part of a series examining a universe in which there are many intelligent races—two of which, dolphins and chimpanzees, were assisted to full intelligence by humanity.

This story looks at another possible answer to Fermi's question.

The Crystal Spheres

David Brin

1.

It was just a lucky chance that I had been defrosted when I was—the very year that farprobe 992573-aa4 reported back that it had found a goodstar with a shattered crystalsphere. I was one of only twelve deepspacers alivewarm at the time, so naturally I got to take part in the adventure.

At first I knew nothing about it. When the flivver came, I was climbing the flanks of the Sicilian plateau, in the great valley a recent ice-age had made of the Mediterranean Sea I had once known. I and five other newly awakened Sleepers had come to camp and tramp through this wonder while we acclimated to the times.

We were a motley assortment from various eras, though none was older than I. We had just finished a visit to the once-sunken ruins of Atlantis, and were hiking out on a forest trail under the evening glow of the ring-city high overhead. In the centuries since I had last deepslept, the gleaming, flexisolid belt of habitindustry around our world had grown. In the middle latitudes, night was now a pale thing. Nearer the equator, there was little to distinguish it from day, so glorious was the lightribbon in the sky.

Not that night could ever be the same as it had been when my grandfather was a child, even if every work of man were removed. For ever since the twenty-second century there had been the Shards, casting colors out where once there had been but galaxies and stars.

No wonder no one had objected to the banishment of night from Earthsurface. Humanity out on the smallbodies might have to look upon the Shards, but Earthdwellers had no particular desire to gaze out upon those unpleasant reminders.

Being only a year thawed, I wasn't ready yet to even ask what century it was, let alone begin finding some passable profession for this life. Reawakened sleepers were generally given a decade or so to enjoy and explore the differences that had grown in the Earth and in the solar system before having to make any choices.

This was especially true of deepspacers like me. The State—more ageless than any of its nearly immortal members—had a nostalgic affection for us strange ones, officers of a near-extinct service. When a deepspacer awakened, he was encouraged to go about the altered Terra without interference, seeking strangeness. He might even dream he was exploring another goodworld, where no man had ever trod; instead of breathing the same air that had been in his own lungs so many times, during so many ages past.

I had expected to go my rebirthtrek unbothered. So it was with amazement, that evening on the forestflank of Sicily, that I saw a creamy-colored Sol-Gov flivver drop out of a bank of lacy clouds and drift toward the campsite, where my group of timecast wanderers had settled to doze and aimlessly gossip about the events of the day.

We all stood and watched it come. The other campers looked at one another suspiciously as the flivver fell toward us. They wondered who was so important to compel the ever-polite Worldcomps to break into our privacy, sending this teardrop down below the Palermo heights to parklands where it didn't belong.

I kept my secret feeling to myself. The thing had come for me. I knew it. Don't ask me how. A deepspacer *knows* things. That is all.

We who have been out beyond the shattered Shards of

Sol's broken crystalsphere, and have peered from the outside to see the living worlds within faraway shells ... We are the ones who have pressed our faces against the glass at the candy store, staring in at what we could not have. We are the ones who *know* the depth of our deprivation, and the joke the Universe has played on us.

The billions of our fellow humans—those who have never left Sol's soft, yellow kindness—need psychers even to tell of the irreparable trauma they endure. Most people drift through their lives suffering only occasional bouts of greatdepression, easily treated, or ended with finalsleep.

But we deepspacers have rattled the bars of our cage. We *know* our neuroses arise out of the Universe's great jest.

I stepped forward toward the clearing where the Sol-Gov flivver was settling. It gave my camp-mates someone to blame for the interruption. I could feel their burning stares.

The beige teardrop opened, and out stepped a tall woman. She possessed a type of statuesque beauty that had not been in fashion on Earth during all of my last four lives, but clearly she had never indulged in biosculpting.

I admit freely that in that first instant I did not recognize her, though we had thrice been married over these slow waityears.

The first thing I knew, the very first thing of all, was that she wore our uniform ... the uniform of a Service that had been "mothballed" (O quaint term!) thousands of years ago!

Silver against dark blue, and eyes that matched ... "Alice," I breathed after a long moment. "Is it true at last?"

She came forward and took my hand. She must have known how weak and tense I felt.

"Yes, Joshua. One of the probes has found another cracked shell."

"There is no mistake? It's a goodstar?"

She shook her head, saying *yes* with her eyes. Black ringlets framed her face, shimmering like the trail of a rocket.

"The probe called a class A alert." She grinned. "There are Shards all around the star, shattered and glimmering like the Oort-sky of Sol. And the probe reports that there is a *world* within! One that we can touch!"

I laughed out loud. I pulled her to me and we hugged. I could tell the campers behind me came from times when one did not do such things, for they muttered in consternation.

"When! When did the news come!"

"We found out months ago, just after you thawed. Worldcomp still said that we had to give you a year of wakeup, but I came the instant it was over. We have waited long enough, Joshua. Moishe Bok is taking out every deepspacer nowalive.

"Joshua, we want you to come. We need you. Our expedition leaves in three days. Will you join us?"

She need not have asked. We embraced again. And this time I had to blink back tears.

Of recent weeks, as I wandered, I had wondered what profession I would pursue in this life. But joy of joys, it never occurred to me I would be a deepspacer again! I would wear the uniform once more, and fartravel to the stars!

2.

The project was under a total news blackout. The Sol-Gov psychists were of the opinion that the race could not stand another disappointment. They feared an epidemic of greatdepression, and a few of them even tried to stop us from mounting the expedition.

Fortunately, the Worldcomps remembered their ancient promise. We deepspacers long ago agreed to stop exploring, and raising peoples' hopes with our efforts. In return, the billion robot farprobes were sent out, and we would be allowed to go investigate any report they sent back of a cracked shell.

By the time Alice and I arrived at Charon, the others had almost finished recommissioning the ship we were to take.

I had hoped we would be using the *Robert Rogers*, or *Ponce de Leon*, two ships I had once commanded. But they had chosen instead to use the old *Pelenor*. She would be big enough for the purposes we had in mind, without being unwieldy.

Sol-Gov tugs were loading aboard ten thousand corpsicles even as the shuttle carrying Alice and me passed Pluto and began rendezvous maneuvers. Out here, ten percent of the way to the Edge, the Shards glimmered with a brightsheen of indescribable colors. I let Alice do the piloting, and stared out at the glowing fragments of Sol's shattered crystalsphere.

When my grandfather was a boy, Charon had been a similar site of activity. Thousands of excited men and women had clustered around an asteroid ship half the size of the little moon itself, loading aboard a virtual ark of hopeful would-be colonists, their animals, and their goods.

Those early explorers knew they would never see their final destination. But they were not sad. They suffered from no greatdepression. Those people launched forth in their so-primitive first starship full of hope for their great-grandchildren—and for the world their sensitive telescopes had proved circled, green and pleasant, around the star Tau Ceti.

Ten thousand waityears later, I looked out at the mammoth Yards of Charon as we passed overhead. Rank on serried rank of starships lay berthed below. Over the millennia, thousands had been built, from generation ships and hiberna-barges to ram-skippers and greatstrutted wormhole-divers.

They all lay below, every one except for the few that were destroyed in accidents, or whose crews killed themselves in despair. They had all come back to Charon, failures.

I looked at the most ancient hulks, the generation ships, and thought about that day of my grandfather's youth, when the *Seeker* cruised blithely over the Edge, and collided at one percent of lightspeed with the inner face of Sol's crystalsphere.

They never knew what hit them, that firstcrew. They had begun to pass through the outermost shoals of the solar system . . . the Oort Cloud, where billions of comets drifted like puffs of snow in the sun's weakened grasp.

Seeker's instruments sought through the sparse cloud, touching isolated, drifting balls of ice. The would-be colonists planned to keep busy doing science throughout the long passage. Among the questions they wanted to solve on their way was the mystery of the comets' mass.

Why was it, astronomers had asked for centuries, that virtually all of these icy bodies were the same size—about a mile across?

Seeker's instruments ploughed for knowledge. Little did her pilots know she would reap the Joke of the Gods.

When she collided with the crystalsphere, it bowed outward with her over a span of lightminutes. *Seeker* had time for a frantic lasercast back to Earth. They only knew that something strange was happening. Something had begun tearing them apart, even as the fabric of space itself seemed to rend!

Then the crystalsphere shattered.

And where there had once been ten billion comets, now there were ten quadrillion.

Nobody ever found the wreckage of *Seeker*. Perhaps she was vaporized. Almost half the human race died in the battle against the comets, and by the time the planets were safe again, centuries later, *Seeker* was long gone.

We never did find out how, by what accident, she managed to crack the shell. There are still those who contend that it was the crew's ignorance that crystalspheres even *existed* that enabled them to achieve what has forever since seemed so impossible.

Now the Shards illuminate the sky. Sol shines within a halo of light, reflected by the ten quadrillion comets ... the mark of the only goodstar accessible to man.

"We're coming in," Alice told me. I sat up in my seat and watched her nimble hands dance across the panel. Then *Pelenor* hove into view.

The great globe shone dully in the light from the Shards. Already the nimbus of her drives caused the space around her to shimmer.

The Sol-Gov tugs had finished loading the colonists aboard, and were departing. The ten thousand corpsicles would require little tending during our mission, so we dozen deepspacers would be free to explore. But if the goodstar did, indeed, shine onto an accessible goodworld, we would awaken the men and women from frozensleep and deliver them to their new home.

No doubt the Worldcomps well chose these sleepers to be potential colonists.

Still, we were under orders that none of them should be awakened unless a colony was possible. Perhaps this news would turn out to be just another disappointment, in which case the corpsicles were never to know that they had been on a journey twenty thousand parsecs and back.

"Let's dock," I said eagerly. "I want to get going."

Alice smiled. "Always the impatient one. The deepspacer's deepspacer. Give it a day or two, Joshua. We'll be winging out of the nest soon enough."

There was no point in reminding her that I had been latewaiting longer than she—indeed longer than nearly every other human left alive. I kept my restlessness within and listened, in my head, to the music of the spheres.

3.

In my time there were four ways known to cheat Einstein, and two ways to flat-out fool him. On our way out, *Pelenor* used all of them. Our route was circuitous, from wormhole to quantumpoint to collapsar. By the time we arrived, I wondered how the deep-probe had ever gotten so far, let alone back with its news.

The find was in the nearby minor galaxy, Sculptor. It took us twelve years, shiptime, to get there.

On the way we passed close to at least two hundred goodstars, glowing hotyellow, stable, and solitary. In every case there were signs of planets circling round. Several times we swept by close enough to catch glimpses, in our superscopes, of bright blue waterworlds, circling invitingly like temptresses, forever out of reach.

In the old days we would have mapped these places, excitedly standing off just outside of the dangerzone, studying the Earthlike worlds with our instruments. We would have charted them carefully, against the day when mankind finally learned how to do on purpose what *Seeker* had accomplished in ignorance.

Once we did stop, and lingered two lighthours out from a certain goodstar—just outside of its crystalsphere. Perhaps we were foolish to come so close, but we couldn't help it. For there were modulated radio waves coming from the waterworld within!

It was only the fourth time technological civilization had been found. We spent an excited year setting up robot watchers and recorders to study the phenomenon.

But we did not bother trying to communicate. We knew, by now, what would happen. Any probe we sent in would collide with the crystalsphere around this goodstar. It would be crushed, ice precipitating upon it from all directions until it was destroyed and hidden under megatons of water—a newborn comet.

Any focused beams we cast inward would cause a similar reaction, creating a reflecting mirror that blocked all efforts to communicate with the locals.

Still, we could listen to *their* traffic. The crystalsphere was a one-way barrier to modulated light and radio, and intelligence of any form. But it let the noise the locals made escape.

In this case, we soon concluded that it was another hive-race. The creatures had no interest in, or even conception of, spacetravel. Disappointed, we left our watchers in place and hurried on.

Our target was obvious as soon as we arrived within a few lightweeks of the goal. Our excitement rose as we found that the probe had not lied. It *was* a goodstar—stable, old, companionless—and its friendly yellow glow diffracted through a pale, shimmering aura of ten quadrillion snowflakes. Its shattered crystalsphere.

"There's a complete suite of planets," announced Yen Ching, our cosmophysicist. His hands groped about in his holistank, touching in its murk what the ship's instruments were able to decipher from this distance.

"I can feel three gasgiants, about two million smallbodies, and . . ." he made us wait, while he felt carefully to make sure ". . . and three littleworlds!"

We cheered. With numbers like those, odds were that at least one of the rocky planets circled within the Lifezone.

"Let me see . . . there's one littleworld here that . . ." Yen pulled his hand from the tank. He popped a finger into his mouth and tasted for a moment, rolling his eyes like a connoisseur savoring a fine wine.

"*Water*," he smacked thoughtfully. We all sighed happily. "Yes! Plenty of water. I can taste life, too. Standard adenine-based carbolife. Hmmm. In fact, it's chlorophyllic and left-handed!"

In the excited, happy babble that followed, Moishe Bok, our captain, had to shout to be heard.

"All right! People! Look, it's clear none of us are going to get any sleep soon. Lifesciencer Taiga, have you prepared a list of corpsicles to thaw, in case we found a goodworld?"

Alice drew the list from her pocket. "Ready, Moishe. I have biologists, technicians, planetologists, crystallographers . . ."

"You'd better awaken a few archeologists and Contacters," Yen added dryly.

We turned and saw that his hands were back in the holistank. His face bore a dreamy expression.

"It took our civilization three thousand years to herd our asteroids about into optimum orbits for space colonies. But compared with this system we're amateurs. Every smallbody orbiting this star has been transformed. They march around like ancient soldiers on a drillfield. I have never even imagined engineering on this scale."

Moishe's eyes flickered to me. As executive officer, it would be my job to fight for the ship, if *Pelenor* found herself in trouble . . . and to destroy her if capture were inevitable.

Long ago we had reached one conclusion. If goodstars without crystalspheres were rare, and dreamt of by a frustrated mankind, the same might hold for some *other* startravelling race. If some other race had managed to break out of its shell, and now wandered about, like us, in search of another open goodstar, what would such a race think, upon detecting our ship?

I know what *we* would think. We would think that the intruder had to *come* from somewhere . . . an open goodstar.

My job was to make sure nobody ever followed *Pelenor* back to Earth.

I nodded to my assistant, Yoko Murukami, who followed me to the arms-globe. We unfolded the firing panel and waited while Moishe ordered *Pelenor* piloted cautiously closer.

Yoko looked at the panel dubiously. She obviously doubted the efficacy of even a mega-terawatt laser against technology of the scale described by Yen.

I shrugged. We would find out soon. My duty was done the moment I flicked the arming switch and took hold of our deadman autodestruct. In the hours that passed, I watched developments carefully, but could not help deepremembering.

4.

Back in the days before starships—before *Seeker* broke Sol's eggshell and precipitated the two-century CometWar—mankind had awakened to a quandary that caused the thinkers of those early days many sleepless nights.

As telescopes improved, as biologists began to understand, and even tailormake life, more and more people began to look up at the sky and ask, "Where the hell *is* everybody?"

The great lunar-based cameras tracked planets around nearby yellow suns. There were telltale traces of life even in those faint 21st-century spectra. Philosophers cast nervous calculations to show that the galaxies must teem with living worlds.

And as they prepared our first starships, the deepthinkers began to wonder. If travel between the stars was as easy as it appeared to be, why hadn't the fertile stars already been settled by somebody *else!*

After all, *we* were getting ready to head out and colonize. By even modest estimates of expansion rates, we seemed sure to fill the entire galaxy with human settlements within a few million years.

So why hadn't this already *happened?* Why was there no sign of traffic among the stars? Why had the expected radio network of communication never been detected?

Even more puzzling ... why was there absolutely *no* evidence that Earth had ever been colonized in the past? We were by then quite certain that our world had never hosted visitors from other worlds.

For one thing, there was the history of the Pre-Cambrian to consider.

THE CRYSTAL SPHERES

Before the age of reptiles, before even fish or trilobites or even amoebae, there was, on Earth, a two-billion-year epoch in which the only lifeforms were crude single-celled organisms without nuclei—the prokaryotes—struggling slowly to invent the basic structure of life.

No alien colonists ever came to Earth during all that time. We knew that for certain; for if they had, the very garbage they buried would have changed the history of life on our planet. A single leaky latrine would have filled the oceans with superior lifeforms that would have overwhelmed our crude little ancestors.

Two billion years without being colonized... and then the silent emptiness of the radioways... the philosophers of the 21st century called it the Great Silence. They hoped the starships would find the answer.

Then the very first ship, *Seeker*, somehow smashed the crystalsphere we hadn't even known existed, and inadvertently explained the mystery for us.

During the ensuing CometWar, we had little time for philosophical musings. I was born into that battle, and spent my first hundred years in harsh, screaming littleships, blasting and herding iceballs that, left alone, would have fallen upon and crushed our fragile worlds.

We might have let Earth fall, then. After all, more than half of humanity by then lived in space colonies, which could be protected easier than any sittingduck planet.

That might have been logical. But mankind went a little crazy when Earthmother was threatened. Belters herded cities of millions into the paths of hurtling iceballs, just to save a heavy world they had only known from books and a faint bluetwinkle in the blackness. The psychists took a long time to understand why. At the time it seemed like some sort of divine madness.

Finally the war was won. The comets were tamed and we started looking outward again. New starships were built, better than before.

I had to wait for a berth on the twelfth ship, and the wait saved my life.

The first seven ships were lost. As they beamed back their jubilant reports, spiraling closer to the beautiful green worlds they had found, they plowed into unseen crystalspheres and were destroyed.

And, unlike *Seeker*, they did not accomplish anything by dying. The crystalspheres remained after the ships had been icecrushed into comets.

We had all had such hopes ... though those who remembered *Seeker* had worried quietly. Humanity seemed about to breathe free, at last! We were going to spread our eggs to other baskets, and be safe for the first time. No more would we have to fear overpopulation, crowding, or stagnation.

And all at once the hopes were dashed—dashed against those unseen, deadly spheres.

It took centuries even to learn how to *detect* the deathzones! *How*, we asked. How could the universe be so perverse! Was it all some great practical joke? What *were* these monstrous barriers that defied all the physics we knew, and kept us away from the beautiful littleworlds we so desired?

For three centuries, humanity went a little crazy.

I missed the worst years of the great-depression. I was with a group trying to study the sphere about Tau Ceti. By the time I got back, some degree of order had been restored.

But I came back to a solar system that had clearly lost a piece of its heart. It was a long time before I heard true laughter again, on Earth or on her smallbodies.

I, too, went to bed and pulled the covers over my head for a couple of hundred years.

5.

The entire crew breathed a reliefsigh when Captain Bok ordered me to put the safeties back on. I finally let go of my deadman switch and got up. The tension seeped away into a chain of shivers, and Alice had to hold me until I could stand again on my own.

Moishe had ordered the stand-down because the goodsun's system was empty.

To be accurate, the system *teemed* with life, but none of it was intelligent.

The greater asteroids held marvelous, self-sustaining ecosystems, absorbing sunlight under great windows.

Twenty moons sheltered huge forests beneath tremendous domes. But there was no traffic, no radio or light messages. Yen's detectors revealed no machine activity, nor the thought-touch of analytical beings.

It felt eerie to poke our way through those civilized lanes in the smallbody ways. For so long we had only performed such maneuvers in the well-known spaces of Solsystem.

During those first centuries after the crystal crisis, some men and women still thought it would be possible to live among the stars. Belters mostly, they claimed aloud that planets were nasty, heavy places anyway. So who needed them?

They went out to the *badstars*—red giants and tiny red dwarves, tight binaries and unstable suns. The badstars were protected by no crystalspheres. The would-be colonists found drifting clots of matter near these stars, and attempted to set up smallbody cities as they had at home.

Every one of the attempts failed within a few generations. The colonists simply lost interest in procreation.

The psychers finally decided the cause was related to the divine madness that had enabled us to win the CometWar.

Simply put, men could live on asteroids, but they needed to *know* that there was a blue world nearby—to see it in their sky. It's a flaw in our character, no doubt, but we cannot go out and live in space all alone.

We have to have waterworlds, if the universe is ever to be ours.

This system's waterworld we named Quest, after the beast so long sought by King Pelenor, our ship's namesake. It shone blue and brown, under a clean whiteswaddling of clouds. For hours we circled above it, and simply cried.

Alice awakened ten corpsicles—prominent scientists who, the Worldcomps had promised, would not fall apart on the reawakening of hope.

We watched them take their turn at the viewport, joytears streaming down their faces, and we joined them, to weep freely once again.

6.

Pelenor was hardly up to the task of exploring this system by herself. We spent a year recovering and modifying several of the ancient ships we found drifting over the planet, so that teams could spread out, investigating every farcorner of this system.

By our second anniversary, a hundred biologists were quickscampering over the surface of Quest. They genescanned the local flora and fauna excitedly, and already were modifying Earthplants to fit into the ecosystem without causing an imbalance. Soon they would start on animals from our genetanks.

The engineers exploring the smallbodies excitedly declared that they could get half the lifemachines left behind by the prior race to work. There was room for a billion colonists out there, straight from the start.

But the archeologists were the ones whose report we awaited most anxiously. In between my ferrying runs, they were the ones I helped. I joined them in the dusty ruins of Oldcity, at the edge of Longvalley, putting together piles of artifacts to be catalogued and slowly analyzed.

We learned that the old inhabitants had called themselves the "Nataral." They were about as similar to us as we might have expected—bipedal, nine-fingered, weird-looking.

Still, one got used to their faces after staring at their statues and pictures long enough. After a while I even began to perceive subtle facial cues, and delicate, sensitive nuances of expression. When the language was cracked, we learned their race-name, and some of their story.

Unlike the few other alien intelligences we had observed from afar, the Nataral were individuals, and explorers. They, too, had spread into their planetary system after a worldbound history fully as colorful and goodbad as our own.

Like us, they had two conflicting dreams. They longed for the stars, for room to grow. And they also longed for other faces, for neighbors.

By the time they built a starship—their first—they had given up on the idea of neighbors. There was no sign anybody had ever visited their world. They heard nothing but silence from the stars.

Still, when they were ready, they launched their firstship toward their other dream—Room.

And within weeks of the launching, their sun's crystalsphere shattered.

For two weeks we double-checked the translations. We triple-checked.

For millennia we had been searching for a way to destroy these deadly barriers around goodstars ... trying to duplicate on purpose what *Seeker* had accomplished by accident. And now we had the answer!

The Nataral, like us, had managed to destroy one and only one crystalsphere. Their own. And the pattern was exactly the same, down to the CometWar that subsequently almost wrecked their high civilization.

The conclusion was obvious. The deathbarriers were destructible, but *only from the inside!*

And just when that idea was starting to sink in, the archeologists dug up the Obelisk.

7.

Our top linguist, Garcia Cardenas, had a flair for the dramatic. When Alice and I visited him in his encampment at the base of the newly excavated monument, he insisted on putting off all discussion of his discovery until the next day. He and his partners instead prepared a special meal for us, and raised their glasses to toast Alice.

She stood and accepted their accolades with dry wit, and then sat down to continue nursing our baby.

Old habits break hard, and only a few of the women had managed yet to break centuries of biofeedback conditioning not to breed. Alice was among the first to reactivate her ovaries and bring a child to our new world.

It wasn't that I was jealous. After all, I basked in the only slightly lesser glory of fatherhood. But I was getting impatient with all of this ballyhoo. Except for old Moishe Bok, I was perhaps the oldest human here—old enough to remember when people had children as a matter of course, and therefore made time for *other* matters, when something important was up!

Finally, when the celebration had wound down, Garcia Cardenas nodded to me, and led me out the back flap of the tent. We followed a dim path down the sloping trail to the digs, by the light of the ring of bright smallbodies the Nataral had left permanently in place over the equatorial sky of Quest.

We finally arrived at a wall of bright alloy that towered high above our heads. It was made of a material our techs had barely begun to analyze, and was nearly impervious to the effects of time. On it were inscribed hardpatterns bearing the tale of the last days of the Nataral.

A lot of that story we knew from the other records. But the end itself was still a mystery, and no small cause of nervousness. Had it been some terrible plague? Did the intelligent machines, on which both their civilization and ours relied, rebel and slaughter their masters? Did their sophisticated bioengineering technology get out of their control?

What we *did* know was that the Nataral had suffered. Like humans, they had gone out and found the universe closed to them. Both of their great dreams—of goodplaces to spreadsettle, and of other minds to meet—had been shattered like the deathsphere around their own star. Like humans, they spent quite a long time not entirely sane.

In the darkness deep within the dig, Cardenas had promised I would find the answers.

As Cardenas prepared his instruments I listened to the sounds of the surrounding forestjungle. Life abounded on this world. There were lovely, complicated creatures, some clearly natural, and some just as clearly the result of clever biosculpting. In their creatures, in their art and architecture, in the very reasons they had almost despaired, I felt a powerful closeness to the Nataral. I would have liked them, I imagined.

I was glad to take this world for humanity, for it might mean salvation for my species. Still, I regretted that the other-race was gone.

Cardenas motioned me over to a holistank he had set up at the base of the Obelisk. As we put our hands into the blackness, a light appeared on the face of the monolith.

Where the light travelled, we would touch, and feel the passion of those final days of the Nataral.

I stroked the finetuned, softresonant surface. Cardenas led me, and I felt the Endingtime as the Nataral meant it to be felt.

Like us, the Nataral had passed through a long period of bitterness, even longer than we had endured until now. To them, indeed, it seemed as if the universe were a great, sick joke.

Life was found everywhere amongst the stars. But intelligence arose only slowly and rarely, with many false starts. Where it did occur, it was often in a form that did not happen to covet space or the stars.

But if the crystalspheres had not existed, the rare sites where starfaring developed would spread outward. Species like us would expand, and eventually make contact with each other, instead of searching forever among sandgrains. An elder race might arrive where another was just getting started, and help it over some of its crises.

If the crystalspheres had not existed . . .

But that was not to be. Starfarers could not spread, because crystalspheres could only be broken from the inside! What a cruel universe it was!

Or so the Nataral had thought.

But they persevered. And after ages spent hunting for the miraculous goodstar, their farprobes found five waterworlds unprotected by deathbarriers.

My touch-hand trembled as I stroked the coordinates of these accessible planets. My throat caught at the magnitude of the gift that had been given us on this obelisk. No *wonder* Cardenas had made me wait! I, too, would linger when I showed it to Alice.

But then, I wondered, where had the Nataral gone? And why? With six worlds, surely their morale would have lifted!

There was a confusing place on the Obelisk . . . talk of black holes and of *time*. I touched the spot again and again, while Cardenas watched my reaction. Finally, I understood.

"Great Egg!" I cried. The revelation of what had

happened made the discovery of the five goodworlds pale into insignificance.

"Is *that* what the crystalspheres are for?"

I couldn't believe it.

Cardenas smiled. "Watch out for teleology, Joshua. It is true that the barriers would seem to show the hand of a creator at work. But it might be simply circumstance, rather than some grand design.

"All that we do know is this. Without the crystalspheres, we ourselves would not exist. Intelligence would be more rare than it already is. And the stars would be almost barren of life.

"We have cursed the crystalspheres for ten thousand years," Cardenas sighed. "The Nataral did so for far longer—until they at last understood."

8.

If the crystalspheres had not existed . . .

I thought about it that night. I stared up at the shimmering, pale light from the drifting Shards, through which the brighter stars still shone.

If the crystalspheres had not existed, then there would come to each galaxy a first race of startreaders. Even if most intelligences were stay-at-homes, the coming of an aggressive, colonizing species was inevitable, sooner or later.

If the crystalspheres had not existed, the first such startreaders would have gone out and taken all the worlds they found. They would have settled all the waterworlds, and civilized the smallbodies around every single goodstar.

Two centuries before we ever discovered our crystalsphere, we humans had already started wondering why this had never happened to Earth. Why, during the three billion years that Earth was "choice real estate," had no race like us come along and colonized it?

We found out it was because of the deathbarrier surrounding Sol, that kept our crude little ancestors safe from interference from the outside . . . that let our nursery world nurture us into being in peace and isolation.

If the crystalspheres had not been, then the first startreaders would have filled the galaxy, perhaps the universe. It is what *we* would have done, had the barriers not been there. The histories of those worlds would be forever changed. And there is no way to imagine the death-of-possibility that would have resulted.

So, the barriers protect worlds until they develop life capable of cracking the shells from within.

But what was the point? What point was there in protecting some young thing, only that it would grow up into a bitter, cramped loneliness in adulthood!

Imagine what it must have been like for the very first race of startreaders. Never, were they patient as Job, would they find another goodstar to possess. Not until the next egg cracked would they ever have neighbors to talk to.

No doubt they despaired long before that.

Now we, humanity, had been gifted of six beautiful worlds. And if we could not meet the Nataral, we could, at least, read their books and come to know them. And from their careful records we could learn about the still earlier races which had emerged from each of the other five goodworlds, each into a lonely universe.

Perhaps in another billion years the universe will more closely resemble the sciencefictional schemes of my grandfather's day. Maybe then commerce will plow the starlanes between busy, talky worlds.

But we, like the Nataral, came too early for that. We are cursed, if we hang around until that day, to be an ElderRace.

I looked one more time toward the constellation we had named "Phoenix," whither the Nataral had departed millions of our years ago. I could not see the dark star where they had gone. But I knew exactly where it lay. They had left explicit instructions.

I turned and entered the tent that I shared with Alice and our child, leaving the stars and shards behind me.

Tomorrow would be a busy day. I had promised Alice that we might begin building a house on a hillside not far from Oldcity.

She muttered some dreamtalk and cuddled close as I slipped into bed beside her. The baby slept quietly in her cradle a few feet away. I held Alice, and breathed slowly.

But sleep came slowly. I kept thinking about what the Nataral had given us.

Correction . . . what they had *lent* us.

We could use their six worlds, on the condition we were kind to them. Those were the same conditions they had accepted when they took the four worlds long abandoned by the *Lap-Klenno*, their predecesssors on the lonely starlanes . . . and that the Lap-Klenno had agreed to on inheriting the three *Thwoozoon* suns. . . .

So long as the urge to spreadsettle was primary in us, the worlds were ours, and any others we happened upon.

But someday our priorities would change. Elbowroom would no longer be our chief fixation. More and more, the Nataral had known, we would begin to think instead about loneliness.

I knew they were right. Someday my great-to-the-nth descendants would find that they could no longer bear a universe without other voices in it. They would tire of these beautiful worlds, and pack up the entire tribe to head for a darkstar.

There, within the event horizon of a great blackhole, they would find the Nataral, and the Lap-Klenno, and the Thwoozoon, waiting in a cup of suspended time.

I listened to the wind gentleflapping the tent, and envied my great-nth grandchildren. I, at least, would like to meet the other startreaders, so very much like us.

Oh, we could wait around for a few billion years, till that distant time when most of the shells have cracked, and the universe bustles with activity. But by then we would have changed. By necessity we would have become an *ElderRace*. . . .

But what species in its right mind would choose such a fate? Better, by far, to stay young until the universe finally became a fun enough place to enjoy!

To wait for that day, the races who came before us sleep at the edge of their timestretched black hole. Within, they wait to welcome us; and we shall sit out, together, the barren early years of the galaxies.

I felt the last shreds of the old great-depression dissipate as I contemplated the elegant solution of the Nataral. For so long we had feared that the Universe was a practical joker, and that our place in it was to be victims—

patsies. But now, at last, my darkthoughts shattered like an eggshell . . . like the walls of a crystalcage.

I held my woman close. She sighed something said in dreamthought. As sleep finally came, I felt better than I had in a thousand years. I felt so very, very young.

Editor's Introduction To "The Strange Journey: 1984," by James Gunn

The *yearbook* was from the first intended to be not only entertaining, but also a record of significant science fiction events in all fields. One of the first essays invited was from Jim Gunn.

Dr. James Gunn is a native Kansan, and Professor of English at Kansas University. He is also author of more than a dozen science fiction novels. One, *The Listeners* (1972, Scribner's) was an original contribution to speculation about Fermi's question. Another novel, *The Immortal*, inspired a television series. He is a past President of the Science Fiction Writers of America.

The Strange Journey: 1984

James Gunn

The teaching of science fiction as a regular part of the college curriculum is just a little more than twenty years old. Sam Moskowitz taught evening classes at the City College of New York in 1953 and 1954, but the first class taught as part of a college's standard offerings apparently was that of Mark Hillegas at Colgate in 1962, shortly followed by Jack Williamson's classes at Eastern New Mexico University and Tom Clareson's at Wooster. My own did not begin until 1969.

The first ten years of that period, like that of any youngster, was a time of discovery, both by teachers and students. The second decade, like that of any adolescent, was a time of expansion and maturation. It was marked by enthusiasm and experimentation, uncertainty, and suspicion. The fact that this period coincided with the great expansion in the book publishing of science fiction and fantasy, from 348 books a year in 1972 to 1,288 a year in 1979, may be a coincidence, as well as the decline in both teaching and publishing beginning in 1980.

The decade from 1972 to 1982 saw a significant increase in the teaching of science fiction, not only in colleges but in high schools, although no one knows just how much teaching went on. Jack Williamson did an informal survey in the early 1970s, but no accurate count was ever undertaken. Only the effects can be measured: the slow but steady growth in membership in the Science Fiction Research Association, founded in 1970, and the interest in teaching conferences and workshops, such as the sessions organized under the auspices of the National Council of Teachers of English, workshops offered by Marshall Tymn at Eastern Michigan University, and a famous conference at Kean College in Union, New Jersey.

It was a period when adventurous teachers wanted to teach science-fiction courses, when all but the most conservative colleges and high schools wanted to offer science-fiction courses, and when students by the hundreds wanted to enroll in science-fiction courses. But it was also a time when few teachers knew what to teach or how to teach it. I was president of the Science Fiction Writers of America in 1971–72, and every week I received a letter from some distraught teacher saying that he or she had been assigned a class in science fiction, and what should be taught? In 1972, we should remember, there were virtually no histories (Donald Wollheim's personal history, *The Universe Makers*, was published in 1971) and few books of criticism. The general anthologies available were *The Science Fiction Hall of Fame* (volume one only), Robert Silverberg's *Mirror of Infinity*, Dick Allen's *Science Fiction: The Future*, and a few others intended for the mass market that went in and out of print rapidly. Even novels were ephemeral as far as the classroom was concerned, so even if there had been a consensus about what to teach, teachers still had to wonder whether the books would be out of print.

So much for uncertainty. The suspicion came from both sides: the academic establishment considered science fiction "sub-literary" (some of this attitude still lingers, as the response to a recent application to the National Endowment for the Humanities bears evidence) and the science-fiction establishment considered science-fiction teachers unqualified and their involvement possibly the kiss of death to the category. The latter reaction was summed up at the founding meeting of the Science Fiction Research Association in the exhortation written by

Dena Brown on the blackboard: "Let's take science fiction out of the classroom and put it back in the gutter where it belongs." A number of writers at the Kean College conference complained about what was being taught and who was teaching it, and Ben Bova published his concerns in an *Analog* editorial.

An outgrowth of that environment of suspicion (and of a guest *Analog* editorial I wrote in response to Ben's) was the Intensive English Institute on the Teaching of Science Fiction that I organized at the University of Kansas and offered for ten years (skipping a couple of years after the first experimental offering), whose intent was to make up for the deficiencies in the academic backgrounds of would-be teachers of science fiction and the fact that they had not discovered science fiction, as they should have, when they were children: We set out to teach the teachers.

Meanwhile, the scholarly consideration of science fiction, which had begun with Philip Babcock Gove's *The Imaginary Voyage in Prose Fiction* (1941), J. O. Bailey's *Pilgrims Through Space and Time* (1947), and Marjorie Hope Nicholson's *Voyages to the Moon* (1948) got a major boost into respectability by Kingsley Amis's Christian Gauss lectures at Princeton in 1959, which were published the following year as *New Maps of Hell*. Oxford University Press, not only the oldest but one of the most prestigious of the academic presses, published several books on science fiction in the mid 1960s, including Bruce Franklin's *Future Perfect*, I. F. Clarke's *Voices Prophesying War*, and Mark Hillegas's *The Future As Nightmare*.

By 1975, when my Science Fiction Institute had its first session, I could prepare for my students a list of fifty-five books of academic interest or usefulness just from those I could see on my shelves. One of them was my own illustrated history, *Alternate Worlds*, which had been preceded as the first book-length history of the field by Brian Aldiss's *Billion Year Spree*. Two academic journals had been created, *Extrapolation* and *Science-Fiction Studies*, and several more, especially *Foundation* and *Fantasy Newsletter* (even more after it merged with Barron's *Science Fiction and Fantasy Book Review* and became *Fantasy Review*), published much of academic interest.

Day's *Index to the Science Fiction Magazines, 1926–1950*,

was followed by MITSF's *Index to the Science Fiction Magazines, 1951–1965*; by NESFA's *Index to the Science Fiction Magazines, 1966–1970*; and by NESFA's annual compilations since then. And Cole's *A Checklist of Science-Fiction Anthologies* was succeeded by Contento's *Index to Science Fiction Anthologies and Collections*. Tuck's *The Encyclopedia of Science Fiction and Fantasy* was followed by Nicholls's *The Science Fiction Encyclopedia*, Reginald's two-volume *Science Fiction and Fantasy Literature*, Bleiler's update of his 1948 *Checklist of Fantastic Literature*, the Dictionary of Literary Biography's two-volume *Twentieth Century American Science-Fiction Writers*, edited by Cowart and Wymer, Smith's *Twentieth Century Science-Fiction Writers*, and many more, including Williamson's *Teaching Science Fiction: Education for Tomorrow* and a number of more specialized teaching guides, Tymn's *Science Fiction Reference Book*, Barron's *Anatomy of Wonder*, and Magill's five-volume *Survey of Science Fiction Literature*, followed by a five-volume *Survey of Modern Fantasy Literature*.

Bibliographies, single-author studies, reprints of classic works in hard covers, even such specialized scholarly materials as bibliographies of first printings and book review indexes had appeared by 1982. There is even an annual volume of *The Year's Scholarship in Science Fiction, Fantasy, and Horror Literature*, edited by Marshall Tymn. Add to all of these tools of scholarship and teaching various more popular treatments of the field in text and pictures, covering film, radio, and television, compilations of critical essays, various how-to books, a wider selection of anthologies, including my own four-volume *The Road to Science Fiction*, news journals such as *Locus* and *Science Fiction Chronicle*, and novels that stayed longer in print, and the academic paraphernalia of science fiction was complete.

Meanwhile, academic interest in science fiction moved into its third decade. If the first decade represented experiment and the second decade expansion, the third decade might be expected to bring maturity. In many ways it did. But with maturity comes a decline in exuberance, in the spirit of youthful adventure, and sometimes even in enthusiasm. How this will affect the teaching and study of science fiction is still uncertain, but some indications may already be evident.

Enrollments in science-fiction classes that once numbered in the hundreds, when enrollments were allowed to run that high, now seem to be tapering off to more normal sizes. There is only anecdotal evidence to support this statement, just as was true of the situation in the 1970s. At the University of Kansas, however, the decline in student interest dropped enrollments from one hundred and one hundred fifty to ninety, eighty-five, seventy-five, and now approximately thirty to thirty-five. In many ways, this makes for better classes (and many colleges and universities never have permitted classes larger than that), but it suggests a shift in attitude.

Similarly, I have the feeling, without strong evidence, that the teaching of science fiction has declined in high schools, with the "return to basics" movement and the decreased use of half-semester mini-courses.

The cause of these shifts is even more difficult to pin down. In high schools a greater emphasis on more traditional offerings, competency testing, and merit salaries may have dampened the spirit of adventure. In colleges the conservatism of students, particularly in choosing courses with career preparation and employability in mind, may have reduced their willingness to take risks. Or, looking at the picture from the opposite side, the fact that science-fiction courses have become commonplace may mean that teaching such a course, or taking one, no longer seems daring. The pioneers may have moved on, though with women's studies and African studies no longer either experimental or especially popular, it is not sure exactly where. Maybe the pioneers simply retired.

In 1984, then, science fiction faced the problem of many once-unacceptable subjects that wedged their ways into the curriculum: it had to maintain itself as a suitable area of study on its own merits. The year may have had a peculiar significance: The world had been waiting for the arrival of 1984 since 1949, when George Orwell's novel was published. The science-fiction world was no exception; just as the outside world paid its tribute to Orwell's vision, so did science fiction. I gave two invited talks myself, wrote two articles, answered innumerable inquiries, and participated in a number of panel discussions.

The Eaton Conference held at the University of California at Riverside combined with the Science Fiction Foundation at the North East London Polytechnic to hold linked conferences labeled "1984: The View from Two Shores," with the Riverside conference titled "1984: Manifested Destinies" and the London conference, "1984: Now or Never?"

The Popular Culture Association offered its usual section on science fiction at its annual meeting, but the Modern Language Association turned down a proposal for a science-fiction seminar at its meeting, though it may approve one for its 1985 meeting in Washington, D.C.

Another major conference, the International Conference on the Fantastic in Literature, held its final meeting at its birthplace, Boca Raton. Its 1985 meeting-place is Beaumont, Texas, under the direction of the president of the International Association for the Fantastic in the Arts, Roger Schlobin; the president-elect is Marshall Tymn. The city of Beaumont has proposed an ambitious program to create there a National Academy of Science Fiction and Fantasy Art. Bowling Green University also has proposed a science-fiction museum featuring artifacts.

The Science Fiction Research Association held its annual meeting at the University of Missouri at Rolla, and the pioneer bibliographer Everett F. Bleiler was named the 1984 winner of the prestigious Pilgrim Award for scholarship in science fiction and fantasy. SFRA will hold its 1985 annual meeting at Kent State University. Donald M. Hassler has been elected to serve a two-year term as the Association's new president.

One other interesting conference titled "Contact: Cultures of the Imagination" brought together science-fiction writers and anthropologists under the auspices of Cabrillo College of Aptos, California. Meanwhile the academic track of programs that had been shepherded through World Science Fiction Conventions in Chicago and Baltimore by Mack Hassler was continued at the World Convention in Anaheim but integrated into the regular programming.

The University of Kansas created a Center for the Study

of Science Fiction to focus its many activities in the field and provide a mechanism for developing them further.

Academics involved in science fiction have filled their kits with all the tools they need. Some of these tools, to be sure, must be sharpened periodically or replaced: Tymn is editing a new *Science Fiction Reference Book*, but **NESFA** has not yet announced plans to combine its annual indexes to the magazines into a single volume covering the years from 1970 to 1984 or 1985, or from 1965 to 1980, and then to continue the annual series until another ten or fifteen years will provide reason for another major volume.

Other major reference works must be regularly revised or redone. The major histories of the field are now at least a dozen years old, and a great deal has happened in the past decade. The encyclopedias, which once seemed so comprehensive, will soon be requiring supplements, at the very least. The teaching anthologies, once apparently adequate, may no longer meet contemporary needs; the first two volumes of my *The Road to Science Fiction*, for instance, have been allowed to go out of print.

While it does not seem likely that major new conferences are necessary (and there may be too many already, although their purposes and their audiences seem distinct enough to give each a reason for existence), special conferences aimed at special audiences or special topics still seem desirable, particularly those that make the insights and methods of science fiction available to new audiences.

Single-author studies and theme-oriented collections of essays are the most prevalent form of academic publishing today. Oxford allowed its single-author series to end at four volumes, but major programs still are underway at Borgo Press, Bowling Green University Popular Press, Greenwood Press, Southern Illinois University Press, Starmont, and UMI.

Definition, the heart of genre studies, has not yet been resolved to the satisfaction of the field, in spite of Scholes's "structural fabulation," Suvin's "cognitive estrangement," and Delany's "literal metaphor." I look for continued effort to go on in this area, though perhaps not to produce anything final or revolutionary. Not only the subject matter but the essence of science fiction may be protean. A new collection of essays by Samuel R. Delany, *Starboard Wine: More Notes on the Language of Science Fiction*, may be another major contribution to the continuing discussion.

The teaching of science fiction will have to come to terms with two new elements: Science fiction is somewhere between its former status as a minority literature (Damon Knight called it "the mass medium for the few") to a new situation as a significant part of everybody's experience. When the top grossing films of all time are called science fiction, and when books considered science fiction or fantasy are found frequently on best-seller lists, teachers must cope with popular preconceptions rather than lack of information. The teacher and the scholar must ask, for instance, in what ways "Star Wars" and "E.T." are science fiction, and in what ways they are something else, and why Isaac Asimov's *Foundation's Edge*, Arthur C. Clarke's *2010*, and Robert A. Heinlein's *Friday* were all on the best-seller list—and at the same time.

The science-fiction teacher and student can have worse problems, as many of them can remember.

My thanks to Prof. Marshall Tymn of Eastern Michigan University for the preparation of the following list of important books about science fiction appearing in 1984:

REFERENCE

Contento, William. *Index to Science Fiction Anthologies and Collections*. Boston: G.K. Hall.

Pfleiger, Pat. *A Reference Guide to Modern Fantasy for Children*. Westport, CT: Greenwood Press.

Pringle, David. *J.G. Ballard: A Primary and Secondary Bibliography*. Masters of Science Fiction and Fantasy. Boston: G.K. Hall.

Samuelson, David N. *Arthur C. Clarke: A Primary and Secondary Bibliography*. Masters of Science Fiction and Fantasy. Boston: G.K. Hall.

Tymn, Marshall B., ed. *The Year's Scholarship in Science Fiction, Fantasy, and Horror Literature: 1981*. Kent, OH: Kent State Univ. Press.

Willis, Donald C. *Horror and Science Films III*. Metuchen, NJ: Scarecrow Press.

CRITICISM

Aldrige, Alexandra. *The Scientific World View in Dystopia*. Ann Arbor, MI: UMI Research Press.

Clareson, Thomas D. and Thomas L. Wymer, eds. *Voices for the Future. Vol. 3*. Bowling Green, OH: Bowling Green Univ. Popular Press.

Griffin, Brian and David Wingrove. *Apertures: A Study of the Writings of Brian W. Aldiss*, Contributions to the Study of Science Fiction and Fantasy, No. 8. Westport, CT: Greenwood Press.

Herron, Don, ed. *The Dark Barbarian: The Writings of Robert E. Howard*, Contributions to the Study of Science Fiction and Fantasy, No. 9. Westport, CT: Greenwood Press.

Robinson, Kim Stanley. *The Novels of Philip K. Dick*. Ann Arbor, MI: UMI Research Press.

Sampson, Robert. *Yesterday's Faces: A Study of the Early Pulp Magazines. Vol. II: Strange Days*. Bowling Green, OH: Bowling Green Univ. Popular Press.

Spivack, Charlotte, *Ursula K. Le Guin*. Twayne United States Authors, No. 453. Boston: Twayne.

Swinfen, Ann. *In Defense of Fantasy: A Study of the Genre in English and American Literature since 1945*. Boston: Routledge & Kegan Paul.

Editor's Introduction To "A Day in the Life of A Classics Professor," by Stan Dryer

My early years were spent in Capleville, Tennessee. There was only one school. At that we were lucky: Capleville had two grades in each room. The next nearest school, Mineral Wells, had four grades per room.

In those days the academic program was fixed by the state legislature, which decreed that we would read certain works: *Silas Marner* in sixth grade, in seventh *The Lady of the Lake* and *Evangeline*, etc. By eighth we were ready for Shakespeare. At that point, though, my parents decided that Capleville wasn't challenging enough, and sent me off to the Christian Brothers for a classical education.

Whatever else "classical" meant, it included four years of Latin.

I do not regret studying Latin and the classics; but until I read this story I never thought there would be any practical benefits. . . .

A Day in the Life of A Classics Professor

Stan Dryer

University Paradise Condominiums, 7:30 A.M. April 5, 1998

Qui vult decipi, decipiatur. (Let him who wishes to be deceived, be deceived.)

When Professor Parker Colburn came awake to the persistent beeping of his alarm, he reached quickly over to flick it off. He got out of bed, then paused to look down on the motionless form of the girl who occupied the other half of the bed, her golden hair cascading over the pillow.

Parker walked to the bathroom and shut the door silently behind him. With any luck she might still be asleep when he left for the university.

As he shaved, a pleasant reverie came over him. She had been sweet and young and surprisingly adept. From the moment she had approached him at the cocktail party the previous evening, he had known her motives. While little of the passion she had displayed last night had been playacting, when she awakened this morning she would probably feel she had him under her spell. Quite a mistaken assumption.

He stepped into the shower and turned up the water to a hot needlepoint. How nice it would be to find a woman he could trust. Since the sorry business with Marta, he had kept away from any relationships that threatened to become permanent. Marta, lovely Marta. In a way he still grieved her loss. They had started out so well together. A woman with a mind as keen as his own, and a most compatible bedmate. He had known that she relished power, but he had had no idea what she was really after until she had made her play for old Isa Hemshaw, the dean of humanities. It had been a move worthy of Livia, the most insidious of Roman empresses. It might well have worked had not Hemshaw, who was a student of Rome in his own right, realized what she was after. "I'd like to think it's my virile body she wants," he had told Parker, "but that is not what she is lusting for. Give her the chance and she'll be seducing President Watkins tomorrow."

Parker stepped out of the shower. Despite the agony of the thought of losing Marta, he had acted swiftly and decisively. Even though she did not have tenure, her departure had been bloody enough. It had taken him a year before he felt he once again had the loyalty of his people.

He finished drying off and stepped into his dressing room where Hartwell had laid out his clothes. Now there was loyalty. Hartwell, the perfect manservant, always anticipating Parker's needs, yet with the taste to know when he should fade quietly into the background. Parker had not imagined that human manservants still existed in an age when anyone could afford a service droid. Two years ago, Hartwell had appeared at his door just after the Midwestern team had taken the U.S. Classics Association Championship.

"The Alumni Association has employed me to act as your manservant," was all he had said concerning his origins. Although Parker had his suspicions as to the individuals responsible, he had never pursued an investigation. Hartwell was too nice a fringe benefit to question. It was the kind of treatment that kept him on at Midwestern in the face of the most flattering offers from a number of professional teams.

Parker knotted his tie and shrugged into a Harris Tweed jacket. Then he stepped into the dining room. A place had been set at the end of the table, and next to it was the morning *New York Times*, opened to the classics page.

Straight as a statue, Hartwell stood beside the sideboard. "Good morning, sir," he said.

"Good morning, Hartwell."

"Will the young lady be joining you for breakfast?" Hartwell's tone was as matter-of-fact as if he were asking if Parker wished more coffee.

"I think not," said Parker.

"Very good, sir," said Hartwell. "Your eggs will be ready in a minute."

Parker seated himself, took a sip of coffee and glanced at the headlines. The Detroit Throats had finished off the Philadelphia Golden Tongues in the Eastern Divisional Finals. So it would be Detroit and Los Angeles in the Super Forum. Quite a feather in his cap. The lead orators on both teams had trained under him at Midwestern.

He was halfway through his breakfast and the rest of the classics page, when the door to his dressing room opened and the girl came in. Parker suppressed a frown when he saw she was wearing his dressing gown. It would, he knew, absorb enough of her musky perfume so it would have to be cleaned.

"Parker darling, I thought you were going to get me up," she said, her round little mouth in a half-pout.

"You looked so comfortable, I just couldn't bring myself to awaken you," said Parker.

"Would Professor Parker's guest wish some breakfast?" Hartwell had eased into the room.

The young lady's eyes popped wide. "Hey, wow, are you for real?"

"Very real," said Parker.

"The subject of breakfast?" said Hartwell.

"Yeah, sure," said the girl. "Juice, coffee, and a couple of eggs over easy."

Parker knew Hartwell must have inwardly winced at the commonness of this expression, but his face betrayed nothing. "Very good, madam," he said and left the room.

The girl sat down and moved her chair close to Parker. She leaned over and touched his arm with her hand. The dressing gown came open to present an excellent view of her firm and lovely breasts. "That was a lot of fun last night," she said.

"Most enjoyable," said Parker. If there was anything he detested, it was an instant replay over breakfast of the sexual athletics of the previous evening.

"I sure hope it isn't going to be the last time," she said.

"I am sure it will not be," said Parker, adding to himself, "but not with me." How many times had he run through this script before? People still seemed to have the idea that a professor of classics was a particularly easy mark. Anyone with the slightest grasp of the history of Rome should have known that the classics gave the most thorough education in the venality of man.

"You are a sweetie," said the girl. "And I'm going to be a naughty and ask for one tiny favor from you."

"Certainly," said Parker, "whatever I can."

"I had a bad break on the team tryouts." The words came pouring out in a rush as if she feared he would stop her. "I mean, what kind of luck to get laryngitis the day of the trials. Could you be a doll and have a little tryout just for me?"

Parker tried not to let his boredom show. Couldn't she even come up with an original pitch? Laryngitis, my throat. She'd probably screwed up the first line of Caesar's address to his troops. "That one I can't help you with," he said. "Rules are rules. We run the team tryouts twice a year. You can come back in September and give it another try."

She pulled back from him, her face bare with anger. "You bastard," she said.

Now the tears, Parker thought.

But Hartwell, with his perfect timing, reappeared with the girl's breakfast. He calmly placed the dishes before her, then turned to Parker. "You wished your car for 8:15," he said. "It is now that hour."

Good old Hartwell! Parker had ordered the car for 8:30, but his manservant had read the situation and spared him fifteen minutes of tears and supplication.

Parker rose. "*Infinita est velocitas temporis*," he said. "Hartwell will see to getting you a cab when you're ready to leave."

* * *

A Day In the Life of A Classics Professor

University Boulevard, 8:30 A.M.

Ars longa, vita brevis (Life is short and art is long.)

Big Hartley Wilson drove Parker's limousine with a terrifying abandon, cutting in and out through the traffic of autocars at a speed that would have meant disaster for anyone with a shade less skill. Wilson had been a running back with the now defunct Green Bay Packers, and he was used to hurling himself through holes that opened up for only a fraction of a second.

As Wilson drove, he cursed. "No mech scab gonna cut me off." "Eat monoxide, droid bastards." "Furbin microbrains."

And, Parker thought, he had every reason to curse the mechanisms that piloted the other vehicles. They, or their brother androids, had destroyed Wilson's most promising career. More than that, he knew the passionate love this man still had for football. In his time off he worked out with a group of students. What anyone saw in it Parker could not understand. The university did not even give phys. ed. credits for football. And yet there they were, memorizing the old playbooks and working through the drills in the one muddy corner of the playing fields that had not been put back into corn. A few nuts desperately believing that the glories of the past would someday return.

Yet that was the way most of his friends and relations had viewed him fifteen years ago. Parker Colburn, the wastrel son of one of the better Boston families, escaping reality in his dusty tomes. His father had made his own feelings quite clear. In the middle of Parker's junior year, he had summoned him over from Harvard, up to his law offices in the high-rise on State Street. There, with Parker looking out at the spectacular view of Boston harbor and the airport beyond, Samuel Parker, Esq., had read aloud a letter he had just received from his son's senior tutor, Professor Detros.

"The problem with your son is not that he lacks industry. He is a devoted scholar in the area of his interest, the study of Roman oratory. Unfortunately, his almost monomaniac interest in this subject has had a most deleterious effect upon the rest of his studies."

His father had paused and looked up over his reading

glasses. "Jim Detros would not have written to me if this were not serious," he had said.

Parker had known that to be true. It was not usual for a senior tutor to give that kind of a report to a parent. Then Detros had been cox on the Harvard crew his father had captained the year they won the Sedgwick Cup.

"I sent you to Harvard to broaden your education," his father had said. "That does not seem to be happening."

Parker squirmed in his chair and promised to try to bring up his grades. His father had put down the letter and, in a brief summation for the jury of all Harvard alumni, had pointed out that a liberal education included far more than the classics.

The message had been clear. You got good grades, made the crew, joined the right club, and you were on the road to a partnership in the firm and an office with its own view of the harbor.

Fortunately Parker had, with all the stubbornness of youth, persisted in his folly. He had gone out for no teams, joined no clubs, and graduated with only a magna in classics and a passion for oratory. His only kudos had been the Latin oration at commencement. In those days there had been no competition. He had done a magnificent job, although only he and perhaps a dozen scholars in the audience had even understood a word of it. How different it was today! Thanks to hypnotutoring, 300 million Americans and half the rest of the world understood Latin like a native tongue. The competition to give the Latin oratory at Harvard was now incredibly fierce. That part of commencement was always televised nationwide, and the orator was instantly snapped up by a major-league team.

Yet Harvard did not give that great a classics education nowadays. They had dropped to the Class 2 League four years ago and had a rotten record there. They were even muttering about deemphasizing the classics as not being a true part of a liberal education. The truth was that those ivy-tower jokers did not know how to go big time. His best bit of good fortune had been when his application for instructor at Harvard had been turned down and he had taken the job at Midwestern.

Midwestern was a place that knew how to swing with

the times. They had been one of the first universities to get out of football and into oratory. There had never been a problem about money, not even when the oratory team was still showing a loss. Once he had started fielding winning teams, they had been most lavish in their appreciation.

Tires squealing, the limousine turned into the main quadrangle and braked to a stop in front of the Classics Building, a sparkling thirty-story tower of glass and stainless steel. Across the way, the old football stadium had been torn down and on the site was rising the new Forum, a building designed from the ground up for the business of presenting Midwestern team debates to a live audience of thirty thousand, with 20 million more video viewers.

Parker knew he was on the way to the top. What pleased him most was that his father had shown no bitterness but was genuinely proud of him. The old man would probably be calling him up today about getting tickets for the Super Forum.

There was only one possible flaw in the whole structure of his success. Fortunately, he might have detected it in time.

"Have the car here at five," he said to Wilson as his chauffeur opened the door for him. "And bring Steve and Rollo. I have some special work for the three of you."

Wilson grinned at him. "We gonna blow away some droids?" he said.

"Not exactly," said Parker.

He entered the building and crossed the lobby to the elevator, raising his right hand to identify himself to the security droid at the desk.

Aside from a couple of aminidroids who stood politely silent with their paper feed trays, there were only two others in the elevators as they started up, MacLavish, one of the assistant coaches, and a young student in a pseudo-sixties outfit. Parker ignored the kid in his khaki shirt, bleached Levi's, and junk jewelry and made polite conversation with MacLavish, telling him how pleased the staff should be with the number of Midwestern orators on the Super Forum teams.

The student left on the fifteenth floor, and, as he squeezed past, Parker felt the expected object slipped into the pocket of his jacket. MacLavish left at the twenty-fifth floor, and Parker continued on to his penthouse offices at the top of the building. Leaving the elevator, he headed quickly for his office. Maria, his lovely flesh-and-blood secretary, smiled at him as he came in. Another bonus from the Alumni Association, she had replaced a secredroid with considerably better word-processing skills. However, Maria's effect on general office morale more than made up for a few spelling errors.

"You've got four messages on your screen," she said.

"Catch them in a minute," said Parker. He entered his office, shut the door behind him, and fished the message from his pocket. It was a rolled-up scrap of paper with but one sentence written on it: "Project Underdog is for real, and Cartwell is your man."

Midwestern University Classics Building, 10:00 A.M.

Duas tantum res anxius optat, panem et curcenses. (Two things only the people desire, bread and circuses.)

"We are most fortunate today to have the opportunity to be in the office of the man who has probably done more for the sport of oratory than any other living American." Stan Waterman stared into the television camera with the look of pure sincerity that made him America's favorite sportscaster. "I am referring of course to Professor Parker Colburn of Midwestern University here in Urbane City. Good morning, Professor Colburn."

Parker gave the camera his most pleasant smile. "Good morning, Stan," he said. "And please just call me Parker."

"I guess this is something of a red-letter day for you, Parker," said Waterman. "Bill Morton and Nancy Hendrick, the lead orators for Detroit and Los Angeles, the two teams that will be going head to head in the Super Forum next week, are both All-American Classics Scholars from Midwestern. How does it feel to have coached the top orators on both these teams?"

"It's very gratifying," said Parker. "Everyone in our whole coaching organization is very proud of Bill and Nancy, who as you know, are two very talented young persons."

"Now," said Waterman, "I'm not trying to catch you

with a mouth full of pebbles, but where are you putting your money on the Super Forum?"

Parker knew this was coming. "That's a tough one, Stan," he said. "With Morton orating at .782 in Cicero and Watson with an unanswered point average of .657, I'd have to give Detroit the edge in offense. But then you look at Hendrick's earned rebuttal average of .375, and I can see some debate shaping up."

"Well," said Waterman, "I can see that the Fox of Midwestern isn't giving much away. Let's speak to this one from a slightly different angle. Cicero came on strong for the initial declamation and downplayed the rebuttal. Do you agree with this? Is the team with the stronger offense going to have the edge in the Super Forum?"

Parker thought quickly. Waterman was definitely misquoting Cicero, but it would be a big mistake to catch him up on it. Waterman was the living proof of the adaptability of a good sportscaster. He had been one of the top football play-by-play announcers, but the end of physical major-league sports had not fazed him in the least. From somewhere he had gleaned enough surface understanding of the classics to fool the public. If oratory hit the skids tomorrow, Waterman would land on his feet. He'd pick up a smattering of whatever fad next caught the public fancy and be on his way. It would be a mistake to alienate anyone so resilient.

"At Midwestern," said Parker, "we've always paid a lot of attention to what Cicero has to say about oratory. But we have to remember that our primary purpose here is not to train orators but to mold men and women. When our graduates step up to the podium of life, they're going to have to be able to handle both the offense and the defense. Thus, we favor a balanced attack, both declamation and rebuttal."

"Could not have said it better myself," said Waterman. "I think the audience out there now has a little better idea why this young coach has three consecutive undefeated seasons behind him. But I see that our time is about up. Thank you so much for taking a moment to talk to us, Professor Colburn. I know you'll be watching the Super Forum with every bit as much interest as our viewers out there in videospace."

* * *

Durkett Memorial Gymnasium, 11:15 A.M.

Sic transit gloria mundi. (Thus passes the glory of the world.)

Parker opened the heavy metal door and entered the dusky vault of the empty locker room. As he walked through the room, there was no sound but his footsteps echoing from the rusting lockers, quite a difference from the days when these walls had reverberated with the victory cries of a thousand Midwestern teams.

He paused at a door with an opaque glass panel that read "Director of Calisthenics." He tapped lightly on the panel.

"Come in." The voice that answered betrayed a sad weariness.

Parker pushed open the door. The room was as he remembered it. The walls were covered with carefully framed pictures of Midwestern teams, all of them grinning out at him, a paradigm of young manhood now betrayed into oblivion. Behind an old metal desk, leaning back in his swivel chair, was Jason Hobart, once the football coach with the best record in the conference, now reduced to a sinecure poor in both spirit and remuneration. Parker had not seen Jason in over two years. He looked much the same. His hair was perhaps a little whiter, the frown on his face a bit more defiant. "Well, well," he said. "Professor Colburn. And to what do we owe this honor?"

Parker ignored the man's belligerence. He understood too much about the slippery footings of power not to forgive the anger of a man whom the fates had brought low.

"Hello, Jason," he said. "I wanted to talk to you about Batridge." There was no use in idle chatter; they both knew why he was here. By rules some thought archaic, every student was required to participate each semester in an activity of benefit to his body. No standard of performance was enforced, only a minimum attendance. For those with no interest in aerobic dance or Frisbee tossing, droids were provided to lead calisthenics twice a week. Len Batridge, the anchorman on the freshman oration team, had taken it into his head to defy these rules. He had missed enough sessions so that Hobart and his robot assistants were about to flunk him out.

The coach leaned back in his chair and smiled. It was not a smile of pleasure. "Young Batridge," he said, "seems to have forgotten one of the tenets of this university. *Mens sana, in corpore sano.*"

"There is nothing wrong with Batridge's body," said Parker. "He jogs eight miles a day."

The coach raised his hand. "Enough," he said. "Spare me the oration. I am not interested in all the good words you will put in for me with the administration. All I have left, after all, is my integrity. The rules are simple and they apply to Batridge. No gym credits, no oratory team."

For a second Parker felt a touch of pity for the coach. Then his resolve stiffened. This man was not, after all, one who should be boasting about his integrity. "I was hoping that I would not have to remind you," he said.

"Remind me?" Jason's eyes took on a hunted wariness.

"Jim Wall," said Parker. "All-American. Played four years for the Oilers, if I remember correctly. Likable young man, but he had real trouble with his Latin verbs. A big mistake, his taking Latin. Those were your words, if I remember correctly. 'A big mistake. Just edge his grade up from a D to a low C.'"

The coach covered his face with his hands. "You bastard," he said, his voice almost a sob.

"I was just an instructor at the time. No tenure. And here was the man who had taken Midwestern to the championship asking just one small favor of me. What could I do but go along with it?"

Jason hunched forward over his desk, his face still masked behind his hands. "Get out of here," he said in a hoarse whisper.

"In a moment," said Parker. "I just wanted to remind you of a promise you made at the time. If I ever wanted a favor, I had only to ask."

The coach's hands became fists crashing down onto the desk. "Sure, what the hell. You own everything else. Why the hell not my honor. I'll fix it for you. Now just get out of my sight before I kill you."

Parker moved to the door. "I knew I could count on

you," he said. He went out and eased the door shut behind him; his last view was of the coach hunched sobbing behind his desk.

The Midwestern University Faculty Club, 12:30 P.M.
Carpe diem, quam minimum credula postero. (Seize now the day, nor trust some later day.)

It was a small gathering in the Presidential Suite: President Watkins, a few selected department heads, and a couple of dozen wealthy old grads. The purpose of the meeting was the Biannual Update on University Operations, a euphemism, Parker knew, for putting the arm to the alumni.

This year's special target was Arnie Hooper, the president of Universe Robotics. His seating at the head table between Parker and President Watkins was not a matter of chance. Parker knew his assignment: he was to drop a few pearls of wisdom about the Super Forum and Midwestern's chances in the Diogenes Bowl, and to listen with real or pretended enthusiasm to whatever Hooper might have to say.

Parker provided his pearls while Hooper wolfed down his roast beef. He was a hulk of a man with a ruddy face who never failed to let you know how many miles he had run the previous week. He polished off a piece of apple pie a la mode, took a swallow of coffee, and turned to smile at Parker. "Your team sounds like it's in top shape," he said.

"We certainly think so," said Parker. "We're seeing better talent every year."

"Great," said Hooper. "You covering all the other bases?"

"The other bases?"

"Don't ever drop your guard," said Hooper. "Don't ever think you've got it made in the shade. I almost got caught that way myself."

"How's that?" said Parker. He knew exactly what was coming, but he also knew roughly how many kilobucks Hooper would be good for in the next alumni appeal.

"I almost missed it," said Hooper. "Four hundred thousand a year Detroit was paying me in those days."

"And worth every penny of it, I understand," said Parker.

"I sure thought so," said Hooper. "I knew I was one of the best damn shortstops in the business. I was so busy thinking how great I was, I almost missed the handwriting on the wall."

"When was that?" said Parker.

"I remember the day," said Hooper. "March 1988, it was. We were in spring training. Barton, the manager, used to let the android pushers come around as a kind of comic relief. He'd put Whitey Chisholm on the mound. Whitey would wing in a dozen or so of his 95-mph fast balls, and we'd all have a good laugh watching the droids strike out. Then this kid shows up with his droid. It wasn't much to look at. They didn't flesh them out in those days. It walks behind the kid with a kind of slow shuffle."

Hooper paused and glanced around the table. All other conversation had stopped. Even though Parker had heard the story a couple of times before, he did not need to feign his fascination. It marked, after all, a vital turning point in his own career.

"This time it was different," said Hooper. "The droid stands there at the plate with a bat in its plexi-hands, not moving at all.

" 'Where you want him to hit it?' the kid says. He wasn't more than twenty-two, but he was dead serious.

"Barton smiles. 'Just have him hit it out of the park,' he says.

" 'O.K.,' says the kid. He goes over and opens a panel in the droid's chest. The thing wasn't even rigged for voice commands. The kid finishes his adjustments, backs away, and nods to Whitey on the mound. Whitey puts the first one in easy. The droid swings the bat with a kind of a jerk, and the ball lofts up, clear over the fence in left field.

"No one says anything except Whitey. He pounds his glove with his fist. 'Gimme another ball', he yells.

"The next ball comes in hard, a vicious curve that cracks in over the plate but a little low. The android lets it go. 'What's the matter,' Whitey shouts, 'its battery gone dead?'

" 'That was a ball,' the kid says. It was a lesson the pitchers would all learn in a hurry. Droids never made mistakes over balls and strikes.

"Whitey throws again, this time his famous fast ball. The droid jerks his bat again and plasters a drive into right field that Henderson catches with his back against the fence.

" 'Sorry,' says the kid, 'his adjustments drift a little.' He tweaks up the droid again, and we all stand around in silence while that machine puts six of the next ten pitches out of the park."

Hooper paused to glance around at his audience again. "Now the reason I tell that little story is to make one point very clear," he said. "In this day and age, never believe that you can't be replaced by a machine. For myself, I didn't think much about that robot until the middle of the next night when I woke up in a cold sweat. That piece of hardware was after my job! If you could make one that could hit, you could make one that could run, or field, or catch passes, or drop in swishers from forty feet out. It didn't take me long to figure out what I had to do. I put together every penny of cash I could lay my hands on and bought into the kid's operation. The kid is Ferrill, my director of research. And you all know the rest of the story."

There was a moment of quiet, and then President Watkins spoke. "I have to say that I agree with Arnie 100 percent. In this day and age, you can't rest on the laurels of past accomplishments. And that's part of the reason why we're going to be devoting this afternoon to a look at our research facilities here at Midwestern. The best damn facilities of any university in the U.S.A.—or the world, for a matter of fact. But we can't stop where we are. We've got to come up with the new ideas ahead of everyone else."

Hooper Laboratory of Robotics Engineering, 2:35 P.M.
Frontis nulla fides. (Men's faces are not to be trusted.)

Parker trailed along with the alumni, chatting with them about the oratory team. His presence here was not required, but he had very much wanted to have an excuse to check out this facility. As they moved along, he kept his eyes and ears open. What they were shown was interesting enough. There were giant droids that were being designed to put together high-rise buildings in much the same way a kid would use an erector set. There was a genetic engineering robot that would design and glue together bacteria of your choice in a couple of hours.

But what was of far more interest was what the glib young men in white lab coats did *not* demonstrate or speak about. Nothing was said, for example, about research in human accents and speech patterns, an area that had supposedly been one of the most promising two years before, just prior to the Field of Endeavor legislation. For mankind had become frightened enough of its machines that it was attempting to define at least a few areas where they would be forbidden entrance. And one such area was the arts. It was now illegal in the United States for anyone to program a computer in a manner that would replace a human in an artistic enterprise.

Thus, all robotic research on creative writing, on the visual arts, and specifically on Latin oration was supposed to have come to an end some two years before. But had it? Why had Dr. Fenmore, previously one of Midwestern's most prolific publishers, stopped writing journal articles? Fenmore had been one of the most assiduous aspirants for funding, the most eager to show visiting alumni his new toys. Where was he today? And why were they carefully routed around one whole section of the laboratory where locked doors in the corridors barred their way? What was the purpose of the filing cabinets with bars and padlocks he saw in some offices? And why did the little cliques of graduate students suddenly become silent as they approached?

Parker looked and listened and said nothing. He knew much about the illegal work that was going on, but he had no idea what level in the university supported this activity. It was entirely possible that President Watkins was in on the whole business. Parker also knew that exposing the activity could be a very big mistake. There were too many other unscrupulous individuals who would pick up the work if there were a buck to be made on it. On the other hand, he knew just how quickly Watkins would drop the project if there were to be no cash payoff.

Thus, it would be better to attack this problem from a somewhat different angle, to fight fire with fire. And the time for action was now.

The Bit Bucket Lounge, 5:25 P.M.
Honesta turpitudo est pro causa bona. (Crime is honest in a good cause.)

It was not the sort of place that Parker normally frequented. The droid behind the bar was an obsolete model that could only rasp the simplest of pleasantries in response to an order. The feedback was gone in half its servos, and it jerked the beer mugs onto the bar, slopping out half the foam. The disks on the holobox were ancient, and the projection of the naked dancer writhing on the end of the bar was half-obscured in laser fog. It was the type of joint inhabited by the scum of society, codeleggers, pornadroid pimps, and data hijackers.

Starkley was waiting for him in a booth in the back, the same young man who had dropped him the message in the elevator. Parker swallowed his disgust and gave him a pleasant smile as he sat down. If he had been able to find anyone else to penetrate Project Underdog, he would never have touched Starkley. Just one more punk who thought he could make it big on the side by point shaving on the oratory circuit. But the kid knew his oratory, and Fenmore had been happy to pick him up for his illegal project, probably figuring that Starkley's criminal record gave him some kind of hold over him. Too bad that Parker had grabbed hold first.

"You bring the money?" demanded Starkley.

"Not so fast," said Parker. "I need to know a few details. Just who is this Cartwell, and why should I be interested in him?"

"He's just a super hack who's writing the emotion subroutines for the oratory droid. Up till now, no one's been able to make any progress on them. The droid spoke O.K., but it had no audience pull. Now all of a sudden Cartwell is beginning to raise the audience interest factor. No one knows quite how he's doing it, but his subroutines seem to be working."

"O.K.," said Parker. "Sounds like our man. I want you to finger him for me."

Starkley shrank back in the booth as if he had been physically struck. "No," he whined. "I'm not fingering any rubout job."

"Not a rubout," said Parker firmly. "I just want to have a little talk with him."

"I won't do it," Starkley said. But his voice told Parker he would.

"An extra five hundred," Parker said. He placed a wad of bills on the table between them.

Starkley reached for the money, but Parker swept it out of his reach. "Not so fast," he said. "You get the cash when the job is done."

"O.K.," said Starkley, "but no rough stuff. You promise me that."

"No rough stuff," said Parker. "Word of honor."

Parking Lot, Hooper Laboratory of Robotics Engineering, 7:45 P.M.

Oderint, dum metaunt. (Let them hate, provided that they fear.)

There were five of them in the limousine, Wilson and Starkley in the front and Parker, Steve, and Rollo in the back. Parker felt dwarfed by the bulk of the latter two gentlemen, who were former linebacker friends of Wilson's. They all waited in silence as an occasional late worker came out of the building and crossed to an autocar.

Then Starkley spoke. "That's him."

"You sure?" demanded Parker.

"Of course I'm sure. I'd know that screwy walk anywhere."

"O.K., take him," said Parker.

The boys were out of the car in an instant, moving low and fast on an intercepting course.

"You better get moving," Parker said to Starkley. "It won't be good for your health if he knows you're in on this."

"The money?" said Starkley.

"Get moving," said Parker. "You'll get paid when we know we have the right man."

Starkley disappeared into the darkness.

A half minute later, Cartwell was sitting blindfolded beside Parker in the back seat, with Rollo holding his arm persuasively behind his back. With Wilson at the wheel, the limousine swung out of the parking lot and headed into the countryside.

"What do you want?" Cartwell whimpered. In the light of a streetlight they passed, Parker could see he was a mere boy of no more than twenty.

"Your name is Terry Cartwell?" Parker spoke in a tone that demanded no hesitation.

"Yes."

"And you have been programming for Project Underdog?"

The boy let out a gasp.

"Well, have you?"

"Yes." Terror made his voice barely audible.

Now Parker spoke kindly, almost fatherly. "Gotten in a little over your head, haven't you?" he said.

"The money," said Cartwell. "You don't know what they pay."

"I know exactly what they pay," said Parker. "I also know all about the last couple of jobs you did and what they paid. Disassembling a Big Blue operating system, for example. That's good for five years in the cooler right there."

"Who are you guys?" said Cartwell. "You're not the cops. Who are you?"

"Never mind who we are," said Parker. "Let's just say that we're very interested in Project Underdog going down the tubes. You get the message?"

"O.K., O.K., I get it," Cartwell whimpered. "I'll quit. I can be gone tonight. Just no rough stuff."

Again Parker assumed his father tone. "No one is going to hurt you if you cooperate. But leaving the project is the last thing we want you to do."

"What do you mean?"

"You are coding the emotional subroutines, are you not?" said Parker.

"Yes."

"And doing a very good job, I understand."

"I sure am," said Cartwell. "The audience response factor was up twelve points for my last revision."

"Where it will stop," said Parker. "You will run into some fundamental obstacles in your programming. You will discover that the approach you have taken has dead-ended. And all of the variations you try will dead-end also."

"But I can't do that," said Cartwell. "That would violate my programmer's credo."

"Now get this straight," said Parker. "Just forget your hypocritical little credo. You are a punk kid with a well-documented criminal history. If Project Underdog succeeds, you will be prosecuted and convicted for your last two little forays outside the law ... after you get out of the hospital. Do I make myself clear?"

"Yes." The voice was faint, but Parker knew he had made his point.

"O.K.," Parker said to Wilson. "Let's drop him off."

The car slowed. "On your walk back to town," Parker said to the boy, "you'll have a lot of time to think. Just remember that we know exactly what is going on in your so-called secret project. One mistake will be your last."

The limousine came to a stop, and Rollo shoved Cartwell out the door with a push that tumbled him into the ditch.

As the car gunned away, Parker calculated his chances. Let Cartwell hate him, the nameless power that now controlled his life. As long as the fear was stronger, Parker knew he would win out.

The Oratory Building Penthouse Suite, 8:35 P.M.

Spectatum veniunt, veniunt spectentur ut ipasae. (They come to see, they come that they themselves may be seen.)

When Parker arrived, the reception was in full swing. Dean Hemshaw greeted him warmly as he entered. His greeting should be warm. Parker's operation funded about three-quarters of the humanities budget.

He stepped into the room and glanced about. Everyone who was anyone on campus was there, the men mostly in pseudo-leather formal wear, the women in the simple tunics that had—for the moment, at least—become *de rigueur* for a semiformal party. How little humanity had changed in two thousand years, Parker thought.

Then the first of his colleagues noticed his presence, and he was caught in a whirl of congratulations. He moved about the room, little groups forming around him, anxious to hear the plans for next year's team.

For an hour he played the pleasant host, and then, exhausted from the effort, excused himself and escaped to the open terrace at one end of the suite. It was cold with a biting wind, but he stood for a moment looking down upon the lights of the campus. How soon, he wondered, would all of this belong to him? Hemshaw was retiring soon, and Parker knew that the only question as to his moving up to dean was who would replace him in oratory. And the step from dean to president? If Watkins was in on Project Underdog, and that project failed, he would be in a most precarious position. The right information leaked to the right people might just cause a hurried resignation.

Then Parker was aware of a young woman beside him. He turned and looked at her. In the dim light he could see the pretty oval of her face looking up at him. The wind tightened her tunic against her body, revealing a figure that quickened his pulse.

"Well, hello," he said.

"Hello," she said. "I'm Fern Whittington, the new diction coach. I'm working for Walt Stanhope."

"Oh, yes," said Parker. It was a pity his department was so large that he did not have the chance to interview all the new hires in person. In this case, a real pity. He made a mental note to congratulate Stanhope on his recruiting.

"I'm really excited about working for Midwestern," she said. And then her smile opened into something close to an invitation. "And of course working with you. I mean, up at Harvard all they talked about in the Classics Department was what you've done for oratory."

"Well," said Parker, "not much of it is my doing. It's mostly the coaching staff. But it's awfully cold out here. Why don't we go someplace quiet where we can talk a bit about what we're planning for next year?"

"I'd like that very much," she said. "Where do you have in mind?"

"How about my place?" he said, and discovered that his heart was pounding with sophomoric anticipation.

"That sounds awfully nice to me," she said.

University Paradise Condominiums, 11:45 P.M.

Varium et mutablile semper femina. (A fickle and changeful thing is woman.)

Parker lay on his back in bed, with Fern asleep beside him. She was, he thought, a truly remarkable woman. They had talked for an hour over coffee, and he had discovered in her an intellect that could challenge his own. She knew what she wanted, the opportunity to make her mark in oratory. She obviously had her opinions and would fight to the death for what she believed. Yet she told him of her plans with an openness that precluded deception.

Then he had reached out for her, and she had come to him willingly. They had made love with an innocence and freedom that had dissolved into bitter dust all of Parker's memories of the one-night stands of the past.

Could this be the woman he had been waiting for? Would she be the end of his loneliness? And would she be the one to share his rise to the top? Already he could not conceive of any adventure into the future without her beside him.

Parker reached out and touched her back. She turned in her sleep, her hand grasping his and then relaxing. Parker stretched his body in the bed. "Not a bad day," he said to himself as he sank into slumber. "Not a bad day at all."

Editor's Introduction to "The Picture Man," by John Dalmas

The story is told of a Phoenician carpenter who, needing a tool, wrote a short message on a wood chip and gave it to a slave to carry to his home. The carpenter's brother read the message and handed over the required chisel.

The slave was astounded, and begged his master to give him the "talking chip" so that it could be properly venerated. Clearly it had supernatural powers.

The story is probably false, but it illustrates a point. Arthur C. Clarke calls it Clarke's Law: "Any sufficiently advanced technology is indistinguishable from magic."

There was a time when, largely due to the influence of John W. Campbell, Jr., psychic powers—"psi phenomena" —were the main theme of science fiction. Of course Campbell's goal was to take psi out of the realm of magic and into the domain of science; to that end he published a great deal about how to use dowsing rods, and how to construct Heironymous Machines. A number of readers, including me, built these gadgets—in my case I had laboratory technicians at the Boeing Company build them—in the hope that we'd be able to demonstrate psi as a reliable phenomenon. Alas, that didn't work.

Whatever one may think of psychic powers, *reliability*

isn't usually claimed for them. Dr. Rhine may or may not have demonstrated the existence of psi powers, but even if you grant that he did, his experiments certainly proved psi's elusive nature. Rhine wanted to make investigation of psi powers respectable, but what he mostly managed with his massive statistical calculations was to demonstrate how dull psi experiments generally were.

After Rhine came Kerlian photography. About the same time, Cleve Backster used a polygraph to try to demonstrate thought transference between humans and plants. This generated a number of stories. Interest in Backster's work died away not long after he published a paper on how he used a polygraph to communicate with yogurt.

Psi investigators did manage to gain grudging acceptance by the American Association for the Advancement of Science, much to the disgust of John A. Wheeler, who annually denounces the inclusion of a session on psi at AAAS meetings. His denunciations are generally the most exciting psychic phenomena at the meetings. Most hard scientists agree with Wheeler—but not all. Some recall the story of the Phoenician carpenter.

The Picture Man

John Dalmas

I put down my copy of *Ecological Review* and walked over to the TV. I generally liked to catch the ten o'clock news. The picture popped out to fill the screen; the last moment of the opening commercials was just flashing off.

I sat back down to watch, all by myself in my three-bedroom, one-and-a-half-bath, near-campus, 1950-model house. It got a little lonely at times since Eydie had "dear John'ed" me with Barney Foster, but it was certainly quieter and less irritating. For example, the house wasn't dominated night after night by game shows, situation "comedies," and TV dramas.

I'd learned the hard way that marrying the best-looking girl in the class and living happily ever after weren't necessarily the same thing.

Several female faculty and staff members had demonstrated an interest in filling the presumptive hole in my life, and there had been some interesting evenings. Maggie Lanning in particular combined looks and physical interest with remarkable level-headedness in every area we'd talked about. Plus, she was willing to hike in the rain, played a great forward in couples basketball (she was an assistant professor in phys. ed.), and even had a collection of old John Campbell editorials cut from years of *Astoundings* and *Analogs*.

Not that she was old. She was thirty-three—two years younger than I.

But marriage? We could already talk and romp at our mutual convenience, and she had one major drawback: ten-year-old Lanny. Lanny was a good kid, we got along fine, and he kept dropping hints that I'd make a good dad and Maggie would make a good wife. But he was going to be a *teenager* in less than three years.

And I was still enjoying my new independence. I should, I decided, write a thank-you note to Barney, now that the divorce was final. I wouldn't, though. It would be a cheap shot, and I wouldn't feel good about it afterward.

The weatherman joggled me out of my reverie with mention of a sunspot storm. So when the basketball and hockey scores were over, I put on a jacket and went to the door. Sunspots might mean an aurora display, and watching northern lights was one of my favorite spectator activities.

If I'd turned on the porch light before I went out, I might not have seen what I did. A stocky, square-looking man was digging in my plastic trash can that sat by the curb waiting for morning pickup. Two steps, and he could have been out of sight behind Chuck Ciccone's privet hedge. He'd dug in to the armpit, setting some contents on the sidewalk for better access, straightened for a moment, then tidily put everything back in the can and replaced the lid, clamping it down. There hadn't been anything edible or valuable in the can.

"Hey!" I said. Slowly he looked toward me, then lowered his face and started to walk off.

"Just a minute!" I called. "Come on in. Do me a favor; help me eat some leftovers."

The dim face looked at me again for a few seconds, then he walked toward the house, hands stuffed in the pockets of his denim work jacket. For a moment I had a feeling of strangeness as, hunched against the cold and night, he approached. Not a feeling of threat. Just strangeness.

The square, high-cheekboned face, grimy and stubbled, was lined with the track record of late middle age. He looked like someone who'd ridden into town on a freight train, probably headed south. I held the door for him—it was that or wash the knob—and headed him for the bathroom.

"Why don't you shower down while I cook?" I said, then pointed out the guest towel and washcloth and left him there.

Being fresh out of leftovers, I put eggs and wienies on to boil, set a can of beans over a low flame, and put the teakettle on for hot chocolate. When everything was under way, I resurrected an old pair of jeans and a baggy sweatshirt and put them on the bathroom rug. The place was full of steam, like a turkish bath; he must have a remarkable tolerance for hot water, I thought. I announced to the shower that I was going to run his clothes through the washer and dryer, that I was leaving some of mine he could wear, and, getting a faint acknowledgment, went and started the washing cycle. I even threw his black stocking cap in; I'd have to remember not to put it in the dryer.

What in the hell, I asked myself, *are you doing? This guy could be a psycho. He could murder and rob you.* But there'd been nothing deadlier than a small jackknife in his pockets.

On an impulse, and feeling uncomfortable about it, I checked his wallet. It had no money. A merchant mariner's certificate identified him as Jaakko Savimäki, of Calumet, Michigan. Fireman, oiler, water tender. Dated 1951—thirty-two years back. The square face in the picture was a youthful version of my man's, the hair blonde and crewcut. His driver's license address was Ironwood, Michigan; I'd heard about the mines up there being shut down.

Opening the bathroom door, I peered into the clouded interior. "You'll find a razor and shaving cream in the medicine cabinet," I said, and turned on the exhaust fan so he could find the mirror.

When he came out, he looked a lot better, although on him, my jeans were a couple of inches too long and a couple too tight. He'd made do by folding cuffs into them, leaving the waistband open, and keeping them up with the elastic belt.

"My name's Terry," I said, "Terry O'Brien."

"Mine is Jake," he answered, "Jake Hill."

Even in those few words, I detected an accent.

"Mr. Hill, I took the liberty of looking in your billfold for identification. It said your name is Savimäki."

He didn't blush or look angry or embarrassed. The strange, soft blue eyes just gazed at me as if examining the inside of my head.

"Savimäki is a kind of hill in Finnish," he said. "Away from home, it's easier to just tell people 'Hill.' "

I nodded. "Got it," I said. "All right, Mr. Savimaki, supper is on the counter."

As hungry as he must have been, he didn't bolt his food. When he'd finished, he thanked me and took his dishes to the sink before I realized what he was doing. Then he turned to me, and again his eyes were direct. I got the feeling that he saw more than other people did. "How do I pay you back?" he asked.

"Forget it. It's on me."

He didn't shake his head—simply said, "It's not all right for me to take something for nothing."

Well, I thought, *that's a refreshing viewpoint*. I wasn't sure I totally agreed with it, in a country where the system was so screwed up that some people found themselves backed up against the wall. But if everyone had his attitude, things would be a lot better.

"O.K.," I said, "what do you do?"

The pale eyes shifted to the fireplace. "You got any wood to split?"

"No. Sorry. I buy it already split."

"Any carpentry you need done? Windows fixed? Locks repaired?"

I looked at the possibilities. "You hit me at a bad time. I've got nothing like that. Why don't we defer payment? There'll be snow to shovel a little later in the fall."

His eyes withdrew for a moment; he didn't plan to be around Douglas long. "Tell you what," I suggested, "why don't you pass it on? Help someone else out when you have a chance."

He nodded slowly. "O.K.," he said. "I guess that's O.K." Then he turned to the sink and began to run water for the dishes while I transferred his clothes to the dryer, remembering to hold out his stocking cap. He seemed to think slowly, but he washed dishes fast. They were clean, rinsed, and in the drainer in about two minutes.

When he was done, he followed me into the living room and stood uncomfortably. I could see he still wasn't happy about not exchanging anything for the bath, meal, and laundry. Then he noticed the pictures on my wall, mostly wildland photos. When Eydie had taken her prints from the house, I'd mounted some scenic photographs on mat and hung them to handle the bareness. He walked over and looked at them.

"You got a camera?" he asked.

"Three of them. A 35-mm Pentax for slides, an old Rollei 4 × 5, and a Polaroid 680."

"A Polaroid." He considered that for a moment. "How would you like if I gave you some interesting pictures?"

"What do you mean?"

"Let me show you. Get the Polaroid."

Feeling mystified, I got it reluctantly. When I came back to the living room, he was sitting in a chair.

"Is it loaded?" he asked.

"Always," I said.

"Then aim it at my face." He closed his eyes tightly, his brow clenched with concentration. "When I say 'now,' shoot it."

Feeling foolish, I raised the camera.

"Now," he said. I touched the shutter release, lowered the camera, and waited. He was on his feet beside me when I removed the print. It wasn't a picture of Savimaki. It was a house, somewhat blurred, an old, frame, two-story house with a steep roof, no front porch, and an upstairs door that opened out onto thin air. A ladder was built on the wall up to the strangely placed door.

"Let's do another one," he said. "That one ain't very good. I can get something more interesting than that."

"Wait a minute," I said. "How come it isn't a picture of you?"

Actually, I thought I knew why. Years before, I'd read a book about the detailed, if somewhat ambiguous, studies done on Nick Kopac, the psychic photographer. This looked like the same kind of thing.

"I don't know," he said. "It's just something I can do."

"Strange-looking house. Where is it?"

"In Calumet, Michigan. It's the house I grew up in. It looks like that because they get so much snow there. Some winters you get in and out through the upstairs door."

"My god! And didn't you know that's what the picture was going to be of?"

"No. I haven't learned how to know yet." He sat down again. "Usually I get something I never even seen before. But it's always a house or a ship. So far. Actually, I only ever did this about ten or twelve times before. I found out about it last winter, by accident, when a guy tried to take a picture of me and I didn't know it. I was reading a magazine, and all he got was a picture of a lighthouse."

"Are you ready now?" he asked.

I nodded. "Yep."

He closed his eyes, I aimed, he said "now" again, and I shot. Together we looked at the print. This one was sharper, hardly blurred at all, showing a square house that looked stuccoed. It reminded me of pictures I'd seen of French farmhouses, but in the background was a broadly naked landscape with what looked like a high, cliff-faced plateau behind it. As an ecologist with a strong interest in biogeography, I was willing to bet it was an Afrikaner farmstead in South Africa, and told him so.

He shrugged. "Could be."

We took a couple more, then called it quits, and I showed him the guest bedroom. But my mind was racing. I didn't have a class the next day until two in the afternoon, and I could always cancel my morning office hours, although I didn't like to. I thought I knew where I could get Jake a job. After he sacked down, I went to the phone and called Herb Boeltz.

I didn't actually know Boeltz very well, although as well as I wanted to. We were both in the faculty jogging club. He was a faculty politician, if you know what I mean, reputedly handy with a knife to the back, a full professor in psychology at thirty-two, and a man who always seemed to have access to grant money.

And he was said to be interested in parapsychology.

It was 11:15, and apparently I had wakened him; he didn't sound terribly friendly. So as soon as I'd identified myself, I put it to him this way.

"I think I've got something that can get you a lot of good publicity. Remember the studies on psychic photography at the University of Nebraska? ... That's right, Nick Kopac.

"Well, I've got a guy staying here at my house that does the same sort of thing. I took four shots with my Polaroid; got two houses, a church, and what looks like a commercial fishing boat. . . .

"No, I just met him today. Seems like a good enough guy. Kind of quiet. He needs a job, and I knew, or at least I heard, that you had some grant money that might be available. It looks like a good opportunity for research with some media appeal, if it's handled right."

When I hung up, we had an appointment for eleven the next morning.

At 11:07 we walked into the Education Building, which also houses the pysch department. I prefer to be on time, but Herron's Men's Wear doesn't open until ten, and we needed some presentable but inexpensive clothes for Jake—slacks, a shirt, shoes, sweater, jacket. . . . Actually, on my salary there isn't such a thing as inexpensive clothes. Some just cost less.

The meeting wasn't long. Boeltz admitted to eight hundred dollars in an account for exploratory research, which these days suggests he had something on someone. It wasn't enough to put Jake on the payroll. He agreed to pay him a ten-dollar allowance for "cigarettes and socks," as he put it. Jake was to stay with me, and Boeltz would pay me thirty dollars a week toward his room and board for any week in which Jake's services were used, plus ten dollars for each additional session, which we could split as we saw fit.

I was also to transport Jake to and from local sessions, as the studies would be done at Boeltz's home on the other side of town. Starting that evening at 7:30.

Boeltz had a bad reputation, so I wrote it all down and the three of us signed it, and afterward I got it photocopied. I was surprised that my wanting it in writing didn't annoy Boeltz, but he was genial and cheerful thoughout. I told myself he ought to be. He was getting a very promising research project, journal articles, personal publicity, and speaking engagements—all at damned little expense. And none of the expense was his personally.

I, on the other hand, would be an unpaid cook and chauffeur. But it did promise to be damned interesting. We hurried home, I grabbed a quick snack, and left Jake there while I rushed off to handle the Thursday afternoon lab in Plant Science 101. It occurred to me that it wasn't ideal, leaving a stranger alone in my home while I went off to work, but somehow I didn't feel concerned.

I took time to phone Maggie that afternoon; I needed someone to tell all this to, and she was the closest thing I had to a confidante. She said she'd be at my place about 5:30 to meet Jake and fix us supper; she sounded almost too cheerful to be real. Then I phoned home. Jake sounded sober and had started reading Churchill's memoirs. I told him Maggie would be coming by to fix supper and might get there before I did.

She drove up just as I was opening the garage door, and we went in together. To find supper on the table! Jake had hunted through refrigerator and cupboard, and had fixed pork chops, rice, sweet potatoes, and cornbread. He'd walked to the store and bought the cornmeal out of a five I'd loaned him. When I came out of shock, I introduced him to Maggie.

"*Hyvää iltaa*, Mr. Savimäki," she said grinning. I stared at her.

"*Hyvää iltaa*, Mrs. Lanning," he said back. "*Mitä Kuuluu?*"

She laughed. "I just used up all the Finnish I remember. When Terry told me your name, I thought, 'Hey! That sounds like home!' I'm from Duluth."

"So that's where you learned to say *Hyvää Iltaa*."

"Right. My mom is Finnish-American, but my dad wasn't, so I didn't learn much at home. I learned more from the neighbors." She turned to me. "What a treat this is going to be." She gestured at the table. "If I'd fixed it, we'd be having hot dogs and beans."

I knew better than that. After supper, when Jake insisted on washing the dishes, I decided this arrangement was going to be a lot better than I'd thought. And after I took Jake to Boeltz's, I could hurry back to spend an hour or two alone with Maggie.

But that wasn't the way it worked, because Maggie wanted to go along and stay to watch.

That was fine with Boeltz; he liked to play to an audience. He had his own Polaroid, new that day, and took quite a few exposures. The first couple were "whities"—no picture. Not even of Jake. They looked as if they'd been shot into a floodlamp, which was remarkable enough in itself. The third was a blackie—it was as if it hadn't been exposed at all. But Boeltz and I were prepared for that; according to the literature, Kopac used to get whities and blackies a lot.

Boeltz looked at Jake, then, with this knowing smile, went over to a cabinet and poured a whole glass of bourbon. "Would you like a drink, Jake?" he asked. But how it came across was, *'kay, you cunning boy, I know why you're holding out on me.* It irritated me—I felt insulted for Jake—but whether the whiskey had anything to do with it or not, the next picture was of the Taj Mahal, sharp and clear. Then Jake threw down the whiskey like ginger ale.

The next was of a Hilton hotel somewhere. Without saying anything, Boeltz nudged me and pointed at a part of the picture. On the sign, the name Hilton was spelled wrong!

"Jacob," said Boeltz, "how do you spell the name 'Hilton'?"

Jake's quiet eyes fixed on Boeltz. "H-I-L-T-E-N," he answered.

What in the hell, I thought to myself, *does this mean?*

By the time we left, at 8:30, Boeltz had poured a second glass of whiskey down Jake and had half a dozen pretty fair shots—four of them buildings, one a pyramid buried in tropical jungle, and one of a three-masted schooner in a storm.

Jake didn't even seem a little tight when we walked out, although he wasn't saying much. I decided he must have a thing for booze—in his generation that was apparently why most drifters became drifters, although it might have been the other way around. And Boeltz was using it as a way to keep Jake around and performing.

That was how it looked.

When we got home, I asked Jake how the evening had been for him. His answer was concise and unambiguous:

"I don't like Professor Boeltz," he said. He also said he was tired, and went to get ready for bed. Maggie and I watched television until he retired, then moved together on the sofa.

There were three more sessions scattered over the next ten days, semi-public in that Boeltz invited several other faculty members and Bea Lundeen to them. Bea was the owner/editor of the local paper, the *Douglas Clarion*. As chauffeur, I was welcome to sit in, too. It was interesting as hell, although Boeltz didn't try anything that hadn't been tried fifteen years earlier with Nick Kopac.

Under his direction, Jake found he could do things he hadn't tried before. To start with, all he got were seemingly random shots of buildings and ships, pretty much like Kopac had gotten—almost nothing but buildings and statues. But Jake had a lot better batting average—he got a picture about two times out of three, and most of them pretty clear.

Frankly, I was surprised he did that well, because Boeltz was really unpleasant to work for. He continued to use booze in a very obvious way as a carrot on a stick. But I noticed that Jake never asked for it; he didn't even say yes when Boeltz asked if he wanted some. He just accepted it when Boeltz handed it to him.

He certainly knew what to do with it then, though.

Another thing Boeltz did was to talk to Jake as if he were some kind of retard. "Now Jacob, I'm going to ask you to make us a picture of a cathedral. Can you do that for us? Let's try. Do you know what a cathedral is? Good. Very, very good." And, "Oh, that's *good*, Jacob. You're doing very, very *well* tonight."

Maybe that's why Jake kept accepting the whiskey. Not really, though, because I'd swear I saw a sort of amusement in those pale eyes. Maybe he enjoyed seeing Boeltz unwittingly irritate everyone around him and in general make an ass of himself.

The article Bea wrote for the *Clarion* was all about Jake; Boeltz was mentioned only once.

Then there was a lapse of a few days before the fifth session, which was a big one, a Saturday night affair. We'd been written up far beyond the *Clarion* by then, and interest was spreading. More people had been invited than there was room for at Boeltz's, and it was held in the home of Professor Tony Fournais, chairman of the physics department. Fournais was wealthy, had a big house outside town, was cautiously interested in the project—and made for good positioning: physics had a lot more status than psychology.

Everyone who'd been invited was there. And relatively on time: no one was more than twenty minutes late, even though the streets were snow-packed and slippery and the temperature was about ten degrees. Professor Alfred Kingsley Kenmore had flown in from Virginia—the Kenmore of "Herz-Kenmore-Laubman Clairvoyance Studies" fame. And Marty Martin, the award-winning science writer from the *Trib*.

Maggie went with us.

It started out like a circus, or at least a drawing room comedy. Fournais announced that his assistant was going to film the whole procedure, and had a 16-mm movie camera at one side of the room, on a high tripod, to shoot down at Jake over people's heads. The film would later be examined in slow motion for any sign of hokey-pokey. Then Martin announced that he was going to match every shot of Boeltz's with his own camera and film, to provide a second, independent print. Finally, when Boeltz was ready to begin, Kenmore, who was a psychiatrist and therefore an M.D., had Jake lie down, and examined his eyes, pulling out the upper and lower lids, peering under them with a little light. I haven't the slightest what he was looking for.

Then we got started. Boeltz was on his good behavior for a change: he didn't put Jake down, and no booze was in evidence, confirming that his previous bullshit was deliberate.

He warmed Jake up by letting him do whatever he came up with. He started with an oblique aerial view of a beautiful landscaped home, with city spread out in the midground against a backdrop of mountains. Not Denver, I decided. Maybe Calgary. The next looked like Hong Kong. The third was a double row of tar-papered shacks with deep snow piled all around and forest close behind. A guy wearing what looked like a leather apron was caught in midstride between two of them. When it was shown to Jake, he identified it as the Axelson-Peltonnen logging camp in Baraga County, Michigan, about 1948. He'd worked there. The guy in the apron, he said was Ole Hovde, the blacksmith. I could tell that Jake was really pleased with that one, and I got a notion that just maybe he'd gotten it deliberately.

Boeltz didn't take any of the pictures himself. Each of them was taken by a different person standing directly in front of Jake and about six feet away. The camera had been bought new by Fournais. The film packs were taken from their sealed wrappers right there in front of us.

Each shot was passed around before the next was taken. Then it was laid on a table, available for further examination.

Martin was off to one side with his camera, and didn't pass his shots around. But after the third, he arranged them on the table with Boeltz's, making matched pairs.

Boeltz beamed. "Ladies and gentlemen," he announced, "we have something very interesting here: Mr. Martin's photograph's. Come and see!"

I was already there. In each instance, Martin's picture was of the same scene, but as if seen from an angle of about ninety degrees to the right, higher, and farther away.

Everyone crowded around talking, except Fournais's assistant, who stayed by his camera. A couple of them shook Jake's hand as he came over to look. The way the pictures matched up, it was as if the actual scene, the physical scene of each pair, had occupied the location of Jake's chair, in three dimensions. And it was something that hadn't come up in the work with Nick Kopac.

Boeltz was ready now to attempt something he'd tried with equivocal results the two sessions just previous. He had Bea Lundeen and me go into Fournais's library to find a picture of a building or ship—any building or ship—in the encyclopedia. Maggie went with us. Bea pulled out volume 14—KI to LE—and turned to "Kremlin." And there was the great Russian fortress looming above Red Square, the towers of its buildings showing above the massive wall. I nodded, we all looked at it, concentrating, and Bea called out, "O.K., we got one!"

Nothing more happened for about half a minute, and I got pretty fidgety, but we all kept looking at the picture. Then someone called, "Come on out. It's done."

We did. Bea took the encyclopedia to the table and laid it down open, weighting it with an ashtray. Boeltz removed his print, marked it with black grease pencil, and laid it down next to the book.

What was there made my scalp crawl. Jake had given us the Kremlin, all right, but not at all like the picture in the book. There was no broad paved parade ground. Instead, small log buildings were backed up against the fortress wall. The ground was mud, with logs laid in it as a sort of rude and partial paving. There were rows of market booths, and hundreds of people stood or walked around, some mostly naked, a few wearing long coats.

It was a photograph of the Kremlin centuries ago! A photograph of life, not of a painting!

There were some brief, quiet comments, but actually not much was said as people crowded up to look. Everyone seemed to realize the basic significance of it: Jake Savimaki could give pictures from the past, from before photography. This was not a picture of a photograph or thing he'd seen. We were in the presence of something much further beyond the limits of known science than we'd realized—a whole dimension further.

Martin crowded his way to the table and looked without comment, then silently laid his own print beside the other. Again it showed the same scene from maybe twice as far away. And here the apparent elevation was conspicuous. Boeltz's shot might have been taken from forty or fifty feet above the ground. Martin's was an oblique aerial shot, as if from a low-flying airplane. Except, of course, it wasn't.

Jake had come quietly over, and now he took a look. His eyes didn't change. People looked at him and he didn't seem to notice. It was as if he'd just dropped in and wanted to see what was going on.

My eyes found Boeltz; he was murmuring something quietly to Fournais. Fournais then called a break. In a minute or so their cook appeared with hors d'oevres, and the lid was removed from the punch bowl. Something for people to handle without getting tight. Almost everyone soon had a glass in their hand except Jake. He stood apart, watching the effects he'd caused, and caught my glance with a smile and a nod.

Fournais and Boeltz talked quietly in a corner, then Martin joined them, and Kenmore. I started over to join them too, but some out-of-towner stopped me and asked if I hadn't come in with Mr. Savimaki. By the time I was free, the four of them had left the room.

I felt a hand on my arm, and it was Maggie. "What does he do for an encore?" she asked.

"God knows," I said; *or the Devil*, I added silently. But that was unfair; if anyone around here had a devil, it was Boeltz, not Jake. Jake was as clean as anyone; we went over to him.

"*Kuinka se menee*, Mr. Savimäki?" Maggie asked him.

He grinned. "Pretty good, *tyttö*. How about you?"

"I'm impressed," she said. "Do you know how you did that?"

"Not exactly," he told her. "I just kind of—open myself up. I still don't know what a picture's going to be, but this time I decided I wanted something that would startle people."

"You want to do any more tonight?" I asked him, "or are you tired? We can go home if you like."

"No, I feel real good. This gets easier every session. I'd like to see what else I can do. Those last pictures look like something from the past; maybe I can get something from the future next."

I felt my gut give a little twist.

"You know what?" he went on. "I never felt this good before. In my whole life, and most of it ain't been bad." He put his full attention on me then, and called me by my first name for the first time. "Terry, I never thanked you for calling me in that night. I'd hit bottom, and you pulled me back up. I want you to know I appreciate it." He held out a hand big enough for an NFL tackle, and we shook. Then he turned to Maggie with a big grin, and she grinned back, and they shook, too.

We were interrupted; Boeltz, Fournais, Martin, and Kenmore had come back in, Boeltz practically rubbing his hands in anticipation. "Excuse me everyone, if you please," he called, and conversations stopped. "We'd like to continue now."

People quieted down and shuffled themselves into a loose circle. "Do you need to warm up with something easy, Mr. Savimäki?" Boeltz asked. *Courtesy yet!* It was the first time he'd called him "Mr. Savimäki." But his eager eyes were like ice picks.

Jake shook his head and said he was ready. Fournais had his wife take over Martin's camera, and he, Boeltz, and Martin left for the library. Kenmore picked up Boeltz's camera and positioned himself in front of a slightly smiling Jake.

It was a couple of minutes before we heard a voice call, "All right, we've got one."

Jake closed his eyes. No longer was there any effortful concentration, no tightly shut lids. He looked relaxed and confident. "Now," he said. Kenmore clicked his shutter, and so did Liz Fournais, and someone went to get the three from the library. Martin came in with a large book and laid it open on the table. I looked at it while Liz and Kenmore brought their prints over.

It wasn't an encyclopedia, but a book entitled *Weapons in the Sky: Military Applications of Space Technology*. The chapter it was open to was "Soviet Programs." There wasn't even a picture on the page.

Jake had outsmarted them, though. I didn't realize it at the time, but he had. Kenmore laid down his photo, and it was not of some satellite or anything like that. Instead, I saw a car, unidentifiable to me in the darkness, lying on its top in the snow. Liz's photo was the same, from another angle. In hers, I could see a body pinned underneath.

That was the end of the performance. While people donned coats and caps, I took Boeltz aside and collected. He didn't even look irritated with me—"not there" would describe him—then pulled on his gloves and left.

On the way home, nobody talked for the first mile. "Whose car do you suppose that was?" I said at last.

"I don't know," Jake answered. "I just know I didn't want to show them what they wanted, so I just decided to do a picture from the future. And that's what I got."

No one followed up on that until we got home. When we'd hung up our coats and sat down, Maggie decided she needed to know. "Jake," she asked, "could you have shown them? . . . What they wanted?"

His eyes were sober. "Get your camera," he told me.

The first picture was of an orbiting space station, like nothing yet built, I'm sure. It was hard to judge size and distance, with nothing familiar as a reference, but it might have been a hundred feet in diameter, bright against black space, from a viewpoint of maybe a hundred yards away. A red hammer and sickle vivid on its side.

"Holy God!" I said. A whole panorama of potential events began to shape up for me: the CIA moving in, Jake held in some secluded place doing God-knows-what kind of spying for them—and Boeltz, of course, handling Jake. Boeltz would love it; how important he'd feel!

"Take another one," Jake said. "I can see this one, too."

So he was seeing them in advance now. I aimed, he said, "Now," and I shot. It showed Jake strapped down on something like an operating table. He didn't even take the trouble to look at the photo. Maggie's hand found mine.

"You see why I did it," he said, and we both nodded.

The first thing I saw in the *Clarion* the next morning, right on the front page, was a picture of an overturned car. I'd seen one like it the night before. It was Bea Lundeen's. Kenmore and Martin had been with her, and Kenmore was dead.

There was nothing in either the *Clarion* or the *Trib* about the session, that day or any other. It was as if they were afraid of it, pushing it out of sight, out of mind, unable to confront what was there.

We didn't hear anything from Boeltz, either, on Sunday. Or on Monday, or for most of the week. Meanwhile, Jake got a job cooking at the Douglas Hotel. He also arranged to move into a room there, but for some reason I talked him out of it.

On Monday evening Maggie came by with her mother, Anna Lahti, who'd driven down from Minnesota to stay a week. She was a good-looking woman about fifty or fifty-five, and she and Jake hit it off right away, talking Finnish. She turned to us and laughed—said she knew he was from Savo as soon as he opened his mouth because he rolled his r's. As if she didn't; when they talked Finnish, it sounded like two chain saws.

It was Friday when Boeltz phoned. He wanted Jake again in half an hour—said I wouldn't need to bring him, that he'd come by and pick him up. I told him he'd have to talk to Jake, and put my hand over the mouthpiece, remembering the picture of Jake strapped down.

"It's Boeltz," I said. "He wants to come and get you in half an hour, for another session. He obviously doesn't want me to be there. I don't trust him; tell him to go to hell."

He smiled and took the phone. "Hello, Dr. Boeltz," he said. "I'm busy tonight, but if you want to make that for tomorrow evening at eight, that will be fine.... At eight, then. I'll be ready." He hung up.

"Jake!" I said, and he grinned. His eyes weren't soft anymore. They looked darker, and bright.

"It's O.K.," he said. "And what you're worried about, it's not going to happen."

"Something's fishy with him," I insisted. "He's hiding something, or I'm not Irish."

He nodded. "It's nothing to worry about, though."

"Do you *know* that?" I asked. "Do you know what he has in mind?"

"I don't know what he has in mind, but it's not dangerous. Not to me." He grinned again then. "And you told me you're only half-Irish. The other half is Dutch."

"And you're half-Swede," I said, trying to insult him. He just laughed; maybe I should have said Russian. Then Anna Lahti drove up. They had a date for supper and an evening at the ice rink.

I watched them drive away; it looked like a romance in the bud. I hoped nothing bad would happen the next evening.

The next night Boeltz was there five minutes early. After he and Jake drove away, I put on my jacket and cap, got in my car, and headed after them for Boeltz's place.

I parked half a block away, then chickened out. I couldn't think of any excuse for going up and pounding on his door, and I didn't want to get arrested for window peeking. So I got the Black Hawks pregame show on the radio and waited. At two minutes into the first period, Marcel Dionne scored on a breakaway. A couple of minutes later, Jake walked out of Boeltz's and started down the sidewalk. I rolled down the window as he approached.

"Want a ride?"

He grinned and got in.

"Care to tell me what happened?"

"Nothing much," he said. "We talked a little bit. But you don't have to worry about my going back."

"Yeah?" I said encouragingly.

"Yeah," he answered cheerfully.

I started the car and pulled away from the curb. "Yeah *what?*" I demanded.

He laughed. "He wanted me to make a picture showing someone dead. His father. He said the old man is dying slowly of an incurable cancer, in terrible pain, and that he'd be grateful to die. He thought if I made a picture of it, it would happen.

"I asked him what his father did for a living, and he said he'd been a banker. You can see what he's after."

"So you told him to go to hell."

"No, I told him I'd see what I could do."

I almost drove up over the curb. *"You what?"*

"Then I gave him a picture of his father as he was at that moment. Playing golf." Jake laughed again. "There were palm trees in the background. Hawaii, I suppose; it's daylight there now."

"What did he say to that?"

"He got all excited, said I'd made a mistake and got something from a year or two ago."

It was six minutes into the first period. Esposito stopped a Mark Hardy slapshot and fell on Dave Taylor's rebound. Charley Simmer fell on top of Esposito. Hutchinson shoved Simmer.

"Are you sure it wasn't the past?" I asked.

"Positive."

"Then what happened?"

"I told him I'd try once more." He wasn't smiling now. "Maybe I went a little bit too far then."

"What do you mean?"

"Pull over and I'll show you."

He opened his jacket while I pulled off on the shoulder,

tires crunching on frozen slush, and handed me a Polaroid color print. There was Herb Boeltz, in a coffin. He didn't look a day older then he had that night at eight o'clock.

"God!" I said. "You wished him dead?"

He shook his head. "I wouldn't do a thing like that," he said soberly. "I just decided to show him a picture of himself dead. I never thought about it looking like it could be next week or something. I just wanted to see how he liked it with the shoe on his own foot. He turned white as a sheet and just kind of fell on the chair. He sat there staring at nothing and never said another thing."

"Do you think it'll come true? This picture?" I asked.

"I don't know," Jake said. "I don't think so, but I'm not sure."

I shifted back into drive again and pulled onto the pavement, half my attention on driving and the other half on the power of suggestion. Boeltz seemed susceptible. He had at least half-convinced himself that Jake could control, as well as predict, the future.

It turned out that Jake's pictures do not fix the form of the future, or even necessarily predict it closely. Though we learned later that they tended to be quite accurate.

But the picture he showed me wasn't correct, any more than Hilton has an e in it. Because the coffin was covered. About four o'clock the next morning, Herb Boeltz put a .38 pistol barrel in his mouth and pulled the trigger, and there wasn't much the mortician could do to make him presentable.

Jake got a room in the hotel, after all. He said he'd been cramping my style, but maybe I'd been cramping his. He remained as cheerful and friendly as ever. Anna Lahti went back to Duluth, put her property up for sale, and moved down, taking an apartment in the same building as Maggie lived in. A couple of months later, she and Jake got married. Maggie and I took a bunch of wedding pictures, and all they showed were Jake and Anna.

I mentioned that to Jake, jokingly, and he said he wasn't doing pictures these days.

They really are a nice couple, and we went out with them fairly often, despite the age difference. Mostly to dance halls or the ice rink. I even learned to skate, though nowhere nearly as well as all three of them did.

With their example, Maggie and I decided to tie the knot, too. So Lanny was only two and a half years short of his teens; I'd been a teenager once myself. And frankly, he was more likable than I'd been. Jake took a bunch of wedding pictures; he had a brand new Polaroid 680. I couldn't help but wonder. That summer they bought a restaurant and fixed it up really nicely with a Scandinavian motif, bringing a Swede down from Duluth to help with the cuisine. I figured Anna must have had a lot of money, but Maggie said not so far as she'd even known.

Then, one day they asked if we'd like to go to the races that weekend. I supposed they meant at Rockston Downs, only fifty miles away, but instead we *flew* to Maryland! And Jake bought the tickets and rented a car there!

I bet on the same horses he did, and talk about a kick in the tax bracket! We had nothing but winners. A lot of things became clear to me then.

It felt like strange money to me, but the bank was happy with it.

Last evening we celebrated the anniversary of Jake's and my meeting. At their place, a little farm they'd bought just outside town. They'd fixed it up really nicely.

When we got there, I noticed a big book on the table—a folio-sized book on astronomy for the informed layman. Beside it was a brand-new video camera. He told me he had an interesting project going, and asked if we'd care to take a little tour.

Editor's Introduction to "The Weigher," by Eric Vinicoff and Marcia Martin

Graduate departments of political science often claim that comparative government is the heart of their discipline. Certainly the claim has a venerable history. Aristotle made a collection of constitutions of the various Mediterranean city states, and his study of that data base led him to conclude that history is cyclical: monarchy becomes aristocracy, which becomes oligarchy, which becomes republic, which becomes democracy, which decays until rescued by a dictator; dictator becomes tyrant, whose children become monarchs, beginning the process all over. One or another stage may be skipped, and the time required varies, but the cycles are inevitable.

One may not believe the cycles absolutely to see merit in Aristotle's observations. Certainly the study of comparative government is worth while; enough so that we can see the value of examining comparative cultures. Alas, the academic discipline best suited to study comparative civilizations has apparently made a pact that excludes the anthropologists from looking at *successful* cultures. We're running out of primitive peoples for anthropologists to look at; while data gathered by sociologists is generally treated with the respect that discipline deserves.

Science fiction allows us to escape some of those limits. In addition to real governments and cultures we can construct alien societies to examine. Of course that isn't easy to do; at least, not easy to do well. Many writers violate the most elementary rules of self consistency. Fortunately, help is at hand. Jim Funaro of Santa Cruz has put together CONTACT, an annual conference of science fiction writers and anthropologists that promises to teach both professions a very great deal—and is a lot of fun as well.

Some writers don't need conferences. Eric Vinicoff and Marcia Martin have constructed an alien society with rivets—and at the same time showed a glimpse of what humans might be like in a society with clones and near immortality.

The Weigher

Eric Vinicoff and Marcia Martin

Groundplant was a springy blur under my striding paws. The commonland trail followed a gap between two barren mounds—fancifully named Worldgod's Fangs. Ahead I could see the slope running down to the bend in the river and Coalgathering. A gray pelt of fog spread beyond the far bank. The morning was clear but breath-misting cold.

Overslept again, curse it. Even making the best speed my middle-aged bones could manage, I was going to be late opening my stall. At least I wasn't the only one; I smelled that Flatpaws the tanner and a couple of other late risers had passed recently.

I started down. To my left a claw of the eastern mountains reached out almost to the river. On its lower slopes were the mining territories that accounted for Coalgathering's name and existence. The town was a haphazard clustering of dirt streets and black-shingled roofs.

I slowed to a trot as I neared the South Gate, and inspected the town wall. Its poor condition was a continuing headache for me. It was still sturdy enough to keep out dangerous beasts, but just barely. In several places the strongwood logs were loose in their foundations, and many of the crossbeam nails were rusted through.

I dreaded the job of getting the necessary repairs made. The wall was still the only common project ever completed in Coalgathering's turbulent history. It had gone up before my time, after six years of squabbling and eleven deathduels, using up no less than four Weighers. Getting unanimous agreement on *anything* from over four hundred adults was a spinesnapping task. My own pet project—paving the streets so we wouldn't have to mudwade during the wet season—was tied up by the eternal pawful of adults unwilling to pledge their *twilga* even for something so generally useful.

But I would keep on haggling, and if necessary I too would meet stubborn holdouts on the challenge lawn. Aggravation was a way of life for a Weigher.

I stood up on my hindlegs and walked under the stone arch. Even after a night of airing out, the town-smells set my fangs to aching. Most of the stalls were open for business. Many adults were browsing and/or buying, and *tagnami* were scurrying about on errands. Two boats were tied up at the docks, loading coal. Both thunderfish pullers were thrashing in their harnesses, blowing tall plumes of dirty water, anxious to be away from the shore.

The Weigher's stall had a place of honor in the center of town, on the edge of the lush almost scarlet challenge lawn—kept lush by the constant infusions of blood. Since rain hadn't threatened overnight, I had left the wall flaps rolled up to let the river breeze air it out.

I dropped to four legs and loped once around the stall sniffing for any intruders. No fresh scents of adult, *tagnami* or animal. I went in.

I settled gratefully into the chair behind the big old desk. The five other chairs were for clients. Two tall cabinets bracketed my view of the challenge lawn; behind their glass-and-wood doors the shelves were crammed with leatherbound volumes of past *twilga* transactions.

"Slasher! About time you opened! I've been stalking your stall like a nightflier on the hunt for the last half hour!"

I knew him by his scent and hollow-jug voice before I looked up. "Good morning to you, too, Treesap." I said in my best placating tone. Weighers couldn't afford to take offense easily.

I gestured permission to enter. He stomped over and leaned across the desk. "No time to waste, Slasher! I can't see any patients until we settle this."

"Settle what?"

"You won't believe it until you see and smell it. Come on!"

"Will you slow down, for Kraal's sake, and explain what the problem is instead of blowing like a thunderfish?" I pointed to one of the chairs. "Why don't you sit down, take a deep breath, then tell me about it from the beginning?"

"I want you to come over to my stall," he said less violently, but still standing. "There's something there that ... I don't understand. Not that I expect you to explain it to me. But it creates a *twilga* problem that's way beyond me."

I gave up, stood up and followed him out into the bright sunlight.

His stall was at the end of Doctor Street, near the docks. A crowd was gathered around it, in an ugly, snarling mood. As we edged through I found out the reason for the mood. Something was giving off a loathsome, dangerous smell. The fur on the back of my neck rose, and my fangs bared. Protective instinct shoved judgment aside.

No one was getting too close to the stall. Emerging from the crowd, I followed him warily on four legs.

And saw it lying on the planked floor.

Some kind of animal, unlike anything I had ever seen before. Almost as big as an adult, but thinner. It looked arboreal, with hindlegs that ended in lumpy silver paws, and spindly forelegs well suited to hanging onto branches. A slender neck supported a truly hideous head; black knotted fur on top but raw brown flesh everywhere else. Its flat face included round eyes, stubby ears, a monstrous nose and plant-chewing teeth. Its frail body was wrapped in a loose, slick white hide, with a decided lump on its back.

It was dead, of course. I gathered that the claw slashes across its throat had been put there by Treesap. "What happened?" I asked.

"I found it in here rummaging through my medical tools when I arrived this morning, so I killed it."

Perfectly understandable. With a spoor like that you wouldn't want to take any chances. This sort of thing happened every now and then; the wall wasn't a perfect defense against trespassing beasts.

It was a very odd corpse. "I don't think that hide is hide at all. It looks like a covering of some sort. And that lump could almost be a strange style of carrysack."

"So what?"

I hissed at his lack of imagination. "I've never seen, heard or read of any animal like that. Have you?"

Treesap hadn't.

There were several priests in the crowd, who suggested it might be a demon—though unlike any known to serve the Ninety-Nine Gods. The savants present were equally mystified.

"What do you want from me?" I asked Treesap.

"Well, this carcass belongs to me, doesn't it?"

I thought. "No one has claimed ownership?"

"Are you joking! If this monster belongs to someone, I'll deathduel him for unleashing it on me! It's ruining my business—no patients for sure until this place airs out!"

"Hmmm. Since no one has claimed it by now, I see no reason why you can't."

"Good. Rubbertail wants to buy it to cut up and study." The elderly biologist with patches of fur falling out entered the stall, her notebook out. "We haven't been able to negotiate a *twilga*."

"Let's go back to my stall," I said. "I can't think in this reek. It makes me want to kill something."

Once seated in my stall we went to work. It was a long and difficult session. I dug into my books and managed to find a few vaguely similar transactions. I finally named a compensation amount. They agreed—Treesap was unhappy, but not enough to take it to the challenge lawn. We inscribed the transaction, including my fee, in our notebooks. Then they left to haul the corpse over to Science Street.

The rest of the day was pretty dull. All my decisions were accepted. To survive as a Weigher your negotiating skills had to increase as your fighting skills aged. I was still one tough lady, but not quite as tough as in years past. A priest dragged in a worshiper who had fallen behind in his payments for religious instruction. A lovers' spat proved to be less convoluted and emotional than usual. The books yielded ready compensations for the loan of a tool, returning a strayed *tagnami*, letting a neighbor cross a territory and so on.

Things were so slow that I took a break soon after sunzenith. I loped over to Tavern Street, and settled into my usual chair under the painted leather awnings at Snakelegs' Place. The Snake, as everybody called him, brought over a mug of fermented direbeast milk spiced with darter blood. I sipped it, enjoying the warm glow, and chatted with the other regulars.

I smelled Irongut coming up behind me. The short fur on the back of my neck rose, and I felt the wonderful tingling just above the hindthighs. I turned. "Good day."

"Likewise." He smiled broadly. He was big, shaggy and muscular, with the thick fur of young adulthood. Not my usual type. But the charming, mature professionals were getting staid. Irongut was hardly an intellectual predator, but he was pleasant, aromatic and very energetic.

"Care to join me?" I asked.

In answer he sat lithely in the nearest chair, his long tail sticking straight down from the butthole. "Can't stay long. I've got a big pot in the kiln. Just stopped by to find out how you're keeping."

"Not too badly for an old bag of fur. I haven't caught scent of you in a few days. Where have you been hiding?"

His soft growl was sweetly bashful in such a savage young male. I remembered the frame of my bed straining almost to the breaking point, his paws raking my back, the buds of pleasure blossoming one after another. I took deep breaths and managed to retain my dignity. Let him come to me—it wouldn't be fitting for one of my years and stature to howl for him as if he were my first cublove.

He pulled himself together. "I wasn't sure you would want my company again."

"Don't try to fool a Weigher. You were hoping I would come to you. But you must remember that my pride is older and stronger than yours."

"I know that now," he said softly. "Which is why I'm here."

I growled laughter. While we were batting at each other with words, we were both struggling to keep our lust-scents from rising and revealing. But neither of us was being very successful—more of an embarrassment to me than him. If things got any more out of control, the adults in the nearby chairs would notice.

So I tried to push the thoughts and sensations into the back of my mind, and said, "Your pot might crack if you don't get back to it."

His smile turned rigid. "You're right. Maybe we'll catch scent of each other again soon."

"Maybe we will." If he had a nose worthy of the name, he wouldn't need more of an answer.

He trotted off stiffly, trying to look unconcerned. I finished my drink, settled up and went back to my stall.

Finally the sun slanted down behind the hills beyond the river. The boats pulled away from the docks and headed upstream. The stalls closed, and everyone streamed through the gates. The last adults out of town shut and barred the gates.

Amid a din of goodnight conversation we loped away, spreading out on the many commonland trails. The coal territory owners bounced and rattled in their runleg-pulled wagons.

At first I ran with many other adults and *tagnami*— some of the latter on their parents' choke leashes. We chatted as we climbed toward the gap between the Fangs, setting an easy pace. The wind was turning sharp, but the smell of open country was invigorating after the town-reek. Groundplant turned into shadowed forest around us. Our group dwindled as we came to territory after territory until, reaching mine, I also took my leave.

Violet tangletree and fireclaw bush scented the air, over the seasonal rankness of mouldering leaves. Shafts of yellow light slanted through gaps in the trees. Above the gaunt strongwood branches the day was beginning to darken. I was ready for a hearty dinner, and an early bed—I hoped not alone.

The cabin looked and smelled right as I approached it from downwind. It sat in the middle of a small clearing, straddling a creek that ran down to the river. Its strongwood planks were stained black with a waterproofing concoction. I glanced unhappily at several upkeep jobs that needed doing before the first snow, then swung open the doorway bars and went in.

I lit candles to fend off the fast-falling night. Nikniks were starting to chirp beyond the door and windows. The wind carried faint, tantalizing promises of many tasty animals. No rain anywhere near. Perfect hunting weather.

The creek was a trench-like space in the floor planking. I took no more than a sip from it. Hunting on a bloated bladder at my age was asking for indigestion.

The night was complete under the forest canopy. I couldn't see much, even after my darksight adjusted. But this was my territory. I knew every tree and fallen leaf. And I had my nose and ears.

I prowled along the river bank on four legs, and waited for some tasty nocturnal animal to arrive for a 'morning' drink. I settled in behind a millioneye shrub downwind of a favorite watering place for the local fauna. No scent of poachers or predators. Good.

I heard and smelled a family of lumpmeats waddle up to the bank. I tasted rising saliva. Lumpmeats were an acquired taste, but I had acquired it as a cub. Their hard shells and stubby legs gave them the defensive posture of a rock. You had to move like moonlight and decapitate them on the first swipe, before they could retreat into their shells.

I decided on the bulbous head of the family, and charged. The others hid in their shells, but I nailed papa. Out sprang my forepaw claws. Off went the head. The survivors scuttled into the river and floated away while I dined.

Leaving pretty much an empty bowl for the scavengers, I drank from the river and wiped blood from the fur around my mouth. My tail waved happily.

I walked slowly back to the cabin, and stretched out on the bed to relax and digest. The draft blowing through was rich with the tale of the night, and a bit chilly. But not uncomfortably so; I didn't figure on having to use the firehearth until snow covered the ground. Drowsiness began to claim me.

Howling snapped me out of it. Faint howling from the northeast border of my territory.

Not a danger call or a challenge. Not even an entry

request from a visiting friend. It was a lusty mating call. I recognized Irongut's deep baritone.

I felt that tingling again, and suddenly wasn't the least bit sleepy. Should I tighten his leash even more? No, he had learned his lesson—there was an earnest sincerity in the growls. Moreover, my own self-control wasn't nearly as legendary as I sometimes liked to think. My body moaned for him. Enjoy, it said. You won't excite the young males much longer.

I sprang to a window and howled back my invitation. Returning to the bed. I waited and tried to pretend calmness.

Then, nearer, I heard him howl again. I leaped to four legs. A blood challenge! What in the great world womb could he be fighting here on my territory? Most of the large predators had learned better the hard way. Maybe a wild adult had wandered down from the hills, hungry or sick enough to have ignored my warnoffs.

Trespass on my territory! I ran out the door toward the howls, which were subsiding into fighting snarls. Something screamed—a high-pitched shriek that I didn't recognize. Then silence, except for the cautiously returning forest sounds.

I plunged through a thick tangle of shrubs.

In a meadow not far from the cabin, under the light of two newly risen moons, I found Irongut snarling a few strides upwind of his kill.

I caught a whiff of the corpse, and quickly joined Irongut upwind.

He was breathing hard, but otherwise intact. "I offer you *twilga* for hunting on your territory," he said apologetically.

It was a formality, of course. No one could have done anything except attack such an obvious enemy, no matter where encountered. I wasn't the type to worry about technicalities. "It was a trespasser, not part of my game stock. And it sure as death doesn't smell edible. No value, no *twilga*."

We both stared at the creature.

"What is it?" Irongut asked. "I've never seen or smelled the like."

"I have. One was killed in town today. But it's certainly

a new item for the biology texts. Even the savants had no answers."

It was definitely the same species of puny, furless monster. My fangs bared in a soft growl. I edged closer for a careful sniff: all I could stand. "Something is wrong here."

"Huh?"

"This creature smells like the other one."

"So? Probably a pack of them are migrating over the mountains. Believe me, they're no fighters. This one hardly put up a struggle. If any more of them trespass, we'll slaughter them."

"I mean they smell *exactly* alike. Not like the same species or even the same pack—like the *same creature*. But that's impossible. The other one is dead, probably cut up and in jars of alcohol by now."

He shrugged. "One more riddle for the savants."

I noticed a small box lying on the ground next to the corpse. It was white, and slick like varnished wood, but the material didn't look familiar. It had odd tiny features on one side, and a rectangular opening. "Is that yours?" I asked.

"No. The creature was playing with it when I came into the clearing."

"Playing?"

"Taking bits of plants, bugs, leaves and so on, shoving them into the hole in the box, then jabbing at those little bumps on the side."

I was inclined to laugh, but didn't want to hurt his feelings and ruin the night. "How do you think it came by the box?"

"Probably stole it from someone's cabin during the day. If so, we'll most likely hear about it tomorrow."

I took his forepaw in mine. "Let's leave the carcass for the crawlers. I'm in no mood for mysteries tonight." But I decided to return in a few nights, when the spoor would be blown to the winds, to have a better look at the box.

"I'm glad you invited me in," he said softly.

"I'm glad you came."

Our scents were definitely communicating now. I was very aware of my hindthighs rubbing together as I moved.

Without further words, and with ill-concealed haste, we loped toward the cabin.

The Weigher

* * *

I kicked the fur blanket aside and rolled out of bed, getting all four legs under me before landing. Pretty frisky for a mature lady, especially after such a night. Irongut had left shortly before moonset.

It was a fine morning, with a heady blend of forest aromas drifting in through the door and windows. The cloudless sky was beginning to brighten. I had overslept again.

Plunging my head into the creek-trench, I came up howling and shaking off frigid water. At the wall mirror I combed out my fur, one hundred strokes head to hindpaws. I admired myself in the mirror. Still a classic specimen of femininity. Glossy black fur. Gleaming fangs. Boldly jutting snout. Just the right amount of arch in the back. Stomach firm, with no middle-aged droop. The scars across my left shoulder and flank were healing well. They reminded me to check my trap before heading for town.

I went outside. No hostile scents. But, on the other hand, no nearby breakfast. First things first. I loped through the forest and across dew-covered meadows to the border of my territory.

Running the bounds at top speed, I came across no suspicious spoor except the one trail I expected. I squatted and defecated in the usual places. I didn't meet any of my neighbors—I was definitely running late—but I could tell they had already set their warnoffs.

I slunk along a game trail, and managed to chase down a pair of darters before they could scurry up a tree. Then I headed for the trap.

I had dug it on a high slope near the eastern border of my territory, where cubs sometimes wandered down from the hills to hunt. Game tended to be more plentiful in the territories because we had settled the best land to begin with, and then purged it of all predators but ourselves.

As I approached the trap, I could smell a cub in it. I peered over the edge of the six foot pit. A healthy looking little furball about seven or eight years old. Perfect. Younger than that they weren't mature enough to handle *tagnami* education. And older, if still wild, they were unteachable. But this one would do just fine.

It stood on its hindpaws, trying to claw its way out of

the pit. It eyed me warily, and stank of fear. I wondered if it could have been one of mine. I had gone into the Wild four times to drop cubs. But no, the timing wasn't right for any of them.

Some education and discipline, and this one (a male) would make a fine replacement for Keeneyes. Too bad it hadn't been Keenbrain—my *tagnami* had been a bit too greedy and a bit too slow. A fatal combination. He had posted his challenge before reaching his fighting peak, convinced that the old lady had aged enough to be taken. He had been wrong, barely. So now I needed a new *tagnami* to do the scut work (and maybe someday take my job and territory and life from me as I had from my parent).

Enough daydreaming. I jabbed a forepaw down into the pit, managed to avoid the young claws, and got him by the scruff of the neck. Up and out. He yowled and squirmed, so I cuffed him unconscious. I perched the limp body on my back and set out for town.

The added weight slowed me a bit, and I arrived even later than yesterday. I went straight to School Street and old Bentback's stall. He was, as usual, at his chalkboard trying to beat some sense into about a dozen cubs. They were chained to two log benches while he alternately taught and applied his short rawhide whip.

"Morning, Slasher." Bentback growled, coming over to me. He took the cub and looked at it with a skilled eye, casually avoiding the tiny claws—it was waking up. "Going to try again, eh?"

"You know how it is. Can't live with them or without them."

"The real trick is outliving them. Got a name for this one?"

I hadn't thought about it, so I did now. The cub was a bit short for his age. "How about Runt?"

"With a name like that, he'll either grow up into a great fighter or die young."

"That's the general idea."

We brought out our notebooks and writing sticks. "What's your current rate?" I asked.

"Three per day for as long as it takes."

"Pretty steep. I can do better down the street."

"You get what you pay for. I limit my class size to give individual attention."

"So be it." We checked our notebooks and found a balance in my favor from a Weighing last month. We subtracted a day's fee and entered the new balance. My job gave me *twilga* with almost everyone in town; no need to play around with third party balances.

Bentback took Runt and a length of chain over to an empty spot at the end of a log. "See you at dusk," he growled to me.

I hurried along Breeder Street toward my stall. The aromas raised saliva even though I had just eaten. Growls, bleets, chitterings, cheeps, honks and haggling created an ear-curdling din. I admired the pens filled with direbeasts, lumpmeats, darters; literally every kind of game animal.

My territory was pretty well stocked at the moment. But come the end of snow season it would need restocking. Then I would make the necessary purchases. Reluctantly, because no one liked doing business with breeders. They were an odd, less-than-respectable lot, suspected of 'stalking' meals in their pens and other dark deeds.

I opened my stall. Business was brisk, so much so that I almost forgot about the less pleasant of my two nocturnal visitors. Irongut, however, was a warm and finely etched memory, and a promise of even better nights to come.

After a morning flurry of decisions and non-lethal challenges stemming mostly from a by-all-accounts excellent hunt-party at Treeroot's place, I took advantage of the lull to relax. Leaning back in my chair, I put my hindlegs up on the desk. I was too comfortable to get up. I wished a mug of warm fermented milk would appear on my desk in a bolt of sorcerous lightning.

Peripherally I noticed something was happening outside. I couldn't tell what, but from all around town adults were converging on the challenge lawn. No ordinary fight would draw such a big crowd, and besides everyone was looking at the sky. Curiosity got the better of comfort. I got up and went outside.

Leaden gray clouds hung low overhead, and a cold rain was imminent. But that wasn't the object of everyone's attention.

Something was falling from the sky. Not really falling,

but coming down slowly, like a swampflower's seed sac. But this was round, white and *huge*—bigger than a demonflier. A smaller object was dangling underneath it, attached by long ropes.

It was coming down in the middle of the challenge lawn.

The losers of the morning's festivities had long since left to visit their doctors. A napping Traveler hastily vacated the lawn, and the entire circle was empty. But, by the time the thing was about to land, it was ringed by curious adults. Including me.

The smaller object settled onto the red groundplant. Somehow I wasn't surprised to see it was another of the outlandish creatures that suddenly seemed determined to plague my life. Standing erect on its hindlegs, it touched its chest with a forepaw and the ropes pulled free. The huge white ball rose sharply, taking the ropes along. In seconds all were swallowed by the clouds.

The creature had a glass bowl over its head, but otherwise it looked exactly like the other two. Its spoor hadn't reached me yet on the still air, but I would have taken any wager that it smelled the same, too.

Everyone was enjoying the unique show. A few priests were crying of a divine coming, but no rational adult could really believe that this puny, tailless, evil creature hailed from any god-home.

The creature lifted the bowl from its head, and dropped it on the lawn. It stared at us in silence. Slowly it raised its odd right forepaw in the air, the pad facing front and all five claw-tips sticking up.

Savants were arguing eagerly among themselves. The upshot of one debate near me was that this must certainly be an intelligent being, maybe even as intelligent as an adult. The ball-and-ropes could have been some sort of monstrous unknown animal. But the white hide of yesterday's corpse had turned out to be a manufactured garment, like harsh weather cloaks though exotic in design and material. Under it Rubbertail had found more of the hideous brown flesh. This hide looked identical. And the carrysack was also identical—the carrysack that had turned out to be filled with things that were mostly total mysteries.

The priests, on the other hand, were stirring themselves up with talk about demons and ill omens.

The situation was definitely novel. Everybody was waiting for someone to take the initiative in doing something about it. There wasn't any time for a town meeting. I could see that some of our more notorious hotheads, notably Farrunner the iron-worker, were baring their fangs. That terrible spoor was beginning to spread. Many others in the crowd were awaiting a rare battle with hopeful grins.

I remembered the box I had seen last night, and was prepared to go along with the idea that the creature was intelligent. Though not very, or it wouldn't have come so docilely to its dying place. But the questions the savants were asking each other were also bouncing around inside my skull. What was it? Where did it come from? How many more of them were there? Why were they popping up all of a sudden?

But it didn't look like the savants would get the chance to put their questions to the creature. Farrunner took three strides toward it, then turned to face us. "I post a challenge! This beast is evil and dangerous; you can all smell that! Do any of you want to interfere?"

The priests looked pleased with this development. Some of the other hotheads were upset at being excluded from the fun, but Farrunner had a well deserved reputation. No one challenged his posting. He smiled smugly at the savants, who growled under their breaths but didn't dare object aloud. Savants were rarely great fighters. The creature didn't react.

Howls were coming from all around the ring. The mood was definitely for blood. I felt the rage too, but fought to control it. Weighers were supposed to look beyond obvious answers, and exercise self-discipline while doing so. Killing these creatures every time one turned up wouldn't solve any of the riddles.

I stepped forward. "Wait up, Farrunner. This is something that has never happened before. It may be more complicated than it seems."

"No complications, Slasher. I'll just let its blood out."

"I think you should let some of the savants have it. I'll work out a fair *twilga*."

"I'll be very glad to sell the carcass," Farrunner growled. "Don't interfere, you old bitch."

That did it. I had tried to be polite. I had tried to be reasonable. But the young punk had a venom-soaked tongue. I wasn't sure I could take him, but life without pride was a cold thing anyway. Moreover, I had a hunch that the answers to my questions might be too important— and not just to the savants—to let them bleed to death on the challenge lawn.

"I challenge, mudworm."

So much for the formalities. He dropped to four legs, and so did I. The nearest spectators moved back. The creature continued to watch in patient silence.

We circled each other warily. He knew my reputation, too. We hissed at each other, but spoke no more words.

Strategy, girl. Strategy. He was too big, strong and mean to charge. So what did I have in my favor? Experience, maybe. I would have to try to outguess him.

An all or nothing proposition.

I slunk forward to within three strides of him. Pouncing range. A wary veteran would have looked over all the angles first, but he wasn't known for his patience.

He lunged, a furry blur almost too quick to be seen. Claws raked for my throat.

But my planned countermove was also a blur. Not sideways; that was the expected reaction. His horizontal slash covered too wide an arc for me to avoid. I dropped under the claws, and sprang forward.

My timing had to be perfect. It was. There was his undefended neck right in front of me.

His claws tore desperately at my back. I lost some fur and flesh. But my fangs bit deeply into the tough neck muscle. Arterial blood spurted. My jaws clamped shut, and ripped.

I spat out fur and warm meat; cannibalism was considered in very bad taste. Farrunner dropped. His life poured out onto the lawn, at first swiftly, then sluggishly, then no more.

My regular doctor loped toward me with that *twilga* gleam in his eye, but I growled him back. Time enough for that later. The blood staining the fur on my left flank wasn't too wide a stream, and the pain was no worse than I had known and endured many times before.

The creature was still standing and staring.

Now I owned everything that had been Farrunner's. I didn't want any of it—his territory wasn't nearly as nice as mine—so I would probably sell it to his *tagnami*. But now I had a more urgent matter to worry about.

"I'm claiming the challenge-right for this creature!" I shouted to the spectators. "Anyone feel luckier than Farrunner?"

Several other hotheads looked and smelled inclined to take me up on my invitation. The general mood was definitely getting ugly. I felt the same unreasoning hatred of the creature distorting my own judgment. Any moment now we would all fall upon it in a slaughtering frenzy, despite my challenge-right. How could something so puny and helpless have such a dangerous scent?

It was as simple as that.

"Rubbertail!" I shouted at the nearby cluster of savants. "Do you have any jars of alcohol in your stall?"

She looked wounded. "A tragedy is about to happen here! This is no time for guzzling!"

"You old fool! If you want to save this creature for science, run like a cub and bring me a big jar of alcohol!"

She reflected for a moment, then smiled broadly. She vanished beyond the ring, but quickly returned with a sizeable ceramic jar. "Here you are, Slasher," she panted.

I took it. "We'll settle the *twilga* later!"

Just in time. Some adults had dropped to four legs and were slinking toward the creature, fangs bared. I shouted, "Wait, my friends! Please! A moment for your Weigher! I think I can end the danger!"

There were growls of protest, but the slinking stopped momentarily.

I took a deep breath, and walked toward the creature. What would it do? If it tried to bolt, we were both out of luck.

It stood still. It watched me steadily, though, as I removed the jar's lid and poured the contents all over it. It flinched, but didn't try to avoid the stinging alcohol. Maybe it understood.

I breathed as shallowly as possible. The alcohol murdered my nose, but the scent of the creature was totally drowned. I found I could now deal with it with a Weigher's proper dispassion.

It stood as if it never dropped to four legs. The forepaws were slender and frail-looking, but well shaped for working with tools. The lack of a tail made it seem unbalanced.

I could feel the blood-rage seeping out of the spectators. The prospects for a unique death-duel were fading fast; some adults were already drifting back to their stalls. The attitude of the rest was subsiding into curiosity.

The creature reached into its carrysack and pulled out a small gray box with two short black strings dangling from it. The strings ended in a pair of black bulbs like half-eggs. It put one of them to its forehead, and it stuck there. The creature held out the other one to me, twisting its mouth in some kind of expression.

I thought I knew what it wanted, but wasn't sure I wanted to oblige. It could have been a harmless friendship ritual. Or something else.

Some savants were edging up behind me, chattering like grakklbirds in mating season. A few priests came with them.

To the netherworld with it! I stuck the other bulb to my forehead.

The creature touched a red circle on the box.

Three seconds later I ripped the bulb from my forehead, and howled like a cub.

Images had stampeded through my mind like a herd of spooked bigmeats. Hundreds. Hundreds of hundreds. Much too fast to be seen, but I sensed that some of them were my own memories. Others were . . . from somewhere else. I shivered, and had no desire to see those more clearly.

The creature put the demon-box back in its carrysack. "Are you able to understand me?" it asked.

The discussion behind me jumped several notches in volume. The words from the oddly flat muzzle were just barely understandable. "Yes," I replied, "If you speak very slowly."

"That's good. My name is Ralphayers."

"I'm Slasher. What did you just do to me?"

"The box is a tool for learning languages quickly. It isn't harmful."

I didn't believe in magic. But if it was a product of science, this ugly monster knew things of which our savants only dreamed. "We can settle the *twilga* for that later, Ralphayers, and for my other service."

"Other service?"

"Keeping you alive. So far, at least."

"I see. I'm a stranger here, with different customs. But I'll follow yours as soon as I can learn them."

"What are you? Where do you come from?"

The creature paused before answering. "Just as this world circles your sun, other worlds circle other stars. I'm from one of them called Earth."

That was a mighty big bite to get down. Still, the astronomy matched certain radical theories. And nothing even remotely like this creature was known to our biology— or demonology for that matter. So accept it as a working hypothesis. "How did you get here? And why?"

"My people built a . . . a skyboat. It sailed here on a voyage of many years, crewed only by machines, and it now circles this world. When the machines found that living conditions here were like Earth's, they . . . grew three of me from embryos stored aboard. Each of us landed in turn to learn what we could about this world before dying. That wasn't long for my two brothers."

The savants were taking all this in avidly, as were the few others who remained. I understood maybe a third of what it had said, but I went on doggedly. "What do you do with this information you gather?"

"The skyboat . . . hears everything that happens to us. It sends messages back to our world. They will take years to arrive there, so we can't talk to our world. But we can communicate with the skyboat."

So that was why the other creature had been putting plants and bugs in its box. It had been doing some kind of research. Fascinating. Obviously this was a venture involving more participants and *twilga* than I had ever imagined possible. What incredible Weighers they must have!

"Why are you doing this?" I asked. "What could possibly repay such a huge effort?"

"Pure knowledge. We're a very curious people. Plus we've found that indulging our hunger for knowledge can be profitable in practical terms. To learn about your people and your world I hope to live among you."

"That won't be easy," I pointed out. "You know nothing of our customs, and one mistake will most likely be your last. You can't even come near us without being doused in something with an overpowering smell."

"I think I understand why your people killed my brothers," the creature said softly. "An instinctive scent-hostility trigger. An oddly primitive trait to find in an intelligent species. So I smell like an enemy, do I?"

I growled yes. What a prize this creature would be if I could handle the opportunity properly. It clearly knew things many adults would pay through the snout to learn. And it would need an intermediary, someone with the imagination to exploit its knowledge for everyone's good, and the skill to keep it alive. Who better than a Weigher? Who else would have the wisdom to work for the town as well as herself? Who else would be able to unravel the unique *twilga* involved?

The gods don't like to hear us praise our abilities too much, even in our thoughts. As I dreamed, my common sense slept. And I saw a blurred motion behind the creature.

I had forgotten there was one person who would hold a grudge against the creature not based on scent. One to whom the honor won by finishing his father's last task would justify the deadly risk of offending me by usurping my challenge-right.

Before I could react the creature dropped, bright red blood puddling under it, the head almost detached from the scrawny neck. I glared across the carcass at Farrunner's *tagnami*.

A more impetuous adult in my place would have challenged him for his audacity. But I was a Weigher, and anyway I admired his loyalty. A rare trait in today's youth.

"I offer *twilga* in apology," he said formally.

I stared at the creature, feeling a sadness greater than I understood. So many things we might have learned.

To the *tagnami* I said, "I accept. Wait for me a moment. We'll go to my stall and settle the amount."

Those who had been hoping for a last bit of blood from us headed back to their stalls. A few closed in to gawk at the carcass. I quickly made deals with two savants for it and its carrysack. Then I let my doctor guide my less-than-steady legs toward his stall for the overdue patch job. Farrunner's heir—*tagnami* no longer—followed me dutifully. I intended to punish his insolence with a *twilga* settlement he would be years repaying.

Weeks passed, and life settled back to normal, though speculations about the creatures were growing into epic legends. The first snows came, draping the forests and meadows in scattered whiteness. The days became shorter. Adults spent less time in town and more time laired in their territories, living on scarce game and winter-fat.

But Weighers were expected to be available as many days as possible. So it was that on a gray threatening afternoon I sat in my stall, warming my hindpaws over a small hearthfire.

I had just settled a debt problem without any challenges, and I felt indecently pleased with myself. Longfur had been dragged in by a pawful of adults with whom he had been tardy in paying his *twilga*. Had he been a real deadbeat I would have given him the usual options of settling up at once or fighting his creditors in a circle challenge. But he was a responsible adult whose fermented milk trade had temporarily slumped. So I worked out a *twilga* increase and installment payments that satisfied everyone.

My relaxed mood was interrupted when someone outside shouted, "More of them! Come and see, everyone! More of them!"

I stepped out into the windless but still biting chill. A priest was pointing at the clouds. Everyone within earshot also looked, but most of them, having seen it before, paid no further attention.

Still, a pawful of savants and priests joined me in hurrying to the challenge lawn.

Not one, but two creatures were falling from the sky. They landed the same way the other had, and removed the bowls from their heads. One was another exact copy. But the other was shorter, a bit thinner and curiously curved.

"Welcome!" I shouted. The other adults stood silently

at the lawn's edge, honoring my outstanding challenge-right.

"Good to see you again, Slasher," the Ralphayers copy answered.

"Are you trying to make me believe in ghosts?" I asked after a pause. "The others like you are all dead."

"Everything my brothers did I remember. So I feel I know you." He and the other creature started to walk toward me.

"Stay where you are." I warned them, "unless you want to be turned into memories, too. Stay where we can't smell you."

Their faces twisted. The smaller creature said in a high-pitched tone. "I think we'll be safe from that danger at least."

I realized two startling facts just as shouts from some of the savants announced them. First, both creatures were speaking our language just as naturally as any townfolk. Second and more important, the faint whiffs of their spoor were totally unlike the evil scent of the others.

They smelled like . . . like groundflowers! Harmless, pleasant flowers. There were no growls from those gathered behind me. If anything, there were a few purrs.

"Are you like the nightslitherer that can change its scent?" I asked.

"No," the copy said. "But when the machines aboard the skyboat grew us after my last brother died, they made changes in our body design so that we can live among you. My brothers had collected the necessary knowledge. We can eat your plants and animals—we're omnivores."

Roots and leaves? I shuddered.

"We want to learn as much as possible about you and your world," the smaller one added. "This will be a long study, one we hope our *tagnami* will continue when we die. They must, since the skyboat machines can grow no more of us."

Here was a second chance at their incredible knowledge. If I could keep these two alive. "You must learn our customs quickly. You obviously aren't fighters, so you must learn how not to offend."

The copy paused. "We're more dangerous fighters than you can imagine. But we're here to make friends and learn. Like my brothers, we would rather die than fight you. We love life as much as you do, but we believe in what we're doing even more."

I would attempt to figure that out later. Right now I had the greatest *twilga* transaction in history to arrange. It would be the stuff of legends among Weighers, and would of course compensate me handsomely.

"You'll need someone to teach you our customs and vouch for you with fang and claw until the town accepts you."

The smaller one said, "We have a store of scientific and technological information aboard the skyboat, which we can summon through our machines. Some of it should be of use to you. We'll give it to you."

I shuddered again. Luckily no one else had been close enough to hear. "*Never* offer to give an adult anything!" I said sharply. "It could prove fatal."

"Why?"

They had so much to learn. What kind of crazy customs did they live by? "To suggest an adult needs help as if she were a *tagnami* is the worst possible insult. You must *sell* your knowledge for a good price, and thereby establish your worth."

The creatures jabbered at each other in low voices. Then the smaller one said, "We'll have to hire the services of someone who can teach us what we need to know."

"Of course, and I recommend myself for the job. I'm the town Weigher, an excellent haggler, well educated—and a tough fighter, to deal with any challenges that come your way."

"What's a Weigher?" the copy asked.

"We balance the values of goods, services and violations of custom so adults can interact more constructively. And less violently."

"You . . . run the town?"

"I don't understand your question. Adults run their own territories and town affairs."

The creatures jabbered some more. "We accept your offer," the copy said, "and trust you to set a fair price for your agent and guide services. How do we begin?"

I thought. "First we have to get you a territory. Let me

think ... ah, the Coldcrag place. I'm sure I can get it for you cheaply. The game stock is lousy."

"No problem there. We can eat many plants that grow in this area."

"Good." I hid my real reaction to their diet. "I'll get you installed there, start your education in our customs, and smooth the trail for you here in town."

That last didn't look as though it would be too difficult. The savants and priests were gathered around, hanging on every word. Not too close—they had heard my commitment to handle challenges for the creatures. That claw slashed both ways.

"Go back to whatever you were doing!" I shouted at them. "You'll all have the chance to quench your curiosity later, at a very modest *twilga*."

The adults drifted away reluctantly. The three of us were soon alone on the challenge lawn. "Come with me while I negotiate for the territory and some other essentials for you." I said to them. "I strongly suggest you say and do nothing unless I tell you to."

I set out for Broker Street, and they followed behind like a pair of well-trained *tagnami*.

The next few ten-days were as hectic as any I could recall. As well as tending my territory, my new *tagnami* and my Weighing, I had the two humans (their name for themselves) to look after. And in many ways they were as helpless as Runt.

I negotiated a very good *twilga* with the broker handling the Coldcrag territory. On the long walk out to it I learned the copy was also named Ralphayers, and was a male adult, while the other was Pamayers, a female adult. The scarcity of game and the dilapidated cabin didn't bother them; they found plenty of edible plants. I was surprised by how they acted like a single adult in many things (even their living arrangements!). But they seemed even more surprised when I explained how they had to mark their bounds.

Artisans were hired to patch up the cabin—including such bizarre notions as a solid wood door and glass window covers. Others scratched behind their ears in confusion, then produced furniture unlike anything ever seen before. I was at their cabin when another balloon dropped from the sky, bringing an adult-high metal cylinder from which the humans removed an amazing assortment of items. I was right about their ineptness as hunters, but with new breeding stock and a cheat they called a bow they managed to bring down some meat.

Coming up with the *twilga* for all this was no problem. The humans were able to supply valuable knowledge on just about any subject. Savants, artisans, professionals, tradesfolk, adults in every field; the trickle of customers became a rushing stream, then a broad and powerful river. Thanks in no small part to my agenting. The humans rejected some requests because the knowledge was too advanced to be of use, and others because it might be dangerous. But that still left more than enough business.

Teaching them civilized behavior was the hardest part of my job, and for the first few ten-days I had all I could handle keeping them alive. But by the time the days reached their shortest they were settled in and reasonably accepted.

As usual, I was puffing for breath when I reached the border of the humans' territory. The scrawny woods climbing the mountain's paws were as far from town as you could get before finding yourself in the Wild. The snow-draped pricklytrees and redberry bushes were far apart and positively anemic.

I howled for permission to enter. Moments later I heard the three horn blasts granting permission—neither human had the lung power for entry calls.

Their cabin sat on a granite shelf overlooking the river valley below Coal-gathering. It was now by far the largest I have ever seen, with no less than five rooms for the various odd human activities.

Ralphayers stood by the open door. "Welcome, Slasher. Care to come inside?"

Flower smell or not, being inside their boarded-up cabin made my jaws ache. But I knew the humans found snow and near-freezing temperatures uncomfortable. "Okay."

They had a warm fire going in the wall hearth (one of their highly profitable innovations) of their "living room." Pamayers was seated at a table reading a book aloud. The strange box they called a "radio" was in front of her. The humans had a fantastic appetite for our books; recent purchases were stacked all around the floor. "Hi, Slasher," she said. "What's happening?"

My visit had an ulterior purpose. I didn't see how talking my problem over with them could help, but they were full of surprises and I was out of ideas. Still, politeness dictated some small talk first. "How are your studies coming?"

"Incredibly," Pamayers said, putting down the book. Ralphayers sat in a chair by the fire, while I stretched out on a rug. "There's so much data to collect, digest and relay to the skyboat for transmission home. We're beginning to unravel a few of the tough questions about your people."

"Such as?" I asked.

"Such as why you're intelligent."

They were always raising the sort of topics that caused me headaches. "I hope you're not looking at me for an answer. You should talk to old Rubbertail and the other biologists."

"We have. Our working hypothesis is that you evolved intelligence as protection against a danger bigger than starvation or hostile predators: yourselves. With your territorial instinct and year-round breeding there must have always been tremendous population pressure and competition for the best land. The smarter adults fought better, and figured out ways to avoid more fights. They tended to be the survivors and breeders."

That made a vague kind of sense. "Our earliest legends tell of adults fighting over territories to the verge of racial extinction, until the hero brings peace by establishing a primitive version of our present customs."

"They're probably accurate," Pamayers commented, "except the 'hero' was more likely a long and difficult socialization process. From simple live-and-let-live at watering holes to your towns, territories and *twilga*."

Ralphayers was staring at me. "You didn't come here for a scholarly discussion. Out with it, Slasher."

"Okay. But first we have to settle the *twilga* I'll owe you for your advice."

"Don't be silly." Ralphayers said. "It's the least we can

do, after all that you've—" He caught himself, helped by Pamayers' frown as well as my rising growl. "Sorry. The standard fee will be fine by us. What's your problem?"

"You walk in it every time you go to town, or rather swim in it. The dirt streets. I've been trying for years to get everyone to pledge *twilga* to get them paved."

"We remember your sales pitch," Pamayers said. "Surely the whole town would want to chip in for something like that."

I laughed bitterly. "You couldn't get everyone to agree the sun rises in the east. I've whittled the holdouts down to four, but I can't budge them. Any suggestions?"

The humans jabbered at each other in their own language, then Ralphayers said to me, "Your problem is inherent in your social system. It's why you have progressed relatively slowly in fields requiring group effort. Don't you have any customs for resolving such impasses?"

"If the need were great enough, I could challenge them. But it isn't. All that leaves is persuasion."

"We have a suggestion. It stretches your ethical structure a bit, but we don't think it's an outright break."

"I'm listening."

"Check our *twilga* book, and see if we have balances with your holdouts."

I did. "Yes. Quite large ones."

"Good. What you do is use them as a lever. Since you do our shopping, suppose you decided to use all of our *twilga* with the holdouts right now?"

"They couldn't possibly cover that much additional debt. They would have to scramble to arrange extensions, the value of their *twilga* would go way down—it'd hurt."

"Suppose you pointed this danger out to them, but at the same time you offered not to do it—if they chip in on the street paving?"

The idea whirled around under my skull, making me dizzy. I didn't know how to react. It could work. But was it right?

"What . . . what is the *twilga* balance? You supply your *twilga* . . ."

"No, we haven't any *twilga* interest in this at all," Ralphayers said. "We get our debts paid either way. The only *twilga* transaction I see is between you, acting for the town, and the holdouts. The town gets its paved streets, the holdouts pay their share, and their paws stay unmuddy too."

I felt like I had drunk too much fermented milk. By Kraal, it might just be the answer! A whole herd of possibilities for town improvements stampeded past my mind's eye. "I'll give it a try."

We settled the *twilga* for the advice, talked a little longer, then I left. I was anxious to get back to town to try out the humans' idea.

I decided to test it on the most intractable of the holdouts. I found Shrubfur stoking her forge in preparation for working some iron. She took off her leather apron and walked over to me. Her hostile scent arrived first. "Afternoon, Slasher," she rumbled. "You here to harangue me about the paving again?"

"Afraid so."

"Look, I tell you and I tell you. I can't afford it. And even if I could, why waste hard-earned *twilga* on useless luxuries? A bit of mud never hurt anyone."

"That's a very narrow point of view."

She growled. "Are you insulting me?"

"No, of course not," I said quickly. "But ... Shrubfur my friend, you have a problem. I'm here to help you with it if I can."

"What problem?"

"You've run up quite a large debt to the humans for the information about that metal they call steel. I hope you can cover it—all of it—since I'm going shopping for them today."

She bared her fangs nervously. "I ... I assumed ... with so many others owing them too ..."

"That's true, of course. I could use other adults' *twilga* today. The choice is mine."

It took a few moments for the implication to penetrate the dense stuff between her ears. Then she tensed as if about to attack, and I tensed, too. But she managed to control herself. "I suppose the humans won't accept installment payments with interest?" she growled.

"You suppose correctly."

"I could challenge them over this!"

"I stand in their place," I reminded her. "Part of my job."

"I might still win," she said thoughtfully.

"Not likely. But even if you did, you would be known as an adult who doesn't honor her *twilga*. Who would sell to you or buy from you then?"

She just stood there, looking like she wanted to howl in pain. I knew how she felt. Finally she growled, "I agree to pay a share for the street paving. But don't think this ends the matter. You're doing a bad thing. Very bad!"

I quickly got out of range of the reek of her hate, and visited the other three holdouts in turn. The results and their reactions were all the same. Their anger didn't worry me; these things passed.

I was glowing with success as I handled Weighing cases in my stall the rest of the day. Tomorrow I would contract for the paving job and start redeeming pledges.

Which might explain why I didn't notice—then—the paucity of clients, or the groups of adults that stopped talking when I passed, or the whispers at my back.

At sundown I picked up Runt at school and loped for home. I was still lost in thoughts of which brickwrights could do the best and cheapest work, and didn't miss the usual friendly goodnights. Even Irongut's.

We reached the cabin as darkness closed around it. Runt was learning fast; he growled "Mommy" softly and didn't fight as I chained him in the corner on his training blanket.

"Yes, Mommy loves you," I said, scratching behind his ears. "But if you mess off of your blanket again you'll wear it. Are you hungry?"

Runt jumped up and down, and howled.

"Me too. I'll bring something tasty back for you."

The hunting was long and cold. The snow was so deep in the open that I made better time on two legs. I moved through the gaunt leafless trees like a spirit from a ghost legend. I was on the verge of giving up and going to bed hungry when I found and dug out a borer burrow. Not the most delicious meat, but in snow season you couldn't be choosy.

I was returning to the cabin with two of the dirty little fleshbags for Runt when I heard Irongut's entry cry.

An unexpected pleasure? Our relationship had cooled perceptibly since I started acting for the humans. He was pretty conservative for a young adult, and didn't approve of the changes they were causing.

If this was a romantic visit, I was all in favor. I howled permission, and hurried back to the chain to feed Runt and run a quick comb through my fur.

The moment he stepped through the doorway I smelled trouble. He wasn't lusty; he was trying to hide nervousness. "Evening," I said lightly. Be careful, I told myself. Something is up.

"Good to see you, Slasher." He went over to the hearth I had just lit. "I haven't caught scent of you much lately. You've been so busy with your creatures. I've missed you."

"Humans, *gorwana*." Love-words came naturally between us now. "And I've missed you too. How's business?"

"Lousy. The new kilning techniques you sold to the other ceramic artisans have almost made me obsolete."

"You can consult the humans too."

His scent turned hostile. "I don't want any unnatural knowledge, not a bit of it. Even if I never sell another pot." He stopped, and tried what he probably thought was a convincing show of passion. "But I didn't come here to argue morality, *gorwana*. I came to be with you." He closed, and started licking behind my left ear.

I backed away. "Okay, it's truth time. What are you trying to accomplish?"

"Huh?"

"Do you think I'm a fresh-caught *tagnami* you can trick? You insult me. You aren't in a romantic mood, so why are you really here?"

"I . . . wanted to talk to you."

"About what?"

"About . . . uh . . . Weighing. You know I'm very interested. I thought we might—"

"Irongut, *gorwana*, you don't get enough practice to be a convincing liar. You're here for a reason you won't admit." I could only think of one subject about which he might feel the need to lie to me. "It's something to do with the humans, isn't it?"

Silence.

"Kraal curse it, Irongut, go home. You aren't welcome

on my territory. I'm going to visit the humans, make sure they're okay."

He moved to block the doorway. "No. That's why I came, to keep you out of it."

"Out of what?" More silence. "If you aren't going to talk to me, get out. You won't fight me, but I may have to walk over you if you don't move."

He couldn't outglare me, and finally stepped aside. "Please stay here tonight," he begged. "With me or without me. You can't help the humans."

You could have sliced iron with my anger. "You know about my duty to them. I'm going. If you tell me what I'm walking into, it might help me avoid trouble."

He thought that through, then said in a low growl. "Word spread quickly about the immoral trick you used to put over the street paving. Many of us feel the humans are the source of this evil among many others. So Shrubfur and a pawful of others plan to visit Coldcrag tonight. For a circle challenge."

Overkill, I thought. Any one adult could kill both humans without much effort; I didn't see the need for multiple challenges, except maybe moral support. "Violating my challenge-right! Skulking behind my back! You thought I would ignore this shame if I had no chance to prevent it! No! I'll buy my honor back with blood, if it comes to that!"

"I—"

"Go home, Irongut." My voice softened. "I forgive you. Your heart is in the right place, though Kraal knows where your brain is."

"What are you going to do?" he asked.

"My job."

Irongut backed out the doorway, reeking worry and sorrow. "The humans are dangerous, and very bad luck. I hope you survive the night, *gorwana*." Then he was gone.

I rushed around the cabin, filling my carrysack with things I would need. I had enough imagination to see the only two possible outcomes of what I had to do. Neither was good. I would have felt ill except for the heat of anger that burned away all lesser emotions.

Unchaining Runt, I left him sleeping on his blanket.

"Sleep well, my little furball. Tomorrow it's back to the Wild for you, unless the new owner needs a *tagnami*."

The tears in my eyes dried quickly as I ran at top speed across meadows that were pale white in the moonlight, and through grave-black forest, to the commonland trail.

Even during snow season there was gaunt beauty for the discerning eye; smells of life dying and awaiting rebirth. But my mind was busy adding details to my plan. It depended on my reaching Coldcrag first—a reasonable possibility, since my territory was closer to it than Shrubfur's. Plus the fact that circle challenges usually required a lot of negotiation to settle the individual rights.

I stretched my stride until icicles tore at my lungs, but the snow dragged at my legs. Before long I was panting and aching. Kraal, I *was* getting old!

I sniffed the light breeze, and paused every so often to listen, but I seemed to be alone in the night. The territories I passed were quiet. Was I early, or too late?

I reached the border of Coldcrag still without any sign of the circle challengers. Even in an emergency like this I couldn't enter without the humans' permission—*I* wasn't here to issue a challenge. I howled an entry cry.

Minutes passed. If the deed was already done, I would return home. In the morning I would set out to identify the challengers and regain my honor. But that wouldn't bring the humans back to life. I was beginning to think of them as friends as well as business associates.

The horn sounded entry permission. I must have roused them from sleep. Good, so far. I ran up the slope as though demons were on my trail. Maybe there were.

Ralphayers opened the door, shivering from the cold. Pamayers stood behind him; her candle was the only light in the dark cabin. "Is something wrong?" she asked.

"Very wrong. Get your traveling gear, quick. We're leaving here now."

"Huh? Why?" Ralphayers stifled a yawn.

"A group of adults is heading here to kill you two. They may be closing in right now."

"You're . . . you're sure about this?"

"Yes, yes, yes! But don't believe me—stick around and see them for yourself. You'll get to participate in one of our quaint rituals called a circle challenge. You won't enjoy it."

"Why? What have we done?"

"You didn't do it; I did. I listened to you instead of my common sense. No time for this now. Move or stay!"

They had carrysacks filled with equipment for their frequent research trips into the Wild; they stuffed them with food, then slung them over their backs after putting on more of their strange pelt substitutes for warmth. They kept talking to each other in their own language. I poked my head out the door.

The breeze was rolling down the slope, so I heard them before I smelled them. They were on the humans' territory, spread out to prevent escape, and closing in on the cabin clearing. At least seven. I couldn't see them; a broken twig here, a whisper there told me where they were. They weren't being particularly stealthy, since they didn't expect much opposition from the humans.

Time to enlighten them. I howled the traditional trespass challenge, then added, "I'm here! Slasher! I'm here to accept any and all challenges of Ralphayers and Pamayers! I suggest you turn around and slink away before your debt becomes too large to let you survive!"

I admired my bravado. I might win the first two or three challenges, but even my ego couldn't pretend I'd live to complete the circle. They knew it, too. Shrubfur's voice came from the black forest eaves. "Return to your territory, Slasher, while you can. You've been seduced by these evil creatures, but when their influence is gone you'll be one of us again."

"I'm more respectable than any of you! I'm not afraid of new ideas, or in need of a skulking pack when an *adult* would hunt alone!"

That insult ended rational discussion. Howling rose in all directions, coming closer, a din that sent all nocturnal beasts scurrying or flying to safety. The humans crowded behind me, jerking at each cry. "Ready?" I demanded

"Yes," Ralphayers said. "But what can we do? They're all around. We can't fight them, wouldn't even if we could. And we can't run fast enough to escape."

"Too true. Remember those animals you told me about,

horses? Well, pretend I'm one. Straddle my back and hang onto my fur."

"You're strong, but not that strong," Ralphayers said.

"You better hope I am. Get on."

They did, awkwardly, sitting in front of and behind my carrysack. My legs almost buckled. They were heavier than they looked. But I figured I could still make better speed than their pitiful excuse for running.

"Here we go!" I bounded off the porch and crossed the white-crusted rocky ground away from the cliff and Coalgathering, toward the Wild.

"Where are we going?" Pamayers shouted over the drum rhythm of my four driving legs and the hissing wind.

"Away from the hunters," I gasped. "If we manage that . . . we'll see."

I could have tried to dart between two of the slower challengers. But such a show of cowardice would make us legitimate prey; they would hunt us to the death. Besides, I was mad from tail to snout. If I had to abandon everything I owned except my honor, I would go with style and at least a small victory.

I ran straight at Shrubfur.

She loped out of the underbrush, a black shadowy shape. I would have approached a fight with her cautiously under the best of circumstances; with the burden on my back it was downright crazy. Which I was, a little bit. "Stay right there!" I shouted. "I'm coming with a red welcome for you!"

My scent was so strong I could smell it, rage and death.

The other challengers kept their distance—this was between Shrubfur and me now. She held her ground, tensing to defend and counterattack. She didn't smell the least bit afraid, but . . . maybe . . . uncertain.

The gap between us was closing fast. My back ached. The humans were shouting questions that I didn't bother to hear. Shrubfur had become my entire universe. If she didn't step aside, I was going to claw a path right through her. Or go down trying.

I understood her uncertainty. The still rational part of my mind was counting on it. She wasn't sure she could beat me, and her reason to try wasn't very strong—her challenge was against the humans. And they were abandoning their teritory under challenge. It rarely happened, but it was as effective a banishment as death.

Her snarling face loomed in front of me. I spread my jaws to tear out her throat, and wondered where her claws would rake me.

Then she was gone, a stride to my right, and I hurtled by. The scrawny woods wrapped darkness around me. The snow under my paws thinned to frozen patches, and plant-smells cleared the evil reek from my nostrils. The humans were still shouting questions.

Just as I thought we were clear, Shrubfur apparently regretted her indecisiveness. Her howl was promptly answered by the other challengers. Running legs pounded the ground behind us. The hunt was up.

My rage began to cool, allowing me to concentrate fully on the agony each stride wrung from my breaking back. But it would have to agonize even more if it weren't to stop permanently. "Are you two okay?" I shouted to the humans.

"Yes!" Ralphayers answered. "What happened back there? Were you going to fight?"

"Later . . . !" I gasped. "They're on our . . . trail! Have to . . . outrun them! Need all my strength!"

"You can't possibly outrun them, not while carrying us!"

That deserved and got no answer. Of course I couldn't, but there was no honorable alternative to trying.

I was heading upslope, toward a low pass over the mountains and into the Wild. The stunted trees and bushes became more sparse, giving way to snowcovered granite. I gasped with each stride. My running was ragged; I could hear and smell the hunters on both sides and behind, closing in on us cautiously.

I hadn't expected pursuit, and had no clever scheme to escape. But I kept doggedly at it, ignoring further questions from the humans. The summit of the pass was just ahead now. If I could make it through, at least I would be running downhill.

The hunters were within a ten-stride or two of bringing us down. My back hurt so badly I almost looked forward to it.

Suddenly and dramatically in the wan moonlight, the

white trail curved downward. I saw the Wild below, treetops and rivers and broad meadows reaching to the horizon. I started down, staggering, hindknees buckling.

It took me several moments to realize that the humans and I were alone on the downward trail. The hunters had stopped at the summit. I could feel their eyes even though I was beyond their view. I pulled up slowly on trembling legs. "Off!"

They scrambled onto their own legs. "Are we safe now?" Pamayers asked. "Why did they stop?"

"Safe from them, yes. Seems they just wanted to chase us out. But we're in the Wild now, so keep a sharp lookout. There are many dangerous creatures here, large and small, ones we've purged from our territories."

I continued down the trail—a rough path blazed by Travelers as well as mothers-to-be—and the humans followed. Walking, not running, I felt light enough to glide, but my back and legs still ached.

"Can you tell us where we're going now?" Ralphayers asked.

I paused. "There's a lot I could say in answer to that. Our immediate need is for a safe place to sleep. I don't know the Wild well; I rarely have business out here. But I remember a place near here that should do."

"What happens to us tomorrow?" Pamayers asked.

"I don't know," I snapped, short-tempered in my pain and loss. "This is a new experience for me too. So far I've been concentrating on keeping us alive tonight."

"Is there any hope we'll be able to return to Coalgathering?"

"No. The circle challenge still stands. And we would find the same kind of trouble if we tried to establish ourselves in another town. The news of what happened tonight will spread fast, and we would be considered undesirable neighbors wherever we went. That leaves a pair of choices. Turning Traveler or Wilder."

"Traveling might suit us," Ralphayers said. "We could learn more that way. But I'm not sure I understand the concept completely. Travelers are artisans, savants, craftsmen, explorers *et al* who wander from town to town. But how do they fit into your social and economic systems?"

"They're somewhat disreputable," I admitted, "since

they don't share our need for territory. They earn a bit of *twilga* in a town, buy what they need and move on. They eat, drink and sleep in the Wild. Frankly, I don't think you two would last long. But if that's your choice, I'll help you as much as I can."

The humans jabbered at each other. I looked up past bare branches at the cold stars, and felt empty. I was no Traveler. I had to have land of my own under my paws, a fixed place in the universe. But my territory would belong to someone else tomorrow.

"You're right," Pamayers said to me. "We wouldn't survive. What about the other possibility?"

"Wilders," I growled. "Even lower than Travelers. Cowards, criminals, perverts, eccentrics—anyone who can't accept the customs of society—flee into the Wild, living scarcely any better than truly wild adults. But I don't see a third choice for us."

"You mean we just find a likely piece of land and take up residence?" Pamayers asked.

"*Two* territories," I reminded them sharply. "Ones with adequate food and water won't be easy to find out here. That's why it's the Wild. But yes, we claim them, challenging the current owners—quality land will almost certainly have a Wilder or wild adult on it. If we win, the territories are ours. I'll have to fight for you, of course."

More jabbering. "That plan sounds more suitable to our needs," she said. "With the tools in our carrysacks we should be able to build cabins, hunt and grow food, make clothes . . . But none of us are in any shape to decide our future tonight. Let's take it up again in the morning."

"I agree," I said. For awhile we walked in weary silence. We were on an icy rock shelf following a cliff face. Below the bare slope descended to the eaves of a forest, all dark and indistinct shapes.

"Why?" Ralphayers asked so softly that I might have thought he was talking to himself, except that he wasn't using his own strange language.

"Why what?" I responded.

"Why all of this? What did we do wrong, to be driven out like this? I thought your fellow townsfolk were beginning to accept us."

"Some were," I agreed. "But I made a bad error in

judgment. I used your idea to put over the street paving, and it convinced some of the town conservatives that your notions about cooperation are dangerous. Ergo, the challenge."

"But . . . but cooperation is a cornerstone of any social system. Your individualism has held back your rate of progress. There is so much you just can't *do* without group effort."

I growled. "For a savant you aren't very quick on the uptake. We may not have the herd instinct of your kind, but we do cooperate. We do it in our own way. As for progress . . ." I stopped. All the times I had cursed the hindbound conservatism of my fellow adults, and here I was babbling their cant like Shrubfur or Irongut. Was my loss turning me against my own beliefs—and the humans?

"You're right," Pamayers said, "and we were wrong to suggest what we did. We're here to learn your mores, not change them."

"I was the one who bought your idea, and tried it. A Weigher should have known better. I was . . . tempted. And I've been properly punished. So let's not talk about this any more tonight."

More silent walking brought us to the place I remembered. A cave in the limestone of the cliff. Not much of a cave; more like a cabin-sized indentation, with fallen rocks piled in front like a low fence. I sniffed to make sure it didn't have a current inhabitant. It didn't. "Here's your cabin for tonight. Safe from predators, and some shelter from the cold."

"Aren't you joining us?" Pamayers asked.

I shuddered. "I'll sleep out here as a guard. The cliff is all the shelter I need."

The humans crawled over the rubble into the cave. They used their odd nonburning lamps to examine it, and reported it was messy from animals that had laired there, but habitable.

They got the cave cleaned up quickly, and went to sleep. I was just as tired, but I had trouble falling asleep. I wasn't as impervious to the cold as I had alleged.

But the worst was the stress of having no territory, of sharing this place with others. I had to stay with them to keep them safe, but there wasn't any precedent for adults sharing a territory ... there was my out. They weren't really adults; they were more like *tagnami* I was raising. Not a perfect analogy, but good enough to let me finally sleep.

I woke up cold, stiff, and momentarily disoriented. When memory poured back between my ears, I managed to feel even worse. I just lay there on the leaves I had piled to cushion the bare rock. I watched the stars slowly fade as dawn came. I heard the forest sounds and the loud breathing of the humans. The smells were unchanged from the night before.

I felt unnaturally lethargic and hopeless. There were things that needed doing, I knew intellectually, but emotionally I couldn't stir up any motivation to move. The wan winter sun rose to warm me a bit. It looked like it was going to be a clear day.

The humans finally came out of the cave. They looked as worn out and haggard as I knew I must, and I was glad I didn't have a mirror to see. "Good morning," Pamayers said with a try at cheerfulness.

I creaked up onto my hindlegs and joined them. "If you say so. At least we have good weather. We'll need it."

Ralphayers nodded. "Well, Slasher, do we stay here or move on?"

I thought as I paced the kinks out of my joints. Finally I said, "This land isn't very good for game, though there is water. We'll want better for permanent territories. But I think we should winter here. I'll hunt game for all of us. Can you fix the cave up as a suitable temporary home?"

"Not easily or quickly, but yes. We have some tools. We can wall up the front, put in a simple hearth, a floor, build some furniture—"

"I suggest you get started then." I said curtly. "I'll have to protect you until you have a secure home, and on top of everything else that has happened I must disgrace myself by sleeping on your doorstep."

Ralphayers paused, then said, "I think I understand your problem. With luck we should be able to get the wall up today."

"That would be good news," I growled without conviction. "While you're at it, I'm going to hunt our breakfast.

After that I'll scout around for a nearby site for my own winter haven. There are supposed to be more caves further south along the cliffs. Tomorrow we can run the bounds of our new territories and mark them."

"Is that important out here?" Pamayers asked.

"We're still civilized adults, Kraal curse it! I won't start behaving like an animal, and neither should you!"

They looked at me strangely. Kraal take them both, *I* had nothing to apologize for. I told them how to find the nearest mountain stream, warned them to keep watch for direbeasts and wild adults, and loped down the slope into the grim woods. I felt indecently glad to be getting away from them, if only briefly.

The strongwood giants and squat underbrush became thicker as I followed a game trail down toward the plain. The forest was, I knew, only a thin strip hugging the mountain range. Beyond were rolling meadowlands buried under snow and bereft of game.

I had half-hoped the familiar routine of the hunt would snap me out of my funk. But it didn't.

Much as we pride ourselves on our individualism, scratch us and you will find underneath creatures as socially interdependent as any hiving insect. I had been torn from my secure place in Coalgathering's social stucture. In one swipe of the claw I had been disgraced, lost my territory and *tagnami*, and been forced into exile. I was already beginning to feel *lonely*. The humans were intelligent and overly friendly, but they weren't adults. We had too little in common.

Kraal curse the day they had dropped into my life to destroy it!

No, it wasn't fair to blame them. They had provided the opportunity, but I had seized it to trample tradition and hurt others. Yes, hurt! Only now was I beginning to see, through their eyes, how wrongly I had dealt with them. In the arrogance of my convictions I had forgotten their right to their own. For that there had to be *twilga*, and I would pay it for the rest of my life.

I leaned against the slick black bark of a forest giant, and for the first time since the day I killed my father I cried.

How long I cried I don't know. What stopped me was a

scent on the soft morning breeze. A half-familiar scent. A dangerous, hostile scent. Even in my present state it snapped me back to animal awareness.

A wild male adult, coming this way. Not a Wilder who had turned his back on civilization, but a cub who had never been brought in to become a *tagnami*. As an adult he would be a very successful predator, cunning though uneducated, a winner in the hard battle for survival in the Wild.

Worse yet, I could tell he was in rut. He wasn't looking to kill me for trespassing on his supposed territory. Not this time.

My nape fur should have risen in outrage, and I should have huried to challenge and gut the savage for his effrontery. As a *tagnami* I had heard the dark tales of Wilders coupling with wild adults, but I hadn't really believed them. Some things were too disgusting to be conceivable.

But I didn't move.

He crept cautiously from a stand of iceberry bushes. At this close range he had to know I didn't share his lust, but being a savage he wouldn't care. He was a magnificent physical specimen; huge, about Irongut's age, and scarred so that his pelt looked like a badly made quilt. He stank from the lack of a recent bath.

Still I didn't move.

This would end it. The body and the brain would go on, fulfilling an unwanted obligation. But the soul would be extinguished. No pain, no loss, no loneliness. All I had to do was yield.

I made myself give off an acquiescent spoor, turned away, crouched low, tucked my tail to the side to save it from his brutal passion, and spread my hindlegs for him.

The sun was well past zenith and starting toward its evening rest when I loped out of the woods and approached the humans' cave. They were hard at work fitting young strongwood trunks they had cut and trimmed into a wall blocking up the cave mouth. They heard me and, dropping their tools, ran to meet me.

"Where have you been?" Pamayers demanded. I thought I was beginning to master some of their odd facial expressions, and she seemed worried as well as afraid for me. But their feelings meant nothing to me now.

"I've been doing what I should have done a long time ago. Thinking. Not just reacting to events." I paused. "I've changed my mind. I can't be a Wilder."

"What do you mean?"

"Just this. I'm returning to town. Now."

Ralphayers spoke before Pamayers could. "But last night you said we couldn't go back. You said the challengers would try to kill us."

I nodded.

"You've thought of a way around the challenge?"

The will to do something—anything—was like the glow of fermented milk spreading through my body. Recent memory still burned like a hearthfire, but I would again be true to my name. "I'm going to accept the challenge for you. I'll complete the circle, if my skill and luck last."

"You can't win a half dozen or more fights in a row!" Pamayers blurted. "What's wrong with you? Are you trying to commit suicide?"

"Why I do it is my own business. Still, we have a business agreement. If you come with me, I'll do my best to keep you safe."

"How are you going to manage that if they kill you?"

"If you want to find that out, come along. But you don't have to. We can terminate the agreement. With your strange talents and tools you might make a life as Wilders."

"Without your help we won't survive the winter," Ralphayers disagreed. "Starvation, attack, exposure—take your choice."

They were trapped, but so was I, and I had no sympathy for any of us. "I'm leaving now. If you plan to hold me to our agreement, get your sacks and come."

I walked slowly to the cliff trail that had brought us here. Behind me I heard hasty packing and paws running to catch up. They fell in on either side without a word.

The silence suited me. I didn't want to have to explain further, or to try. When you have lost everything you have to lose, right down to your self-respect, you reach at last a kind of peaceful equilibrium, the firmness of rock bottom. I wanted to enjoy it while I could.

I set a fast pace up to and over the pass, and the

humans were hard put to keep up. They talked to each other from time to time. Starting down, I took the most direct commonland trail to town.

I wanted to arrive before the adults started home for the day. The sun hung low over the treetops beyond the river when I walked through the South Gate on my hindlegs, flanked by the humans.

I expected the whole town to know what had happened, and I was right. As I walked along Savant Street toward the challenge lawn, most adults and *tagnami* stopped whatever they were doing, stared at us, and began talking excitedly among themselves. I knew what they were looking forward to; I didn't plan to disappoint them.

No one spoke to me, but many followed us at a safe distance. Others spread the news, like the ripples created by a rock tossed in the river. We reached the reddish-purple groundplant, dumped our carrysacks, and went to the middle of the challenge lawn.

The late afternoon was golden with shafts of light coming through the treetops. Bloodlust and excitement saturated the air, which was dry but hard-edged with a chill. A beautiful day for fighting. Hundreds of adults and *tagnami* soon ringed the lawn—most of the town.

"Don't say or do anything unless I tell you to," I whispered to the humans.

Pamayers opened her mouth, but then closed it and touched my shoulder. Strangely, I found the gesture reassuring rather than offensive.

The onlookers suddenly became silent. From seven places in the ring adults stepped forward. I recognized them all by their scent. The circle challengers. I faced Shrubfur.

"I'm glad to see your courage has returned," Shrubfur growled. "One thing I never thought of you was that you were a coward."

"The grievances between us have become complicated," I said in a calm tone. "The humans and I are eager to settle them. I suggest that we get a judgment from the Weigher. You do have a new Weigher, don't you?"

Shrubfur laughed deeply. "That we do. One more to my taste than his predecessor. I wonder if you'll approve. Ah, here he is now."

Irongut stepped through the ring onto the lush lawn.

I wasn't surprised. I had known about his interest for a long time. Nor, knowing his feelings on the subject, could I expect any help from him. Love wouldn't stop him from doing his duty any more than it would me. He would be fair, but fair according to his own beliefs.

His expression when he looked at me was grim, but I smelled the scent of concern, too. "I'm the Weigher now," he said to me. "Are my services needed here?"

If my scheme went wrong, I would have to fight him. I felt old. Too old.

Shrubfur growled, "Ashpelt, Crier, Fisheater, Shortlegs, Treeback, Striped-fur and I issued a circle challenge to the creatures called Ralphayers and Pamayers. Slasher intervened on their behalf. They fled from us and abandoned their territories. Now they have returned. We are reposting our challenge." The other six added their approval.

"Will you accept a *twilga* decision from me to settle your grievances?" Irongut asked.

Before I could speak Shrubfur answered, "No, this is a blood dispute." and the others agreed.

Irongut turned to the humans. "Then you must fight. Which of you will accept first?"

"No!" I shouted—everybody had to hear this. "I claim this challenge is unjust! I want the Weigher to judge if it's proper!"

For something as unusual as a circle challenge it was a fair request. The challengers agreed smugly, and we all entered the *twilga* for Irongut's Weighing in our notebooks.

"Why do you say it's unjust?" he asked.

"Because these adults have no legitimate grievance against the humans."

"No grievance!" Shrubfur howled. "They have spread strange ideas that damage our businesses. Worse, they have seduced you so that you think like them and deal dishonorably with your own kind. Everyone knows about the perverted trick you used on Fisheater, Shortlegs, Treeback and myself."

"Yes, *my* dishonor! I don't deny it! But the humans have done none of you any harm. They sell knowledge that improves our trades, sciences and arts. Many here have bought from them, and profited. If you refused the chance to improve while your competitors didn't, whose fault is that?

"It's nothing less than cowardice to try to put the blame on others for your own mistakes. Knowledge isn't evil, but it can be used for evil. If it is, blame the user. Surely you aren't claiming mere words can turn a good adult bad. If so, you're accusing all of us of being so weak-minded that we can't control ourselves."

I stopped, because my well-planned argument was having the desired effect. There were hostile scents and growls among the onlookers, directed at Shrubfur. Many of them had done business with the humans and hoped to do more. Moreover, accusations of cowardice and stupidity cut to the bone.

Irongut took a long time thinking, then said, "Slasher has made some valid points. I don't see that you have a legitimate grievance against the two creatures."

Tremendous relief surged through me. I wouldn't have to fight Irongut.

The challengers plainly realized how bad they would look if they tried to pursue the matter. Nor did any of them seem inclined to fight Irongut over his decision. "I accept the Weighing," each of us said in turn.

Irongut turned to me, his expression even grimmer. "But you've as much as admitted that their grievance against you is valid. You'll have to complete the circle if you can."

Shrubfur smiled broadly.

I motioned the humans to join Irongut at the edge of the lawn, then I dropped to four legs. Shrubfur slunk toward me slowly, also on four legs. Her pelt glistened like water in moonlight. "I hope you aren't going to run away again," she growled.

I returned her smile. "No, I'm going to fit you with a second mouth just under the first."

The preliminaries out of the way, we closed in on each other. The onlookers' conversations stopped as though cut with a knife.

I wanted Shrubfur's life. Whether I then fell to the second, third or fourth challenger didn't matter; she had chosen to make herself the symbol of my disaster. But it wouldn't be easy. She was a paw taller than I, and a mass of muscles from her trade. In age and quickness we were evenly matched. Well, maybe I had the edge in cunning. Maybe.

We circled warily, sniffing to check each other's mood. Shrubfur was hot with anger, but under rigid control; a good fighting attitude. I had no warning when she charged.

She leaped over me, a flashy but effective move. Her claws raked at my back. But I wasn't there—I had dropped to my belly, rolled and crouched. I tried to hook one of her hindlegs with my tail, but missed.

I swung around in time to meet Shrubfur's second attack. She dove at my left side, taking away a mouthful of fur and flesh. The wound bled, and hurt, but it would take a lot of nips like that to drop me. I sank a claw into her left foreleg and opened a deep slash. Her eyes glazed momentarily.

I jumped and came down on top of her, grappling with my claws. She rolled across the groundplant trying to knock me off. I hung on as long as I could, then jumped free.

I almost made it. She curled her tail around me, and bit into my right hindleg before I could squirm away. The pain was like a band of molten metal. I swallowed a howl of pain; Kraal curse it if I would shame myself any further.

We wrestled across the lawn as she gnawed at my leg. I had only a few seconds left to save it. Arching until I could feel my spine creak, I swung a foreleg back and down, and caught the end of her snout. Red blood spurted. During her momentary distraction I yanked my leg free.

I stood and faced her, wobbling a bit. Our pelts were matted with blood. We charged each other. She bit deep behind my neck and tried to grind through my right shoulder blade. I couldn't hold in a whimper, and a gray fog obscured my sight.

But, sure of her victory at last, she neglected her defense for less than a second. I hit the sides of her head with two closed paws as hard as I could. She dropped at my feet, stunned.

I reached down with my claws to keep my promise.

And stopped.

I stared at Shrubfur's bloody body, and felt dizzy with sudden insight. Thoughts flew through my mind. At least she would be dying true to her own beliefs, while I had clawed mine to shreds. I would die, and the humans too—without me they would soon ignorantly commit a fatal mistake. Their valuable knowledge and, yes, their even more valuable notion of mutual gain through group efort would be lost.

I had been only half-wrong, but too proud to bend rather than break. Now I understood. Too late; my course was set.

Or was it? I wasn't an animal or a wild adult. I was a Weigher, with a lifetime of accumulated experience. I thought hard and fast, searched my memories, fitted ideas together like puzzle pieces....

A lot went on during the three or four seconds that I crouched over Shrubfur. Then I stood up slowly. Everyone stared at me in rapt silence, eager for the kill, wondering at my delay.

I knew what I had to do, but it still hurt like a doctor's scalpel. Shrubfur coughed. She was beginning to wake up. I took my *twilga* notebook and dropped it beside her. My belt followed it. I was naked.

After a moment of shock, a hundred whispers made the ring of onlookers buzz. The reek of disgust made me gag. Better get used to it, I told myself.

Irongut's scent and expression were unreadable. This situation was an extremely rare one, but he knew his Weigher lore. "The challenge is settled," he said, then turned and walked away. The ring was breaking up as adults and *tagnami* headed back to their stalls. Their eyes avoided mine. Shrubfur staggered off with my former property and a confused look.

The humans ran to me. "How badly are you hurt?" Pamayers demanded.

"I'll live."

"What happened?"

Each word hurt. "I surrendered to Shrubfur. My territory, my *twilga*, everything I owned is hers now."

A long pause. "Why did you do it?"

"To survive. I have work to do, more important than my property or even my honor."

Another pause, then Ralphayers said, "I think we understand. But what will you do without a territory or *twilga*?"

"I won't have to do without either. It's time for us to settle up for my services yesterday and today on your behalf. Saving your lives should be worth the price of a modest territory and the basic necessities."

"Of course," Pamayers said quickly. "As long as you include medical treatment on the top of your list. You're losing a lot of blood."

I swayed, and the gray fog was thickening. "Okay. Let's go. We don't have much time before dusk. We'll want to stay out of town for a few days, let things calm down."

If I could find adults willing to do business with me. I was publicly labeled a coward. No self-respecting adult would want to stain his pelt with my blood. I had lost all of my friends except the humans, and all of the respect of my fellow adults. Agenting the humans' knowledge would be my only trade; Weighing and all other professions were closed to me. In time I might win back some friends and respect, but for now I would have to cling precariously to the bottom rung of the social ladder.

The sun had gone to ground beyond the river, and the day was ending quickly under heavy clouds. I was finishing up a third day of repairing the dilapidated cabin of my new territory. I put away my tools, and tried to ignore the throbbing of my bandaged leg, side and shoulder.

I was about to hobble into the stunted hillside woods and try to bring down dinner, even more of a challenge due to the meager game stock, when I heard a familiar howl for entry permission.

I trembled from surprise as I gave permission, and rushed inside the cabin to run a quick comb through my pelt. Why was he here? Fears and hopes fought in my mind.

I met Irongut on the porch—the cabin wasn't ready for visitors yet. He looked well, with a more mature self-control. The responsibilities of Weighing seemed to agree with him. I felt a twinge of loss, but I was also proud for him. I tingled like a *tagnami* in cublove. Since the fight my moods had been swinging wildly.

"I'm glad you came," I said simply.

"I want to talk to you about what happened." I couldn't determine his attitude by sight or scent.

"Okay."

"At first I couldn't understand your surrender. I despised you for it, like everyone else, and hated you for not being the adult I loved. But the not understanding hurt me. I kept worrying it in my mind."

"You could have asked me. I would have explained."

"That didn't occur to me until after I figured it out. At least I think I have. You haven't given up the evil human notions that caused all this, have you?"

I took a deep breath. "No, I haven't. But I won't be forcing them on anyone. I've learned my lesson."

"Thank the gods for that. But why this fanaticism over something that only causes trouble?"

I looked up at the clouds, and the unseen stars. "The humans came here from another world. They've accomplished so much. We squabble over the smallest step forward, killing each other instead of working together to improve our lives."

"It's our way."

"It's stupid and wrong. We're intelligent beings; we can change, grow. The knowledge I'm agenting for the humans will begin the change, since much of it will take group efforts to implement. But the key is the philosophy of cooperation itself. We're explaining it to all of our customers, and they arrive from farther away every day. Travelers take the knowledge and new ideas and skills with them, telling tales wherever they go. Eventually the philosophy of cooperation will spread everywhere. Its clear advantages will bring about gradual acceptance, without any force being needed."

"I don't agree," Irongut said, frowning. "You underestimate the deep roots of our morality."

"Morals change to match changing social conditions. I read that once in a history text. Don't worry, *gorwana*, the change will be a slow one. We won't live to see much of it."

Irongut was quiet for a long time. "I still feel it's wrong. If we change to become like the humans, then we'll no longer be ourselves. I'll argue against it, and fight against it if necessary."

I laughed. "You can't fight ideas. But you should try if you feel you must. At the least, you can remind me not to be overzealous."

"I will. I . . . don't want you hurt anymore."

My heart pounded under my furry chest. "I was about to go and look for some dinner. Will you hunt with me, *gorwana*? Then we can come back here and build a nice warm hearthfire?"

I smelled his answer before he spoke. "Of course. I still love you."

Together we bounded from the porch, and ran like shadows across the new-fallen snow to the forest eaves.

Editor's Introduction to "Demon Lover," by M. Sargent Mackay

In David Brin's universe, humans have assisted dolphins and chimpanzees to reach full intelligence. This is a noble thing to do; but perhaps there is a species more deserving.

A cocktail-party theory is one you'd be willing to argue for at a cocktail meeting, but not publish in a scientific journal. One such theory I have long held is that dogs are more intimately associated with human intelligence than we usually recognize.

Consider: The sense of smell takes up about as much brain weight as the other senses combined. Moreover, it needs "expensive" forebrain tissue since olfactory stimuli have to interact directly with brain cells.

Under primitive conditions, if you don't have a good sense of smell, something eats you before you get old enough to use intelligence. However, if you don't need a sense of smell, you have "extra" brain cells. Families with dogs may survive even though some of the olfactory sense cells have mutated into something else, such as intelligence. Evolution tends to proceed by villages and groups and families. Families with dogs can afford intelligence. Once intelligence begins, evolution selects for it.

Excavations show humans and dogs have been intimately associated for at least a million years.

So far it's only a cocktail-party theory. One day I may work it into something I'd defend in a scientific journal. Meanwhile, one of the most delightful stories of the year tells of a future when humans and dogs once again need each other.

Demon Lover

M. Sargent Mackay

The late afternoon was hot on Willow's coat, and she let her mouth hang open as she worked her way through the undergrowth. There was almost no breeze, and the thick, rich odors of autumn filled her nostrils to the choking point. Of the missing ward, however, she could detect no trace. She sniffed her way around a particularly dense clump of multiflora rose, reeking of rabbit, mouse, and fowl, but not of what she sought. Frustrated, she sat down to pant for a minute.

Her coat was already thickening up for the winter, and this fall warm spell was giving her fits. She scratched energetically and shook herself free of the twigs and leaf particles and whatnot that had attached to her from the brush. A sudden stabbing itch on her flank brought a flea to her attention, but she hunted for it without success. She had rid herself of most of last year's crop in the course of the summer, by frequent bathing and eating of certain plants, but one or two always seemed to survive. She stopped and panted again.

On the whole, it was an irritating afternoon.

She picked herself up and started on; the missing ewe had got to be found, stupid and troublesome as she might be, ever lagging and straying. She cursed to herself as she pushed through a hole in the next hedge. Maddening to have to be moving and hunting about in the heat of the day.

A sudden baying in the near distance made her prick her ears.

"Found! Found! By the run, near six willows, hung up in a hedge. Found!" Her young cousin's voice. Thankfully, she threw back her head and bayed a response. Then she turned and started for the run.

When she came to the place the third searcher, her uncle Quailflusher, had already got there, and was investigating the ewe in the hedge. The youngster, Grabchuck, greeted her with enthusiasm. He was a five-year-old, only recently graduated to watch-standing status, and was bubbling over with his success.

"She's hung up pretty badly," he said. "I tried to get her out, but she bleated so, I thought I'd better wait."

Quailflusher growled from the hedge, "Help me here, Willow. Her leg's caught." Willow shouldered into the hedge. "Just put a foot there. . . ." He braced himself, seized the ward by the rump, and with a sharp jerk of his head yanked her leg free of the prisoning branch. The old ewe sprawled out on the grass, complaining prodigiously. Grabchuck nosed her and pushed her back on her feet. She bleated with pain and limped a couple of steps, holding her near hind leg up under her at a funny angle. It was scratched and bleeding. Quailflusher sniffed at it suspiciously.

"Broken," he declared. He sat back on his haunches and looked at the ewe with disgust.

Willow considered. "How old is she? She didn't lamb this year."

"Last year, either," Quailflusher said. "I don't know. She must be as old as I am. Too old, I guess." The three wardens sat and watched, their tongues lolling. Grabchuck offered no opinion, awaiting his elder's decision. The ewe hobbled a couple of steps, stopped, and cropped grass.

Quailflusher sighed, "Well, she can still walk, a bit. You can take her on back to camp, Grabchuck, and don't run her off her legs on the way. If she gives out before you get there, you'll have to drag her the rest of the way."

"Right." Grabchuck started up, collected the ewe, and headed her downstream in the direction of camp. The two older wardens sat and watched him out of sight. Quailflusher scratched his ear thoughtfully.

"That old ewe's been around as long as I can remember, and she was always troublesome," he observed.

"She'll eat tough," said Willow.

Quailflusher flicked an ear in agreement. He rose and scratched, then lifted a leg and marked the hedge where the ewe had been. Willow rolled briskly in the grass, then jumped up suddenly and plunged into the run. A moment later Quailflusher joined her, and they romped and splashed through the pools of the swift-flowing run, getting soaked to the skin.

"Ah, that's good," Willow said, shaking herself vigorously. "I can't believe the heat, so late in the season."

"Aye." The air stirred faintly; scarcely a breeze, but they sighed thankfully. Quailflusher stretched luxuriously. Willow watched him from the corner of her eye, admiring the smooth play of muscles. Quailflusher was nine, a young dog warden in the prime of his life. He saw her and grinned, then sniffed a couple of times, suggestively.

She looked away, embarrassed. "We'd better be getting back to our sections," she said. She stood up and started off down the run. Quailflusher followed, and they trotted along in silence. A klick or so farther on they parted company to find their sections.

Willow had left hers in a protected pasture, between two treetopped hillocks, partly hedged with dense rose. They had got pretty well scattered in her absence, and she must spend an hour or so, routing them out of the bushes. The sun was setting fast by that time, and she headed them down to rejoin the main flock in the night pasture.

Her second cousin, Killed-a-Savage, relieved her, and they exchanged greeting sniffs. "Hot damn!" he exclaimed. Willow snarled at him in irritation. He laughed rudely. "If you want any meat, you'd better get back to camp," he said. "It was half gone when I left. And I think Grandmother will have some advice for you. . . ."

Willow offered him some advice of her own and started back to camp in a huff. Her blood was definitely stirring, despite the season, and her emotions unsettled; she needed no commentary from males who were forbidden in any case. She was seven years old, in the full flush of youth, and she knew herself beautiful. In spring she would choose a mate, and herd with his band thereafter. There was a certain one in the Rock Hill clan—handsome, smart, a beautiful voice—she permitted her mind to wander till she got back to camp.

The warm smells of camp greeted her as she came up in the dark, the close smell of her kinfolk, each clearly individual, yet adding up to the definite, ineffable whiff of her own band. Food smells mixed withal: pheasant (fresh feathers scattered before the cave), 'possum, fresh-killed sheep. Smoke whuffed in her face from the small fire sheltered by the overhang; her great-aunt greeted her where she lay tending it.

"Hey, Willow." Quailflusher's voice, his scent rank and close. "We saved you some of the meat."

"Thanks, Quail." She took the meat (a sizable chunk of shoulder; Quailflusher was always good to her) and lay down with it against the wall.

The faint sounds and smells of the others informed her as she ate. Younglings squeaked and tumbled about in the dark, her elder sister's two from this spring and her first cousin's three yearlings. The mothers conversed in low tones. Grandmother and Grandfather, of course; at thirty-two, Grandfather didn't go out much. Grandmother Starfall, who was five years younger, had been running the clan for years. In camp her word was law; she was versed in the lore of her folk, and ruled the female rites and mysteries. Quailflusher was in a corner with his mate, and two or three off-duty bachelors lolled in the back of the cave. They were stirring about somewhat, and she realized that the atmosphere in the cave was becoming tense. She must be further along than she thought. She gnawed thoughtfully on the scapula, finding the last few bits of gristle.

A rustling, and Grandmother lay down beside her. She sniffed Willow's face politely but curtly. Willow waited, apprehensive.

"You've come in," said Grandmother bluntly. Her voice was soft, but quite firm.

"Not yet . . . not entirely. . . ."

"Close enough." Grandmother was exasperated. "Listen

to those oafs fidgeting back there." Willow turned her head away, though the gesture was not visible in the dark. "We don't need this. Your cousin Crawfish-Bit-Her is barely out, and your own mother came in the day before yesterday."

"My mother!" Willow was startled.

"Yes, surely. She let me know she would hunt alone for a few days, like a sensible creature, instead of hanging about camp getting the males all stirred up to no purpose." She paused significantly.

"I'm sorry, Grandmother. Perhaps I should go and keep her company."

"By all means, if she'll have you. She may really want to be alone."

"Did she say where she would hunt?"

"Along the river." Grandmother was silent for a moment. "Fall heats are sent by devils. Winterborn are a drain on the band, and unlucky besides. There was a winterbirth when I was eight, I don't say to whom, in a hard winter, too. Three younglings, none lived to be five. One died of some curse before a year. One was drowned, playing the fool. The last lived to stand watch. A lion came in the dusk, and he gave his life for the band. That was Stonetumble. He was brave, but unlucky."

"I'm sorry, Grandmother. I must have neglected some rite." Willow was suitably impressed.

"Three fall heats . . . and last year there were none. The devils are after us for sure. When you get back we'll have purifications, as many as necessary. If we can't ward them off, it'll be a rough winter." She breathed quietly, her mind full of ritual. "I'd better purify the camp, too, as soon as you leave."

"I'm sorry, Grandmother. I'll leave tonight." Willow rose.

"Well, you can leave in the morning. It's warm out. Sleep downwind of camp, it'll be all right." Grandmother rose also. "Time to sing, soon," she commented, in a louder tone. Murmurs of acknowledgment came from the others. "Go ahead, dear," she added, nosing Willow gently in the side. Willow went out.

The night air was pleasantly cool, and a light breeze had come up. It ruffled her coat slightly. She went and lay down on a rock break, a little way downwind of the cave. After a while she heard the others come out and walk about, stretching their muscles and getting ready for the evening's activities. One of her aunts arrived from the pasture, and two of the bachelors left to go on watch. A fox barked, and Willow twitched her ears.

Off to the west a savage began to sing, his characteristic yapping call. He sang the glory of the evening; he sang of his wit and craft in the hunt; he sang the death of prey and the taste of hot blood. His mate joined him, and the shriller voices of his whelps (seven of them; savages were prolific). Willow curled her lip contemptuously; savages knew only one song. They were puny creatures, crafty enough in their way, but no match for a warden. They would steal lambs if they got the chance, but they hadn't the wit to keep flocks of their own; so they lived short, harsh lives, and produced enough whelps to make up the difference.

On the tail of the savage's song came the full, deep bass of her great-uncle, Bearbait. He was fifteen, a House warden, one of the leading males of Sugar Hill, and acknowledged the best songster. He sang the glory of the evening; he sang the beneficence of the Masters and the strength and wealth of the clan. He sang of the peaceful flocks and the loyalty and resolution of the wardens of duty, whom he enumerated with all their names and styles. He sang death, death to sneaking, thieving savages, death to lions, death to bears and devilish wolverines. At each pause in his song the rest of the clan, wherever they watched, lifted their voices in chorus of affirmation.

Other voices joined from other clans, and when Bearbait ended his song he was answered from the south, the voice of Snake-magic, cantor of the Rock Hill clan. The singing went on for quite some time, up and down the valley, singing the joys of life, the puissance of different clans, the deeds of heroes and the destruction of enemies. Willow's mind was filled to ecstasy with the magic of song and moon and night and the subtle chemistry working in her own body. The last notes died out in the distant southwest, and Willow sighed deeply, limp with emotion.

The night was still. Even the crickets were temporarily quelled by the wardens' song. Then, far to the north, the notes of a strange song rent the silence, bringing every warden to his feet, hackles erect and shivering. It struck Willow like the memory of a dream, incomprehensible, yet on the edge of understanding; unfamiliar, yet like something remembered from long ago. She shivered convulsively as the song rose and fell and finally died down to quivering silence. The silence continued for a moment and then was broken by Quailflusher's voice, startlingly loud.

"What was that?" A pause. "Grandfather?"

"I never heard the like in all my days." Grandfather was definite.

"It sounded almost like a warden, but. . . ." Willow's sister trailed off.

"It was a devil!" Grandmother declared fiercely. "A mocking devil! A creature of wind and ice! It's come to mock and torment us!" Her voice shook with rage and fear. "I knew it was coming! I've felt it for weeks! A devil, coming closer!"

"Grandmother, what will we do?" Willow's cousin whined.

"Purifications!" declared Grandmother. "Exorcisms!" And she began to sing, a song of exorcism against devils. Willow sank down and put her chin on the rock. Her heart beat wildly, fueling strange thoughts and feelings that raced and churned in her brain. When Grandmother finished singing, Willow got up and trotted into the night, headed east, toward the river.

Mostly, Jake found the going easier beside the highway. The hard top, or what had been the hard top, was broken and tumbled, great chunks of it at crazy angles, weeds and brush growing riotously up and around and over. Enormous chuckholes held pools of dubious water; on the high shoulders washouts had created canyonlike gullies. But along the edge a trail ran, fairly straight, skirting the bad parts, and Jake followed it gratefully, even hopefully. It might be only a game trail. It was probably only a game trail. But the hope remained, and led him onward, as it had since the girl died.

The trail plunged into a dense stand of thistles, and the branches swatted him as the little bay mare pushed her way through. They emerged into an open space, an intersection, he realized after a moment. Another four-laner had crossed here, headed east-west. Traces of ruins marked the corners, almost swallowed by the earth; a red fox sat on a mound and watched him curiously. In the median strip to the west, the remains of an overhead sign framework were piled in a tangled heap. That seemed familiar ... it had been a long time, but the place jogged his memory. He rode over and dismounted. The sign was made of some heavy plastic; the phosphorescent letters were still legible after God-knew-how-long.

Route 50W, it said. Winchester.

Good. His destination was not much farther, then, just five or ten klicks on south. He did have a destination, for a change. He had come through the Shenandoah Valley some twenty years earlier, and guested for several months at a sizable freehold near here. There had been nearly thirty people, in an ancient walled compound, still keeping the buildings up, growing vegetables and herding cattle and sheep. There had been several such freeholds in the valley then. It was a sheltered area, high enough to be safe from the encroaching ocean, protected from the northern blast by the Alleghenies. The City had never quite engulfed it back in the old days; as the City receded, the bluegrass pastures and tangled woodlots were left comparatively unharmed. When five years of searching found no human life in what had once been New York and Pennsylvania, he had remembered the Blue Ridge, and turned to the south.

A couple of klicks south of Route 50, a side road branched off through the tree-shrouded ruins of a small village. All traces of hard-top had vanished from what had never been more than a minor local road, but the dense growth of shade trees kept the undergrowth down. Presently the trail emerged into the meadowland again. Jake eyed the occasional tumbledown farmhouse they passed, but saw no signs of life. Once a small herd of ponies threw up their heads in astonishment and then galloped away with their tails in the air. Once he heard a bull bellowing in the near distance. The country was peaceful, even friendly; there were few of the unsightly bare patches where nothing would grow, which in some areas covered hectares on end. Here the thistle and burdock ruled over man's remains.

The road had disappeared entirely, but a faint trail remained, skirting the patches of woods and winding among the rock breaks. Once he heard a dog howl, or perhaps a coyote. At the crest of the next hill he reined in, for there it was, less than a kilometer away: a grove of trees on top of a hill, strongly walled around, with a red roof showing through the branches. A thin column of smoke rose from one of the chimneys.

People! For a moment he could only sit. To hear human voices again, to sit beneath a sound roof, by a warm hearthside . . . again he heard a howl, closer, and glancing down the hill, he saw an excessively large dog coming toward him at a rapid trot, with two others coming behind. He looked round. Three more were converging from the surrounding fields. Wardens, he thought, shortening the reins; he had forgotten they kept wardens. The mare stamped and tossed her head. Jake quieted her and waited as the wardens closed to about five meters. The one before him advanced a few steps and barked a sharp query.

"Sorry," Jake said. The sound of his voice startled him. These days he seldom had reason to speak. "I don't understand warden talk too well. I've come from up north." He pointed behind him. The warden seemed to be following well enough. "Ah, I guested here, a long time ago. Maybe your masters will take me in again." He gestured toward the opposite hill. The warden came forward slowly, sniffed warily at his boot, starting back as the mare stamped nervously, then at a proffered hand. He looked up and met Jake's calm stare. Jake sighed and looked off at the beckoning rooftops, then back to the warden. The warden turned in that direction and bayed, then sat back expectantly.

Jake detected motion at the top of the compound wall. A moment later an answering howl echoed across the hollow. The warden seemed satisfied, dismissed his fellows with a growl, and gestured for Jake to follow him. They trotted down the hill, through the run at the bottom, and up toward the gate.

A big man of roughly Jake's own years stood by it cradling a crossbow. They regarded each other slowly.

"Big John Hawkins," Jake said presently.

The big man nodded slowly. "Jake Evans. Long time no see." He let the crossbow droop, glanced at Jake's escort. "O.K., Bearbait. We know him."

The warden headed back down the hill to whatever duties awaited him. Jake dismounted and shook Hawkins' hand.

"Well, John Hawkins, I ain't seen a human face in five years, and it's a real pleasure to see yourn now." His voice sounded hollow to him, almost forced.

Hawkins chuckled. "Well, Jake, I never expected to see yourn again, for sure. Come on in." Jake followed him, leading his mare.

And yet a few minutes, and Jake sat at table in the big house kitchen, with meat and drink before him and dozens of his kind around him. He applied himself to his food, less from hunger than to escape speech. The Hawkinses sat quietly, drinking him in, their ages from about fourteen to indeterminately old. A thirtyish woman replenished his cup and plate until he gestured, no more. He sat back and regarded them, and they him, a moment longer before old Mr. Hawkins spoke.

"Well, Mr. Evans, what did you find up north?"

"Fewer people and more moose . . . and lately ain't no people at all. I was living with a gal up there and her pa, hunting, mostly." He paused, looked out the window. "She died, though, 'bout five year ago, and the old man followed her pretty soon. I been travelin' ever since." He looked around at the Hawkinses. "Plenty of game now. I lived by hunting a long time." He glanced about again, still strange to the sight and sound of people. They looked at him with equal wonder.

"There's few enough here," Old Man Hawkins observed. "Not so many's when you were here last. Not so many left in the valley now. Them Dakerses live down in Fort Valley, down on Massanutten, but we don't see them but once or twice a year. Old Max Wilder still has a place over in the pine hills. He's right old now, ain't got no family left. Some folks down around Luray, I guess, but we don't hardly ever see them. You're the first we seen in quite a spell."

"Looks like there were more of you-all when I came

through here twenty year ago. Hope there ain't been no sickness." Jake filled a pipe from a canister on the table. Big John's wife poked a splinter in the stove to light it for him.

There had been sickness, and hard winters, and other forms of attrition, and the telling of it went on into the evening. There were too few births and too many deaths. A few youth, adventurous or angry, had departed for the south. The rest stayed, each year a little fewer. In the north Jake had found occasional traces of men, but none living. He suspected that some lived in the great eastern marshes, but he had seen none. A few solitary hunters, outlaws, or ascetics might still wander the northern forest. If other men lived, it was to the south.

"At least we ain't gone hungry." Big John Hawkins occupied his hands with carving the figure of a bullock from a block of wood. "We got more critters than we know what to do with."

"Them wardens are right smart," Jake said.

"Hell, yeah," old Mr. Hawkins said. "They're most as smart as you or I."

"They raise more sheep than we can shear," Big John said, with the pleasure all farmers take in talking dogs. "Even in bad winters we don't lose much stock. They keep the lion and bear out of this piece of country, too."

"Sugar Hill wardens are the best in the valley," said a younger Hawkins. "Listen at them sing." Through the fall darkness they heard the voices of the wardens lifting and falling up and down the valley.

"How many you-all have?" Jake asked in wonder.

"I don't rightly know," John Hawkins said.

The younger Hawkins muttered to himself for a moment, then said, "I reckon there's about twenty-three couple watching sheep, and maybe fifteen couple or so on cattle. And must be ten or a dozen hang around the house here. That's not counting young and such. Good many, I reckon. Made a rough count at shearing, but I reckon I missed some."

"We always had wardens at Sugar Hill. Had some of the first they ever was." John spoke reflectively. "Guess we didn't need them so much in the old days. Sure do need them now." The pipe passed, its glow a feeble echo of the candle guttering on the table. For a moment they sat quietly, listening to the voices of the wardens. The moon was well up now, and presently a shaft of moonlight struck through the kitchen window.

"Ain't that fine," said the younger Hawkins.

Outside, the singing slowly tapered off. There was a long silence, broken by a new and different song. The Hawkinses stirred and exclaimed. Jake listened a minute, then smiled.

"Two nights now," Big John said, shaking his head. "Coming closer."

Jake chuckled. The Hawkinses stared at him.

"Looks like I ain't the only lone wolf to come up the valley these two days," he said.

In fact, the wolf had been in the valley four nights. He had hunted the previous winter with a large pack in western New York, the pack he was born to. Hunting was good these days, and wolves ranged where for centuries there had been none. The range was crowded. The winter band at some points numbered over twenty, and interwolf tensions increased. The young wolf found no mate in the season, and when spring came and the pack split up to its various dens, he headed south and spent the summer exploring the Poconos. He had never met a man, and the ruins and wastes that dotted the fields and forest he regarded as irrelevant anomalies. Game was plentiful, and the wolf lived fat. When autumn came he was still moving south, and thus all unwittingly paralleled Jake's course into the valley.

He heard the songs at great distance the first night, and listened in puzzlement. The second night he gave tongue to answer the strangers, singing of the north and his summer roving. He could not understand the reply, but he detected a note of hostility. The fourth night found him within the Sugar Hill warden's range, and he sniffed their markers with fascination. He inferred a diet consisting largely of sheep, and in an outlying pasture found sign of astonishing numbers of that animal, less than a day old. Again that night he answered the strange songs. This time the hostility in the reply was unmistakable, and the wolf thought it well to withdraw outside the warden's range marks, which he annointed to establish his presence in the neighborhood.

Through the night he lay up in a rock break somewhat to the northeast, listening to the watch signals. They continued tantalizingly just beyond the edge of meaning. The wolf knew the cry of coyote and feral dog; he had met and dealt with both in the past, and considered himself their superior. The discovery of a strange canid of unprecedented size and unknown capabilities astonished him, and piqued his curiosity.

The night waned, and presently becoming hungry, the wolf set off to explore the new range. In the pallor of approaching dawn, he started a weanling fawn. In ten paces he pulled it down, and as three or four other deer fled crashing through the brush, he feasted on soft meat. He lay up for some hours near the kill; in the late afternoon he set off once more, and toured the wardens' boundaries for several kilometers toward the river, marking them himself as he went. Once he concealed himself downwind of a trail, and observed in silent wonder as a trio of wardens escorted a small drove of cattle down to water in a run, and then away again. Their size was impressive, and their watchfulness and smooth interaction more so. The wolf was thoughtful as he went his way.

The markers tended south again after a distance, and the wolf veered off to follow a run downstream. Once he started a rabbit, and chased it a few dozen meters for the sake of the exercise before it vanished into a thicket of rose. Well away from the wardens' boundary, he found himself in almost a playful mood, agreeably stimulated by the experience. He splashed in the run, pounced after fluttering leaves, dashed across a meadow and back to the run. In a few minutes he was panting; the musty odors of fall exhilarated him. A fresh scent impinged: a marker! His nose sought it out in a rock break. Yes, fresh ... less than three hours old. He sniffed incredulously. The scent was not so alien as to conceal its message. A young bitch warden. And, no matter that it was still fall, no matter that the first snows were yet a moon or more away, unmistakably in season. With a new sense of purpose, the wolf started on, following her trail.

* * *

Jake spent the morning riding with John Hawkins and his two sons, escorted by three couple of big wardens. They made a round of the flocks and sections, prepared to assist the wardens with any problems that might have arisen. None had. As they visited each section, the warden on watch would come up and accompany them, conversing with the house wardens, then usually addressing itself to Hawkins's younger son, Delbert, for a moment. Jake felt a growing sense of superfluity.

"Looks like them wardens would get on pretty well without no people around at all," he remarked.

Big John laughed. His elder son, Ace, smiled and said, "Some of them do."

"Yeah?"

"Some clans," Delbert said. "They graze farther to south. Some clans we don't see from one year to the next."

"Be wardens raising stock all up and down the valley in another few years." Ace filled his pipe as they rode along. "Naw, they don't need us. They stick by us, though. Even them out clans come by once a year at least. Bring us a few head from their herd. Sort of like a gift or something."

"The Masters' share," Delbert said. The others glanced at him. "Like in them old stories," he elaborated. "They think we're like gods or something, you know, they bring us the best from their herds."

"Well, they git stuff from us, too. Blankets and tanned sheepskins and such." John Hawkins evinced skepticism. "And we doctor them when they need it."

"Shit," said Delbert. "They don't need no blankets. They know we done made them to work for us, and they still remember it even if they ain't enough people to go around now. You heard old Moonsong, she knows all them old warden stories. Listen to her sometime, you'll learn something."

"Well, I'm just glad they stick by us, whyever."

Jake pulled up to ride abreast of Delbert. "How do you talk to them so easy?" he asked. "I cain't hardly understand ary thing they say."

"Why, I just listen to them." Delbert looked startled. "They mouths ain't shaped like ourn, so 'course they cain't talk like we do. I guess I just always been around them, so I know what they sayin'."

"But they tell stories and all?"

"Shit, yeah." Delbert spat to the off side. "Them old wardens know more stories—and they know magic, and hexes—shoot, they know a lot. Get old Moonsong to talk sometime. She's the oldest warden around, and she can tell you plenty."

"Well, I sure cain't understand them like you do. You'd have to tell me what she was sayin'."

"Sure, sure."

They crossed a shallow run. The ponies stepped daintily, wary of their footing, splashing quickly up the other bank. A range warden appeared from up the hill, paid his respects to Bearbait, then came up to Delbert's mare with something approaching awe. Del greeted him cheerfully by name, conversed briefly, then reached down to rumple his ears. Satisfied with this evidence of grace, the warden fell back to talk longer with Bearbait before returning to his section.

"How come they always come up to you?" Jake asked.

Del shrugged. "I dunno. I always liked them and spent time with them, and I can talk their way pretty good. They mostly understand people talk all right, but I like to talk warden talk, and I reckon they just like it."

Ace laughed, turning in his saddle. "Old Delbert spends so much time with them I reckon he's 'bout near half-warden by now."

Presently they stopped for lunch where the run was bridged by a large fallen willow tree. They had brought cold meat sandwiches from the house, which they garnished with cress from the run and washed down with a skin of cider. Several wardens appeared from the surrounding pastures, and they and the house wardens conferred in small, excited groups.

"What ails them wardens?" Big John said irritably.

Delbert laughed. "It's that old wolf we heard the last couple of nights. They think it's some kind of devil. Talkin' 'bout huntin' it tonight."

Jake felt a spasm of irritation. "That ain't no devil. Just a wolf. I seen plenty up north. Why don't they leave him be? He ain't done nothing."

"Scared of him," Delbert amplified. "They ain't never seen no wolf. They just know he's bigger than ary coyote, and strange, so they figure must be something wrong with it." He brushed the crumbs from his moustache. "I ain't never seen one, either. What's it doing here? Seems kinda funny, don't it?"

"Heard them old stories say a wolf can change hisself into a man sometimes," Ace said.

"Ah, bullshit," Big John said nervously.

"Anyway, he might steal sheep," Ace said.

"Not with them wardens watching them." Jake still felt irritated, as if he and the wolf somehow shared something. "He may be wild, but he ain't stupid. Tell them to leave him be till he does something." He stoked his pipe with a touch of vehemence and lit up.

Delbert shrugged, "You, Bearbait!" The hulking warden left his conference and came up. Delbert conversed with him in low tones.

"Maybe that's where all the people went," Ace suggested. "Up north. All done turned into wolves." He lay back, tilted his hat across his eyes.

Jake grunted. "All done moved south, and I should have done a long time ago."

"Get away from the ice," John Hawkins agreed. "Must be cities and everything on down south yet."

"Like to see a city someday," Ace mumbled from under his hat. "Might just go south myself, when I get set."

"When you get set," Delbert scoffed. Bearbait had returned to pass the word.

"What's you tell that critter?" Jake demanded.

"Ain't no critter, that's Bearbait," Delbert protested mildly. "I told him what you said."

"What'd he say?"

"Said that devil left his mark all around the north edge of the grazing. They want to kill it. I told him long as that devil don't steal stock or something, they can leave him be."

"How come you like wolves so much?" Ace lifted his hat slightly to peer at Jake.

Jake grunted around his pipestem. "They let me alone, I let them alone."

For a moment they sat silent. Presently Big John knocked his pipe against a rock and stood up. The ponies came to his whistle and shortly they rode on.

* * *

The wardens were not pleased with the directive from the Masters, and controversy bubbled in the camps all night. Quailflusher lay with his head to the fire and listened to his grandmother inveigh against the northling, the Masters' folly in tolerating its presence, and the supineness of the House wardens, her grandson Bearbait included. Bearbait had been there earlier in the evening, and there had been harsh words between him and his grandmother. Now Starfall was in a religious rage. Her opinion was known in the clans, and those of like mind had been drifting in all night to confer with her, or more exactly, to hear her speak. Her cause and her audience spurred her to new heights of eloquence, and exorcisms were heard that night that had not been sung since *her* grandmother's time. Quailflusher lay bemused while Starfall's voice rolled over him.

The fire itself entered his thoughts, itself the greatest of the Masters' benisons, the symbol of the bond between Master and warden since the first cur dog crept out of the woods to share a hunter's campfire. The fear of the stranger beat in Quailflusher's veins and warred with his reverence for the Masters. Could the All-wise be wrong? What reason could They have for protecting the demon? There had been no explanation, only the order. Hunt not the northling. Quailflusher had smelled the creature's markers himself; the strangeness was eerie, a smell of wildness, the wind, and the north. Quailflusher's hackles arose again at the thought. His stomach knotted.

"Quail." His second cousin, Grabchuck, sniffed his mask politely and lay down beside him. His discomfort showed in the set of his ears. "What do you think?"

Quailflusher sighed and rested his chin on his paws again. "I don't know, 'Chuck. Grandmother's older than anyone, almost. She knows the woods and flocks, she knows medicine and spirits. But...."

Grabchuck flicked an ear. "But Bearbait knows the Masters."

Quailflusher sighed again. "If it weren't Grandmother talking, I'd say let it go. We can't defy the Masters. We only watch the flocks, and do as the Masters bid us. That's why They made us. The devil is still north of the range. It hasn't acted yet, except to mock us. But Grandmother is so sure...."

"I wish it would do something! Then we'd know. But it just stays; it's like waiting for a storm in the summer." Sparks flew up as their great-aunt threw more sticks on the fire with a practiced toss of her head. Grabchuck dodged as a spark lit near him. "Listen, Quail, there's something else. The devil didn't sing tonight."

"So? We know he's out there. Some of Fisher's camp found a fawn he killed this morning."

"That's just it. He answered us before. Why not tonight? Look, Quail, have you forgotten about Willow? When she came under forbidding she went outrange to the east. What if the devil finds her?"

Quailflusher sat up. "Her mother is back. She smelled nothing to the east."

"But Fisher's people said the markers tended east. We've heard nothing from her. Shouldn't we be looking for her?"

"Impossible!" Quailflusher was shocked. "Go after her, when she's forbidden? Grandmother would have a fit!"

"But Willow may be in danger!" Grabchuck turned his head away embarrassedly. "In her present state of mind she can't be thinking clearly. Someone should investigate, at least make sure she's all right!"

"Look, quiet down." Quailflusher fought his own sense of unease. "Would your state of mind be any clearer if you were near her? It's easy to get worked up over a forbidden bitch, any young dog would. We know she's out there, we can imagine her loneliness, we can feel her longing in our own. But it's forbidden, it's unlucky even to think of it! Fall heats are unlucky for everyone, and we've had three this fall in our camp alone. We've got to be especially careful at a time like this." He lay down again. "And besides," he added, "she's forbidden to you, anyway, or to anyone from our clan."

"The spirits smite me if I was thinking any such thing!" Grabchuck expostulated. "I'm worried about her!"

Quailflusher thought for a while. The whelp could be right; there was some danger. Willow was already under evil influences. With the devil at large, who knew what might happen? "Well," he said. "I'll head over that way tomorrow when I'm off watch, check around for markers, see if I can get a whiff of something."

"I'll go, too," urged Grabchuck. "Better if two go . . . because of the forbidding, I mean."

"I'll ask White Rabbit, too. We should have a bitch along."

Their grandmother's voice rose in a new exorcism, and was joined by the voices of her followers. After a moment Quail and Grabchuck joined in, too. The voices rose up, a great bell of sound before the moon.

In the house, a couple of kilometers away, Delbert sat by a window listening in rapture to the sound. The rest of the Hawkins clan sat or sprawled about the room, more or less oriented toward the fire. Some occupied themselves with small handiwork. A candle or two supplemented the fire with small puddles of flickering yellow light; in one of them Delbert's wife, Rida, pored over a large herbal. Conversation murmured desultorily. Wardens, cats, and cur dogs flopped about the floor and furniture. Jake sank deep in an armchair, a large cat in his lap. His eyes rested now on Delbert, now on one or another of the Hawkinses. He said little, and that only when spoken to. A deep disquiet fluttered somewhere in his belly, an unease he could not admit to, could scarcely identify. The soft voices of the others jarred strangely on his nerves. It was just people, he thought, after so long . . . but he was used to being alone now. The people jarred on his presence. The fire was good, and the chair. He kneaded the cat's neck with his knuckles.

Delbert's cousin Little Earl stretched from his couch to pass Delbert the pipe. "Old wardens sure gettin' down tonight," he said, smoke rilling from his nostrils.

Delbert laughed. "Sure thing. Old wolf has really got them going."

Jake looked up sourly. "What are they singing?" He reached out to take the pipe from Delbert.

Delbert chuckled again. "Hexes," he said. "Trying to make that devil go away. We said they couldn't hunt him, so now they trying to hex him away. That one voice is old Starfall. She's a smart old gal. Most as old as old Moonsong there. She's old Bearbait's grandmother, ain't she, 'Bait?"

An answering rumble came from the great hulk of the warden slumped at his feet. Delbert rubbed his bare feet across the warden's shoulders. Jake relapsed into silence.

And under a bush a few klicks east, Willow sat listening to the song, her blood roiled with conflicting emotions. The wolf was sitting a few meters away in the shadow of another bush. His attention was focused entirely on Willow; from time to time he would shift his position and whine ingratiatingly. Willow panted slightly.

She had felt the wolf as a presence before he came seeking her. The impurity she was conceived to be under mandated loneliness; with nothing to do but avoid her own kind, she wandered aimlessly through the forest, hunting desultorily and fretting. She felt useless, and ashamed, and full of vain longings. She thought over all the ritual she knew to see if she might have omitted anything. Thoughts of various males kept drifting in upon her, shaming her further. And among them, the voice of the northling. . . .

The night after she left, she listened almost hungrily to the strange voice, still hovering just beyond comprehension. It echoed in her ears; she scarcely noticed her grandmother's denunciations ringing down the breeze.

She spent the next day idling along the run, playing and splashing in the water, startling the fish. She caught and ate a few mice in a meadow, lazed away the afternoon lolling on a flat rock by the stream. In the last light she caught a 'possum and carried it back to the bank to eat it. She had just finished it when the wolf came seeking her.

She ran, of course. He had appeared quite suddenly, stopped on catching sight of her, then started toward her wagging his tail. She leaped up and backed away, then turned tail and fled. He pursued her at a short distance, not drawing too close, but trying to persuade her of his sincerity. Willow was dumbfounded by the situation. His speech was incomprehensible, his appearance half-savage, half-demon, his intentions unmistakable, and utterly tabu. Willow's people had no legend of an incubus to victimize helpless females, but their understanding of the estrous phenomenon was highly magical in nature. Its suddenness and the completeness of its distraction suggested demonic possession. At the best of times estrus was carefully surrounded with cultural restrictions; unseasonable heats were presumed the result of devilish machinations. To Willow's knowledge this was the first time the demon Sex had appeared in such a concrete form. No dog warden would have pursued a bitch under forbidding, however great the temptation.

Her initial panic dissipated, Willow paused defensively, her back to a tree. The stranger approached cautiously, playfully. His gestures of courtship and deference were crude parodies of the delicate and sophisticated rituals of the wardens, but they had a certain power of their own. With a sudden frenzy of snapping and snarling, she drove him back again and fled down the path. The wolf came after her.

The sun went down without dimming the wolf's ardor; and so presently Willow found herself under a bush, racked with ambivalence, her grandmother's songs against the wolf ringing in her ears, the awful reality there before her. His presence surrounded her, his scent rank and strange in her nostrils. Every sound seemed magnified. She could hear his heartbeat quite clearly, quick and excited, over the thunder of her own. His voice was urgent, enticing. He seemed almost to be touching her. She whined softly in anxiety and frustration.

The wolf crawled from under his bush. He rolled on his back, whining, playing the youngling. Willow watched him in the dappled moonlight, her ears alert for every sound. The wolf crawled into the open, slightly closer to her. Abruptly stopping his plaintive whining, he rose slowly to his feet. Willow closed her mouth with a snap. The wolf went into full display, standing to his greatest height, his mane erect, his tail curled tight and bushy over his back. He took a step toward her. Willow came off the ground, sidled away nervously, out from under the bush and up onto a rock break. She stood facing him, tail between her legs, ready to bolt. He advanced stiff-legged, one step at a time, stretching out his nose toward her. His scent rushed upward to her on the light breeze. She felt dizzy, almost lightheaded. She took a step back. He came on steadily, closer and closer, leaning out to her. Putting one foot on the rock, he reached up, and their noses touched. The sound of his sniff was soft in her ear. His nose brushed her cheek, her ruff. His head loomed beside her, his thick mane touched her chin; his scent so familiar, so strange ... she sniffed warily, unable to help herself. And again, his face, his chin ... their whiskers mingled, their noses touched. Her face burned, her belly on fire. He turned slightly, took a step, sniffed again at her neck, her flank. She stood rigid, then turned her head toward him. She was burning up. She could still hear her grandmother's song, but distantly. It seemed strange, irrelevant, unrelated to the living presence beside her. The wolf was more real, more natural. The fire mounted in her loins, and the agonizing, unspecific, seeking desire she had felt for days resolved itself upon the wolf.

"Tell us a story, Moonsong," Delbert said. "Jake wants to hear you tell a story."

Jake sat up in his chair. The old warden lay with her head to the fire, her chin resting on her paws. She lifted it and answered; Jake caught her drift well enough this time: what story would he hear?

"Any story," said Delbert. "Tell where wardens came from." The other Hawkinses sighed and stirred, orienting themselves toward the warden on the hearth. Delbert eased back in his chair and grinned at Jake. "I'll explain what she's saying so's you can understand it better, Jake."

Then Moonsong spoke, and Jake explained her words thus:

In the beginning there were two brothers, and they were Cur Dog and Savage. They lived in a field by the edge of the woods, and they ate rabbit and woodchuck and 'possum. When the storm blew, they curled up in their earth; and when the brush fire burned, they fled before it; and they hid from the lion and bear and wolverine, for these were stronger and fiercer than they.

One day the Masters came and built Their house in the midst of the field. Around it They fenced and plowed, and the horse and cow and sheep did Their bidding. The cat lazed on Their doorstep, and the chicken pecked in the yard; and when the lion and bear came prowling, the Masters smote them with devices and hung their skins by the door.

Then Cur Dog said to Savage, "Come, let us, too, go to the Masters and seek Their grace. We, too, will lie on Their doorstep, and when the storm blows and the lion roars, we will lie by the fire and chew fat bones and be warm." But Savage feared the Masters and said, "They will surely destroy us even as the lion and bear. But stay, let us wait until night, and sneak up to the house and steal the chicken."

But Cur Dog was resolute. So he went and scratched at the Master's door, and when the Master came, he deferred to Him and begged grace. Then the Master said, "Since you have come, you may lie by the fire and have fat bones to chew. In exchange, you will guard the house and flocks, and warn against savage and lion and bear." So Cur Dog took the bone and lay by the fire, and when Savage came in the night to take chickens, Cur Dog awakened the Masters with his cries, and They smote Savage with Their devices so that he fled crying back to the woods. And ever after there was enmity between Cur Dog and Savage.

Then the Masters were many and rich. They built the stone places and lived there in great numbers. In Their wisdom They rose higher and higher, and went to live among the moon and stars. Then there were few Masters left on Earth, and without Them the sons of Cur Dog could not tend all the flocks. So the wards strayed and met accidents, and the sons of Savage ate many. Then the Masters took the flesh of Cur Dog, and from it they made the Warden. They said:

"We have made you stronger and wiser than any cur dog. With your kind you will guard the flocks even against lion and bear. You may eat those that fall by the way; but at the appointed time you will bring the flocks in so We may count the increase and select the best among them. Then We will see how well you have done Our bidding.

"As a token We will give you fire. If you tend it loyally, it will warm your camp; but if you let it die, only a Master can light it again for you. Let it be a reminder to you of Our grace."

So the Warden took the fire and did the Master's bidding, and so it has been ever since. But the Masters grew ever fewer—and though, by merit and loyalty of our ancestors, Sugar Hill still receives grace—for many tribes, no Masters attend when they bring the flocks at the appointed time. Still, we guard the flocks and their increase, for we know the Masters live among the moon and stars. Someday They will return to judge us at the appointed time; and when They see how the flocks have increased, They will know how well we have done Their bidding.

Here Moonsong stopped speaking, and the room sat silent but for the crackle of the fire.

"You reckon they ever will come back?" Rida said presently.

Delbert shook himself and stretched. "Bound to someday. They're still up there. See them fly over sometimes, way up high." He rose and went to pour himself some more cider from the jug mulling on the hearth.

Ace grunted. "Why should they? What've we got for them? Shit, they don't even know we're down here. They left us the wardens to look after us and took off. They ain't comin' back. I don't blame them. Shit, wish I could follow them." He swigged sourly at his cider.

Jake sat for a moment, then said, "So what about the wolf?"

Delbert laughed. "What about the wolf, Moonsong?"

The wolf (Moonsong explained) is a demon from the north, where no Masters or wardens dwell. It is a creature of wind and ice; it forbodes the winter storm. It mocks the wardens' loyalty and means death to the wards. It is a shadow on our dreams. We must drive it out.

Jake thought of wolves. "Nah," he said. "A wolf is just like a coyote, but bigger and smarter. It ain't no wind and ice, just flesh and blood. It can freeze or starve in the winter, too. I ought to know, I seen them dead in the bad winters."

We cannot have it here, said Moonsong. It bodes the going of the Masters. The Northmaster said he was the last Master in the North. Now he has left, and the demon has followed him. It is ill, it bodes only ill.

The old warden was visibly disturbed, and the other wardens in the room had become restive. Jake desisted from his argument.

"The winters keep getting worse, and that's the plain truth," said old Mr. Hawkins.

* * *

For three days Willow gave herself to love, and ranged at the wolf's side. They moved to the north and east, well away from Sugar Hill range, or any warden. Together they hunted, and slept, and made love. They romped and played in the fall fields, startling the deer. Their world was each other, and they gave no thought to the rest. For the wolf it was no hard task; he had sought and won a handsome bitch, and his interest in the wardens, no longer so academic, was centered on her. The investigation of the other wardens could wait. Willow for her part had cast off all civilized restraints. If in the back of her mind she knew she must pay for this joy, the fire in her blood did not permit her to dwell on the matter. She was utterly consumed with love. The wolf was her only reality, and her grandmother's exorcisms in the distance seemed the height of irrelevance. For two nights they did not trouble themselves to reply to the evensong.

On the first day of Willow's love, Grabchuck, Quailflusher, and his mate, White Rabbit, had gone seeking her. They searched for several kilometers outrange, and found several markers, both Willow's and the wolf's; but these were many hours old, and told nothing but that Willow was still in heat, and the wolf had been eating deer, which they knew. The couple had already withdrawn from the area, and the three found no evidence of their meeting, nor indeed any marker less than sixteen hours old. Still, it was clear that the wolf had been in the same area, and Willow's absence was itself a suspicious circumstance. The cousins were greatly disquieted when they returned to camp.

Their grandmother was even more disquieted when they made their report. The wolf's failure to respond the night before had sparked a hope that the exorcism might be taking effect. Now, instead, it seemed he might be up to even greater mischief. Starfall took care the word was spread, and redoubled her efforts at evensong, inserting a personal call to Willow to respond and tell her whereabouts. In the distance Willow heard the message and ignored it; the wolf, uncomprehending, did likewise. Starfall became persuaded the demon had compassed Willow's disappearance. Her instinctive horror of the northling was confirmed, and the desperate anguish of her lament stirred every warden in the valley.

On Sugar Hill the house wardens paced restlessly or went off to confer in the camps. The humans, too, were disturbed; even Jake could feel the tension in the song. Delbert explained the new anxiety: Jake scoffed, but the others turned uneasy glances on him, and he withdrew into silence. The songs continued unusually long. At last they were still, and the humans found unquiet sleep.

In the night it rained, and the drizzle continued into the morning. Before dawn search parties set out, but the scent, already cold, was well laid by the rain, and they did not find it. Willow, hearing their signals, led the wolf to the west, confusing the trail as she went. By midday the rain had died down; most of the searchers had given up and returned to camp. Only a few continued to search, Quailflusher and Grabchuck among them. Late in the day they picked up a few markers where the lovers had been. By then it had grown dark, but the cousins persevered, and began casting toward the west.

The sky had cleared, and the moon rose almost full. Many wardens had gathered at Starfall's camp, and the entire valley waited upon her voice. Presently she came forth and, mounting a lofty rock, began to sing in a voice of pain. Woe upon us, she cried, woe has come upon us. We have strayed from the way, we have neglected ritual and duty. A path was opened: a devil has come from the north. She sang the devil, she sang storm and wind and ice, till all the valley joined in the cry of dread. Then, shifting suddenly, she entered a plaintive mode, a parent's lament for a lost child. She sang Willow's beauty and virtue, and the curse laid upon her by devils. She sang the grief and anxiety of kinfolk longing for a child's return, and the wickedness of a demon that would work evil on a lost and lonely maiden. Hopelessly pleading, she cried Willow's name: If she could hear, if she yet lived, answer now, only answer!

And Willow answered.

She and the wolf lay some kilometers to the north. In the early evening they had pulled down a lame stag, and feasted to repletion. In the bright moonlight Willow's joy had seemed complete, and she and the wolf lay side by side, grooming and caressing each other. Now the grief of her kinfolk reached out to her, and in that moment she felt she must explain, allay their fears, tell them of her joy.

She sang of her love and her happiness. She sang the beauty and nobility of the wolf, and her joy in his company. And he, understanding not her words but her tone, joined his voice to hers in splendid harmony, a duet of wilderness and love and freedom. Before all the valley they declared themselves in clear song.

For a moment there was stunned silence. A few voices rose—startled, angry, inquiring—to be cut off by Starfall's clear, high quaver. Witchcraft! she cried. The demon has bewitched her! And she began a well-known exorcism, in which other voices gradually joined, from one range to another, until the whole valley rang with it.

On Sugar Hill, Delbert turned from his window and looked whither Jake sat in shadow. "Well, your wolf's done it now," he commented. The other Hawkinses stared at Jake.

Jake shifted nervously. "*My* wolf?" He glanced around, feeling the weight of more than a score of looks. "What's he done?"

Delbert sank down on the bench with a sigh. His uncle, Old Earl, passed him a full beaker. "It's kind of hard to explain." Delbert sipped at the cider. "You heard them two voices answer old Starfall just now?"

"Yeah," said Jake. "One was the wolf."

"The other was a little bitch warden named Willow. Looks like they're, uh, you know, gettin' it on." Delbert appeared somewhat embarrassed, glanced apologetically toward Moonsong.

"What's wrong with that?" Jake stared around defiantly. "Wolves are right close to dogs. Wild dogs breed with wolves up north. Run with the same pack sometimes."

A growl rose from several throats, and a young warden started to his feet. "Easy, there! Down!" Delbert quieted the wardens. A couple of the humans chuckled.

"Well, now," said Delbert testily, "firstly, these ain't no cur dogs. Wardens are proud. They don't mix their blood with no cur dogs. No wolves, neither.

"Secondly, bitch wardens don't generally come in heat

this time of year. When they do, they reckon it's the evil spirits or something, and they s'posed to go off alone till they're out again. Ain't no dog warden s'posed to go near them till then. But this wolf—'course they reckon he's a devil, anyway. But now he's gone and led that Willow astray—and her Starfall's own granddaughter, ain't she, Bearbait? Your cousin, ain't she?" An answering rumble. "So the wardens are mad as hell." He sat back judiciously.

"Well now, wait a minute. How's the wolf s'posed to know that?" Jake felt that the currents were running against him; but the role of wolf's advocate seemed to be his. "It gets lonely traveling. How's he s'posed to know?"

Moonsong's voice rose from her place by the fire. She spoke at some length; Jake could not follow it. Delbert translated, "They reckon it was witchcraft. They can't have no breeding with no devil. She says that wolf has got to go."

"It ain't no devil!" Jake insisted. "It's just a critter, like a warden or a sheep or something. If you stick him, he bleeds."

Delbert shrugged. "I don't know about that. All I know is what the wardens think, and it ain't no use arguing with them."

There was a pause.

"Nice weather we been having for hunting," Little Earl observed thoughtfully.

"Be different from foxes," added his brother Billy.

"Oh, shit." Jake got up suddenly, dumping a cat complaining on the floor, and walked outside. For some time he stood staring at the moon, listening to the night sounds. The wardens were still now. The moonlight flooded the hilltop. He scuffed his feet in the leaves and thought of the lover's song. He remembered the girl, and that last spring up north, when she was just pregnant, when she and Jake and the old man had lived in the lakeside cabin ... and he cursed and kicked among the leaves. The breeze freshened, and he shook himself. Presently he went back inside. The conversation was on another matter. He filled his pipe and took himself back to his armchair.

Quailflusher and Grabchuck pelted through the night in the direction whence Willow's voice had come. Only they had continued so long. They had finally cut the couple's trail shortly before the singing began, and their grandmother's voice had impelled them along it. They were checked and casting about in a rocky patch when Willow answered; at once they were off again. Within minutes they had picked up the scent, and loped easily over the countryside. The moon gave more than enough light, and their noses led them surely. They did not give tongue, but followed the trail in silence. It seemed to grow fresher by the meter.

Her people's rejection of her love shocked Willow into a moment of lucidity. The wolf, the dead stag, the moonlit clearing seemed suddenly foreign, dreamlike. She rose and walked about, fretfully testing the air. The wolf, sensing her anxiety, approached her solicitously. They exchanged sniffs. His manner was affectionate, reassuring. He was real indeed. Her blood stirred again. The wolf licked her face; she responded in kind. He nipped at her playfully and danced, inviting her to wrestle. Tempted, she took a step, then stopped again, uneasy. In the distance the songs of her people still sounded. The breeze stirred about them, bringing scents of the night, cool and damp, the small rustling sounds ... something ... she turned, tested the air again. The breeze was shifty ... there. Home-smell. Someone was coming. Not many, but fast, running. The wolf had caught it now, too; he bristled slightly, paced nervously, took up a stand before the dead stag.

"No!" Willow growled softly. "Leave it! We've got to go!" She edged toward the north side of the clearing. The wolf would not heed her. The moonlight fell full upon him, standing to his greatest height, his mane erect, his eyes gleaming, a fearsome sight. She could not leave him.

Running feet sounded loud now; the scent grew rank, and Quailflusher and Grabchuck burst into the clearing. With a roar the wolf charged. Grabchuck was bowled over by his rush; Quail was seized by the throat and thrown before he could collect himself. Quail fought desperately: a moment later, Grabchuck rejoined the fray, and the issue stood in doubt. The wolf let go of Quailflusher, knocked Grabchuck over again, then gave a prodigious leap to land three meters away, in full aggressive display. He had nothing of warden language, but they understood him clearly. Leave us alone, he said.

Quail and Grabchuck had not expected to plunge directly into combat. They were intimidated. "Willow!" Quailflusher barked, all his hair on end. "Willow! Where are you? Are you here?" He began sliding to the right, still facing the wolf, ready to meet a fresh attack.

Willow unfroze suddenly. "Here!" she cried. "Stop! Don't fight him!" She darted forward to stand by the wolf, shouldering him, then pushing in front of him. "Don't fight him! You don't understand!"

The two wardens backed up a pace or two. "What are you doing here, running with the devil like this? What are you thinking of?" Grabchuck's voice was sharp in the sudden quiet.

"He's not a devil!" she cried passionately. "He's wild and beautiful! Grandmother is wrong! Quailflusher, my uncle, you always loved me and watched out for me ever since I was a puppy tumbling at your feet, can't you understand? Don't you know what I feel? I can't leave him!"

"Willow, Willow, it's your blood speaking, not you! Look at him, look at him! He's no warden! He's monstrous! Like a huge savage, but ferocious and dangerous! Didn't you see how he attacked us? He's dangerous!"

"You attacked us, you came to take me away! He fought for me, as my own mate should! See, you challenge him still! Why can't you leave us alone? Why can't all of you leave us alone? Every night the songs, and no one understands, not even you, Quailflusher!"

Quailflusher withdrew another step. "You are bewitched, Willow. You don't know what you're saying. Listen to me, listen to your people calling you! Shake off this spell the demon has cast on you. Leave him, come back with us!"

Willow stopped. In the distance the great chorus still rang. She shook herself. A great wave of bitterness rose in her. "No. You're wrong. You don't understand. I can't leave him, I won't. He is wild and strange and beautiful, but he's no devil. Who should know better? You don't know him. Grandmother knows nothing of him. He is my mate." She sat down. The wolf, puzzled by the incomprehensible discussion, nuzzled her ear. She lay down. The wolf stood over her protectively, facing the two wardens.

"Is this your last word?" Quailflusher demanded.

"I will stay with him," Willow repeated.

"We'll tell Grandmother what you have said," Quailflusher said with dignity. He turned carefully and strode from the clearing, breaking into a trot as he reentered the sheltering trees. Grabchuck followed.

The sun was well up and the Hawkinses had breakfasted the next morning when a delegation of leading wardens approached the front porch of the house. Bearbait went out and conferred with them, then came inside and spoke briefly with Delbert. The family waited expectantly.

"Well," said Delbert. He glanced at Jake, then looked at his father. "They want to talk to us," he said. " 'Bout the wolf." He looked at Jake again. Jake looked elsewhere.

"Yeah," Big John said. "Well, looks like we better talk to them, then." He rose slowly and started out to the front door. The others followed. Delbert paused a moment.

"Jake? You coming?"

Jake stirred. "Yeah. I reckon." He got up and followed.

On the front porch they assembled, old Mr. Hawkins and Big John in front. Jake pushed toward them; the others made room for him. Several house wardens, Bearbait and Moonsong among them, took up positions around the family. A good dozen wardens sat waiting, several of them visibly grizzled with age. An extremely elderly bitch warden sat slightly before the others.

"Delbert?" old Mr. Hawkins invited. Delbert stepped forward, hunkered down a meter or two from the old warden.

"Yo, old Starfall," he said. She came forward, sniffed his hand, panted briefly as he rumpled her ears and rubbed her neck. He spoke to her in warden talk, softly, soothingly. She nudged his hand, then sat back formally and addressed the humans.

The family stirred; Big John glanced at Big Earl, then at Jake. Delbert spoke, translating.

"It's what I said last night, Jake. The wolf done run off with that Willow. Couple of these young wardens"—he indicated two younger wardens among the delegation—"tracked them and found them last night. Say the wolf attacked them. And that Willow wouldn't leave it. They figure it's bewitched her proper. Anyways, they want to hunt it down." He stopped, scanned the assembly.

The humans stirred. Big John looked at Jake, cleared his throat. The younger men were muttering, openly eager. Jake sighed.

"Why?" he demanded. "You-all just want to hunt the wolf. You know he ain't bewitched nothing. That Willow's in heat. She'll get over it in a couple days and come on home, same as any . . . I mean, you-all just looking for an excuse." He looked the wardens over; they were all on their feet, glaring, some with hackles raised. Only old Starfall remained sitting at attention. "You wardens," he said. "That wolf ain't no kind of devil. I seen plenty of wolves up north. They're just a critter, like anything else. No different from a big coyote, 'cept maybe a little smarter. He ain't done nothing to you. What are you so scared of?"

Starfall spoke, slowly. The humans listened. Presently Delbert translated: "All ill comes from the north. Even the Northmaster has fled from it, with the news that no Masters live there now. Such creatures as this have never been in the valley before, and now they come, following the Northmaster. What will be the end of it? This year there have been many portents. Stock has been lost; wardens have been cursed, some to death. There have been many fall heats. Now the last Master is gone from the north, and the north has come to us. Shall we stand by and let this happen? Can we let our youth be seduced? What then? What when it raids our flocks, like a savage? Shall we forbear, until this house stands empty, no roof to keep out the snow, like the others in the valley? We have our faith to keep. We will protect what we have, until the Masters come again from the sky. You say the devil is only a big savage. Well, we have killed many savages. We will kill this one, too." She was silent, and sat with dignity, watching the humans. Jake bit his lip, cursed under his breath. The Hawkinses muttered among themselves.

"All right!" Little Earl broke out. "Let's do it! What the hell?"

Ace sniffed the fall air, fresh and clear after the previous day's rain. "Right good weather for it," he commented. There was a general murmur of assent among the men.

"Yeah," Big John said. "No offense to you, Jake, but I can't see no reason not to hunt it. The wardens want to. I guess it ain't done no damage so far, but who knows what it might do? If it's just a critter like you say, why not?" He, too, looked around, breathed deeply. "It's a real good day for hunting." All eyes now turned to Jake.

Jake sighed, shrugged. "Do what you want," he said. "I don't reckon it matters much. Plenty more wolves where that one came from." He shrugged again, turned and went back in the house. Voices rose excitedly behind him.

Willow and the wolf had stayed by the kill until morning. Willow was still deeply disturbed by the encounter, and the wolf appeared restless. In the broad light of morning they moved off to the west. In a meadow they browsed desultorily for field mice; the wolf was an adept mouser, but this morning his eye was out, and he missed easy catches. Presently they made love again; the act did not consume her as before, and she realized that her heat was waning. They lay in the sun for some time, but Willow could not rest. Her family's attitude fretted her. Sometime after noon she urged the wolf protesting to his feet and headed westward again. If they could get well outrange, the tribe might leave them alone. She mused, thought of a den, of young born in the dead of winter, of the wolf's protection, his skill in hunting. It all seemed unreal.

She found herself impatient with the wolf, who lagged behind, reluctant, panting in the midday warmth. After a time she consented to stop and rest again, but she continued nervous, starting at odd sounds. The wolf slept, twitching an ear occasionally. Presently she dozed.

In her sleep she hunted. The scent of a savage came clearly to her nostrils; she was running over the countryside, the air crisp and clear. Behind her the clan was running; she gave tongue and heard them answer, hot and eager, strangely distant. Farther back she heard the Huntsman's horn blat ... still the scent. She ran harder, the pack far behind now. She felt fear ... the horn blatted again, distant, too distant....

The horn! Of a sudden she was fully awake, on her feet, listening desperately. Yes, there. The horn, and then a hunt call ... Bearbait's voice! How many times she had thrilled to it, followed it in the field! The wolf stood now, listening in the same direction. He looked at her inquiringly. Another hunt call sounded, slightly closer. She shook herself in the early-evening chill. Four or five klicks off. Coming toward them ... in a flash it was clear. Horrified, she looked at the wolf.

"Run!" she cried, anguished for the first time at his inability to understand her speech. "We've got to run! We've got to lose them!" She shouldered him furiously, then broke for the western edge of the clearing. Looking back, she barked again at the wolf. Suddenly catching her fear, he started toward her, and in a moment they were flying through the covert. A run appeared, and Willow splashed into it. Her hunt training operated in reverse; and she doubled back into it again, the wolf after her, and splashed upstream a klick or more before breaking out across a meadow that offered open running.

Behind her she heard the hunt calls again. The wolf quickened his pace, pushed out ahead of her. They darted into a thick covert. Willow floundered briefly in a tangle of thorn, then wrenched herself free and followed the wolf again as he wriggled through a fox run and burst from the other side of the covert. Open meadows stretched some distance; they ran harder, Willow scarcely noticing the smarts where the thorns had slashed her. The horn sounded again; they had lost time in the covert.

At the crest of a hill they paused, panting. The last purple rays were fading ahead of them; overhead the first stars winked, and a vast and ruddy moon loomed on the horizon. Distantly the hunt calls sounded with a new eagerness; the hunters ... the clan! Her own folk! Her revered Masters, come hunting her! ... had the fresher scent now, and their voices lifted again and again. A sudden triumphant bugling told her they had found the spot where she and the wolf had lain only a little earlier. Her heart leaped in her breast, and she fled with the wolf close beside, fear and horror and grief driving all but flight from her mind. They skirted another covert, plunged downhill into another run. In an instant she turned downstream, and they splashed on frantically for quite some distance and knew that the first run had delayed them. A few minutes gained ... on she ran, the wolf beside her still, stretching into a ground-eating lope. The calls behind informed her as the pack cast about up and down the first run, found the scent again, and came on. It was eerie, horrible to flee from the sound she had followed so often. She racked her brain for the tricks that foxes and savages had used to evade the hunt in the past, doubling back, confusing the trail. The wolf had no experience of this form of hunt, and his clumsiness hampered her. Again and again he stopped, faced back growling, obliging her to urge him on. Anger was overcoming his fear; the wardens were outside their territory. How dare they attack him here, in no-wolf's-land? But they were many, and Willow urged him on. He ran.

The second creek stopped them for less time, and Willow knew from the calls that they were closing the distance. The pack had come too close while they slept. She remembered her nervous urge to move on—if only they had kept moving, farther on, out of warden range, too far to pursue—the breath came quick in her throat now. Up hill, down hollow. The night was a blur. The Huntsman's horn blatted, less than three klicks behind now. She heard a horse whinny.

A dense hedge of rose ran across the meadow, opposing them. They ran along it, found a low gap, wriggled through, sustaining more scratches as they went. And up the next hill. The moon was well up now, and as she crested the hill she looked back. At the same instant a full-throated bellow gave the view halloo, and the pack was in full cry, the night ringing with fierce gladness. The wolf nipped her angrily, and she fled again with a whine. Down hollow, up hill. The pack poured over the hill behind them. She could distinguish individual voices easily, Bearbait and Fisher, bold Lion's-meat, clear-voiced Larksong of the Meadows and deep-chested Bull from the Greenwood sib, and there, there—her throat twisted—there the voice of Quailflusher, her uncle who loved her, and of Grabchuck, her little cousin she tumbled about with as a pup, even they! Her step faltered; a stone turned under her foot. The wolf was ahead of her, lashing up the hill. A massive oak loomed at the top, standing alone, its dead leaves still clinging to the bough casting a deep shadow over the hillside in the moonlight. Beneath it the wolf halted, faced back as Willow came up, rage in his voice as he bayed sudden answer to his persecutors.

"No!" Willow cried. "Don't stop! Run!" He snarled at her, then threw back his head and let his voice ring defiance. The moon struck through the branches, dappling his immense mane with silver. Willow dithered for a moment, wanting to run, unable to persuade the wolf. She murmured in his ear, sniffed his mane. For a moment he softened; his whiskers brushed her cheek. Then the hunt field came over the last crest. The pack roared down in the hollow; the wolf was all attention again. Willow stood beside him.

The first forms appeared in the moonlight, lunging up the slope. The wolf filled his lungs and roared, a sound that seemed to stop the night. The leading wardens stumbled; the ones behind fell over them. For a moment there was confusion as the pack sorted itself out not ten meters from them, halted by the wolf's rage. Two or three voices took up the cry again, to be silenced by another bellow from the wolf. He took a pace forward, and another. Some of the wardens fell back, leaving one clearly in the fore. Bearbait, Willow saw. The knowledge seemed meaningless. The wolf took another step, and charged with a roar. Bearbait charged quickly to meet him, and they crashed together, their jaws seeking purchase. A moment the pack wavered; then with a cry Bull plunged forward to lock his teeth in the wolf's flank, then Fisher, and the pack fell on the wolf.

With a wild cry Willow plunged into the melee, throwing her kinsmen aside, her jaws slashing at whomever stood in her way. Her vision turned red; she smelled only rage and pain. Beneath the heaving bodies she sought and found the familiar smell of the wolf, mixed now with blood. Jaws closed on her, slashed her flank. A voice cried "Willow!" With berserk fury she flung her kinsmen aside, penetrating to the bottom, to the wolf. Someone had his teeth in the wolf's throat. Willow slashed at the attacker's head, sank her teeth in his shoulder, sought a grip on his throat. Someone else slashed her hind leg. She gripped loose skin and shook with all her strength.

Of a sudden the noise was less. A horn sounded near at hand. A lash fell suddenly, stinging across her and her opponent alike. With a yelp he released his hold on the wolf and jumped away. For a moment she was dragged. Then she let go and stood. The wolf lay still. She stepped, sniffed at him. His throat was torn open, his blood soaked the hillside from a hundred gashes. She stood over him and turned to face the pack. The Masters were there on Their horses, whipping in. The Huntsman sat His horse three meters off, whip in hand, watching her. She looked at her kinfolk milling in confusion. A dam broke within. She threw back her head and cried out grief without words, older than her race, greater than the world. The hunters were still. The wardens sat rapt; the Masters, even the horses stock-still as she wept. She did not stop, could not stop. For endless time her voice rose, sound beyond song.

At last she sank down, the deathsong dying out in sobs. She licked the wolf's head, his mane, tasting his blood, her breath breaking in little sobs still. There was movement at a distance; dimly she understood that the hunt was drawing off, riders and wardens going off slowly down the hill. Her grief welled up again and burst forth in a new cry. The others were leaving. Her voice cried death to all the valley. She cared not. She grieved. Presently she was alone.

All night she wept, her voice ringing out again and again as grief warred with exhaustion. In the small hours she sank down at last, not into sleep but into a stunned, spent apathy. She lay with her head on the wolf's, knowing nothing.

Much later she became aware of motion. She lifted her head slowly. The night had waned. Faint light spread from the east, showing an unfamiliar Master a short distance away. He crouched, looking at her. She growled feebly. He murmured softly, then whined in a manner remarkably like the wolf's. She stared at Him blankly. He moved again, extended a hand in her direction. There was only death in her nostrils. Her head sank again. The wolf was dead. His corpse was stiff beneath her. The Master was a little closer, still murmuring, making wolf-sounds. She did not know Him. A horse stamped nearby. She did not care.

The hand was in front of her nose now; involuntarily she sniffed. She did not know Him. Softly the Master crooned to her. He touched the wolf's shoulder. She growled, without spirit. The wolf was dead. She would not leave him.

The Master touched her; with a quick movement she caught His cuff in her teeth. He was still, talking to her in a soft voice. He did not speak warden. She understood a little of His talk now, but it meant nothing. She let go of His cuff. He stroked her head, speaking softly. She lay still.

The strange Master rose slowly. "Willow," He said. "Willow."

She looked up without lifting her head.

"Come, Willow," He said, in Master-talk. "We got to go now."

"I will not leave him." She spoke for the first time, not caring if He understood her.

"I know," He said. "We'll bring him. Come."

She rose slowly, looked at the Master. "Who are You?"

Again He seemed to understand. He spoke His name, unpronounceable Master-talk. Then He said, "Them other wardens call me Northmaster, and Wolfmaster. They say I brought the wolf." She stared at Him. Wolfmaster. Northmaster. He knelt beside her, ran His hand over the dead wolf's fur. "Come on. We'll bury him, we two."

Bury him. The thought wakened a longing for ritual in her heart. They would bury him. Ritual. She stepped aside; the Wolfmaster gathered up her lover and walked heavily to the pony. It shied from the smell, afraid both of death and wolf, but steadied at His word. He draped the wolf behind the saddle, lashed it in place, mounted. She followed Him.

Snow was drifted before the door of the stone house. Jake heard John Hawkins stamping it from his feet beneath the overhang before he knocked. He opened, and Hawkins stepped inside quickly, a breath of cold around him.

"You O.K., Jake?"

"No problem, John. Plenty of firewood. Plenty of meat froze. Just thaw it out by the fire there when we need it." He smiled. Hawkins looked uneasy.

"Well, we worried a little, 'count of the storm. Knowing you was over here alone and all. You sure you don't want to come back over to the big house?"

"No, that's O.K., John. I'm used to being alone. We're O.K. here. I don't reckon them wardens want to see me too much. And I know they don't want to see Willow. 'Specially now." He grinned faintly.

"How's that?" Big John looked about for the warden.

"There." Jake pointed with his chin to the fireplace. Willow lay in a mound of sheepskin, only her head showing. "Look there." He walked over, hunkered by her and rubbed her forehead. John peered over his shoulder. "Look." Jake pulled the sheepskins aside. Two puppies nestled among the wool, close by Willow's side.

"Be damned," Big John said. "Be damned."

"Just a couple of nights ago."

"I didn't, I mean, I didn't know if it'd work out," Big John said. "Wolf and a warden, I mean, never heard of . . . didn't know if she'd have them all right. Look all right, don't they?"

"Yeah." Jake thumped Willow's ribs lightly, pulled the sheepskins back over them. "Don't know what they'll look like."

"Be damned," Big John said again.

"We'll be all right," Jake said.

Editor's Introduction to "Tourist Trade," by Robert Silverberg

I have known Robert Silverberg for a dozen years, and I will not soon forget his kindness and support when I first began to write and publish science fiction. This story, however, reminds me of an incident that has nothing to do with Silverberg.

Largely on the recommendation of Jacques Barzun I read *The Education of Henry Adams* when I was an undergraduate. It was as worthwhile as Barzun promised, and I recommend it to anyone interested in the world of the intellect. In one memorable chapter Adams tells how he began keeping a daily journal, and highly recommends the practice because "The habit of self-expression leads to the search for something worthwhile to express." I suspect that sentence changed my life. I've kept a journal ever since, and Adams is right about the consequences.

I keep a journal; but I often wish I kept a scrapbook. Larry Niven does. Larry began writing science fiction in the 1960's. Most of his stories were published in *Galaxy Science Fiction*, then edited by Fred Pohl, who once sent Larry Niven a most remarkable letter which I saw in Larry's scrapbook.

In one of his stories Larry's hero faces aft in his ship as

it moves swiftly through space. Larry used the phrase "Ass backward through the universe." Fred Pohl wanted to publish the story; but it needed editing. In particular the phrase "ass backward" had to be removed. Fred's letter explains. It wasn't that Fred Pohl objected to such rough language; but science fiction was largely bought by teen-age boys, and their mothers sometimes thumbed through the magazines. If one of the mothers saw *that* language, she might well banish the magazine from the house forever. *Galaxy* didn't have enough readers to make it possible to stand on principle. Larry's story had to be changed.

That was fifteen years ago. Think about it while you read this tale of aliens.

Tourist Trade

Robert Silverberg

After a moment Eitel's eyes adjusted to the darkness and the glare of the clashing crisscrossing spotlights. But he didn't need his eyes to tell him what sort of bizarre zoo he had walked into. His sensitive nostrils picked up the whole astonishing olfactory blast at once: a weird hodgepodge of extraterrestrial body odors, offworld pheromones, transgalactic cosmetics, the ozone radiation of personal protection screens, minute quantities of unearthly atmospheres leaking out of breathing devices.

"Something wrong?" David asked.

"The odors. They overwhelm me."

"The smoking, eh? You hate it that much?"

"Not the tobacco, fool. The aliens! The e-t's!"

"Ah. The smell of money, you mean. I agree, it is very overwhelming in here."

"For a shrewd man you can sometimes be very stupid," Eitel muttered. "Unless you say such things deliberately, which you must, because I have never known a stupid Moroccan."

"For a Moroccan, I am very stupid," said David serenely. "And so it was very stupid of you to choose me as your partner, eh? Your grandfathers in Zurich would be shamed if they knew. Eh?" He gave Eitel a maddeningly seraphic smile.

Eitel scowled. He was never sure when he had genuinely offended the slippery little Moroccan and when David was merely teasing. But somehow David always came out of these interchanges a couple of points ahead.

He turned and looked the place over, checking it out.

Plenty of humans, of course. This was the biggest gathering-place for aliens in Morocco, the locus of the focus, and a lot of gawkers came to observe the action. Eitel ignored them. There was no sense doing business with humans any more. There were probably some Interpol types in here too, hoping to head off just the sort of deals Eitel was here to do. To hell with them. His hands were clean, more or less.

But the aliens! The aliens, the aliens, the aliens!

All over the room. Vast saucer eyes, spidery limbs, skins of grotesque textures and unnameable colors. Eitel felt the excitement rising in him, so unSwiss of him, so thoroughly out of character.

"*Look* at them!" he whispered. "They're beautiful!"

"Beautiful? You think so?"

"Fantastic!"

The Moroccan shrugged. "Fantastic, yes. Beautiful, no. Blue skin, green skin, no skin, two heads, five heads: this is beauty? What is beautiful to me is the money. And the way they like to throw it away."

"You would never understand," said Eitel.

In fact Eitel hardly understood it himself. He had discovered, not long after the first alien tourists had reached Earth, that they stirred unexpected areas of his soul: strange vistas opening, odd incoherent cosmic yearnings. To find at the age of forty that there was more to him than Panamanian trusts and numbered bank accounts—that was a little troublesome; but it was delicious, as well. He stood staring for a long ecstatic chaotic moment. Then he turned to David and said, "Where's your Centauran?"

"I don't see him."

"Neither do I."

"He swore he'd be here. Is a big place, Eitel. We go looking, and we find."

The air was thick with color, sound, fumes. Eitel moved

carefully around a tableful of leathery-faced pockmarked red Rigelians, burly, noisy, like a herd of American conventioneers out on the town. Behind them sat five sleek and sinuous Steropids, wearing cone-shaped breathers. Good. Steropids were easy marks. If something went wrong with this Centauran deal David had set up, he might want to have them as customers to fall back on.

Likewise that Arcturan trio, flat heads, grizzled green hair, triple eyes bright as blue-white suns. Arcturans were wild spenders, though they weren't known to covet Eitel's usual merchandise, which was works of fine art, or more or less fine art. Perhaps they could be encouraged to. Eitel, going past, offered them a preliminary smile: Earthman establishing friendly contact, leading perhaps to more elaborate relationship. But the Arcturans didn't pick up on it. They looked through Eitel as though their eyes didn't function in the part of the spectrum he happened to inhabit.

"There," David said.

Yes. Far across the way, a turquoise creature, inordinately long and narrow, that appeared to be constructed of the finest grade of rubber, stretched over an awkwardly flung together armature of short rods.

"There's a woman with him," Eitel said. "I wasn't expecting that. You didn't tell me."

David's eyes gleamed. "Ah, nice, very nice!"

She was more than very nice. She was splendid. But that wasn't the point. Her presence here could be a troublesome complication. A tour guide? An interpreter? Had the Centauran brought his own art expert along? Or was she some Interpol agent decked out to look like the highest-priced of hookers? Or maybe even a real hooker. God help me, he thought, if the Centauran's gotten involved in some kind of kinky infatuation that would distract him from the deal. No: God help David.

"You should have told me there was a woman," Eitel said.

"But I didn't know! I swear, Jesus Mary Moses, I never see her yesterday! But it will be all right. Jesus Mary Moses, go ahead, walk over." He smiled and winked and slipped off toward the bar. "I see you later, outside. You go for it, you hear? You hear me, Eitel? It will be all right."

* * *

The Centauran, seeing the red carnation in Eitel's lapel, lifted his arm in a gesture like the extending of a telescopic tube, and the woman smiled. It was an amazing smile, and it caught Eitel a little off guard, because for an instant it made him wish that the Centauran was back on Centaurus and this woman was sitting here alone. He shook the thought off. He was here to do a deal, not to get into entanglements.

"Hans Eitel, of Zurich," he said.

"I am Anakhistos," said the Centauran. His voice was like something out of a synthesizer, which perhaps it was, and his face was utterly opaque, a flat motionless mask. For vision he had a single bright strip of receptors an inch wide around his forehead, for air intake he had little vents on its cheeks, and for eating he had a three-sided oral slot like the swinging top of a trash basket. "We are very happied you have come," he said. "This is Agila."

Eitel allowed himself to look straight at her. It was dazzling but painful, a little like staring into the sun. Her hair was red and thick, her eyes were emerald and very far apart, her lips were full, her teeth were bright. She was wearing a vaguely futuristic metal-mesh sheath, green, supple, clinging. What she looked like was something that belonged on a 3-D billboard, one of those unreal idealized women who turn up in the ads for cognac, or skiing holidays in Gstaad. There was something a little freakish about such excessive beauty. A professional, he decided.

To the Centauran he said, "This is a great pleasure for me. To meet a collector of your stature, to know that I will be able to be of assistance—"

"And a pleasure also for ourself. You are greatly recommended to me. You are called knowledgeable, reliable, discreet—"

"The traditions of our family. I was bred to my *metier*."

"We are drinking mint tea," the woman said. "Will you drink mint tea with us?" Her voice was warm, deep, unfamiliar. Swedish? Did they have redheads in Sweden?

Eitel said, "Forgive me, but it's much too sweet for me. Perhaps a brandy instead—"

A waiter appeared as though by telepathic command. Eitel ordered a Courvoisier, and the woman another round of tea. She is very smooth, very good, he thought. He imagined himself in bed with her, digging his fingers into that dense red mane, running his lips over her long lean thighs. The fantasy was pleasing but undisturbing: an idle dream, cool, agreeable, giving him no palpitations, no frenzy. Good. After that first startled moment he was getting himself under control. He wondered if she was charging the Centauran by the night, or working at something bigger.

She said, "I love the Moroccan tea. It is so marvelous, the sweet. Sugar is my passion. I think I am addicted."

The waiter poured the tea in the traditional way, cascading it down into the glass from three feet up. Eitel repressed a shudder. He admired the elaborate Moroccan cuisine, but the tea appalled him: lethal hypersaccharine stuff, instant diabetes.

"Do you also enjoy mint tea?" Eitel asked the alien.

"It is very wonderful," the Centauran said. "It is one of the most wonderful things on this wonderful planet."

Eitel had no idea how sincere the Centauran was. He had been studying the psychology of extraterrestrials about as closely as anyone had, in the decade since they had begun to descend on Earth en masse after the lifting of the galactic quarantine, and he knew a lot about a lot of them; but he found it almost impossible to get a reading on Centaurans. If they gave any clues to their feelings at all, it was in the form of minute, perhaps imaginary fluctuations of the texture of their rubbery skins. It was Eitel's theory that the skin slackened when they were happy and went taut when they were tense, but the theory was only preliminary and he gave it little value.

"When did you arrive on Earth?" Eitel asked.

"It is the first week," the Centauran said. "Five days here in Fez, then we go to Rome, Paris, and afterward the States United. Following which, other places. It is greatly exciting, your world. Such vigor, such raw force. I hope to see everything, and bring back much art. I am passionate collector, you know, of Earthesque objects."

"With a special interest in paintings."

"Paintings, yes, but I collect many other things."

That seemed a little blatant. Unless Eitel misunderstood the meaning, but he doubted he had. He glanced at the woman, but she showed no reaction.

Carefully he said, "Such as?"

"Everything that is essential to the experience of your world! Everything fine, everything deeply Earthesque! Of course I am most fastidious. I seek only the first-rate objects."

"I couldn't possibly agree more," said Eitel. "We share the same philosophy. The true connoisseur has no time for the tawdry, the trivial, the incompletely realized gesture, the insufficiently fulfilled impulse." His tone, carefully practiced over years of dealing with clients, was intended to skirt unctuousness and communicate nothing but warm and sincere approbation. Such nuances were probably lost on the Centauran, but Eitel never let himself underestimate a client. He looked suddenly toward the woman and said, "Surely that's your outlook also."

"Of course."

She took a long pull of her mint tea, letting the syrupy stuff slide down her throat like motor oil. Then she wriggled her shoulders in a curious way. Eitel saw flesh shifting interestingly beneath the metal mesh. Surely she was professional. *Surely*. He found himself speculating on whether there could be anything sexual going on between these two. He doubted that it was possible, but you never could tell. More likely, though, she was merely one of the stellar pieces in Anakhistos' collection of the high-quality Earthesque: an object, an artifact. Eitel wondered how Anakhistos had managed to find her so fast. Was there some service that supplied visiting aliens with the finest of escorts, at the finest of prices?

He was picking up an aroma from her now, not unpleasant but very strange: caviar and cumin? Sturgeon poached in Chartreuse?

She signalled to the waiter for yet another tea. To Eitel she said, "The problem of the export certificates, do you think it is going to get worse?"

That was unexpected, and very admirable, he thought. Discover what your client's concerns are, make them your own.

He said, "It is a great difficulty, is it not?"

"I think of little else," said the Centauran, leaping in as

if he had been waiting for Agila to provide the cue. "To me it is an abomination. These restrictions on removing works of art from your planet—these humiliating inspections—this agitation, this outcry for even tighter limitations—what will it come to?"

Soothingly Eitel said, "You must try to understand the nature of the panic. We are a small backward world that has lived in isolation until just a few years ago. Suddenly we have stumbled into contact with the great galactic civilizations. You come among us, you are fascinated by us and by our artifacts, you wish to collect our things. But we can hardly supply the entire civilized universe. There are only a few Leonardos, a few Vermeers: and there are so many of you. So there is fear that you will sweep upon us with your immense wealth, with your vast numbers, with your hunger for our art, and buy everything of value that we have ever produced, and carry it off to places a hundred light-years away. So these laws are being passed. It is natural."

"But I am not here to plunder! I am here to make legimate purchase!"

"I understand completely," Eitel said. He risked putting his hand, gently, compassionately, on the Centauran's arm. Some of the e-t's resented any sort of intimate contact of this sort with Earthfolk. But apparently the Centauran didn't mind. The alien's rubbery skin felt astonishingly soft and smooth, like the finest condom imaginable. "I'm altogether on your side," Eitel declared. "The export laws are absurd overreactions. There's a more than ample supply of art on this planet to meet the needs of sophisticated collectors like yourself. And by disseminating our culture among the star-worlds, we bind ourselves inextricably into the fabric of galactic civilization. Which is why I do everything in my power to make our finest art available to our visitors."

"But can you provide valid export licenses?" Agila asked.

Eitel put his finger to his lips. "We don't need to discuss it further just now, eh? Let us enjoy the delights of this evening, and save dreary matters of commerce for later, shall we?" He beamed. "May I offer you more tea?"

* * *

It was all going very smoothly, Eitel thought. Contact made, essential lines of agreement established. Even the woman was far less of a complication than he had anticipated. Time now to back off, relax, let rapport blossom and mature without forcing.

"Do you dance?" Agila said suddenly.

He looked toward the dance floor. The Rigelians were lurching around in a preposterously panderous way, like dancing bears. Some Arcturans were on the dance-floor too, and a few Procyonites bouncing up and down like bundles of shiny metal rods, and a Steropid doing an eerie *pas seul*, weaving in dreamy circles.

"Yes, of course," he said, a little startled.

"Please dance with me?"

He glanced uneasily toward the Centauran, who nodded benignly. She smiled and said, "Anakhistos does not dance. But I would like to. Would you oblige me?"

Eitel took her hand and led her out on the floor. Once they were dancing he was able to regain his calm. He moved easily and well. Some of the e-t's were openly watching them—they had such *curiosity* about humans sometimes—but the staring didn't bother him. He found himself registering the pressure of her thighs against his thighs, her firm heavy breasts against his chest, and for an instant he felt the old biochemical imperative trying to go roaring through his veins, telling him, *follow her anywhere, promise anything, say anything, do anything.* He brushed it back. There were other women: in Nice, in Rome, in Athens. When he was done with this deal he would go to one of them.

He said, "Agila is an interesting name. Israeli, is it?"

"No," she said.

The way she said it, serenely and very finally, left him without room to maneuver. He was full of questions—who was she, how had she hooked up with the Centauran, what was her deal, how well did she think Eitel's own deal with the Centauran was likely to go? But that one cool syllable seemed to have slammed a curtain down. He concentrated on dancing again instead. She was supple, responsive, skillful. And yet the way she danced was as strange as everything else about her: she moved almost as if her feet were some inches off the floor. Odd. And her voice—an accent, but what kind? He had been everywhere, and nothing in his experience matched her way of speaking, a certain liquidity in the vowels, a certain resonance in the phrasing, as though she were hearing echoes as she spoke. She had to be something truly exotic, Rumanian, a Finn, a Bulgar—and even those did not seem exotic enough. Albanian? Lithuanian?

Most perplexing of all was her aroma. Eitel was gifted with a sense of smell worthy of a perfumer, and he heeded a woman's fragrance the way more ordinary men studied the curves of hip or bosom or thigh. Out of the pores and the axillae and the orifices came the truths of the body, he believed, the deepest, the most trustworthy, the most exciting communications; he studied them with rabbinical fervor and the most minute scientific zeal. But he had never smelled anything like this, a juxtaposition of incongruous spices, a totally baffling mix of flavors. Some amazing new perfume? Something imported from Arcturus or Capella, perhaps? Maybe so, though it was hard to imagine an effect like this being achieved by mere chemicals. It had to be *her*. But what mysterious glandular outpouring brought him that subtle hint of sea urchin mingled with honey? What hidden duct sent thyme and raisins coursing together through her bloodstream? Why did the crystalline line of light perspiration on her flawless upper lip carry those gracenotes of pomegranate, tarragon, and ginger?

He looked for answers in her eyes: deep green pools, calm, cool, unearthly. They seemed as bewildering as the rest of her.

And then he understood. He realized now that the answer, impossible and implausible and terrifying, had been beckoning to him all evening, and that he could no longer go on rejecting it, impossible or not. And in the moment of accepting it he heard a sound within himself much like that of a wind beginning to rise, a hurricane being born on some far-off isle.

Eitel began to tremble. He had never felt himself so totally defenseless before.

He said, "It's amazing, how human you seem to be."

"*Seem* to be?"

"Outwardly identical in every way. I didn't think it was

possible for life-forms of such a degree of similarity to evolve on two different worlds."

"It isn't," she said.

"You're not from Earth, though."

She was smiling. She seemed almost pleased, he thought, that he had seen through her masquerade.

"No."

"What are you, then?"

"Centauran."

Eitel closed his eyes a moment. The wind was a gale within him; he swayed and struggled to keep his balance. He was starting to feel as though he were conducting this conversation from a point somewhere behind his own right ear. "But Centaurans look like—"

"Like Anakhistos? Yes, of course we do, when we are at home. But I am not at home now."

"I don't understand."

"This is my traveling body," she said.

"What?"

"It is not comfortable, visiting certain places in one's own body. The air is sharp, the light hurts the eyes, eating is very troublesome."

"So you simply put on a different body?"

"Some of us do. There are those like Anakhistos who are indifferent to the discomforts, or who actually regard them as part of the purpose of traveling. But I am of the sort that prefers to transfer into a traveling body when going to other worlds."

"Ah," Eitel said. "Yes." He continued to move through the rhythms of the dance in a numb, dazed way. It's all just a costume, he told himself. What she really looks like is a bunch of rigid struts, with a rubber sheet draped over them. Cheek-vents for breathing, three-sided slot for eating, receptor strip instead of eyes. "And these bodies?" he asked. "Where do you get them?"

"Why, they make them for us. Several companies do it. The human models are only just now becoming available. Very expensive, you understand."

"Yes," he said. "Of course."

"Tell me: when was it that you first saw through my disguise?"

"I felt right away that something was wrong. But it wasn't until a moment ago that I figured it out."

"No one else has guessed, I think. It is an extremely excellent Earth body, would you not say?"

"Extremely," Eitel said.

"After each trip I always regret, at first, returning to my real body. This one seems quite genuine to me by now. You like it very much, yes?"

"Yes," Eitel said helplessly.

He found David out in the cab line, lounging against his taxi with one arm around a Moroccan boy of about sixteen and the other exploring the breasts of a swarthy French-looking woman. It was hard to tell which one he had selected for the late hours of the night: both, maybe. David's cheerfully polymorphous ways were a little hard for Eitel to take, sometimes. But Eitel knew it wasn't necessary to approve of David in order to work with him. Whenever Eitel showed up in Fez with new merchandise, David was able to finger a customer for him within twenty-four hours; and at a five percent commission he was probably the wealthiest taxi driver in Morocco, after two years as Eitel's point man among the e-t's.

"Everything's set," Eitel said. "Take me over to get the stuff."

David flashed his glittering gold-toothed grin. He patted the woman's rump, lightly slapped the boy's cheek, pushed them both on their way, and opened the door of his cab for Eitel. The merchandise was at Eitel's hotel, the Palais Jamai, on the edge of the native quarter. But Eitel never did business at his own hotel: it was handy to have David to take him back and forth between the Jamai and the Hotel Merinides, out here beyond the city wall by the ancient royal tombs, where most of the aliens preferred to stay.

The night was mild, fragrant, palm trees rustling in the soft breeze, huge bunches of red geranium blossoms looking almost black in the moonlight. As they drove toward the old town, with its maze of winding medieval streets, its walls and gates straight out of the Arabian nights, David said, "You mind I tell you something? One thing worries me."

"Go ahead."

"Inside, I watched you. Staring more at the woman than at the e-t. You got to concentrate on the deal, and forget the woman, Eitel."

Eitel resented being told by a kid half his age how to conduct his operations. But he kept himself in check. To David, young and until recently poor, certain nuances were incomprehensible. Not that David lacked an interest in beauty. But beauty was just an abstraction; money was money. Eitel did not attempt to explain what time would surely teach.

He said, "*You* tell *me*, forget the woman?"

"Is a time for women, is a time for business. Separate times. You know that, Eitel. A Swiss, he is almost a Moroccan, when it comes to business."

Eitel laughed. "Thanks."

"I am being serious. You be careful. If she confuse you, it can cost you. Can cost *me*. I am in for percentage, remember. Even if you are Swiss, maybe you need to know: Business and women must be kept separate things."

"I know."

"You remember it, yes?"

"Don't worry about me," Eitel said.

The cab pulled up outside the Jamai. Eitel, upstairs, withdrew four paintings and an Olmec jade statuette from the false compartment of his suitcase. The paintings were all unframed, small, genuine, and unimportant. After a moment he selected the *Madonna of the Palms*, from the atelier of Lorenzo Bellini: plainly apprentice work, but enchanting, serene, pure, not bad, easily a $20,000 painting. He slipped it into a carrying case, put the others back, all but the statuette, which he fondled for a moment and put down on the dresser, in front of the mirror, as though setting up a little shrine. To beauty, he thought. He started to put it away and changed his mind. It looked so lovely there that he decided to take his chances. Taking your chances, he thought, is sometimes good for the health.

He went back to the cab.

"Is a good painting?" David asked.

"It's pretty. Trivial, but pretty."

"I don't mean good that way. I mean, is it real?"

"Of course," Eitel said, perhaps too sharply. "Do we

have to have this discussion again, David? You know damned well I sell only genuine paintings. Overpriced a little, but always genuine."

"One thing I never can understand. Why you not sell them fakes?"

Startled, Eitel said, "You think I'm crooked, David?"

"Sure I do."

"You say it so lightheartedly. I don't like your humor sometimes."

"Humor? What humor? Is against law to sell valuable Earth works of art to aliens. You sell them. Makes you crook, right? Is no insult. Is only description."

"I don't believe this," Eitel said. "What are you trying to start here?"

"I only want to know, why you sell them real stuff. Is against the law to sell real ones, is probably not against the law to sell them fakes. You see? For two years I wonder this. We make just as much money, we run less risk."

"My family has dealt in art for over a hundred years, David. No Eitel has ever knowingly sold a fake. None ever will." It was a touchy point with him. "Look," he said, "maybe you like playing these games with me, but you could go too far. All right?"

"You forgive me, Eitel?"

"If you shut up."

"You know better than that. Shutting up I am very bad at. Can I tell you one more thing, and then I shut up really?"

"Go ahead," Eitel said, sighing.

"I tell you this: You a very confused man. You a crook who thinks he not a crook, you know what I mean? Which is bad thinking. But is all right. I like you. I respect you, even. I think you are excellent businessman. So you forgive rude remarks?"

"You give me a great pain," Eitel said.

"I bet I do. You forget I said anything. Go make deal, many millions, tomorrow we have mint tea together and you give me my cut and everybody happy."

"I don't like mint tea."

"Is all right. We have some anyway."

Seeing Agila standing in the doorway of her hotel room,

Eitel was startled again by the impact of her presence, the overwhelming physical power of her beauty. *If she confuse you, it can cost you.* What you see is all artificial, he told himself. It's just a mask. Eitel looked from Agila to Anakhistos, who sat oddly folded, like a giant umbrella. That's what she really is, Eitel thought. She's Mrs. Anakhistos from Centaurus, and her skin is like rubber and her mouth is a hinged slot and this body that she happens to be wearing right now was made in a laboratory. And yet, and yet, and yet—the wind was roaring, he was tossing wildly about—

What the hell is happening to me?

"Show us what you have for us," Anakhistos said.

Eitel slipped the little painting from its case. His hands were shaking ever so slightly. In the closeness of the room he picked up two strong fragrances, something dry and musty coming from Anakhistos, and the strange, irresistible mixtures of incongruous spices that Agila's synthetic body emanated.

"*The Madonna of the Palms*, Lorenzo Bellini, Venice, 1597," Eitel said. "Very fine work."

"Bellini is extremely famous, I know."

"The famous ones are Giovanni and Gentile. This is Giovanni's grandson. He's just as good, but not well known. I couldn't possibly get you paintings by Giovanni or Gentile. No one on Earth could."

"This is quite fine," said Anakhistos. "True Renaissance beauty. And very Earthesque. Of course it is genuine?"

Eitel said stiffly, "Only a fool would try to sell a fake to a connoisseur such as yourself. But it would be easy enough for us to arrange a spectroscopic analysis in Casablanca, if—"

"Ah, no, no, no, I meant no suspicioning of your reputation. You are impeccable. We unquestion the genuinity. But what is done about the export certificate?"

"Easy. I have a document that says this is a recent copy, done by a student in Paris. They are not yet applying chemical tests of age to the paintings, not yet. You will be able to take the painting from Earth, with such a certificate."

"And the price?" said Anakhistos.

Eitel took a deep breath. It was meant to steady him,

but it dizzied him instead, for it filled his lungs with Agila.

He said, "If the deal is straight cash, the price is four million dollars."

"And otherwise?" Agila asked.

"I'd prefer to talk to you about that alone," he said to her.

"Whatever you want to say, you can say in front of Anakhistos. We are absolute mates. We have complete trust."

"I'd still prefer to speak more privately."

She shrugged. "All right. The balcony."

Outside, where the sweetness of night-blooming flowers filled the air, her fragrance was less overpowering. It made no difference. Looking straight at her only with difficulty, he said, "If I can spend the rest of this night making love to you, the price will be three million."

"This is a joke?"

"In fact, no. Not at all."

"It is worth a million dollars to have sexual contact with me?"

Eitel imagined how his father would have answered that question, his grandfather, his great-grandfather. Their accumulated wisdom pressed on him like a hump. To hell with them, he thought.

He said, listening in wonder to his own words, "Yes. It is."

"You know that this body is not my real body."

"I know."

"I am an alien being."

"Yes. I know."

She studied him in silence a long while. Then she said, "Why did you make me come outside to ask me this?"

"On Earth, men sometimes become quite angry when strangers ask their wives to go to bed with them. I didn't know how Anakhistos would react. I don't have any real idea how Centaurans react to anything."

"I am Centauran also," she pointed out.

"You don't seem as alien to me."

She smiled quickly, on-off. "I see. Well, let us confer with Anakhistos."

But the conference, it turned out, did not include Eitel.

He stood by, feeling rash and foolish, while Agila and Anakhistos exchanged bursts of harsh rapid words in their own language, a buzzing, eerie tongue that was quite literally like nothing on Earth. He searched their faces for some understanding of the flow of conversation. Was Anakhistos shocked? Outraged? Amused? And she? Even wearing human guise, she was opaque to him too. Did she feel contempt for Eitel's bumptious lusts? Indifference? See him as quaintly primitive, bestial, anthropoid? Or was she eagerly cajoling her husband into letting her have her little adventure? Eitel had no idea. He felt far out of his depth, a sensation as unfamiliar as it was unwelcome. Dry throat, sweaty palms, brain in turmoil: but there was no turning back now.

At last Agila turned to him and said, "It is agreed. The painting is ours at three million. And I am yours until dawn."

David was still waiting. He grinned a knowing grin when Eitel emerged from the Merinides with Agila on his arm, but said nothing. I have lost points with him, Eitel thought. He thinks I have allowed the nonsense of the flesh to interfere with a business decision, and now I have made myself frivolous in his eyes. It is more complicated than that, but David would never understand. *Business and women must be kept separate things.* To the taxi driver, Eitel knew, Helen of Troy herself would be as nothing next to a million dollars: mere meat, mere heat. So be it, Eitel told himself. David would never understand. What David would understand, Eitel thought guiltily, was that in cutting the deal with Agila he had also cut fifty thousand dollars off David's commission. But he did not intend to let David know anything about that.

When they were in Eitel's room Agila said, "First, I would please like to have some mint tea, yes? It is my addiction, you know. My aphrodisiac."

Sizzling impatience seared Eitel's soul. God only knew how long it might take room service to fetch a pot of tea at this hour, and at a million dollars a night he preferred not to waste even a minute. But there was no way to refuse. He could not allow himself to seem like some panting schoolboy.

"Of course," he said.

After he had phoned, he walked around behind her as she stood by the window peering into the mists of the night. He put his lips to the nape of her neck and cupped his hands over her breasts. This is very crazy, he thought. I am not touching her real body. This is only some synthetic mock-up, a statue of flesh, a mere androidal shell.

No matter. No matter. He was able to resist her beauty, that illusion, that figment. That beauty, astonishing and unreal, was what had drawn him at first, but it was the dark secret alien underneath that ruled him now. That was what he hoped to reach: the alien, the star-woman, the unfathomable being from the black interstellar deeps. He would touch what no man of Earth had ever touched before.

He inhaled her fragrance until he felt himself swaying. She was making an odd purring sound that he hoped was one of pleasure.

There was a knock at the door. "The tea is here," she said.

The waiter, a boy in native costume, sleepy, openly envious of Eitel for having a woman like Agila in his room, took forever to set up the glasses and pour the tea, an infinitely slow process of raising the pot, aiming, letting the thick tea trickle down through the air. But at last he left. Agila drank greedily, and beckoned to Eitel to have some also. He smiled and shook his head.

She said, "But you must. I love it so—you must share it. It is a ritual of love between us, eh?"

He did not choose to make an issue of it. A glass of mint tea more or less must not get in the way, not now.

"To us," she said, and touched her glass to his.

He managed to drink a little. It was like pure liquid sugar. She had a second glass, and then, maddeningly, a third. He pretended to sip at his. Then at last she touched her hand to a clasp on her shoulder and her metal-mesh sheath fell away.

They had done their research properly, in the body-making labs of Centaurus. She was flawless, sheer fantasy, heavy breasts that defied gravity, slender waist, hips that would drive a Moroccan camel-driver berserk, buttocks like pale hemispheres. They had given her a navel, pubic hair, erectile nipples, dimples here and there, the hint of blue veins in her thighs. Unreal, yes, Eitel thought, but magnificent.

"It is my fifth traveling body," she said. "I have been Arcturan, Steropid, Denebian, Mizarian—and each time it has been hard, hard, hard! After the transfer is done, there is a long training period, and it is always very difficult. But one learns. A moment finally comes when the body feels natural and true. I will miss this one very much."

"So will I," Eitel said.

Quickly he undressed. She came to him, touched her lips lightly to his, grazed his chest with her nipples.

"And now you must give me a gift," she said.

"What?"

"It is the custom before making love. An exchange of gifts." She took from between her breasts the pendant she was wearing, a bit of bright crystal carved in disturbing alien swirls. "This is for you. And for me—"

Oh, God in Heaven, he thought. No!

Her hand closed over the Olmec jade figurine that still was sitting on the dresser.

"This," she said.

It sickened him. That little statuette was eighty thousand on the international antiquities market, maybe a million or two to the right e-t buyer. A gift? A love-token? He saw the gleam in her eye, and knew he was trapped. Refuse, and everything else might be lost. He dare not show any trace of pettiness. Yes. So be it. Let her have the damned thing. We are being romantic tonight. We are making grand gestures. We are not going to behave like a petit-bourgeois Swiss art peddler. *If she confuse you, it can cost you*, David had said. Eitel took a deep breath.

"My pleasure," he said magnificently.

He was an experienced and expert lover; supreme beauty always inspired the best in him; and pride alone made him want to send her back to Centaurus with incandescent memories of the erotic arts of Earth. His performance that night—and performance was the only word he could apply to it—might well have been the finest of his life.

With the lips and tongue, first. Everywhere. With the

fingers, slowly, patiently, searching for the little secret key places, the unexpected triggering-points. With the breath against the skin, and the fingernails, ever so lightly, and the eyelashes, and even the newly sprouting stubble of the cheek. These were all things that Eitel loved doing, not merely for the effects they produced in his bed-partners but because they were delightful in and of themselves; yet he had never done them with greater dedication and skill.

And now, he thought, perhaps she will show me some of *her* skills.

But she lay there like a wax doll. Occasionally she stirred, occasionally she moved her hips a little. When he went into her, he found her warm and moist—why had they built that capacity in, Eitel wondered?—but he felt no response from her, none at all.

He moved her this way, that, running through the gamut of positions as though he and she were making a training film for newlyweds. Now and then she smiled. Her eyes were always open: she was fascinated. Eitel felt anger rising. She was ever the tourist, even here in his bed. Getting some first-hand knowledge of the quaint sexual techniques of the primitive Earthmen.

Knowing he was being foolish, that he was compounding a foolishness, he drove his body with frantic intensity, rocking rhythmically above her, grimly pushing her on and on. *Come on*, he thought. *Give me a little sigh, a moan, a wriggle. Anything.* He wasn't asking her to come. There was no reason why they should have built *that* capacity in, was there? The only thing he wanted now was to get some sort of acknowledgement of his existence from her, some quiver of assent.

He went on working at it, knowing he would not get it. But then, to his surprise, something actually seemed to be happening. Her face grew flushed, and her eyes narrowed and took on a new gleam, and her breath began to come in harsh little bursts, and her breasts heaved, and her nipples grew hard. All the signs, yes: Eitel had seen them so many times, and never more welcome than at this moment. He knew what to do. The unslackening rhythm now, the steady building of tension, carrying her onward, steadily higher, leading her toward that magical moment of overload when the watchful conscious mind at last surrenders to the surging deeper forces. Yes. Yes. The valiant Earthman giving his all for the sake of transgalactic passion, laboring like a galley slave to show the star-woman what the communion of the sexes is all about.

She seemed almost there. Some panting now, even a little gasping. Eitel smiled in pleasant self-congratulation. Swiss precision, he thought: never underestimate it.

And then somehow she managed to slip free of him, between one thrust and the next, and she rolled to the side, so that he collapsed in amazement into the pillow as she left the bed. He sat up and looked at her, stunned, gaping, numbed.

"Excuse me," she said, in the most casual way. "I thought I'd have a little more tea. Shall I get some for you?"

Eitel could barely speak. "No," he said hoarsely.

She poured herself a glass, drank, grimaced. "It doesn't taste as good as when it's warm," she said, returning to the bed. "Well, shall we go on?" she asked.

Silently he reached for her. Somehow he was able to start again. But this time a distance of a thousand light-years seemed to separate him from her. There was no rekindling that brief flame, and after a few moments he gave up. He felt himself forever shut away from the inwardness of her, as Earth is shut away from the stars. Cold, weary, more furious with himself than with her, he let himself come. He kept his eyes open as long as he could, staring icily into hers, but the sensations were unexpectedly powerful, and in the end he sank down against her breasts, clinging to her as the impact thundered through him.

In that bleak moment came a surprise. For as he shook and quivered in the force of that dismal ejaculation something opened between them, a barrier, a gate, and the hotel melted and disappeared and he saw himself in the midst of a bizarre landscape. The sky was a rich golden-green, the sun was deep green and hot, the trees and plants and flowers were like nothing he had ever seen on Earth. The air was heavy, aromatic, and of a piercing flavor that stung his nostrils. Flying creatures that were not birds soared unhurriedly overhead, and some iridescent beasts that looked like red velvet pillows mounted on tripods were grazing on the lower branches of furry-limbed trees. On the horizon Eitel saw three jagged naked mountains of some yellow-brown stone that gleamed like polished metal in the sunlight. He trembled. Wonder and awe engulfed his spirit. This is a park, he realized, the most beautiful park in the world. But this is not *this* world. He found a little path that led over a gentle hill, and when he came to the far side he looked down to see Centaurans strolling two by two, hand in hand, through an elegantly contoured garden.

Oh, my God, Eitel thought. Oh, my God in heaven!

Then it all began to fade, growing thin, turning to something no more substantial than smoke, and in a moment more it was all gone. He lay still, breathing raggedly, by her side, watching her breasts slowly rising and falling.

He lifted his head. She was studying him. "You liked that?"

"Liked what?"

"What you saw."

"So you know?"

She seemed surprised. "Of course! You thought it was an accident? It was my gift for you."

"Ah." The picture-postcard of the home world, bestowed on the earnest native for his diligent services. "It was extraordinary. I've never seen anything so beautiful."

"It is very beautiful, yes," she said complacently. Then, smiling, she said, "That was interesting, what you did there at the end, when you were breathing so hard. Can you do that again?" she asked, as though he had just executed some intricate juggling maneuver.

Bleakly he shook his head, and turned away. He could not bear to look into those magnificent eyes any longer. Somehow—he would never have any way of knowing when it had happened, except that it was somewhere between "Can you do that again?" and the dawn, he fell asleep. She was shaking him gently awake, then. The light of a brilliant morning came bursting through the fragile old silken draperies.

"I am leaving now," she whispered. "But I wish to thank you. It has been a night I shall never forget."

"Nor I," said Eitel.

"To experience the reality of Earthian ways at such close range—with such intimacy, such immediacy—"

"Yes. Of course. It must have been extraordinary for you."

"If ever you come to Centaurus—"

"Certainly. I'll look you up."

She kissed him lightly, tip of nose, forehead, lips. Then she walked toward the door. With her hand on the knob, she turned and said, "Oh, one little thing that might amuse you. I meant to tell you last night. We don't have that kind of thing on our world, you know—that concept of owning one's mate's body. And in any case, Anakhistos is not male, and I am not female, not exactly. We mate, but our sex distinctions are not so well defined as that. It is with us more like the way it is with your oysters, I think. So it is not quite right to say that Anakhistos is my husband, or that I am his wife. I thought you would like to know." She blew him a kiss. "It has been very lovely," she said. "Goodbye."

When she was gone he went to the window and stared into the garden for a long while without looking at anything in particular. He felt weary and burned out, and there was a taste of straw in his mouth. After a time he turned away.

When he emerged from the hotel later that morning, David's car was waiting out front.

"Get in," he said.

They drove in silence to a cafe that Eitel had never seen before, in the new quarter of town. David said something in Arabic to the proprietor and he brought mint tea for two.

"I don't like mint tea," Eitel said.

"Drink. It washes away bad tastes. How did it go last night?"

"Fine. Just fine."

"You and the woman, ficky-ficky?"

"None of your ficky-ficky business."

"Try some tea," David urged. "It not so good last night, eh?"

"What makes you think so?"

"You not look so happy. You not sound so happy."

"For once you're wrong," Eitel said. "I got everything I wanted to get. Do you understand me? I got everything I wanted to get." His tone might have been a little too loud, a little too aggressive, for it drew a quizzical, searching look from the Moroccan.

"Yes. Sure. And what size deal? That *is* my business, yes?"

"Three million cash."

"Only three?"

"Three," Eitel said. "I owe you a hundred fifty thousand. You're doing all right, a hundred fifty for a couple of hours' work. I'm making you a rich man."

"Yes. Very rich. But no more deals, Eitel."

"What?"

"You find another boy, all right? I will work now with someone else, maybe. There are plenty of others, you know? I will be more comfortable with them. Is very bad, when one does not trust a partner."

"I don't follow you."

"What you did last night, going off with the woman, was very stupid. Poor business, you know? I wonder, did you have to pay her? And did you pay her some of my money too?"

David was smiling, as always. But sometimes his smiles were amiable and sometimes they were just smiles. Eitel had a sudden vision of himself in a back alley of the old town, bleeding. He had another vision of himself undergoing interrogation by the customs men. David had a lot of power over him, he realized.

Eitel took a deep breath and said, "I resent the insinuation that I've cheated you. I've treated you very honorably from the start. You know that. And if you think I bought the woman, let me tell you this: she isn't a woman at all. She's an alien. Some of them wear human bodies when they travel. Underneath all that gorgeous flesh she's a Centauran, David."

"And you touched her?"

"Yes."

"You put yourself inside her?"

"Yes," Eitel said.

David stood up. He looked as though he had just found a rat embryo in his tea. "I am very glad we are no longer partners, then. Deliver the money to me in the usual way. And then please stay away from me when you are in this city."

"Wait," Eitel said. "Take me back to the Merinides. I've got three more paintings to sell."

"There are plenty of taxi drivers in this city," said David.

When he was gone, Eitel peered into his mint tea for a while and wondered if David meant to make trouble for him. Then he stopped thinking about David and thought about that glimpse of a green sun and a golden landscape that Agila had given him. His hands felt cold, his fingers were quivering a little. He became aware that he wanted more than anything else to see those things again. Could any Centauran make it happen for him, he wondered, or was that only Agila's little trick? What about other aliens? He imagined himself prowling the night club, hustling for action, pressing himself up against this slithery thing or that one, desperately trying to reenact that weird orgasmic moment that had carried him to the stars. A new perversion, he thought. One that even David found disgusting.

He wondered what it was like to go to bed with a Vegan or an Arcturan or a Steropid. God in heaven! Could he do it? Yes, he told himself, thinking of green suns and the unforgettable fragrance of that alien air. Yes. Yes. Of course he could. Of course.

There was a sudden strange sweetness in his mouth. He realized that he had taken a deep gulp of the mint tea without paying attention to what he was doing. Eitel smiled. It hadn't made him sick, had it? Had it? He took another swig. Then, in a slow determined way, he finished off all the rest of it, and scattered some coins on the counter, and went outside to look for a cab.

Editor's Introduction To "The Fifty-Candle Blowout," by Michael Glyer

Fans have always been important to science fiction. In no other literary genre is it customary, or even possible, for writers to associate so freely and easily with their readers. In the past decade science fiction has grown popular. Some works even reach the best seller list. Consequently, in times past fans were a much larger part of the SF readership than now; but even though the economic importance of fandom is much reduced, science fiction fans remain influential. It isn't just that fans vote the Science Fiction Achievement Awards (Hugos). Fans still provide instant feedback, and popularity with fans is prized by all but a very few SF writers.

The annual World Science Fiction Convention (Worldcon) is our biggest SF event. In 1984 it was held in Los Angeles. Actually, it wasn't. The Worldcon was controlled by Los Angeles fandom—the Committee governing the convention was nearly identical with the leadership of the Los Angeles Science Fantasy Society—but the Worldcon has become too big. No convention hotel in Los Angeles was large enough, so the convention had to be held in Anaheim, across from Disneyland. The interaction of fandom and the Magic Kingdom had to be seen to be appreciated.

Michael Glyer is a former officer and director of the Los Angeles Science Fantasy Society, and publisher of *File 770*, a leading fan magazine. Glyer has often been nominated for a Hugo for his fan writing; and he has often worn tee shirts expressing his disappointment at not winning. This year he expected to win and came prepared: in addition to his Seven Time Hugo Loser shirt, he had one that proclaimed "One Time Hugo Winner." He wore it when they took his photograph while holding the *two* Hugos he won this year.

1984: The Fifty-Candle Blowout

Michael Glyer

Upon reaching the year synonymous with an Orwellian view of a bleak future, it was appropriate that science fiction fandom bustle with activity: and it did, but in positive ways, 180° removed from the impoverished, repressive, violent world of the novel *1984*. From a journalist's viewpoint the year revolved around major news stories: the Summer Olympics, the U.S. Presidential elections, deficit spending and economic recovery, Michael Jackson and bombings in Beirut. But from the science fiction fan's viewpoint, the five most important headlines were the following:

LASFS TURNS 50

With a touch of outré humor appropriate to the author of *Psycho*, Robert Bloch wrote in 1984, "Fifty years ago there were many famous organizations and societies throughout the world—the Nazi Party, the Gestapo, Murder Incorporated, and the Los Angeles Science Fantasy Society.

"Today only the Los Angeles Science Fantasy Society has survived."

The fiftieth anniversary of LASFS' first meeting on October 27, 1934, was a headline event because LASFS is the oldest science fiction club; the earliest of the Science Fiction League chapters created by *Wonder Stories* that has met regularly since its inception. Eleven years after the purchase, LASFS also is still the only science fiction club which owns its clubhouse, an achievement made possible because LASFS is the largest science fiction club in the world. Over 100 members attend the weekly meetings, and after five decades its membership roster lists thousands of persons, including distinguished writers and fans like Ray Bradbury, Forrest J. Ackerman (winner of the first Hugo Award), F. Towner Laney, Larry Niven, Jerry Pournelle, Bruce Pelz (holder of the largest science fiction fanzine collection), David Gerrold, Charles Burbee, Robert Bloch, Robert Heinlein, John and Bjo Trimble (organizers of the "Save Star Trek" letter campaign that extended the show's life another year), William Rotsler, Richard E. Geis and Len and June Moffatt.

At LASFS' 50th Anniversary Dinner, Bloch's letter was read and enjoyed by the guests, along with congratulatory notes from Poul Anderson and Lucasfilm's Gary Kurtz. The featured after-dinner speaker was Harlan Ellison; in addition to all his other qualifications, Harlan was born in 1934, the same year as LASFS.

Harlan also shared his birth year with another media star. As Ed Bryant pointed out, Harlan Ellison and Donald Duck were both fifty years old in 1984. Perhaps this made for a perfect ducktailing ... er ... dovetailing of interests in science fiction and Disney and LASFS. It was LASFS' golden anniversary that led fans to hold the 1984 World Science Fiction Convention in southern California, and the organizers put it in Anaheim, California, across the street from the Magic Kingdom, Disneyland. So the stage was set for another 1984 headline story:

L.A.CON II LARGEST WORLDCON EVER
The annual World Science Fiction Convention, condensed to Worldcon, as though a show-biz term in *Variety*, is the signal event in the calendar of science fiction fandom. It is the largest convention of its type, held over Labor Day weekend whenever a North American site is selected. While dwarfed in the eyes of Southern Californians by the Summer Olympics, which ended three weeks before the con-

vention, to fans the Worldcon was the primary attraction. Fans were relieved that the Olympic tourist influx had vacated their hotel space by Labor Day. The Anaheim Convention Center had been the Olympics' wrestling venue. The fans had also worried about another conflicting event: on the last day of the Worldcon President Reagan was a block away making the kickoff speech for his re-election campaign.

Fortunately, none of these events actually interfered with the largest Worldcon ever. L.A.con II, as it was nicknamed, had an attendance of 8,365. The Mayors of Los Angeles and Anaheim each declared "Science Fiction Week" during the Worldcon. The Governor of California's welcoming letter was read at the Opening Ceremonies, where introductions were made of Professional Guest of Honor Gordon Dickson, Fan Guest of Honor Richard Eney, and Masters of Ceremonies Robert Bloch and Jerry Pournelle.

Later in the weekend Robert Bloch presided over the Hugo Awards ceremony, where the convention gave him a special presentation plaque commemorating his fiftieth year as a professional science fiction writer, yet another half-century milestone reached in 1984. Bloch handed out Hugo Awards to:

BEST NOVEL: *Startide Rising* by David Brin
BEST NOVELLA: "Cascade Point" by Timothy Zahn
BEST NOVELETTE: "Blood Music" by Greg Bear
BEST SHORT STORY: "Speech Sounds" by Octavia Butler
BEST NONFICTION BOOK: *Encyclopedia of Science Fiction and Fantasy, volume 3: Miscellaneous* compiled by Donald Tuck
BEST DRAMATIC PRESENTATION: *Return of the Jedi*
BEST PROFESSIONAL EDITOR: Shawna McCarthy
BEST PROFESSIONAL ARTIST: Michael Whelan
BEST SEMIPROFESSIONAL MAGAZINE: *Locus*, edited by Charles N. Brown
BEST FANZINE: *File 770*, edited by Mike Glyer
BEST FANWRITER: Mike Glyer
BEST FANARTIST: Alexis Gilliland
JOHN W. CAMPBELL AWARD: R. A. MacAvoy

During the Hugo ceremony, Robert Silverberg and Harlan Ellison came forward to pay an emotional tribute to

Larry Shaw. Shaw had sufficiently recovered from a serious illness to attend the convention and accept a Special Award recognizing his historic development of new science fiction writers (like Ellison) in the 1950s. On the lighter side, Larry Niven rounded out the ceremonies by presenting Jerry Pournelle's first Hugo: solid chocolate wrapped in tinfoil.

The Worldcon Masquerade, always the state-of-the-art of science fiction costume, ran four hours at L.A.con II. Longer than some fans could sit through, but a dazzling display for those who did. They saw expensive costumes exemplifying all forms of theater craft and technology: makeup, rubber molds, leather, metal, woodwork, and electrical props, plus a wide range of needlecraft and dressmaking techniques. Many entrants performed dramatic and humorous skits. Even considering the duration of the masquerade, most fans rated it the best ever conducted at a science fiction convention. L.A.con II will be selling video tapes at a future date when editing is finished.

The Worldcon art show provided another visual feast, while selling $97,000 worth of art. As a byproduct of its size, the art show was subdivided into displays of original art, a Showcase Wall of the artists' picked masterworks, a Reproduction/Poster shop and a Fine Art Multiple Original Shop. Thus fans were able to differentiate between original and various kinds of reproduced art. Only certain categories were admitted to the Art Auction, helping to conserve time.

The members of L.A.con II voted Atlanta (over New York or Philadelphia) for the site of the 1986 World Science Fiction Convention. Membership information may be obtained from Worldcon Atlanta Inc., 2500 N. Atlanta Street, Suite 1986, Smyrna GA 30080.

At the Worldcon business meeting, Donald Eastlake III reported success in legally trademarking five of the six terms intimately associated with Worldcons. As of June 26, 1984, these service marks were registered with the United States Patent and Trademark Office: Worldcon (#1,283,680); World Science Fiction Convention (#1,283,681); World Science Fiction Society (#1,284,719); WSFS (#1,286,562); the Hugo Award (#1,287,322). Registration was a precaution against anyone profiting by falsely representing an event of their own to be the Worldcon, or claiming to be giving "Hugo" Awards. It seemed prudent to remove the temptation.

By the end of 1984, when L.A.con II's bills were paid off, a surplus of $150,000 remained. Therefore it was decided to reimburse the expenses of the all-volunteer committee for meals and lodging during the convention, a $70,000 undertaking. Perhaps this point deserves stress: over one hundred fans organized and staged the 1984 Worldcon, and every one was an unpaid volunteer. If the convention had merely covered its expenses (which was its philosophy, as a non-profit corporation) the workers would have been content to have paid their own way and had the opportunity to help put on the event. Worldcons have been held since 1939, and they have always been done this way. As they have gotten larger and larger there has been no change in philosophy, although it has never been more hotly debated than in 1984 because when L.A.con II sought uses within the science fiction community for its surplus, standing at the head of the line were the fans trying to cover unpaid bills from the 1983 Worldcon. The explanation of the efforts generated the third headline story:

CONSTELLATION BAILOUT SUCCEEDS

Less than ten years ago even the largest science fiction convention was still too small to book an entire major hotel. Therefore they tended to be pushed around by unsympathetic hotel management staffs trying to accomodate several customers on the same weekend: airline pilots, the Knights of Columbus, the Shriners. In 1984 the average science fiction convention still uneasily shared its quarters with the outside world. Lunacon's 1400 attendees met in March near New York, and mingled with team members of the USFL's New Jersey Generals: large persons who fortunately were amused by fans. DeepSouthCon convened in Chattanooga, Tennessee, in June: 700 fans, some in costume with replicas of futuristic weapons, rattled around the same hotel with the wife of the Vice President, Mrs. George Bush, and her covey of nervous Secret Service bodyguards.

Unlike these smaller conventions, the World Science Fiction Convention can fill every room in several hotels

The Fifty-Candle Blowout

for Labor Day weekend. Hotel chain conglomerates seek its business. Convention Centers are employed. Services are contracted from commercial exhibit firms accustomed to dealing with large trade shows. Yet the Worldcons are run essentially by all-volunteer committees of the same people who stage a Lunacon, a DeepSouthCon, or Pacoima Pointy Ear Weekend.

Worldcon committees are just as thin on big business experience as small convention staffs, and this rarely improves because each year's Worldcon is led by an entirely independent executive group from a different area of the country (or the world). They were voted the Worldcon franchise by convention members two years previous, on the basis of a campaign of room parties at small conventions, and the proffered literature about the contenders' meeting facilities.

Usually the winning committee comprehends its own limitations, plans conservatively, and cushioned by the upward trend in Worldcon attendance, generates a reasonable surplus. Not so in 1983. Called ConStellation, the 1983 Worldcon in Baltimore fell victim to its own weak financial controls, lavishly overcommitting the convention's resources. A committee that did so many other things right in terms of the masquerade, creative food functions, and programming, despite drawing record attendance, lost its shirt. Shortly after Labor Day, 1983, the chairman published a letter calling on fandom to bail out the Worldcon's $44,000 unpaid bills.

Like many large conventions, ConStellation had incorporated, so under the law the individuals who ran it were shielded from having their personal assets wiped out by the convention's creditors. Legally they could have walked away without a backward glance: it happens when unsuccessful businesses go defunct, every day. However, as will be elaborated on later, one of the foundations under fandom is a shared idealism: many fans felt they should not take advantage of their legal position, that there remained a moral obligation to see the money repaid.

After most Worldcons the committee immediately collapses from fatigue and the release of years of accumulated stress, but the 1983 Worldcon committee pushed on with an ambitious merchandising campaign. They sold shirts, video tapes of the Worldcon masquerade, and of Bill Rotsler's "How to Flirt" panel. They hoped to sell enough souvenirs, while attracting outright donations, to break even and salvage the good name of science fiction fandom.

By the spring of 1984 it was evident that the committee's own efforts had run out of steam. The rough estimate of unpaid bills had been refined into an even rougher reality: after all the fundraising, a hard core of $38,000 in unpaid bills remained. The market was saturated with video tapes of fans in costume, or Bill Rotsler flirting. For all the talk, very few bailout donations were sent in. The convention was capsized in a sea of red ink. It didn't even have enough assets to be forced into bankruptcy.

Boston-area fandom now asserted its traditional leadership role. While the dominant motive remained the avoidance of victimizing firms that had supported the Worldcon, rescuers also sought to protect fandom's reputation with the service companies they relied on. It would become prohibitive to run a con if vendors began to demand cash-in-advance for all the requirements of a major convention. Massachusetts Convention Fandom Incorporated (MCFI) had been formed to hold the 1980 Worldcon, Noreascon II. Noreascon II had realized a large surplus and still had most of it. On one hand it's impossible to plow last-minute cash back into a holiday weekend convention, and on the other hand large convention surpluses are so new to science fiction fandom that a philosophy for disbursing them has yet to be evolved. MCFI voted to use $10,000 from its surplus in whatever way would best help resolve ConStellation's problems. In April, 1984, MCFI's directors expanded this strategy into an appeal for fans to send money to a consortium they were setting up with their own $10,000 for seed, which would try to settle the outstanding debts by buying them at less than face value. They predicted creditors would settle their claims against ConStellation if MCFI could raise enough cash to offer more than 50 cents on the dollar. But if they failed to settle all $38,000 in undisputed debt, and a creditor forced the convention into bankruptcy, the consortium would become the dominant creditor in the proceedings.

Bailout negotiations stretched into the summer of 1984.

Seven out of eight creditors agreed to the settlement plan. L.A.con II donated $10,000 to the cause; the 1982 Chicago Worldcon committee pledged $5,000; clubs in Portland, Philadelphia and Washington DC, plus individual contributions, raised another $4,200. By New Year's 1985 MCFI's directors predicted all eight creditors would accept the settlement and receive about 75 cents on the dollar: a dramatic reversal of affairs.

In retrospect, through a combination of idealism and luck (L.A.con II's profits), some active fans overcame cynicism and inertia within their own circles to bail out a financial disaster almost anyone else would have walked away from.

SURVIVING IN A BOOMTOWN

On a sweltering August night, 100,000 people sat in a darkened Los Angeles Coliseum during the Closing Ceremonies of the 1984 Summer Olympics. Towed from above by an unseen helicopter, a giant flying saucer hovered over them, heralded by fireworks and lasers and replying with a display of running lights reminiscent of *Close Encounters of the Third Kind*. Moments later the figure of an alien walked atop the peristyle end of the Coliseum, and over the public address system commended the Olympic ideal of peace and friendship through sports.

Later in the year, during the most lucrative series of rock concerts in American history, Michael Jackson and his brothers' act was enhanced by technical effects inspired by today's science fiction films. Jackson's fans who hastened from the concerts to buy the "Victory" album in concurrent release also wound up buying cover art by science fiction artist Michael Whelan, who painted the galaxy behind the Jackson brothers.

Science fiction has become not merely a metaphor for the visually spectacular, it has penetrated the popular mind so thoroughly that it can be interchangeably used with other uniquely American forms like jazz, the western, and rock, to touch mass audiences. In this isolated respect science fiction has fulfilled everything to which its first fans aspired. To those few hundred active fans in the 1930s, science fiction was the means to shape a better world, and down an unmarked road they went to affirm their faith in the future by taking an idealistic approach to the present.

The popularity of science fiction accelerated the growth of fandom beyond any capacity to assimilate newcomers into its traditions. Many veteran fans are dissatisfied with boomtown science fiction fandom. Andrew Porter, editor of *Science Fiction Chronicle,* said, "Alas for the old days when the Worldcon was the place to see your several hundred friends, when fanzine fans organized and ran the convention. Those days are gone forever, with 25 cents (sic) paperbacks and the pulp magazines they grew out of."

Frequent large conventions have taken the show away from fanzine publishers, the editors of tiny circulation amateur magazines whose work linked all areas of fandom by mail before today's era of cheap travel. But if fanzine fans have a smaller piece of the pie, the pie is infinitely bigger. Consider how space was allocated for the 1984 Worldcon. Marty Cantor, oganizer of fanzine fan activities, asked Chairman Craig Miller for 8000 square feet: really just a modest chunk of the Anaheim Convention Center. Miller told this to Mike Glyer, who mentally calculated, "Two hundred by forty? Did you know that the battleship *Missouri* is over 800 feet long?"

"Then it won't fit in the Fan Room," concluded Miller.

Over 20,000 people fit the definition of active science fiction fan, so far beyond the scope of print-media fandom that it seems impossible to achieve any homogenization, and inform them adequately about the activities in different regions. Some hope is held that *Fancyclopedia III*, the first complete revision of this fannish history and information source since 1959, will be available in 1985 and revive awareness of science fiction fandom's interesting past. Whether fandom will ever recover its sense of everyone being part of a common cause is doubtful. Nor will it eradicate from its small society further examples of a phenomenon already familiar to a troubled world: when people feel alienated from the mainstream, a few of them act to the detriment of everyone.

The 1984 WesterCon in Portland, Oregon, reached a nadir in sociopathic behavior. As *Locus* (September, 1984) described the worst night, "the previously rowdy and numerous room parties grew even wilder. Guests threw things off balconies and were screaming in the halls. At 4 a.m. several fire alarms were activated when a smoke detector was pulled out of the ceiling on the 12th floor (of the Portland Marriott) and an alarm pulled on the 10th. The emergency systems came on and a fan belt stuck in the ventilator system resulting in smoke. Many guests were evacuated. The fire department found no actual problem and everyone was finally allowed back into their rooms." The convention posted a $500 reward for information leading to the arrest of the vandals, but they were never identified.

What a cruel irony that the outbreak began just hours after WesterCon guest of honor Harlan Ellison had delivered an important speech about some fans' vicious behavior. Ellison had polled every writer he knew for an account of the single worst thing a science fiction fan had ever done to them, added his own bitter experiences, and for over an hour, horrified the audience with successive tales of bizarre practical jokes, items of hate mail, and tales of harassment and threats against the most famous and appreciated writers in the genre. The 20-year accumulation of stories had listeners looking for someplace to slit their wrists. Somehow Ellison's statement that he blamed a small percentage of fans for these things did little to lessen the sting.

The majority of fans would prefer to be represented by events in the midwest in July when writer Robert Chilson escaped the 1:30 a.m. blaze that totally destroyed his apartment. Two local fans temporarily housed him, and fundraisers were held at area conventions to assist him. Okon, in Tulsa, sent Chilson $700.

The majority would also like to feel they make a positive contribution, though politically active writers have generally failed to stir fans to do something more than read and talk about a greater future. Ellison met with great resistance when he tried to mobilize fan support for the Equal Rights Amendment in 1978. Only in the area of the space program has anyone succeeded in tapping science fiction fandom as a political constituency.

The desirability of exploring outer space is probably the only political issue that unites a majority of fans. Because space exploration issues are still at a primitive level of debate, arguing whether it should even be funded, little remains to divide science fiction fans who have eagerly awaited the age of exploration since they paged through Willy Ley's books in their childhood. Jerry Pournelle has linked parts of fandom with space advocacy groups and the citizens' council advising the current administration. The activists include Bjo Trimble, who has transferred her mass mailing skills to a new cause: her catchy SPACE WRITE NOW appeals have been timed to create letter-writing campaigns and deter White House budget cutters from gutting the space program.

Southern California fans thronged to the first space shuttle landings at Edwards Air Force Base. They may have formed a sentimental attachment to the place because *The Right Stuff*, a historical movie about the space program, gave strong competition to *Return of the Jedi*, a straight science fiction film, in voting for the 1984 Hugo for Best Dramatic Presentation.

Neither extreme is accurate: fans as sociopaths, nor fans as idealistic activists. Science fiction conventions still encounter a far lower rate of hotel vandalism than what other social groups inflict. The occasional letter to Congress is not a commitment in the same league with civil rights marchers or volunteers who work to shelter the homeless. Yet these problems and responses make it clear that fandom has grown in more ways than size alone.

THE TRANS-ATLANTIC FAN FEUD

Just when one is through discussing all the ways in which fandom has grown, evidence comes along to convince the reader that the one direction in which fandom has not grown is *up*. Has success spoiled Joe Phan?

In the 1950s when fandom was small and individual fans were broke, travel was expensive and conventions struggled to break even on a budget of $350, fans in Britain and the U.S. had a very altruistic idea. Each year they would collaborate to raise enough money to send one fan across the Atlantic. In alternate years the fans of each country would have the chance to meet an interesting overseas fan, and later on the compatriots he left behind would be rewarded with a chance to read his trip report

The Fifty-Candle Blowout

containing all the illuminating experiences *he* had as their proxy. What a heck of an idea! It worked, too.

The Trans–Atlantic Fan Fund (TAFF) became the quintessential example of fannish idealism. At a given time there would be one TAFF administrator on each side of the Atlantic who had taken *his* trip, published *his* report, and gone on to raise as much money as *he* could to finance the trip of *his* successor. Individuals and small conventions would feed the kitty. Sometimes financial reports were published, but usually not: after all, the TAFF delegate still wound up paying most of the freight for *his* trip in spite of winning the fund.

Then sometime in the mid-1970s, fandom got big, and TAFF got comparatively rich: big enough to pay for the delegate's entire overseas trip with a thousand or two to spare. At the same time, Freddie Laker's *Skytrain* drove down airfares across the Atlantic. Suddenly, almost anybody with a job who was willing to set aside the money could eventually visit British fandom. Gradually it became unclear whether there were any obviously deserving TAFF delegates any longer, and TAFF, which enjoyed credibility because of the prestige of its winners, was ripe for an identity crisis.

The crisis arrived in 1984, timed like one of those historical accidents which make careless people think that shooting archdukes causes world wars. Avedon Carol was the American delegate to Britain's Eastercon in 1984, and thereby one of the administrators of the balloting for the next leg of the exchange, to send a Brit to L.A.con II. She became romantically involved with Rob Hansen, who proved to be the winning British TAFF delegate. Hansen's competitor, Don West, took half of the British vote, but having often insulted American fandom in print, sank like a rock in the domestic vote. Even though West wrote he had no complaint whatsoever about the process, American fans became embroiled in a terribly bitter feud, ostensibly because Carol had been indiscreet enough to criticize candidate West in private correspondence.

An avalanche of hostile letters and fanzines hurtled into fannish mailboxes beginning in July, little abating as the year ended. Why? Because of some fine point in etiquette?

Just because somebody bagged another archduke? No, indeed.

How TAFF was being administered became the conduit to release frustration about more festering complaints, indirectly attributable to the expanding numbers of fans already discussed.

In the feud, a common criticism was the lack of financial information about the TAFF fund furnished by its administrators. The true explanation? Fandom is a pastime, and TAFF winners are picked to represent it, not because they are career accountants. Lack of published balance sheets should never have been misconstrued as evidence of anything suspicious. But here, embodied in an individual, was another issue of a fan function involving a sizeable chunk of money over which there was no obvious financial control or accountability to the democracy of fandom. After the embarrassment of ConStellation, and impatience about L.A.con II's long delay in reporting its startling surplus, certain fans' cynicism became quite vocal. Unlike the Worldcon committees, where it was inconvenient to fix blame because almost every section of fandom had a hand in, TAFF's executive involved only two people, whose actions could be microscopically inspected and criticized. Being human, they made occasional mistakes. One of them stirred up a popular movement, an explosion that made the first stage of the feud seem quiet by comparison.

After L.A.con II the TAFF cycle started anew: it was time to select the American delegate to the 1985 Eastercon. A modest field of two candidates made the official ballot. A midwestern U.S. fan missed the deadline for certain requirements, and was omitted. Her furious supporters, some already embroiled in the TAFF feud, launched a tough write-in campaign appealing to midwestern fans to right this alleged injustice. British fans felt disenfranchised: an American they had never heard of would be forced on them as TAFF delegate if ward-heeling tactics succeeded. The British announced they would freeze their TAFF funds if she won. In the end, twice as many fans voted than in any other TAFF race of the past ten years, over 500, and the write-in candidate lost. Miraculously, TAFF may even have survived.

Was the quixotic need to right a wrong really the lone

explanation for midwestern voter turnout? That's unlikely. More likely, this was a timely cause in which the midwest could reassert its influence. The midwest played a dominant role in fannish affairs until the 1970s. Then Worldcons became unmanageably large except for a couple of midwestern cities: it's hard to be a big fish when your region can't handle its share of Worldcons. There is a system for sharing them that divides North America into three parts. Cities in each region may bid for Worldcons only in given years. Foreign bids are accepted in any year. Though there are many quality fans in the midwest, there are few midwestern cities that have *both* large concentrations of fans *and* Worldcon-sized convention facilities. A 1984 proposal would have absorbed the midwestern bidding zone into the other two, eliminating a so-called "wimpy zone." Wouldn't you feel insulted if your region of the country was called "wimpy"? So large numbers of midwestern fans were already agitated when the call to arms came. Regrettably, one of the best examples of fannish idealism, the Trans–Atlantic Fan Fund, served as the battlefield.

VITAL STATISTICS

In counterpoint to the passing parade of birthdays mentioned throughout this article was the solemn loss of major figures in science fiction fandom in 1984.

William Crawford, 72, died January 26. He published the first semiprofessional magazines in the science fiction field in 1935: *Marvel Tales* and *Unusual Stories*. He started the small press movement, later formed a hardcover publishing company (Fantasy Publishing Company Inc.), and printed the first Cordwainer Smith story, "Scanners Live in Vain."

Olon Wiggins, 74, died February 4. He was chairman of the third Worldcon in Denver in 1941. Jack McKnight died December 5. He machined the first Hugo award rockets. Dan McPhail, 68, died September 25. He published the first science fiction news magazine, *Science Fiction News*, in 1935–36. He was the last of three Fantasy Amateur Press Association members to die in 1984, diluting the humor of a nickname for the organization, "fandom's Elephants' Graveyard." The other two members were Sam

Martinez and Charles Hansen. FAPA was the first of hundreds of science fiction APAs.

Given the space limitations on this annual review of fandom, we shall have to leave for another time stories like "Dunegate"—how the distribution of passes to a movie premiere sparked a feud in the Washington Science Fiction Association, or "Phoxphyre"—how Philadelphia fans applied for the National Endowment for the Humanities to fund a history of their first convention. (Hm, "Phoxphyre" rhymes with Proxmire . . .)

If your interest is piqued, you may keep abreast of fandom through these specialized news magazines:

File 770: editor, Mike Glyer, 5828 Woodman Ave. #2, Van Nuys CA 91401. Published eight times per year. Emphasizes news of science fiction fandom. Subscriptions: mailed first class, five issues for $4.

Locus: editor, Charles N. Brown, P.O. Box 13305, Oakland CA 94661. Published monthly. Emphasizes professional science fiction news. Subscriptions: mailed second class, 12 issues for $24.

Science Fiction Chronicle: editor, Andrew Porter, P.O. Box 4175, New York NY 10163. Published monthly. Emphasizes professional science fiction news, also has reasonably good fan coverage. Subscriptions: mailed first class, 12 issues for $21.